SWEET SURRENDER

"Your mouth is so ripe for kissing. Have you ever
been kissed?"

"I, um, I cannot recall."

Logan's throaty laugh undid Gillian's last remaining shred of propriety. "If you cannot recall, I would
imagine it was not memorable. Tell me, did your Brian ever kiss you?" His mouth slowly descended.

There was no time for doubt or protest. Gillian's
confused mind could only register that his mouth was
cool and firm. Without any provocation from him,
her lips parted to meet his.

"You need to be kissed," he whispered against her
mouth. "You need me. I could teach you so much if
you'd let me." His hand slid lower to explore her soft
curves. "Mmm, so lovely. I would love to feel more of
you."

Gillian was totally lost to his sensual power. Not
thinking of anything but the moment, of the feel of
his hands, freely roaming her satin-clad body, she did
not realize that she was being lowered to the ground.

"Let me touch you, Gillian," he murmured fiercely,
watching her face, her eyes closing in the throes of
first passion, knowing that he could take her right
here, right now . . .

SEDUCTIVE SCOUNDREL

VICTORIA LONDON

ZEBRA BOOKS
KENSINGTON PUBLISHING CORP.

ZEBRA BOOKS

are published by

Kensington Publishing Corp.
475 Park Avenue South
New York, NY 10016

First printing: June, 1989

Printed in the United States of America

TO MY EVERLASTING LOVE — MY HUSBAND
TO MY NEWEST LOVE — MY DAUGHTER

Part One

LONDON, APRIL – JUNE, 1825

Chapter One

April 1825

She was bored. That was the only reason Gillian had decided to stroll around her uncle's home alone. The large stone house and its magnificent gardens were as familiar as her own home in Pall Mall. When the conversation of her friends had become annoyingly familiar, Gillian politely excused herself, leaving Adeline Barrish alone to defend her best friend.

"There she goes," a blonde with cascading curls whispered a trifle too loudly. "She always seems so distracted, so aloof."

"That's what keeps good old Brian intrigued," laughed one of the young men, slapping his friend's back.

The gentlemen stared at her straight satin-clad back as she briskly walked out of the room.

"So unladylike," sniffed one young woman in blue.

"I thought you were her friend?" the blonde challenged her.

"I am. Someone needs to tell her though, that she is not often ladylike. Why—" she languidly fanned herself "—Gillian is almost twenty. She's had her coming-out ball. She's had her international schooling and her father even took her on another trip to France."

"Probably to find a suitable husband," the blonde retorted.

"You're saying that because she turned down your Peter before he asked you to marry him," laughed another young woman.

"If the rumors can be trusted, I believe she has done that to a couple of young men, eh, Brian?" the gentleman teased his friend again, much to Brian's annoyance. He finally excused himself.

"No one knows what she wants, but I would wager all of my prize horses that Lady Gillian Marlowe will be a spinster. I hope she enjoys her freedom," the young woman smoothing the skirts of her blue satin said.

"She does," Adeline Barrish declared at last. "Gillian is my best friend, and I think she would rather remain unmarried than marry someone she could not learn to love and respect. Why, she has told me so herself more than a dozen times."

Adeline's expression became dreamy as it usually did whenever she interpreted something Gillian had said. Gillian was older, more mature, and definitely knew what she wanted. Or rather didn't want, Adeline reconsidered. Nevertheless, like a devoted puppy, Adeline listened and applauded everything about Gillian. In less than a month, Adeline's betrothal to Anthony Palmer would be announced. Palmer was twenty years her senior, fat, balding, his breath wreaking of stale tobacco and liquor. It was her parents' idea of a perfect marriage. Adeline was not strong enough to say what she wanted.

She was not like Gillian, who could be as outspoken as any man. However, Gillian's parents—particularly her father—did not share those sentiments and were pressuring her to find a suitable young man. They hadn't arranged a marriage, though—not yet at least!

Unaware of the silly conversation about her, Gillian wandered into the gardens. The idle gossip and stupidity of her friends often sent her roaming.

Besides, she had a lot on her mind this spring night. Gillian's parents had not arranged a marriage, but time was running out. Just the other morning, her father had launched into his one-sided discussion about marriage. What was wrong with Brian? he asked. He had told her that although she was quite attractive, there were many other attractive women in London, most of whom were a few years younger than she. He wanted to know who would look after her if she did not marry. Being a spinster—for surely she would be called that—precluded many social invitations. She would be an outcast in society. And what would happen after her mother and he died? Who would look after her? Certainly not her older brother, John, for he had his own family to support.

Wrapping her lace shawl tighter around her slim body, Gillian wondered if her father's words were prophetic. Would it be so horrible if she did not marry? Would it be so horrible if she did?

"Damn it all," she cursed aloud. "I cannot tolerate those self-centered fops." Most of the men she knew were very much like her brother. As the sons of wealthy men, they did not know the meaning of work, of exercising one's mind, of the serious side to life. How could they? They drank, gambled, went whoring, and took long holidays. They were vain, arrogant, and often stupid.

Gillian found a secluded stone bench. The swirling gray mist rose ominously around her knees. It was almost impossible to see the graveled path beneath her satin-slippered feet, let alone anything beyond an outstretched hand. But she wasn't concentrating on her location or the weather. Her father had issued an ultimatum today: "Either find a husband within the next year, or I will find one for you."

She knew this time that he was serious. Her mother had remained silent, her usual sympathetic face devoid of any emotion. "You must marry, Gillian. I will not have a spinster for a daughter," she was told. "You should marry Brian."

Interesting way to phrase it, Gillian had thought. Her father did not want to be embarrassed. Was that a reason to marry?

"I don't know anymore," she whispered to no one. "I just don't know." Perhaps if she found a man who was at least six inches taller than she, it might be a suitable marriage. Gillian was tired of looking eye-to-eye with most of her suitors and disgusted with those she looked down on. At least Brian was two inches taller than herself. Why not make height a criterion for marriage? she whimsically decided. It was as good a reason as wealth, or attractiveness, or experience with women.

She hadn't thought about the latter until now. On her last visit, Adeline had made such an issue of experience that Gillian actually put down one of her novels to think of it. Experience. The physical side to a marriage. John had teased her about it once, telling her that she was afraid of losing her virginity, afraid of letting a man have his way with her.

Was she likewise afraid? Gillian had never seriously considered the sex act as a prerequisite to a happy marriage. She didn't know anyone who was happily married—including her parents. They had merely tolerated each other for the last twenty-five years. They must be fond of each other by now, she thought, but

12

did they love each other?

Gillian was ready to return to the ballroom to take another look at the young, eligible men. Foreign Secretary Canning was due to arrive, and she did like talking to him. He was one of the few men who allowed her to talk of politics, of England's future, of the problems with the other countries, particularly America.

She stood to straighten her long dress and smooth a drooping curl. It was then that she heard the crunching of feet along the gravel path, and for some reason she chose not to move, not to make her presence known. The fog-enshrouded shadows loomed closer.

Two elegantly dressed men strolled around the area, heedless of the cool air or the laughing revelers far away. The taller man withdrew two cigars, offering one to his companion before striking the match. The yellow light only briefly outlined his aquiline nose and high forehead. Gillian could not see the color of his eyes or his hair, though he was hatless.

"So, have you any information for me this week?" The upper-class accent was mixed with a trace of something else.

"Yes." He reached into his inside coat pocket, withdrawing a small packet. "Harold said this was extremely important. He warned me to tell you not to be caught with this information, for it will surely hang you."

The taller man's smile went unnoticed. "Bless Harold, always worrying. I wonder if it's because he's so fond of me or my talent."

"Your reputation is becoming legendary."

"I doubt that. But I hope I am helping in some way."

"Your reports of the past have guided many decisions."

"How do you know so much?" The voice was expressionless.

"I know. Harold has told me and he knows." It was spoken with the belief of a trusting child.

"Fear not. There will always be another if I should meet an untimely demise. That's what is so remarkable about our business. You're admired and feared one moment, and the next—" He blew a puff of smoke to make his point. "So hurry, man, we have no time to spare in idle chatter. I must go back inside before I am missed."

"Oh, I am certain you are missed already. With your other talents, well—" the shorter man coughed "—I gather you have a number of female acquaintances."

"How do you know about me?"

"I am aware of much more than you think. But I would never reveal your identity. It is safe with me."

"Meet me in a fortnight next time. I think we should meet in public. How about Hyde Park at five? I usually enjoy a late-afternoon stroll with a little companion on Thursdays."

"What are you going to do with that packet?"

"There is no need to divulge all my secrets, is there?"

"Remember what I said about being caught."

"I will never be caught. Besides, my aim is superb. No one has ever been able to identify me." He spoke with assurance and haughtiness.

"May I ask you another question?" the man asked timidly. The tall man inclined his head, but the gesture was missed in the dark, churning mist.

"Go on, man. Ask your question. If we're not caught, one of us will surely perish from pneumonia."

"I only wanted to know why you do this," he hurriedly said. "I mean, it isn't for the money. Your family's wealth is not a secret. So, is it loyalty to a new country or the sheer danger of it all?"

"Both," the gentleman crisply replied before walking off into the gray-shrouded night.

The man who had said something about being legendary walked away. Oh, if only she could get a close look at one of them, but the mist was so dense, she feared she'd trip over them trying to see better. Judging from the way the arrogant one spoke, Gillian did not doubt he was a killer. Wasn't this grand! She was sitting in the fog, freezing, overhearing a conversation between spies, and she was too frightened to do anything at all.

His cigar must have gone out, for he stopped long enough to relight it. The flame illuminated a diamond "S" stickpin in his cravat.

As he struck the match Gillian thought the entire sky would flare up and she held her breath. Please don't let him see me, she prayed silently, her nails digging deeply into her soft palms.

She had heard part of the conversation and had seen the glittering stickpin. Their voices had been muffled by the sounds within the ballroom and by the night air. They had whispered too much of the time for her to identify either man.

Yet one of them now possessed a valuable packet. Long after he had strolled past, she dared not move from the cold stone bench. Gillian did not feel the damp air seep through her lace shawl. Her once-high curls now limply hung along the sides of her face.

There was a spy in England!

Certainly she was aware that state-inspired intrigue

was prevalent in most societies. Brian had told her that much. Gillian was not that naive. But *she* had overheard the conversation and had seen the exchange of papers. It made her blood run cold and her heart hammer so loudly that Gillian wildly thought the killer would turn around.

Never truly fond of English weather, she thanked God it was so foggy this night. Her life had surely been spared.

Being extremely proud of her heritage and country, she believed that to tell no one of the incident would just as surely incriminate her as another traitor. Lady Gillian Marlowe could not remain silent.

"Whoever you are," she whispered aloud, straightening her rumpled satin dress, "you will be caught. And I will be there when you hang."

Chapter Two

Gillian almost ran into the ballroom, but immediately rejected such an unladylike notion. Her pale blue eyes quickly scanned the crowded area and lit up with delight when she finally found her father talking to none other than the Duke of Wellington. Surely he would know how to catch a spy.

"Father," she rushed up, unmindful of her manners, "I must speak with you."

"My dear, can't you see I am in earnest conversation with my friends?"

She hated when he used that imperious tone with her. "Please excuse my rudeness," she panted to catch her breath, "but I have just witnessed the most unbelievable thing and I simply must . . ."

"Gillian," Lord Marlowe, Earl of Dalton, wearily sighed, "I did not think your year abroad was for naught."

"Let her speak, Charles. She is obviously distressed," remarked the kindly Duke of Wellington.

"I overheard the most," her eyes scanned heavenward for the proper words, "the most treasonous conversation. Outside, in Uncle's gardens. I overheard a conversation between two spies! One was giving something to the other and then the other said, 'Har-

17

vey—I think that was the name—will be pleased,' or no," she waved her hand trying to think clearly, "I know what he said. He said 'your reputation is legendary.' Yes," she brightened, "that was it!"

"Gillian, you are not making any sense." Her father apologetically turned to the duke. "This happens every time she becomes excited. Gillian chatters so much, one forgets what she's trying to say."

His laughter sounded harsh, but Gillian was anxious to explain everything she could recall before forgetting any details.

"Please let me continue. I saw them. No, I mean I heard them. It's so damn, excuse me," she looked at the duke, "I mean it is so horridly dense outside that it is impossible to see at all. But I did hear them. I heard their feet along the graveled path. And I heard the rustling of papers. As if something were exchanged. And then he lit a match, and although I could not see his face, I saw the glitter of a jewel, a diamond initial stickpin. I tell you," she paused to quickly take a deep breath, "they were spies!"

"Gillian," Charles didn't bother to look at her but at the amused Duke of Wellington, "I thought you abandoned your girlish fantasies years ago. You are far too old . . ."

"Father, you must listen to me." She grabbed his coat sleeve, ignoring the curious stares of the people around them. "I am trying to tell you something of monumental importance. There was something about that man, I don't know, perhaps it was his manner of speech. He was so sure of himself. He's a spy, Father! He admitted it. He said he enjoys it. Then the other said something about his wealth and his reputation with women."

"That narrows it down to at least fifty of the most eligible young men in London. I daresay we have not

18

included the older chaps." Her father laughed lightly.

"I am not playing a game, Father. Your Grace," she implored the Duke of Wellington with her pale eyes, "I cannot express how important this must be. Why, the traitor is probably in this room," she gestured widely with her arms. "Are we to do nothing?"

"Gillian, you must stop this nonsense."

"What nonsense?" asked a tall, sandy-haired young man who could not help but overhear the conversation and see the agitated young woman gesturing to the crowded room.

"Ah, Logan. Do join us. My daughter Gillian, you do remember meeting her, don't you? At my son's house last year, or was it a few months ago?" Charles thoughtfully rubbed his chin. "My daughter believes she has discovered traitors right here in my brother's house. Actually," he chuckled, "they were outside in the gardens."

Gillian blushed to the roots of her strawberry-blond hair. How dare her own father talk about her in such an offhand manner.

"Will you excuse me," she stiffly said. "I seem to be making little sense to my father. I know someone who would appreciate my information."

"Please, Lady Gillian, I am interested in your discovery. Would you tell me about it?" He winked at the gentlemen.

Gillian looked up at Lord Logan Hammond, relieved to hear that he was at least interested in her story. Since Logan was much older than those in her circle of friends—over thirty—she rarely saw him except at some grand social function like this one, or at the theater. Yet she knew three things about this tall, extremely handsome man. One, of course, was his looks, causing most women to swoon whenever near him; second, he was good friends with Adeline's older brother; and last, he was even wealthier than her father.

Still, Lord Hammond always frightened her a bit. There was something about him. Perhaps the way he seemed to be so apathetic about everyone around him. His height gave him an advantage. And since Gillian was so conscious of height, she sensed that Lord Hammond enjoyed looking down at people, as if they were inferior to him. That, or he was politely indifferent to everyone.

At this moment, however, all Gillian wanted was someone to believe her. It could have been the devil for all she cared.

Charles Marlowe repeated Gillian's story. "Careful, Logan chap. Gillian could be describing one of your dear friends. Or you!" He laughed uproariously at that notion.

"Did you see these men?" Lord Hammond asked Gillian, appearing somewhat interested.

"No. But I heard something more important. They planned to meet again in two weeks. At Hyde Park. He takes a companion there on Thursdays." Suddenly Gillian was very tired of trying to convince this group of her discovery. Pulling herself up to her full five feet and seven inches, she boldly announced, "It matters not what any of you think. I know what I heard. I only wish I could do something."

"It is most interesting, my dear. We not only have to consider most of the upper-class gentlemen to see if there is a spy among them, but now we must look for him in Hyde Park. Have you ever seen a day during the season that Hyde Park was not crowded in the late afternoon? Why, everyone in London is seen in Hyde Park after five. My daughter is looking for a traitor among hundreds of people." Charles sighed, then laughed aloud. "Most young women of her age are married and probably with a second child. My daughter not only refuses to marry, she continues to harbor childish fantasies."

This time Gillian did not wait to be excused. She could not tolerate her father's boorish behavior. Murmuring a hurried apology, she excused herself and began to weave her way through the dance floor, dashing away unbidden tears. It was sinful that her father had laughed at her, but to announce to all who could hear that his daughter was heading for spinsterhood was more than she could bear. Nor was this the first time he had embarrassed her in public!

She was almost out of the ballroom when someone gently took her elbow. "I believe this is our waltz, my lady."

Gillian looked up into golden eyes. Yes, that was the fourth thing she remembered about him. His golden eyes that could sear a woman's soul yet reveal nothing in return.

"I truly don't need you to rescue me, my lord. I find myself in an untenable position at the moment, but it is nothing unusual for my father. He manages to do that quite often. In fact, he once . . ."

"Do you plan to converse in the middle of the dance floor? Wouldn't you rather allow yourself to be led around the room in a dizzying dance?"

His deep voice was kind. A bit too kind, she thought. "Please, I appreciate your attempt to spare me further embarrassment, but I don't need your sympathy."

"Sympathy?" Logan looked down at her and laughed. Now more heads turned in their direction. "I have been called many things, my dear, but sympathetic has surely not been among them."

Gillian wanted to complain a bit more but was cut off by his firm grasp of her back. Without thinking,

21

she lifted her right arm and allowed him to deftly twirl them around the room to the melodious sounds of a Strauss waltz.

For three minutes, Gillian forgot the humiliating scene with her father and his friends and closed her eyes, allowing the music and the strength of the man securely holding her to control her.

Logan Hammond looked down at the slender woman in his arms. Eyes closed, she did not see the twinkle in his eye and the slight smile bestowed on her. He hadn't really noticed her before this night, before she had nervously chattered to her father and one of the most important men in England, the Duke of Wellington. The story about the spies, the exchange of information, and the meeting in two weeks were all too fantastic to be real. Poor girl, he thought. No one will believe her . . . but he did. She really was a pretty thing, he decided, and quite graceful, too, considering her height.

Whenever Logan noticed a woman, he would look first at her chest — Lady Marlowe's was less than inviting, a little small for his taste — then her mouth. Here she passed his test with high marks. Her mouth was not that small, but delicately rounded, and her sensual lips seemingly invited kisses.

After the music ended, Logan kissed her gloved hand, looked deeply into her blue eyes, and smiled. "You are indeed a rare treasure, my dear. I wish you success in your chase. I would imagine it will not be easy."

"After two more glasses of wine, I may convince myself that I had imagined the whole evening. Anyhow, I suppose Father is right about finding them in Hyde Park. It's a bit like a needle in a haystack, don't you think?" She smiled a trifle sadly, and it briefly bothered Logan to see her so affected by the

22

evening's events.

"Perhaps you will save me another waltz. I hope to be reunited with you before the evening is over."

Not waiting for or expecting a reply, Logan Hammond turned on one booted heel, disappearing into a circle of tittering females.

Gillian was too entranced by his height and powerful frame to notice his right hand slip into the pocket of his dark blue jacket. Certainly she could not have seen his fingers fold around a diamond "S" stickpin, gently rubbing the sharp point before flipping it around and around in his hand.

Chapter Three

He was always looking for some kind of adventure. No scheme was wild enough, no dare too risky. It was the same with women. Logan could recall at least a half-dozen times when he was within a second of being caught with some man's wife.

Less than a week ago he had convinced the Countess of Hartshorn to allow him into her husband's bed during the day, knowing that the earl was expected home within the hour. It added to the excitement and their pleasure. Only Logan had laughed much later as he rode home. He had to remain hidden in Beverly's sitting room listening as she convinced her husband that she had been waiting for his return. Logan recalled the earl's astonished words, "But, dearest, you told me you only wanted me twice a month!"

It was as if he were waiting for the ultimate challenge, the ultimate thrill, the brief brush with death. Logan needed much more than being the Earl of Stanton's errant son. There was more to life than parties, secret tête-à-têtes, gambling, and women.

There were many young gentlemen of the 'ton' who felt similarly. But it went much deeper for Logan. It had become a sickness that pumped furiously through his blood at the oddest times. He refused to waste away in brandy and cards. His family's title and fortune were not enough. He craved adventure and danger.

Within the last five years he had found it. It had given him such pleasure, such satisfaction to know that his services were desperately needed. Never had any of his assignments ended in disaster. Nor would he allow anyone—including an empty-headed, chattering spinster—to ruin his plans.

Lord Logan Hammond, only son of the illustrious and wealthy Earl of Stanton, was an American agent.

It had come to him so matter-of-factly that Logan often wondered why he had never thought of it before. Logan did not feel like a traitor; after all, his mother was originally from Charleston, South Carolina. The family still held land there. Logan had spent most of his adult years in England, studying in the best of schools, learning the finer points of seduction and sophistication.

But it had been his summers in America that conjured up his fondest memories—carefree days spent on his maternal grandfather's plantation outside Charleston. His mother was happiest whenever they had returned to Charleston and it had been her dying wish that Logan continue to spend his summers in Charleston.

Her death had not been sudden. After Logan had returned from school, he and his father had held her hand for months watching the disease waste her lovely features, her hair, and her slender body. His mother had been a beautiful woman—in every way. Unlike the other members of her class, Judith Hammond had taken an active interest in her child's growth. And unlike other ton marriages, his parents had been in love and devoted to each other.

He had been fifteen when Judith died — old enough to understand that life continues, that obligations must be met. Yet he was young enough to feel alone and abandoned. The deep loss became a pain that to this day remained hidden in his heart.

His father had recovered somewhat faster than Logan. Ten years ago, Richard Hammond had married Charlotte Carstairs. Logan did not resent her or his new half sister, Luisa. Charlotte had done everything to make Logan feel wanted and loved, but it was different.

Despite his love for his father and sister and his deep affection for Charlotte, Logan felt alone. Not long after that time, he felt consumed by ennui. His recklessness and bravado reached new heights.

It was not until he had met Harold five years ago that Logan began to feel he had a purpose in life.

At thirty-three, Logan Hammond had become one of the most fearless spies in Europe. There was some altruism in his choice of occupation, but, most of all, it was the lure of danger that had appealed to him. Perhaps it was because he loved the excitement, the adventure, and the brushes with death that his reputation had become so well known. He knew that what he was doing could lead to his own death by hanging if he were ever caught — but Logan rarely considered being caught.

Except tonight. Damn his carelessness. Logan had never come this close to being discovered. So when he overheard the conversation of the Marlowe chit with the Duke of Wellington, Logan knew something would have to be done. Even if it meant a death. With the packet safely hidden, he had approached the group to listen and observe. But now, as he led the tall, slender young woman around the dance floor for the second time that evening, Logan thought better of such extreme action. After all, no one believed the chit and she had even begun to doubt herself.

Nevertheless, he had to find out precisely what she had heard and seen. He would not risk exposure — no matter what the cost.

Before returning Lady Marlowe to her friends, Logan had discarded his plan. Suddenly, it had become a challenge to see just what would happen with this girl. How far would she take this story?

"May I call upon you tomorrow, Lady Marlowe? Perhaps you would like to accompany me to the theater. The Paris Opera Ballet is performing at King's Theater." He looked into her stunned blue eyes and stifled the urge to laugh. She was unbearably impressionable. Logan could not recall the last time he had escorted an unmarried, aristocratic young woman anywhere. His conquests were either married, divorced, or of an entirely different class. Most of his forays ended in a night of lusty passion.

Looking at her slender, satin-clad body, Logan doubted that this young girl would meet any of his prerequisites for a good lover. She was undoubtedly a virgin. She was — or rather her family was — looking for a suitable husband and Logan Hammond had no desire to be anyone's husband.

Nevertheless, the invitation was spoken and the challenge sparked. How much time could he spend with her before she realized who he really was? Was Gillian Marlowe another empty-headed girl? Or could she put her facts and voices together and remember more of the conversation.

"My lord. I said I would be delighted to attend the theater with you." Her soft voice called him back to the present.

"Excellent." He took her hand. "I am looking forward to seeing you tomorrow."

Gillian felt his warm lips through her gloves. There was nothing to say as she watched his tall, muscular frame casually stride over to the Countess of Hartshorn.

"Gillian, I cannot believe my eyes or ears!" Adeline exclaimed. "You and Logan Hammond! Why, he is the most, I mean *the* most lascivious rake in all of London. Perhaps in all the world! God, I should know. My brother is not much better. And the two of them are often together drinking and gambling and," she lowered her voice considerably, "whoring."

"Adeline, I am only going to the theater with him. Lord, what could possibly happen to me?" Gillian nervously pulled on the strings of her silk fan. "He was awfully nice, you know. Perhaps he feels obligated to escort me somewhere. He overheard the most ludicrous conversation with my father and the Duke of Wellington. I think he felt sorry for me," she mused. Her eyes did not leave the back of the dark-blue-clad man across the room.

"Listen to me," Adeline implored. "Lord Hammond does not feel sorry for any human being. He's heartless, Gillian. Haven't you heard the rumors about him? He is a notorious womanizer. Your father would not let you out of the house, let alone ride in a carriage with him."

Gillian finally tore her gaze from Logan and looked at her best friend. "Adeline, you know my father. He would let the devil escort me to a dockside tavern, if it meant marriage. Besides, this might be my last chance."

"Last chance for what? Not for marriage. Logan Hammond is not marrying anyone. He'd rather cuckold half the men in this room than marry."

"Why, Adeline Barrish. I've never heard you talk this way." Gillian smiled brightly. "At least consider

28

this. Before I am either forced to marry a man I do not love, let alone like, or before I must resign myself to spinsterhood, let me experience a little fun." Her eyes located Logan Hammond once more. He was leaning over the countess, whispering something that made her laugh and touch his arm. "I think Lord Hammond knows how to have a little fun."

"I haven't told you about the countess, have I?" Adeline leaned closer to her friend. "Why, I overheard my brother talking to Logan one afternoon in the gardens. They didn't realize they were standing beneath my window, or I am sure Arthur would have closed his big mouth. Well, I heard Logan telling Arthur about the night they dressed in costume and went to the Vauxhall Gardens. And," she began to blush and giggle, "Logan took her to the other end of the gardens, you know, the darkest area, and they . . ." She stopped suddenly.

"What Adeline, what? Finish your story." Gillian took her friend's arm.

"Hello again, Viscount Althorp," Adeline said meaningfully.

Gillian stifled a moan. Brian. Wanting to face the direction of Logan Hammond, Gillian's back was to the larger half of the ballroom. And she failed to see or hear Brian's approach. Wherever Gillian was, Brian Althorp was not far behind. Actually, it was amazing that he hadn't found her sooner than this. It had been that way for as long as she could remember. Being a neighbor and boyhood friend of her older brother John, Brian was as much a part of her childhood as her dolls or favorite pets. He was always there. It unnerved her at times. Of late, he seemed to virtually sneak up on her—like now.

"Good evening, ladies. I noticed you seem to be enjoying your conversation. I wonder who you are gossiping about this time?" His dark eyes scanned the room. "Could it be Lord Hammond? He is a good friend of your brother's, Miss Barrish, is he not?"

"How could you know? I mean, Brian, that is most ungentlemanly of you. You should never ask what ladies are furiously whispering about. It could be about you. Then what would you do?" Gillian scolded.

"I would demand to know what they said."

Despite Brian's airs and good breeding, he sometimes acted as if the only way to obtain a dance or a kiss from a woman was to take it without asking for permission. "That wouldn't help you and you know it. Did you join us for information about Lord Hammond or did you really want to see me?" Gillian asked.

It was easy to make Brian feel uncomfortable. They had seen enough of each other in the last year to know many of the other's weak spots. Gillian never minded. To her it was a pleasant, harmless little game. Still, there were many times when Brian was very nice and thoughtful. Because she viewed him more as a relative than a suitor, Gillian was immune to his handsomeness. Tall and thin, with dark brown hair and eyes, Brian looked every inch the English country gentleman.

Her father, of course, was convinced that Brian should be the one. His position as deputy minister of Foregin Affairs was almost as influential as any appointed position in the Liverpool government. Brian worked closely with Foreign Secretary George Canning. And everyone knew that Canning held most of the power within the government. Lord Liverpool was too ill of late to challenge Canning's authority.

Gillian always paid a good deal of attention to Brian's political conversations with her father—that is, whenever she was permitted to remain in the room. From what she had gathered, Brian not only enjoyed what he was doing but was destined to go even further in the Liverpool government.

One rainy afternoon when he had called on the Marlowes, Gillian had finally asked Brian what specifically he did for Canning.

"Well, my dear, it's a little bit of everything. Mostly administrative, I suppose. But someone must be informed about what the other governments are planning to do in, ah, certain delicate negotiations. I try to know before any official meeting is organized."

"Brian? Isn't that dishonest?"

He had laughed heartily at her, then tried to explain. She had immediately thought he was patronizing her, but held her tongue, lest he decide not to tell her anything at all. Brian had been so circumspect in the last few months that Gillian's curiosity had been truly aroused.

"In the game of international politics, my dear, nothing is dishonest. It is always a matter of protecting one's government. That must come above all else." Gillian did not like the dark gleam in his eyes. It seemed almost unfocused — he could have been talking to anyone.

"Gillian, do you not think there are spies in England?"

Her eyes had rounded in surprise. "I hadn't thought of it. I suppose so. But, Brian, whatever for?"

"Do not be so innocent, my Gillian. There are American agents, Austrian agents, Russian and French agents. And they all want one thing. To know what our government plans to do that will in some way affect their governments. And if," he had that faraway look again, "if one of these agents can influ-

31

ence a decision or leak some information, he will do it regardless of the price."

"What does any of this have to do with you?" Gillian had been perplexed, for Brian never spoke of spies or other government agents.

"It is going to be my responsibility to identify those spies who are in England at this very moment."

She had suddenly felt a chill, but ignored it to ask the next question. "What will you do with these spies?"

Brian had looked at her at last and smiled. "Why, give them a dose of English justice, of course."

That conversation had been her first true awakening to British politics. Things were not as simple as they seemed. Brian had been chosen to look deeper into the political quagmire. He seemed to enjoy it enormously. Gillian's thoughts were abruptly interrupted at the sound of Brian's voice.

"Ladies, will someone please answer my question about Lord Hammond?"

"Oh, Brian." Gillian took his arm. "Don't tell me you want to find out more about his ancestors. His family ties are more impeccable than yours. What could you possibly want with him?"

Brian looked down at her and gently took her elbow. "What could you? He is not for you, my dear."

"Thank you, brother Brian. I shall try to remember that." Gillian laughed. Whenever Brian was at his most serious, Gillian felt most carefree and would tease him mercilessly. "Would you like to escort me to supper? Besides, I have the most fascinating story to tell you. And you had better believe me and not act like my father."

As they were leaving the large ballroom, Gillian could not help but sneak a look in the direction of Logan Hammond. Surrounded by three women, Lord

Hammond did not seem to care that most of the guests were emptying out of the room. His mouth lifted into a slight smile, despite the great distance, and it seemed as if he was laughing at them.

reproduced at the top of this page
was very empty but at the same time. His sister
has helped him as much as she has most difficult
times, because it has been happening at times.

Chapter Four

Gillian was only slightly nervous the following day. She had been escorted many times to the theater by any number of eligible, wealthy young gentlemen. Going with Lord Hammond would be no different, she told herself more than once.

Yet one hour before he was scheduled to arrive, Gillian was still staring into her enormous wardrobe, searching for the right gown, one that didn't make her look too old or too young. It had to make her look sophisticated, but not gaudy or daring. She must have discarded a half dozen gowns before finally settling on one. If it hadn't been for her mother's timely intervention she would probably have not chosen the rose velvet gown.

"Wear it, Gillian. The color suits you," Lady Helena insisted. And after Gillian stood in front of the gilt-edged mirror for the tenth time in as many minutes, she had to agree that the gown was appropriate.

"The bodice isn't too low, is it, Mother? It pushes my bust up and out. And the sleeves are tight. What about jewels? I don't know which jewels to wear with this. My pearls? The single or double strand? What about the earrings? Oh, and the bracelet. Oh, and I forgot to put something in my hair. Oh, my hair," she despaired, fidgeting with the long curls.

"Gillian, dear. Would you please stop talking and listen to me for a moment. And stop tugging at the ribbon on the waistband. You'll pull it off," her mother smiled indulgently. "Here," she handed her daughter the double strand of pearls, "these are perfect, and as for the earrings," she withdrew a box from behind, "I want you to wear these."

Gillian stared at the huge diamond-and-pearl earrings. "Oh, Mother, I cannot wear yours. Why, they are magnificent and so large."

"It is fine. I want you to wear them. Now hurry, dear, I think I hear a coach."

"Oh, God," Gillian moaned, looking about the dress-strewn room. "I hope he isn't too old for me. And he is so," she paused, "so sophisticated. Why, his reputation with women is renowned. In fact, I wonder why Father is permitting Lord Hammond to call on me? How stupid," Gillian frowned, "I know the answer. Father doesn't really care as long as I marry within the year. Isn't that true?"

"Lord Hammond is a fine gentleman. His father and yours are members of the same club. And if you let your father have his way, you will marry someone much older than Lord Hammond. Or Brian."

Lady Helena forced a bright smile. She hated to see her daughter in such a terrible situation. For her part, Helena had more or less accepted the fact that Gillian might never marry. Perhaps it was for the best. Why be wedded to someone you don't love? Most ton marriages were arranged so the money and influence remained within a powerful social strata. She had married because her parents had insisted that Charles Marlowe was perfect for her. And although her marriage to Charles had not been unhappy—they had two nearly grown children, money, and position—it

35

had not been full of laughter and love.

Like many members of the wealthy class, Charles had a few mistresses to satisfy his desires. Helena refused to acknowledge their existence. But she knew, oh yes, she knew, and had spent many nights alone in her huge bed—with the silk tapestries and bedspread and the delicate porcelain pieces along the dressing table—crying for a relationship that could never be, crying for a fantasy man who would hold her fiercely in his arms and kiss her with all the love and passion she craved. Perhaps, Helena wondered for the dozenth time, Gillian was right. Better to remain unwed than live with a loveless marriage.

"Gillian, forget about all of this and have a nice evening." She embraced her daughter. "We will probably see you at the ball after the theater."

"Good. I think I'll need to see a friendly face. Mother, do I look all right? I mean do I look pretty?" Gillian turned away from the full-length cheval glass to her mother.

"You've already asked me that, dear, and yes, you look lovely. Don't scowl at me, I mean every word. You are a very attractive young woman."

"Please, Mother. Why couldn't I look more like you? All we seem to have in common is the same eye color. And my eyes don't stand out like yours because my hair is so pale. Not as dark and rich as yours. Or my height. I'm too tall, too thin, and far too awkward. I never know when to keep quiet and don't seem to share the ladylike interests of most other women. I wonder where I belong."

"Now, darling," Helena took her daughter's hand and met her gaze, "what you are saying is simply untrue. That you are not exactly like the other young ladies of your station is a compliment to you. Be yourself." Helena lovingly smoothed a stray curl. "I often think you need a little more confidence in yourself. You are not like all those other simpering fools, but that does not make you any less beautiful. Lady Gillian Marlowe is unique."

Her mother's smile and quick embrace settled a few uneasy nerves, but it was not enough to keep her hands from trembling when the maid softly knocked on the bedroom door to announce that Lord Hammond was waiting in the library with her father.

"Father has probably offered the dowry by this time. Wish me luck, Mother." Gillian straightened her spine. "I suspect I may need it this evening."

Entering her father's library, Gillian found Lord Hammond and her father deeply engrossed in conversation. Logan seemed quite at ease, lounging in her father's large armchair, his long legs stretched before him. He held a glass of port in one hand and a cigar in another.

"I tell you, Logan, this situation cannot continue. The Spanish government cannot exist much longer. And if our foreign secretary is correct—and I am quite sure that he is—the French have exerted far too great an influence on Spain. And now, with the possibility of losing some of the Spanish colonies in America, the French would like to see nothing better than a chance to gain a stronger foothold in the Americas."

Gillian wanted to clear her throat to announce her presence, but knew the conversation would halt immediately. For some reason, she was curious about what Lord Hammond had to say.

"All of this political talk is tiresome, sir. You know as well as I that there is nothing we can do. Canning will try to exert some influence, but how much is that? And besides," he stifled a yawn, "I am not sure that many people are interested."

"Certainly you are not." Charles harrumphed. "I

do not understand you, lad. You seem to have no interest in politics."

"Should I?"

"Well, yes. Someday you will be sitting in the House of Lords in your father's seat. What will you do then?"

"Considering my father's robust health, I truly doubt that I will be anywhere near Parliament. I believe I have a few more years to enjoy the good life."

Gillian wondered briefly how long it would take before Logan Hammond's face and body would look more like the king's than an eligible, handsome, and fit young man. King George was hidden behind layers of fat, and his face was barely recognizable. Her mother had told her he looked nothing like the man of his youth, when as Prince Regent he was so very attractive. Is this what happens to those aristocratic young men who live to the fullest, enjoying the life of the pampered few who have nothing more to worry about than what to wear to the next ball and which woman to chase?

"It's a shame, Logan. You're wasting your life. Now, you take Gillian's brother John. There is a young man who is interested in politics and government. Lord Althrop has promised him a government position."

"How wonderful," Logan replied, and Gillian was positive his enthusiasm was insincere.

"Ah, excuse me," she coughed politely, "has anyone wondered where I was?"

Logan immediately put out the cigar and straightened out of the chair, swiftly examining her with a golden gaze which Gillian did not notice, for her eyes fixed on the breadth of his shoulders in the dark maroon coat. She forgot to extend her hand in greeting, and not until Logan reached for it did she remember her manners.

He noticed her bright pink blush but ignored it. Charles, of course, did not, and with his usual tact asked, "Where are your manners, Gillian? Do you want Logan to think you have not been brought up in the best of schools?"

Gillian did not know how to respond, but Logan did. "I believe your daughter's grace and beauty speak for themselves, Lord Marlowe. Lady Gillian, I fear our idle chatter has unsettled you. I apologize," he bowed over her hand, "and intend to make it up to you this evening."

She did not know what to say. He was everything the rumor mongers said about him and more, yet Logan was as courteous and solicitous of her comfort and happiness as any devoted suitor. Gillian was pleasantly surprised to know there was a charming and witty quality about him, too.

She could not help but notice the stares and whispers from the surrounding boxes as they entered Logan's theater box.

The King's Theater in the Haymarket was one of the most fashionable centers of entertainment in London. Everyone who wanted to be seen and be a part of the ton was there during the season. Because it was a horseshoe-shaped auditorium and Logan's box was on the first of five tiers, it was impossible not to be seen by the rest of the ton. And Gillian knew it the second Logan led her into the box.

"They must be wondering what you are doing with me," she whispered behind her fan, not really thinking that Logan heard her comment.

"Why? Because you are Lord Marlowe's precious daughter? Unmarred by scandal? Is it so unusual for me to escort a lady to the theater?" He raised a cynical eyebrow, and Gillian could have kissed him in front of the whole audience.

"Oh, no," she breathed. "You misunderstand." Meeting his hard golden eyes she rushed on, "They must be surprised or shocked that you would be seen with *me*. Lady Gillian Marlowe, the spinster."

"Come now," he helped her remove the white fur-lined cloak, "you cannot be serious."

Too entranced with his large hands on her almost-bare shoulders, Gillian briefly forgot what they were discussing. "What? Oh, excuse me. The gossips." She looked at his long fingers, still resting on her shoulders. "Lord Hammond . . ." she began.

"I think you are being unnecessarily formal, don't you agree?" His smile brightened the small box.

"Yes, well . . . Logan," she almost stammered his name, "I think our friends and social acquaintances over there . . ." she looked over to the next box and smiled at Ladies Smythe and Thompson, who immediately looked the other way when Gillian continued to smile. "The ladies are not shocked that I am with you. On the contrary, they are flabbergasted that you are with someone as old and plain as me."

There was a hint of laughter in her merry tone simply because she was having such a wonderful time making the ladies feel uncomfortable. Gillian did not realize how easily the words came to her. They were not meant to tease a compliment from Logan. He recognized the innocence and lack of guile in her tone as soon as she spoke.

Taking her gloved hand in his, Logan helped Gillian into the cushioned seat. For all of the eyes and opera glasses that were trained on them, he made an elaborate effort to make Gillian comfortable and stifled the urge to laugh aloud when his warm lips nearly brushed her bare neck.

Gillian thought she heard some titters, or were they

sighs? Her mind was too befuddled with the feel of his hands and lips to give the matter further thought.

"Let's show these biddies a thing or two this evening, shall we?" he suggested, never thinking that Gillian would have the courage to go along with the game.

Her laughter was as sincere as the clear expression in her eyes. "Why not? I promised myself it was time to have fun—that is, before it is too late."

"Too late?" He leaned closer and the whispers began again. "Why too late?"

"Never mind, Logan. It is silly. And I do want to have a wonderful time this evening. I never thought you to be such a nice man." The temptation to run gloved fingers through his light brown hair was strong enough for Gillian to clasp her hands tightly together.

"If we are to enjoy ourselves this evening, we must set aside the rumors and false impressions. I would like to know more about you. You are," his gaze lowered meaningfully to her chest, "an attractive young woman. I do not know what you have heard about me. Perhaps you will enlighten me over dinner after the theater?"

"But the Sandersons' ball?"

"Forget the ball. I thought you wanted to have a pleasant evening."

It was a challenge that Gillian could not resist. Why not? she asked herself. What difference could any of this make? As long as her father threatened to have his way, Gillian's life would be handed over to Brian or some old goat. Logan Hammond was offering a temporary solution. With an impish smile and wink, Gillian clicked shut her fan. "My lord, I think you are absolutely correct. Will you teach me how to have fun? I fear I have forgotten."

Logan was almost taken in by her winsome smile

and innocent, trustful gaze. It reminded him of his sister Luisa, who could wrap him around her chubby little finger in less than five minutes. But the voice of reason and caution prevailed. This chit could be dangerous to you, Logan. Remember, you don't know how much she overheard in the garden the other night. And to make matters more interesting, she has a devoted admirer in none other than Brian Althorp—better known within Logan's network as the "Vicious Viscount."

A most dangerous foe, or potential one, Althorp was just beginning to recognize his own power. It could be lethal to those who did not support the Liverpool government. It was rumored that Althorp was quite effective with accused traitors. And he showed no mercy to the ones imprisoned and eventually tried for treason—if they ever lived long enough to stand trial. In the last two months, Logan had learned of two men who died under mysterious circumstances before reaching trial. Logan sensed that Brian Althorp was interested in him. He would not still be alive and one of the best agents in England if he were unable to detect trouble before it got too close. Sooner or later, he would have to deal with Althorp.

And the Lady Gillian Marlowe could unwittingly help by keeping Logan apprised of her "friendship" with Althorp, but, in the meantime—ah, in the meantime. Logan stole a glance at the creamy white breasts straining under the rose velvet material. Yes, in the meantime, there was this lovely creature to become better acquainted with. And how could he ignore this new challenge and see how far he could go with Lady Gillian Marlowe. Besides, she was most amusing. The girl had great potential. If there was time, he could teach her so much. She was attractive and probably a good student, but her damn innocence struck a protective chord within him.

As the glaring theater lights were at last dimmed and the crystal chandelier's glow began to diminish, Logan placed Gillian's hand in his lap.

"You will have a most delightful evening. I give you my word." His husky whisper sent shivers down her arms.

For the first time that evening, Gillian forgot to be afraid of the consequences and did not pull her hand away. She was having a memorable time. Life might never be the same after this night and, after all, who cared?

Chapter Five

That evening, and the three successive ones, turned out to be far more pleasant than either Gillian or Logan had imagined. Returning to his club, White's, each night after taking Gillian home, Logan was surprised to find that her image remained with him. It was rare that he could instantly recall a potential conquest's exact features, yet if a canvas were placed in front of him this minute, Logan could paint Gillian's wavy blond hair shot through with red, the full lips ripe for kissing, the high cheekbones and upturned nose sprinkled with freckles, and the smooth white skin that turned bumpy whenever he touched her. She was definitely not unattractive. But what was beginning to disturb him was that Gillian Marlowe was no empty-headed chit, either. Unlike other ladies, Gillian possessed a keen interest in politics and literature and was quite knowledgeable about both. It was a shame, he thought as he stared into his almost empty brandy glass, that he had to so protect himself and could not engage her in a lively conversation, suspecting that Gillian could hold her own as well as any man.

Gillian was a staunch Tory, and seemed genuinely fond of Foreign Secretary Canning—though what anyone could see in him was beyond Logan's ken.

Canning was hot-tempered—Logan knew that first-hand—and loved to drink. True, he was very smart, or rather, *shrewd*. His ample forehead and oval face gave him the look of a scholar. Outwardly, Logan could only pretend mild indifference to Geroge Canning and his politics, even though he was keenly interested in the subjects. No one could know how much political knowledge Logan really possessed. Especially not Lady Gillian Marlowe.

Logan looked down the long, carpeted hallway not really seeing the number of familiar faces wandering about, playing cards, or drinking. Pouring himself another drink, Logan again recalled the fit of her small hand in his. He was becoming fond of Gillian, which was unfortunate. And that reminded Logan of two other problems.

On more than one occasion Gillian had mentioned her friendship with Brian Althorp but had revealed little else. Logan did not want Althorp to become any more curious about him than he was at present. Least of all did he need to be concerned with some suitor's jealous wrath. And Althorp's vengeance would be most untimely and dangerous for his mission. Moreover, Gillian had no idea how dangerous Althorp was.

None of this would matter much longer, for Logan was leaving England on a new assignment which, according to Harold, was of monumental importance. An imminent departure, he supposed, could pose a problem with Gillian. This assignment could take a few months. The ton would naturally think he was off seeing the world again, but he did not know what to do with the Lady Gillian. He had to leave England confident that she knew nothing more about that night, that she couldn't possibly jeopardize Logan's true profession.

So engrossed in his own thoughts, Logan did not realize the import of the conversation behind him until the voices became much louder.

"I tell you, Martin, this has gone too far. Canning will never get Parliament to agree with this wild scheme."

"He will not need Parliament's approval. You sit in the House of Lords, how much do you hear directly from Canning and how much from unofficial conversations?"

"It matters not. If what you are saying is true, it is not going to work. Furthermore, it will only antagonize the Americans. The power remains with the northern states, whether some southerners like it or not."

"Canning has no great fondness for the American Secretary of State, Henry Clay."

"Bah, it's not Clay. Canning doesn't like the Americans. It's really quite that simple."

Logan wished he had been paying attention earlier and silently cursed his lack of control. Behind him were two of the most influential Tories and they were arguing over Canning's policy toward the Americans. And because he had been pining, yes *pining,* dammit, over some attractive chit, Logan had missed some vital information. It served him right for allowing a woman to interfere in his life. Hopefully, the two gentlemen would continue the conversation. With a little luck and a lot more port, they might just give Logan the information he was seeking.

For weeks he had heard of the rumors concerning Canning's policy toward the Americans. Only recently he had learned that Canning was determined not to renew the West Indian treaty with the Americans. It had been a bad mistake for the Americans to let the treaty expire without a new one, but that was more the fault of the American Congress than either President Adams or Clay. However, with the expiration of the treaty, the lucrative trade routes and rights to the West Indies would again be under British control. In exchange for a new treaty, the British wanted exclusive trading rights with the Americans. The timing was poor, for how could the Americans forget so many of the past and present English transgressions and allow exclusivity in trading. What the devil was Canning thinking when he made those demands? Or was it simply that Canning wanted the treaty to expire, wanted to force Clay's hand to negotiate other, more delicate issues? Whether the Americans would really enforce the Monroe Doctrine if England allowed Spain to reclaim its lost colonies was yet to be determined.

"Pardon me, Arthur. But again you are mistaken. I have heard some very disturbing news today and it could have some devastating effects on both our government and America."

Logan snapped out of his romantic stupor to concentrate on the gentleman's last words.

"I have reason to believe that a number of so-called emissaries will be sent to America to find out how strong the union between the northern and southern states is and whether something can be done about it."

"Are you daft, man? Why could Canning think of something as dangerous as that?"

"There is every reason, my friend."

Logan couldn't strain any further without being seen. The man's voice was slurring, and it became increasingly difficult to understand the words. Although he suspected what would be said, Logan wanted confirmation.

"It's a brilliant scheme, you see. If the states could

47

be divided, I mean irrevocably divided, who would support the British? The North or the South?"

"Why, the South, I suppose."

"Correct. And where else could the British regain a toehold, rather, a large foothold, than in the South?"

"I don't believe it."

"You don't have to. I heard it with my own ears this very morning in this very chair. Canning was here, you know. So was that chap Althorp and a number of devoted followers of King George and the Tory government. I heard it. I sat two seats away from Canning when he said those words."

It was Logan's turn to look incredulously at his brandy glass. This was more than he could have hoped for. If he could prove it, the information would be invaluable to Harold and the others.

Ignoring an approaching acquaintance, Logan unfolded his long legs, smoothed his ruffled hair, and headed for the door. There was much to do with the remainder of this evening. With luck, Logan would have something for Harold and still be able to keep both his appointment with his tailor and dinner with Lady Gillian.

Over the next three weeks, Gillian had seen Logan quite often. The afternoon at Hyde Park had come and gone uneventfully. With Logan and his half sister Luisa as companions, they had ridden around the park looking for her mysterious spies. Of course it had been as ridiculous as Charles had predicted. Logan had so much trouble maneuvering the pony phaeton through the crowded lanes that a dozen rendezvous could have transpired before the phaeton was led around one turn.

It mattered not, Gillian decided. Her days and

thoughts had been fully occupied by Logan and the times she would see him again.

It baffled Gillian when Logan condescended to accept her father's invitation for dinner next Tuesday. It was ludicrous, she knew. Charles Marlowe was convinced that Logan could be persuaded to continue courting her, but Gillian knew that was not Logan's intention, no matter how much of a dowry she possessed. Logan was not interested in her money. He had more than enough of his own. So why did her father insist on making a mess of her life? After what would probably be a disastrous dinner, Logan would most likely walk out of her life.

But it did not matter, for she would always treasure the memories of the last three weeks. Gillian had been transported to a euphoric state. Damn her father for interfering and making it end. Once he confronted Logan about marriage, Gillian would not see him again, and she had been having so much fun. Logan proved to be a gentleman with her, despite the rumors. Adeline was positively shocked that Logan had not even kissed her. The most he had done was hold her gloved hand or brush his lips against it. Nothing more than that. But it did not matter to Gillian. For when he sat close to her, when his leg touched hers or his hand brushed her neck, Gillian felt hot and cold simultaneously. Perhaps it was his husky voice, so unlike the foppish men she knew, or his strength, or his strong classic profile, or the delightfully attractive tiny cleft in his chin. Whatever it was, Logan Hammond was the most devastatingly handsome man she had ever known. And he had been paying quite some attention to her since the night of her uncle's ball.

Pacing the confines of her room, Gillian reviewed the events of their first meeting. Strange, she thought, Logan had come to her defense over the matter of the spy. She had tried to talk to Logan about it and he had asked questions—even appeared interested enough to listen to her recital of the entire conversation—but Gillian had recognized polite indifference. Only Brian was still truly interested.

Gillian picked up a white rose. Logan had sent the flowers yesterday, yet they were still as fresh as his smile. But she wasn't thinking of Logan now; no, she was trying to think of Brian.

"Silly goose, ever since you met him your mind has wandered into a thousand different directions at once," she laughed aloud. It was true, but it was so wonderful.

"Brian Althrop." She repeated his name to herself just to divert her concentration. Brian had asked her to tell him the story of the spy at least a dozen times since that night, hoping she could remember something else, or, better, recall some physical feature of either of the two men. Gillian had tried, for the subject was quite interesting to her. Unfortunately, she could not reveal anything different. Brian had told her that he would be at Hyde Park, even though it would be a wasted effort. The traitor would have found out by now. He always did, Brian had told her. "That bastard is always one step ahead of me. But not for long," he had whispered fiercely. "Soon."

Gillian had no idea of what to say. Since Logan's courtship of her, Brian was somehow different, more serious and far more involved in his government position than anything she had ever seen him concerned with before. He was also very jealous. If it hadn't been for her preoccupation with Logan, Gillian would have tried to understand Brian and probably help him. After all, she had been the one to overhear the incriminating conversation. She hadn't been fair to dear Brian. It was time to make up for her abominable behavior. She would make an effort to be kinder to him.

But tonight would be spent with Logan. He had promised to take her to the Vauxhall Gardens. It was a slightly scandalous place, she knew, but it could be so exciting. Besides, she couldn't help but recall the story Adeline had told her about Logan and the Countess of Hartshorn disappearing the last time they were at the Vauxhall Gardens.

It was a delightful evening to spend outdoors. There was a mild breeze and of, course, fog. Every now and then the moon peeked out behind the clouds, giving everything an ethereal gold. Being so near the river, the Vauxhall Gardens were shrouded in fine, swirling mists and the dampness caused Gillian's cheeks to bloom and her hair to curl charmingly about her face.

"You look lovely, Gillian, and robust—the picture of health."

"Robust? No one ever called me robust. Slightly anemic, of sickly pallor, but never robust. I thought that was a word used for the women in Reubens paintings." She took Logan's proffered elbow as they continued to stroll around the area. Gillian could care less that the hem of her silk dress dragged along the wet ground or that the night air chilled her bare arms.

"Are you cold? Here, why don't you wear my coat." Before Gillian could utter another word, Logan had quickly shrugged out of his charcoal-gray coat and placed it around her shoulders. She inhaled his masculine scent. Never again would she smell the essence of lemons and limes and not think of Logan.

Pulling the coat around her, Gillian imagined it was his arms that enfolded her so securely. So lost in thought, she had no idea where Logan was leading her. The number of torches had diminished considerably where they were headed. In fact, by the time they got close to the river, there was hardly any light at all. This was probably the spot where he had taken the countess, but Gillian did not mind. All that mattered was the outline of his face and the contrast of his crisp white shirt and cravat against the night sky.

"What are you thinking about?" His voice was a whisper.

That you will kiss me, she wanted to say, but held her tongue. "I love this kind of night. It is so mysterious and lovely. This evening reminds me of the night we were introduced. Although I must admit I was rather upset that evening. That was when I overheard the traitors' conversation," she continued, not noticing in the slightest how Logan's body had stiffened.

"I wonder if they will be caught."

"I hope so. I would hate to think that I was responsible for allowing them to remain free. I should have been more bold, I suppose." Gillian was not looking at Logan, but at the river, spotted with torchlight and an occasional boat that lazily sailed past.

"Mind if I smoke?" He did not wait for an answer and pulled out a long cigar. "These are the best cigars in the world, I've been told. I had them imported from the Spanish colonies."

She loved to listen to his deep voice. There was something about its tone even when he was nonchalantly asking permission to smoke or inquiring about the weather that Gillian could have sworn he was asking her to undress. The accent was clipped, but not perfectly upper-class English.

The flare of the match illuminated his face. He was still speaking, and Gillian suddenly felt she was being propelled back in time. It was a naggingly familiar scene.

"Gillian? Do you hear me? You seem so lost." He touched her shoulder. "Is there something wrong? Are you very cold?" Logan stared down at her, waiting for the accusation. Noticing the suddenly stiffened back and shake of the golden head, he knew exactly what she was thinking and wanted to test her further. "Perhaps my cigar does offend you." Tossing it to the ground, he deliberately faced her shocked face. "Ah, my dear, you seem troubled about something. May I be of assistance?"

"What?" She lifted her head, but could not see his direct, challenging gaze. The moon swiftly and briefly appeared and Gillian could have sworn he was mocking her.

"I think we should return. I promised Adeline I would look for her. And then, of course, you know Brian will be looking for me." She said the first words that came to mind, and they proved to be a serious mistake.

"Althorp? Why are you suddenly concerned about him?" Logan took her shoulders, intentionally allowing his coat to slide off. "Forgive me." He lowered to retrieve the coat and once again placed it around her shoulders. This time, however, he leaned very close, too close. Gillian was stunned into silence.

"Perhaps I should clasp the button." His voice was husky as his hands touched her smooth neck, then roamed along her arms. "Such soft skin," he murmured. "I wonder . . ." he began.

"What?" she croaked, both terrified and excited about what might happen next.

"Your mouth is so ripe for kissing. Have you ever been kissed?"

"I, um, I cannot recall."

His throaty laugh undid her last remaining shred of propriety. "If you cannot recall, I would imagine it was not memorable. Tell me, did your Brian ever kiss you?" His mouth slowly descended.

She could see the outline of his full lips, imagined the slight cleft in the chin. He was a scant two inches from her mouth. Her heartbeat quickened. Her breath became erratic. She felt lightheaded. If he didn't hold her erect, Gillian did not think she could stand on her own.

He must have known, for Logan's arms tightened around her small waist. "Althorp never kissed you like this."

There was no time for doubt or protest. Gillian's confused mind could only register that his breath faintly smelled of tobacco and that his mouth was cool and firm. Without any provocation from him, her lips parted to meet the contours of his mouth.

"You need to be kissed," he whispered against her mouth. "You need me."

More than anything, she wanted to respond. Her eyes closed, her body leaned into his, and she gave herself up to the inexorable sensations he created with his mouth. Why talk and ruin this dream?

"I could teach you so much if you let me, Gillian," he breathed into her hair. "I like the feel of your lips against mine. Your lips taste so sweet." His hand slid lower and crept inside the gray coat wrapped around her. Before she could take another breath, his hand found the bodice of her dress and gently explored the burgeoning tip of her breast. "Mmm, so lovely. I would love to feel more of you." Again, he took her open mouth and pressed his body into hers, slowly rotating his hips against her. Logan's hand slipped beneath the silk dress to caress her rounded breasts gently.

Gillian was totally lost to his sensuous power. Not thinking of anything but the moment, of the feel of his hands freely roaming her satin-clad body, she did not realize the coat was no longer protecting her and she was being lowered to the ground.

"I must feel all of you. Let me touch you, Gillian," he whispered fiercely. He was watching her face, her eyes closed in the throes of first passion. He knew he could take her right there.

With years of experience in the art of seduction, the coat was perfectly placed on the ground. In a few minutes, she would be his.

"Am I interrupting something, Gillian?"

It was Brian Althorp. Logan would have murdered him on the spot if Gillian hadn't fainted into his arms.

Chapter Six

"What the devil are you doing with my fiancée?"

"Your 'fiancée' is it? I had no idea you two were betrothed. I did not see the announcement," Logan calmly said, seeming to forget that Gillian was lying unconscious in his arms.

The two antagonists faced each other. Brian's anger was palpable, while Logan appeared amused. Only when Gillian moaned did the two remember where they were, and why.

"Unhand her, Hammond." Brian reached for Gillian.

"Gillian chose to be with me this evening, Althorp. I suggest you depart before you cause her to swoon again." At last Logan looked down, noting the rapid blinking of her eyes and feeble attempt to raise one gloved hand to her head.

"Logan?" Gillian was alternately chilled and warm, yet it was not an unpleasant sensation. With Logan's strong arms around her, Gillian decided to make the moment last and nestled her head on his shoulder.

"What do you think you are doing?" a familiar voice barked, reminding Gillian of why she had swooned. "Brian," she groaned softly into Logan's neck.

"Gillian, I demand an answer."

"For goodness' sake, Brian, why are you following me?"

"I am only trying to protect you." His voice seemed to carry in the wind and fog.

"Well, I am fine." Suddenly Gillian remembered where she was, and found it difficult to stifle a giggle. "Excuse me, Logan, I think I feel fine now."

"Do you think you are able to stand?" He sounded solicitous, but Gillian heard the hint of laughter in his question.

"Gillian, do you have any idea of what you are doing? You are about to compromise your reputation with this, this . . ."

"Stop sputtering, Althorp. Is there anything else you wanted to say before Lady Gillian and I depart? I would ask you to join us, but under the circumstances I think it unwise. Don't you?"

Logan, however, did not wait for an answer. Rearranging his discarded jacket about her bare shoulders, Logan firmly took Gillian's elbow and walked farther into the dark night.

"You're headed in the wrong direction!" Brian shouted.

"Are we?" Logan called back before the two disappeared behind a large tree.

"We are not finished, Lord Hammond," Brian swore. Pulling his brown cloak tighter about his shoulders, Brian turned in the opposite direction. "You will not steal anything or anyone from me. This I swear."

If any of the lovers trysting on the grounds saw an angry young man stalk across the gardens, they pretended not to notice. It wasn't any of their business. Quite often one could see a rebuffed, would-be lover stalk away or a frightened woman streak across some path into the warmth and security of the well-lit pavilion.

Certainly the row with Brian Althorp was the furthest thing on Gillian's mind. She would remember tomorrow, but now there was the rest of this enchanting evening to enjoy.

"Gillian, are you feeling well?" Logan's voice was a husky whisper in her ear. "We can go inside."

"No. I'm fine, truly. It is just that Brian startled me. Besides, I think I like the quiet of the open air." They walked towards the river. Gillian wished they could sail away on one of the custom-made private barges she had seen but never been aboard.

"And the company I hope." His arm tightened about her slim waist. With the back of her head leaning against his chest, Gillian could not see his furrowed brow. Damn, how could he possibly make up the lost time. His mind furiously raced over the last twenty minutes. He could have claimed her if it weren't for the fool Althorp. Inwardly, though, Logan knew Althorp was no fool. Nor could he be considered one of Logan's friends, and after this night, would be counted among his enemies. It did not matter, in any case, for Logan would not be in England much longer. If only he could get this girl out of his mind.

He had wanted her. Lord, he could still feel the desire in his loins. Gillian would still be writhing passionately in his arms if it hadn't been for Althorp.

"Were you affianced to him?" His lean fingers stroked some errant curls.

Lost in the sensation, Gillian needed extra moments to think about the question. "Brian? Oh, no, although it would make my father quite happy, I suppose. Brian and I have been as close as siblings over the years. I do care about him. But not in *that* way.

58

He's somewhat overbearing and stuffy. But I am fond of him. And he will come around. He always does."

"Too sure of your conquests, my dear."

"Brian isn't a conquest, Logan." She turned to face him.

"Am I?" He tilted her soft mouth up to his. "Would you like me to continue our previous, ahem," he cleared his throat meaningfully, "exploration?"

This was her moment of truth. Why did Logan have to leave it up to her to decide? Gillian would have liked nothing better than to be driven senseless by Logan's kisses and soft touch. She would have loved to feel his hands roam her naked body. But not here, not on the wet grass to serve as a bed with nothing but a dark jacket to serve as silk sheets.

"Perhaps not." Her pale blue eyes beseeched him. "Not like this. I suppose I am not like Countess Hartshorn. Oh," she pressed a hand to her mouth, "I apologize, I did not mean to mention . . ."

His deep laugh made her look up in surprise. "You seem to know quite a bit about me. Let me guess. Does it have anything to do with your friend Adeline Barrish? I shall have to speak with Arthur."

"Oh, no." She took his arm, realizing that Logan had still not put his jacket on. "It wasn't Arthur's fault. Adeline, well, Adeline overheard a conversation of yours." She sighed heavily. "I do apologize. Sometimes my mouth is faster than my mind."

"I like your mouth." Logan lowered his head to lightly kiss it. "You were made for kissing. But I suppose you are correct, my dear. The Vauxhall Gardens do not suit you. I shall endeavor to find a more romantic setting."

Gillian had no idea if he were jesting. Choosing to forget his words for now, she allowed him to lead her back into the lantern-lit gardens. Logan had not pressed her. Perhaps he cares about me a little, she thought. Or perhaps he is a gentleman underneath that rakish exterior and wild reputation.

What Gillian did not know was that Logan was merely postponing the inevitable. He could read her mind as if she were speaking aloud. By not pressing her, he had won her trust. She would be his in a very short time, if he wanted to pursue her.

But first he would have to attend a dinner with her parents, and that was completely out of character for Logan Hammond. It was one of his rules to never socialize with any relative of his current paramour. Of course Gillian wasn't his lover—yet. Logan never felt any compunction to explain his comings and goings to anyone—let alone a woman. Still, the evening could prove to be enlightening. How much did the Marlowe family know? Lord Marlowe was quite chummy with the Duke of Wellington and most interested in the policies of Foreign Secretary Canning. Gillian's father could be useful.

"He's not coming, I tell you." She stomped across the drawing room.

"Gillian, I am sure there is a suitable explanation. And stop that infernal pacing, you are ruining that fine Aubusson carpet."

"I could have guessed you would be more concerned about the welfare of this silly rug than my total humiliation." Her voice rose sharply.

"Don't be a little fool. Helena, do something about this girl. I swear her temper is worse than mine, and her tongue might be every bit as salty as the dockside sailors."

"Father," Gillian stared at the ornate French clock on the mantel, "it is past eight. I recall telling Lord

Hammond to be here at seven. Do you usually tolerate such rudeness from other dinner guests?"

"Helena," Charles warned again.

"I cannot stop her, Charles. I happen to agree."

Charles threw his newspaper to the floor and stood up to come face-to-face with his daughter, who was only three inches shorter than himself. Although Charles Marlowe had dark eyes, it was said that Gillian's resemblance to him was quite strong. The hair color was similar, and so was the stubborn set of the chin. Even their temperaments were identical, which made it all the more difficult for the two to get along.

Charles cared very much for his children and had a special fondness for Gillian. If only she were married by now. It rankled Lord Marlowe that his pretty, if occasionally stubborn daughter, was not yet married. Unlike most of his friends, whose children were of the same age as Gillian, Charles continually fretted that Gillian was destined for spinsterhood. It meant that she would continue living in his household, receiving his financial support. The stigma was simply too much for a man as socially conscious as Lord Marlowe. It was not right.

What did it matter if Gillian married Lord Hammond—in spite of the lad's reputation. She would be married, and no longer his problem. Let Hammond worry about her—if he stayed home long enough to remember just whom he had married! Why Hammond was interested in Gillian was beyond Charles's ken. Certainly it wasn't for her dowry, for, if the rumors were true, Hammond's family had more than enough money to support most of London's poor.

Charles walked over to the large window, pulling the brown velvet curtain aside while mechanically straightening his embroidered waistcoat over his paunchy stomach. There was no sign of Hammond's coach yet. It was odd, of course, that Hammond was over an hour late for the dinner, but Charles decided it was because of some pressing business or social obligation, both of which he was willing to forgive and certainly could understand.

"Ladies, how do you know Lord Hammond isn't tied up with some estate problem? The Earl of Stanton owns at least three estates that I am aware of. Or perhaps there was some delay because of the House of Lords. I left early because of you!" he growled.

"Charles, was Lord Hammond seen today in Parliament?" Helena quietly asked.

"Ahem, no. But I did not stay too long. As I've said . . ."

"Yes, Father, we heard you. How much longer should we wait?"

Charles glanced at his daughter. She really was pretty. Oh, perhaps not a standout beauty like a number of younger ladies, but Gillian possessed a regal air. She was unusually tall, but as long as she didn't hunch her shoulders, she carried herself quite well. And tonight she looked especially nice in a pale yellow dress with her hair piled in curls. But she was so sad, Charles saw it in her lackluster eyes. He actually felt sorry for her plight.

"I apologize, Gillian. I wanted this to work for you." He saw her doubtful expression. "I am sincere. I think Logan is a nice chap underneath that wild exterior. Come here," he stretched his arms, "let me hold my little girl."

Surprised by her father's unusual tenderness, Gillian forgot her anger and rushed into his arms. It was refreshing to have her father's arms and kind words soothe her. "I have shamed us all," she whispered into his shoulder. "If you want me to marry, I suppose I must."

"Gillian," Charles lifted his daughter's chin, "are you in love with Hammond?"

"I don't know. I have known him less than two months. It's just that I have never felt so much enjoyment with a man. I've never felt that way with Brian. Logan is quite interesting when he is not bored by life, and he knows much more than you think. Except about politics, of course, something you love to discuss. Logan merely tolerates it."

Charles bestowed a rare smile on his daughter. "I think you are fond of him. I hope something favorable will happen."

"And if it doesn't? How long must I wait to hear another lecture, receive another ultimatum about marriage within this year?"

"I shall leave you alone for at least one month," he jested and kissed her brow. "But I think you will not have to fret any more this evening. I hear a coach."

Gillian ran to the window and almost had the curtain pulled aside when Helena reprimanded her to act like a lady.

When Logan was announced, he strode casually into the drawing room as if nothing were amiss. Gillian scrutinized him as if she were seeing a ghost. He looked so handsome in his dark gray coat and trousers that she wanted to melt into his strong embrace and forgive him anything, but her logical mind at last won over her heart. She would hear him first.

"How nice of you to join us Lord Hammond," she icily announced.

"Lord and Lady Marlowe, and Gillian, my dear, I deeply apologize for my tardiness, but my father insisted I handle a business matter, and it took up the entire day. I had no opportunity to contact you, for I only just returned to London, coming directly to your home. I apologize for my appearance as well." Looking down at some imaginary creases in his attire, he addressed himself once more to Lady Helena. "If you wish, we can change our plans for this evening, but I hope you will understand."

Logan looked into Gillian's accusing stare. She did not believe him, but the Marlowes appeared to have swallowed his excuses. He would have to count on their forgiveness to sway the lovely Lady Gillian, and she looked ravishing in that pale yellow watered-silk gown. The lace trimming gave it a virginal quality, but he could see her heaving bosom under the thin material and wondered if it were anger or passion that moved her.

"I defer to my father, Lord Hammond."

Anger, he knew now. Nevertheless, she would be wonderful in bed if he could turn that anger into equally combustible passion.

"Please, Logan, let us begin the evening anew. Helena, will you notify Davis to serve dinner in thirty minutes. I am certain Logan would like a strong drink. Gillian, will you give this to our guest, please?" Her father did not wait for a reply before handing the crystal glass full of Scotch whiskey to her.

Her eyes briefly flashing defiance, Gillian hesitated before quickly taking the glass from her father and spilling some of the contents on the fine Aubusson carpet. Gillian was surprised that her father chose not to admonish her for soiling his precious carpet. Must be our distinguished guest, she decided. One must keep up a good impression if one is to find a suitable husband.

Logan read her thoughts, for as she handed the glass to him, he met her gaze smiling deeply into her pale blue eyes and winked. "Impressions, you know," he murmured for her ears alone.

She would have liked nothing better than to run from this room. Good manners dictated that she remain, but it did not mean she had to forgive him so easily.

Chapter Seven

"Where did your father send you this afternoon? I don't seem to recall you mentioning it." She moved to the sofa across from him. As if she had all the time in the world, Gillian made an elaborate effort of smoothing her gown around her legs, then gently touching an imaginative stray curl. Her eyes, however, did not leave Logan's face. She was waiting for a proper excuse and would sit all night on that sofa until she was satisfied.

"I did not mention it. I was sent to Windsor to confer with an architect. My family is interested in the renovation of two estates." He paused to take a small sip of the potent brew. He would have preferred to down the entire glass in one gulp, but Gillian would have misinterpreted his action for nervousness rather than thirst and impatience.

"It must be so difficult keeping up with one's estates," Gillian drily added. "Father is often preoccupied with these problems. He has allowed my brother John to become involved."

"It was time to see John more involved with the family's interests. It is good to see you finally interested in your father's estates." Charles privately noted how wonderful it was to see Lord Hammond take an

66

interest in something other than clothing, gambling, and women. Perhaps there was some hope for the lad.

"Did you hire an architect?" Gillian's eyes remained fixed on him.

"Well, no. I must find someone who can understand my father's desire for the preservation of the land and surrounding villages, not to mention the complete renovation of a wing on the main house. Difficult task, my dear." His tone was even, but something was still amiss.

"Logan, since when have you become interested in anything other than your own frivolous pastimes?" Gillian nearly bit her tongue for blurting such an impolite question. "Ah, excuse me, Logan, I did not mean . . ." She tried to continue, but Charles cut in.

"Gillian, really. Logan, my daughter often speaks too quickly. I do hope you are not offended."

Noticing a becoming blush creep up her neck to her cheeks, Logan sat back in the chair and smiled. "I think your daughter is delightful. I could never be offended by anything she says."

Charles could not have been more pleased. Imagine that, he thought, Logan is fond of my Gillian. Aside from the American ties on his mother's side, Logan's impressive ancestry could be traced as far back as the signing of the Magna Charta. Not that the Marlowe family history was any less impressive, but oh what a wonderful match this would be. Noticing Gillian's embarrassed smile, Charles knew she, too, cared about Logan.

"Let me propose a toast." Charles raised his glass and faced Logan. "To you, young man, and your family. I hope we have the chance to know you better."

Gillian could have choked on her wine, but Logan

would have laughed. She couldn't bear it if he laughed at her now. Loose tongues ran rampant in the Marlowe family, she decided.

"Thank you, Lord Marlowe. I hope so, too. Much depends on your lovely daughter." Logan looked at Gillian's surprised face and smiled deeply into her eyes. "I would like to toast Gillian. A rare jewel whose depth and beauty have yet to be discovered."

The rest was left unsaid, but Gillian knew from his penetrating stare that Logan wanted to remind her of the other night in the Vauxhall Gardens. She could almost feel his hands on her silk dress, slowly roaming up to the lace bodice. Thank God her father was still in the room, for she would have gladly thrown herself into Logan's hard embrace for a dizzying kiss.

Despite the unpleasant beginning, the evening progressed nicely. Logan was his usual charming self, and even Charles managed a few clever repartees. The conversation was light and no one seemed to be at a loss for words.

Seated across from him, Gillian's view of Logan was partially blocked by a silver candelabra. It gave her the opportunity to study his impeccable dress. Dark colors suited Logan who, contrary to popular London fashion, chose not to dress in bright colors. He did not need any adornments to stand out in a crowded room. The combination of his height, muscular yet lean body, and rugged handsome face, were all he needed to make a room full of women swoon at his nearness. And when Logan laughed, the rich, deep baritone ran through her body like a shot of forbidden whiskey. He was gorgeous, and for some peculiar reason was desirous of her.

It still bothered Gillian, for she could not understand why Logan was suddenly interested in her. There were far more beautiful women than she, and if the rumors were only remotely true, most of them were most willing to share Logan's bed. Yet he had singled her out and it had all started the night of her uncle's ball. It was all so odd, but tonight was not the time to dwell on the matter.

She knew her mother had asked him a question, but Gillian heard nothing. When Logan turned to face Helena, Gillian took great delight in noticing the tiny cleft in his chin.

"Gillian, dear, is there anything else you would like? You have hardly touched your food. I thought turbot was your favorite fish and Cook prepared it with your favorite cream sauce."

It took a full minute and Logan's expectant stare to realize that someone was talking to her. "Pardon me? I'm afraid I was thinking of something else, Mother. I apologize."

"Gillian, your mother only wanted to know if you were still interested in eating. Everyone else is finished, but you haven't touched your food."

Leave it to her father to be specific. "Everything is simply delicious. I had lunch a little later than usual. I apologize once more." To cover her nervousness, Gillian lifted the stemmed wine goblet to her lips, quickly draining its contents.

Logan could not have asked for a better set of circumstances. The evening was progressing nicely. If only he could have arrived on time. Damn Harold for detaining him today. According to Harold, something was afoot in the British cabinet. Foreign Secretary Canning had been scheduled to meet once again with the American emissary, Albert Gallatin, but had canceled the appointment abruptly! That was clearly an insult, but Harold had been only mildly upset about that. Something far worse was afoot.

Harold had proof that some influential Tories were

becoming overly interested in American domestic policy and wanted Logan to obtain the details. It would be vital if his next assignment were to be a success. Lord Charles Marlowe, soon to be the sixth Earl of Suffolk, might unwittingly be of assistance.

Taking a moment to study the faces of the surrounding Marlowes, Logan knew he had charmed all of them, Charles most of all, and for the moment that was more important than either of the ladies. He needed to know how much latitude Althorp was given by Canning over the espionage issue. The opportunity hadn't presented itself. It would, Logan knew, once he and Lord Marlowe were alone. Gillian would have to be the one to open the discussion and he knew just how to accomplish that.

"Gillian, has your friend Viscount Althorp made further investigations about the spy incident?"

"Oh, not that again," Charles groaned. "Logan, you don't really take this matter seriously."

Seeing Gillian's stricken look, Logan felt a slight twinge of regret, but he had to get Charles Marlowe talking and what better way than to anger him over this spy. If it had to be at Gillian's expense, so be it.

"Gillian does and so do I. Don't you, my dear?"

She wanted to throw her wine in his charming face, but the glass was empty. Why was he ruining a pleasant evening? It was the first time in so long that her father had not embarrassed or scolded her. Now Logan had to bring *that* up.

"The matter still troubles me. You all know that," she said quietly. "A traitor is among us. I owe it to my country to do something. But what can I do now?"

"Ah, but it's Althorp who is greatly disturbed. Gillian fueled the fire, so to speak. Althorp is convinced there is a major spy network right here in London and is determined to smash it. He has identified possible traitors, I've been told." Charles had seen Brian at their club the other night and Althorp would not let the matter rest.

"With good reason, Father." Gillian had no intention of repeating the details of the incident, but Logan had other ideas.

"There must be something distinguishing about those men you saw that evening. Perhaps it was their voices."

Throwing him a chilly look, Gillian replied, "The voices were muffled. It was hard to distinguish them. Of course, as each day passes, I can barely remember their conversation, let alone their voices. You know all of that, Logan." It was difficult to mask her exasperation.

Logan wanted this conversation to veer towards another direction. "Well," he noticed the candle wax dripping onto the ivory lace tablecloth, "there's not much you can do, Gillian. The traitors are probably gone by now. But if Brian is as efficient as you say, I am confident he will succeed in finding them." If only he could learn the names on Althorp's list.

If Logan were not so distracted by his desire to encourage Charles to speak, he would have chosen his next words more carefully. But it had become obvious that Charles had his own motive for inviting Logan to dine with the family. He wanted Logan to announce his intentions for Gillian this night.

"By the way, have I mentioned that I must be off on a business holiday to Italy and France? I'll be leaving in a few weeks. I shan't be away longer than two months."

The blood suddenly drained from her face while her heart pounded loudly in her ears. Could she have heard Logan correctly?

It felt as if the mauve-papered walls were unexpectedly closing in on her. Gillian felt claustrophobic. She needed to be alone and away from him. Blinded by his handsomeness and overwhelmed by his attention, Gillian could not think straight as long as he was near. But there was one thing she did know: this had to be Logan's way of begging off. He must have had enough experience with anxious fathers who wanted to marry their daughters off to know when it was time to exit gracefully.

She had harbored no illusions about marriage with Lord Hammond. She only wanted their time together to last longer than a few more weeks. And if her father decided to press Logan for his intentions this night, she would probably never see him again.

"Father, I realize I must be detaining you. Why don't you and Logan withdraw to the library while Mother and I freshen up? I am sure you would like your imported cigar now, Logan. And Father can tell you all about the dreadful parliamentry session. Can't you, Father? After all, there is little else to discuss now, is there?" Certainly her message could not have been more direct.

"Sounds wonderful." Actually it wasn't. Logan noticed her reaction to his impulsive announcement. He should have waited for a private moment to tell her. She was hurt more than angry. If only he could steal a moment alone with her tonight. He wanted to hold her hand and take her into his arms. He did not want passion at the moment—only to give comfort. Suddenly it was important to Logan that Gillian understand he was not leaving her.

He knew she was infatuated with him and with time would fall in love with him if he continued courting her. She was lovely, witty, and a good companion. Given the proper time and circumstances, Logan might have seriously courted Gillian.

Logan tried to send her a sympathetic look, but her icy blue eyes focused on the lace tablecloth. Obviously, she was angered with him and her father, too, for that matter. Gillian did not want her father to bring up the subject of marriage, and he knew why. She was not stupid. She was afraid of losing Logan forever.

Unfortunately, Logan could not hold back time or postpone his assignment.

Chapter Eight

The pounding rain against the damask-curtained window was Gillian's companion, that and the down pillow she clutched in her lap. Leaning against the upholstered headboard, she had abandoned the idea of sleeping hours ago. Glancing at the French mantel clock, Gillian wondered why time had to creep so slowly. Only 3 A.M. Lord, there were too many hours left to think. To think about Logan Hammond and his departure.

It was over. She had known it would happen. So why did she feel an emptiness in the pit of her stomach? Why did she feel so lonely? Her one glorious chance to live life fully was leaving England. Perhaps a more courageous woman would beg him not to go, and if that failed, beg him to take her along. But then the scandal would be too great for her family and no one would ever offer for her hand— not even Brian.

Was she in love with Logan, her father had asked. Perhaps she was in love with the reckless side of him that encouraged a spontaneous response in her or the intuitive side of him that seemed to know her thoughts. If only they could have more time together.

On the other hand, she reasoned, what difference did it make that Logan was leaving England in a few short weeks? There were no guarantees he would continue courting her. Perhaps he was biding his time with her in London until someone else — someone far more beautiful and younger than she — came into his life. He was bound to leave her, she was sure, yet, before he had left this evening, Logan whispered in her ear, "I want to spend some time with you, Gillian — before my departure. Alone. Say yes." He had used that seductive tone for her ears alone. Gillian had shivered and nodded an affirmative response, mindless of the implication of his words.

What did he mean by "alone?" Gillian spent the next hour pondering that one word. Was it possible Logan would ask her to wait for him? How long would he stay away from London? He had said two months, but that was meaningless. Business and holiday, he had said. If it were remotely true, he might be forced to extend his stay. Mayhap the business could be concluded sooner than two months. Would he consider marriage after he returned from his holiday? Or would he remember her at all? With the bevy of French and Italian beauties who most certainly would throw themselves at him, would Logan even recall her name when he returned?

Sighing aloud, Gillian knew he would forget her as soon as he stepped aboard his ship. She was not the kind of woman a man remembers. There was nothing distinctive about her features. She had never been known for a sparkling personality, nor had she given Logan anything to remember.

It was different for her. What memories would she have? There were many, she remembered with a sigh, like the one frantic night of near passion. The times when his long, lean fingers brushed her bare shoulders as he assisted her with her cloak or the impish grin when he seemed genuinely amused by something she had said. She was never bored with Logan.

In three weeks Gillian would be terminally bored and left with her memories. Were they enough to last a lifetime? Would she always wonder what it might have been like if she had allowed Logan to take her virginity?

"Now that would be some memory," she laughed aloud.

As the minutes dragged by, Gillian became obsessed with the notion. Would it matter if she gave herself to him? She knew some girls who were not virgins when they married. She also knew others who had to marry, but what difference did that make? In a few short months, she would have to marry, too, simply because her father wanted it that way. No spinsters in his family.

Why not go into an arranged marriage having experienced what true passion could be? There couldn't possibly be a better teacher than Logan.

By 5 A.M., Gillian had convinced herself that she must be alone with Logan. She must be given the last chance at love.

"No, no, Gillian, not love. Don't confuse passion with love," she told herself more than once. "This is an experiment with life."

By 5:30 she was asleep. There was a tiny smile on her soft lips while she still clutched the pillow to her heart.

If he had known what Gillian was thinking, Logan would have been delighted. It would have saved him many useless hours of worry. As it was, he didn't bother to return to his townhouse until nearly dawn. Immediately after leaving the Marlowes, he had his coachman drive him around town for nearly two hours. Realizing it wasn't kind of him to keep old Henry's arthritic bones in the foggy air, Logan decided to walk to his club. White's wasn't far and the damp air might do him some good.

For some odd reason, Logan could not erase the sight of Gillian's forlorn expression after he'd announced his departure. Foolish girl must have assumed he would continue courting her. She might have been awaiting a proposal—surely her father anticipated as much. Fortunately, Logan had adroitly sidestepped Lord Marlowe's questions. It had been equally obvious that Gillian did not want her father to say one word about marriage. That was their problem, he decided with a shrug. There was nothing he could or would do about it. Gillian would survive. Probably marry Althorp.

"Poor girl," he said aloud, oblivious to the curious expression of a passing acquaintance.

"As drunk as I am," the man said, and continued staggering down the cobblestone street.

Deciding that a strong drink and a chance to win some money at the gaming tables were exactly what he needed, Logan hurried along St. James's Street to his club.

After three snifters of brandy, Logan felt marginally better. Looking around the darkly paneled room, Logan saw his friends and acquaintances immersed in gambling. Drinking and conversation came second and third to their primary passion. Hour after hour, with hats tilted low over their bloodshot eyes, they stooped over the green baize tables. Some were successful, but one would never know. Emotion—whether joy or misery—was never,

ever shown. It was not what a gentleman did, for it showed ill breeding. It mattered not if he lost or win, for he wore the same bored expression.

Many a time Logan had witnessed these same expressionless gentlemen creep away in the early morning to the house of the "Jew" King in Clarges Street to mortgage their estates, or silver, or wives' diamonds. All for some extra cash to be gambled away again the following evening.

It disgusted Logan to see such irresponsible behavior. He would never be like them. Besides, he always won. In everything. Almost.

"Damn," he muttered into his crystal snifter. Gillian's softly rounded body appeared in the glass, and her sweet mouth, just begging him to kiss her passionately. He wanted her. For some ungodly reason, he desired her young, untried body.

His current mistress, Caroline Hartshorn, was baffled by his behavior. He had seen very little of her in the last two months, but when they managed to spend some time alone, Logan behaved—according to Caroline—"damnably distracted." No matter how prettily she pouted or how seductive she was, Logan barely noticed her.

"It's that silly young Marlowe girl, Logan, isn't it?" Caroline had asked after she had contrived to run into him at a friend's rout.

Logan hadn't heard her, for his amber gaze was following Gillian's regal stroll across the room. Logan thought how confident she had become since their "courtship."

"Logan," Caroline's voice had risen with frustration, "you are not paying any attention to me. Why, you haven't noticed my new hairstyle." Countess Hartshorn patted the elaborately coiled dark curls. "Or my new dress. It's your favorite shade of blue, darling," she'd purred. "I wore it especially for you. I imagined your hands unbuttoning the back of this dress and I couldn't stop shaking with desire."

It seemed as if everyone else in the room had noticed the countess's rapturous expression except Logan.

"Logan, damn you. I demand an explanation!" She had grabbed his arm. "I will not allow you to treat me this way."

Reminded at last of the persistent woman at his side, Logan sighed. "Caroline, if I bore you, why don't you attach yourself to Reginald over there. I understand he is quite desirous of establishing a liaison with you. You might prefer his company to mine." Logan had shown no feeling at all for the woman who — for the last five months — had shared his passion.

"Everything they have ever said about you was true. You are a bastard!" Her dark eyes glared with anger and humiliation. "I never should have allowed you into my bed. You are callous, heartless, and cruel."

"My dear, I think you have run out of adjectives. Are you finished?" He coldly stared down at her. "I have some other business to attend to."

Logan had walked off uncaring of her murderous expression and had left her standing alone in the middle of a crowded room.

Now that he thought of it, the scene had been amusing. Caroline only thought she would never talk to him again, but he knew differently. Besides, it didn't matter, he told himself. Glancing back down at the snifter, he realized that someone had refilled it while he was dreaming. Still seated in the large leather armchair, Logan reminded himself that losing Caroline Hartshorn was not too tragic.

"Pardon me, Lord Hammond," a vaguely familiar voice made him look up, "you seem so preoccupied."

"Oh, it's you, Althorp." Logan intentionally omitted the man's title. "I hope I haven't done anything to embarrass you." Logan did not stand up or invite the man to sit across from him.

"May I?" He sat before Logan could respond, studying Lord Hammond's face. He had seen him drink those brandies in quick succession but it appeared as if it was only cold water coursing through Hammond's veins. Brian studied his adversary, believing he could accurately judge a man by his gaze and hands. If both were steady, the man could be a strong opponent. So far, Hammond fit into that category.

"I understand you dined with the Marlowes again this evening." Brian's brown eyes could find no evidence of agitation in Hammond's posture, not even a tiny bead of perspiration upon his brow.

When Logan continued to stare and not respond, Brian was forced to continue. "Have it your way." He slightly inclined his head. "Let me get to the point, Hammond." Leaning forward in another effort to unnerve Hammond, Brian said, "I understand you are leaving our gracious city soon."

Logan raised the brandy to his lips, his eyes never leaving Althorp's thin face.

"You are making this difficult for me, Hammond." Brian cleared his throat. Damn, this libertine has no right to make me uneasy, he thought.

"Am I?" He reached for a cigar.

"Damn you, man, I only want to know what you intend to do about Gillian."

"I beg your pardon?" Logan nodded to a passing friend.

"Look at me. I asked you a question." Brian's voice remained steady, although it was difficult to control his mounting fury.

"I suggest you leave your orders to your lackeys, Althorp. I am not one of them. And as to your asking me about Gillian, I suggest you mind your own business. I told you as much before. I had no idea your memory was deficient." Now Logan leaned forward. "I never saw that scar on your forehead, Althorp." Logan appeared interested in the straight white line from Brian's hairline to temple. "A dueling accident?" he casually inquired.

"Yes, many years ago. The other fellow died. But I did not join you to discuss my duels or scars. I want to know about Gillian."

"You already know, Althorp, since you appear to be so well informed about most things—including my holiday. By the way, who told you about that? Did one of your lackeys bribe one of my servants? Or," he grinned, "is one of my servants in your employ? Is that how you know so much about people? You really are quite efficient, you know." His smile did not reach his eyes.

Somehow Hammond did not sound as if he were passing a compliment. Whenever Brian spoke to him, he had the impression that the bastard sported with him.

Brian made a point of never forgetting or forgiving the faces of those who mocked him.

"I seem to have made an error. You could not possibly be a gentleman. A gentleman does not poach. Particularly with young women."

As Brian rose to leave, Logan could not help but add another taunt. "I think I might ask for her hand, Althorp. I know she would accept eagerly. So would her father. By the way, I could challenge you for those nasty words." He decided to stand, towering over Brian by at least six inches. "I would hate to scar the other side of your face. Moreover, I doubt Gillian would be pleased. For some odd reason, she rather likes you." In a friendly gesture, he placed a strong hand on Althorp's shoulder. "I never said I was a gentleman. Good evening, Althorp. I will give Gillian your warm regards."

As Brian hurried away, Logan fought the desire to strangle the bastard right there in the middle of the sedate White's gaming room. It would give everyone something to remember, he decided. If anyone had the power to infuriate, it was Viscount Althorp. But he didn't want to bother killing anyone, and this one's demise would cause quite a stir in the British cabinet. The last thing Logan wanted was for anyone in the government to remember his name.

Not until he was deeply engrossed in a game of whist did Logan remember his parting remarks to Althorp. To the utter amazement of the three men seated around the table, Logan threw his head back and laughed. He had actually stated an intention to offer for Gillian's hand.

"How utterly preposterous!" he said aloud, still laughing.

"Beg your pardon, Hammond? Do you want to continue or would you rather laugh and talk to yourself while I lose?" his friend Arthur Barrish asked.

"Forgive me, Arthur." Logan slapped his back. "I just thought of the most amusing joke of the night."

"Save it, Logan. I'm busy. Well, are you in or out?"

"In. You know I cannot resist a challenge like this."

Logan won the game and silently drank a toast to Brian Althorp. For the first time that evening, Logan Hammond felt relaxed and carefree. Perhaps being betrothed was not such an awful idea after all. He wouldn't have to think about marrying the girl until he returned from his assignment. Many things could happen in the time he'd be away.

At least he was confident of one thing: Lady Gillian Marlowe would have to wait for his return. So would Brian Althorp.

Chapter Nine

The incessant pounding on the door finally reached Logan's ears.

"For God's sake, what is it?"

"Begging your pardon, my lord, but a young lady is here to see you."

Ignoring the dull throb in his head, Logan sat upright in bed, uncaring of the morning chill on his naked torso. "What time is it?" He ran long fingers through his wavy hair, then vigorously scratched his scalp in an effort to wipe the cobwebs from his brain. The tousled hair settled in different directions on his forehead.

"It is 10 A.M., my lord," his manservant nervously replied. Everyone in the house knew that his lordship hadn't come home until seven. In all the years Webster had been working for the young lord, no one ever disturbed him this early without prior permission. If Lord Hammond had wanted to rise early, he would have let Webster know when he came home.

"For Christ's sake, Webster, you know better than to waken me." He was irritated but could not muster the strength to scold his manservant. No one knew his habits better than old Webster, so something was obviously greatly afoot.

"I do apologize, but the young lady was so insistent and quite nervous that I thought it best to awaken you."

Logan flung the satin sheet aside, exposing the rest of his bare body. "Did she give her name?"

"Lady Gillian Marlowe."

His head fell into his hands. "Oh, not now. What could she want with me this early. Did you say she was nervous?" He looked up at Webster, flicking hair out of his half-closed eyes.

"Quite, my lord. You see, she's here alone."

"Alone? No chaperone? Well then, it must be very important to her. My head does not have the stamina to be scolded for some infraction. I wonder what the deuce is troubling her."

Suddenly last night's words with Althorp rumbled through his mind. Could Althorp have gotten to her this early? Was she expecting a marriage proposal?

"I suppose I must see her. Is she in the drawing room?"

"I thought it best not to let any of the household staff see her. Since she is so obviously a young lady," he emphasized those last two words, "I showed her to the study. It was closer to the front door."

"I understand, Webster," Logan muttered. "Thank you for your concern."

"She's not like the others who show up, now is she, my lord?"

"No, she is not," he smiled, forgiving Webster's outspokenness. He quickly jumped out of the huge four-poster bed, accepting the black silk bathrobe from the manservant.

"Tell her I'll be down shortly. Give her something to eat or drink. Tea. Nothing stronger."

"She did not appear the type to want anything stronger, particularly at this early hour. Not even you drink at this hour. Unless you've been out all night."

"You know me too well, Webster. And I must like you, otherwise I would never tolerate such insubordination."

"Yes, my lord." Webster's wide smile revealed a missing bottom tooth. "I already knew that."

Within ten minutes of Webster's departure, an unshaven Logan descended the curved staircase and entered the study. Forgetting to knock, he quietly entered the small room to find Gillian's straight back to him. One gloved hand held the blue print curtain open just enough to see what was going on outside near Regent's Park.

It was a rare sunny day in London. One golden ray slipped past the curtain settling on Gillian's face. Moving slightly to one side, Logan could now see her delicate, porcelain profile beneath the morning bonnet.

Either the drink had finally gotten to him or Gillian Marlowe was looking more enchanting each time he saw her. Everything about her was in perfect proportion to her height. With her cashmere shawl open, Logan saw the outline of her high, firm breasts through the fine material of the striped pale blue walking gown. She had no idea how she affected him. She was still an innocent in many ways and it delighted him to think he would be the one to initiate her into the finer things in life—not just the physical side.

What a pleasure it would be to take her to his favorite dressmaker and design the finest silk and satin dresses, the flimsiest nightgowns, sheerest undergarments, and fur capes that would enhance every one of her lovely features.

He must have groaned, for Gillian quickly turned to face him, a light flush creeping up her long neck.

"I did not mean to startle you, my dear." Still enjoying the play of the sun against her face, he did not move.

"I apologize, too, my lord, for barging in. May I? It's a trifle warm, I think." She removed the bonnet and placed it on the nearest armchair. "I never thought myself to be so impulsive, but there was something I simply had to discuss with you."

"Well, please, Gillian, make yourself comfortable." He gestured to the black leather armchair. "This is the least formal room in the house. It is where I get most of my paperwork done." He pointed to the messy but large desk. "I hope you don't mind."

Gillian dared not speak. She was so nervous and had no idea how she would phrase her next words. Logan was hardly making it easy for her. Not only was he his usual charming self, but this was the first time Gillian had seen him look as informal as he claimed the room to be.

The white lawn shirt, opened at the neck, exposed a whorl of dark brown chest hair. It was obvious he recently awakened, since he was still unshaven and his hair appeared slightly damp.

"Perhaps this is the wrong time. I did not mean to disturb you." Her voice trembled slightly.

"Please, don't leave now." Logan reached for her hand. "At least stay long enough to remove one glove?"

"I am not used to this."

"Obviously. Which makes it more delightful to tease you." Seeing she could not move, he took her arm, leading her to the chair. "May I offer you some refreshments? I asked Webster to bring my breakfast in here. Do you mind?"

Perhaps he would be so preoccupied with his food, he would not look at her with that melting golden brown gaze. Unconsciously, she tightened the shawl about her.

"Are you suddenly chilled?"

"Um, a little. Logan, I don't know why I came here," she blurted, feeling so foolish she wished she could miraculously disappear.

"Sweetheart, I do not mean to unnerve you. In fact, I am quite pleased that you chose to call on me at all. Although I swear I would have called on you this afternoon." He grinned and she felt her heart forget one beat.

"I wanted to talk to you about last evening."

"Oh? You mean he has seen you already?"

"Who?" Gillian didn't want to be interrupted, since she was trying to muster the courage to speak and not stop until everything was said.

"Althorp."

Logan sat on the wide arm of her chair and Gillian wondered if he could see the tiny beads of perspiration on her nose—a telltale sign of nerves.

"Brian?" She looked up at him. He was so close to her now that she could feel his warm breath on her hair.

"Yes, who else? Are there other suitors I am unaware of, Gillian?" He took such devilish delight in her discomfort that he allowed himself to be sidetracked by her beauty. "By the way, you have a lovely neck. Long and graceful and just begging for a small kiss. May I?"

She wanted to say no, but remained frozen instead. Taking that as permission, he lowered his head, his lips barely touching her neck.

"Ooh. But Logan . . ." She couldn't finish, for as she turned her head to face him, he mistook her gesture as a plea for more and took her lips in another gentle kiss.

"Let me taste you, Gillian," he murmured against her mouth.

Without knowing how it happened, her hair was undone and falling about her shoulders onto his hands. "You are so lovely, Gillian."

"Mmmm, kiss me again." That wasn't Lady Gillian Marlowe speaking, but some silly trollop, she realized.

His low rumble of laughter gave her chills. "You have much to learn, my dear. I cannot wait to teach you."

Taking her lips once more, he insinuated his tongue into her soft mouth. Sensing she was about to fall into him he braced her shoulders letting one hand slowly pull off the cashmere shawl.

"Kiss me, Gillian, like this." Again his tongue played with hers, teasing her until she knew what he wanted of her.

"That's good. You are an apt pupil."

Prepared to take her on the armchair, Logan ignored the soft knocking on the door.

"Your breakfast, my lord. May I bring it in? My lord? Lord Hammond?"

"Ah, my formidable manservant, Webster. He always knows the most propitious moment to make me want to discharge him." Looking down at her dreamy, eager face, he swore to himself he would release Webster this time. "Ah, Gillian, would you excuse me?"

Disentangling himself was the most difficult thing he had to do in quite some time.

"Oh, my God," she groaned. "I must leave." She struggled to rise. Never had she been so mortified by such wanton behavior.

"Wait here." He quickly left her side and opened the study door. "Start packing," he hissed to a grinning Webster, grabbing and nearly unsettling the silver tray held out to him.

"Not again, my lord. Would you like me to bring this in?"

"Get out of here, now." He slammed the door with his booted foot.

"I don't believe this," Gillian sank into the back of the chair. "I have never been so embarrassed in my life. Why did I ever think to come here and discuss my plan with you so early in the morning, and un-chaperoned? Why, if my parents found out, they would crucify me. Oh, forgive my language, it's just that I am so . . ."

"I understand. Please, calm yourself." For one second he thought that if he hadn't interrupted her, she would have babbled for the next ten minutes, without taking a breath. "Gillian," he placed a hand on her head, "it's really quite all right. Nothing would have happened," he lied. "I am not such a cad. Please, look at me."

When she turned, a stray reddish-blond curl caught in the button of his sleeve. "I suppose the only thing to humiliate me further would be if my father saun-tered in your front door. Or better, my mother were with him." She smiled slightly. "Why not add Brian, too."

"No, the worst thing that could happen would be *my* father and that awful gossip Lady Threshall waltzing into the room while I'm still struggling with this damn curl." He tugged on the hair again, finally releasing the errant item.

For the first time that day, they laughed together at the awkwardness and humor of their situation. Logan took note of the color in her cheeks and the bright-ness of her azure eyes and forced himself not to regret locking the door against Webster and the rest of the world.

"I like your laugh, Gillian. It's light and carefree. You should laugh more often."

"So should you. It makes you look years younger." She laughed again upon seeing his startled expression. "I didn't mean it to sound that way, Logan."

"Well, as long as you feel better." Reluctantly, he moved away from her, noting the full breakfast tray and a chance to launch into the subject uppermost on his mind.

"Gillian, love, what did Althorp say to you?" He finished a piece of buttered toast before she could comprehend the question.

"Brian says a lot of things to me. He is very interested in the affairs of state, you now, and I am rather pleased that he likes to talk to me about such matters."

"Indeed?" One dark eyebrow quirked. "Does he reveal state secrets in moments of passion?"

"Why . . ." She shot him a meaningful look, "I assume you are testing me again."

"I am and I am not. Gillian, just what is between you and that government lackey?" Logan didn't notice her sudden scowl, for he concentrated on the three poached eggs, which reminded him of his hunger.

"Brian Althorp is no such thing. Why, Logan, he is a decent, hardworking young man who passionately loves his country and will do whatever is necessary to keep England strong and powerful. What is wrong with that? If you must know, I totally agree with him." Her voice rising with increasing ire, she wanted to say much more, but Logan's raised hand caught her attention at last.

"That was some speech, my dear. I never knew you were such a staunch Tory. If only women were allowed positions in government, you would tell them all what to do." He resumed eating. "Are you certain you wouldn't care to join me? How about some tea? Or hot cocoa? Though I doubt you need anything to steam you further."

"Why are you so flippant all of a sudden? I am quite aware that our government's policies are totally meaningless to you—if you know anything at all about what is going on—but I am surprised that you could misjudge others in such an obviously thoughtless manner."

Gillian stood up, deciding she could not argue with him in his present state. Besides, she wanted to get out of the house now, while all that was undone was her hair. Within seconds, she remedied that by efficiently coiling it in a tight knot.

At last he looked up. Lord, she was angry and oh so appealing. Having never seen her like this, he decided he liked this firebrand. "I did not mean to anger you. Please," he motioned to the chair, "sit down and join me. There is much I want to say to you."

"If you have anything else to say about Brian, I will not listen."

"Why are you so protective of him all of a sudden? Gillian," he raised a suspicious brow, "are you in love with him?"

"With Brian? No, I've already told you that and I've also told you that I have never accepted his proposals. So, why in heaven's name are you badgering me?"

Thinking to take her into his arms, he rose at last. At the moment, all that mattered to him was halting her tirade with a passionate kiss. God, she excited him with her mounting fury. Her eyes alight with anger, he could just picture her passionate responses when his hands and mouth roamed along her naked body. The thought made the blood surge through his veins.

"Gillian," he took her forearms, "what are we arguing about? I only asked you one question about Althorp. I have yet to get an answer and instead am barraged with your patriotic fervor for your country." He cocked his head to one side. "I have much more interesting and exciting ways of spending a lovely June morning." His hands roamed along her bare arms. Logan was quite aware of the effect he was having on her and thought briefly of resuming his previous physical assault on her senses.

Gillian threw her head back and moaned softly. "I am not certain of the issue anymore, but I do know, that, Logan, you can truly anger me!"

"That is wonderful. I hope I can do much more. Now, my love," he held her at arm's length to stare into her wide blue eyes, "did Althorp tell you my intentions?"

"I haven't seen Brian today. He usually calls in the afternoon. Brian spends his morning in his office or at Parliament. Not in bed. Besides, can we leave Brian out of our conversation?"

"I am afraid not. It's because of him that I must tell you what is on my mind."

"Logan . . ." She put one finger on his lips. The bold gesture surprised them both. "I came here for another reason. It has nothing to do with Brian. He's a dear friend, but I have no intention of marrying him."

"I know that. Because you are going to marry me when I return from my holiday."

There was no time to comprehend his statement, for he took her into his hard embrace before claiming her mouth. "This could be a wonderful match. I never knew you possessed such fire," he whispered huskily. "I think there is much about you I don't

93

know. But I am looking forward to discovering every inch, every nuance."

Confident of his ability to make her swoon with passion, Logan was unprepared for her reaction.

Gillian wept. In his arms, on his expensive white lawn shirt, then into his bare neck. He suddenly found himself drenched with tears and at a loss for words.

Chapter Ten

"Gillian," He tilted her face upward, "whatever is the matter?"

Through the haze of tears she managed to focus on the tiny cleft in his chin. He was so handsome and so damn sure of himself.

"Have you discussed this with my father?"

"Your father? Why would I do that?"

"That is the proper thing to do under the circumstances." Turning to his discarded breakfast tray, she took the unused linen napkin and dabbed her eyes.

Logan's loud laugh could be heard in the hallway. "Gillian," he could not suppress a grin, "why would I ask your father's permission when I am seeking yours? If you have no intention of waiting for my return, obviously there is no point in speaking with your father." He firmly took her elbow, guiding her to the armchair.

"I must leave in a matter of weeks. I cannot alter my plans. I merely want to know if you will wait for me. Besides, is this morning a 'proper' social visit?"

Her giggle startled him. "I suppose you are right. But, Logan, why do you want to marry me?"

"Because I find you amusing." At her sudden pout, he continued. "I also find you very attractive, witty, and charming company. I would hate to return from my holiday to find you betrothed to Althorp."

"Not Brian again," she groaned. "Why must you constantly bring his name up in our conversations?"

"Because, my lovely, whether you know it or not, your good friend is in love with you." He tweaked her nose. "Moreover, he is not often a very nice fellow."

"I find both statements hard to believe."

"For your sake, I hope you never have to find out otherwise. I shall not bring his name up any more this morning. So," he took her hand, "what is your answer? Are you interested in changing your title from Lady Gillian Marlowe to Lady Gillian Hammond? Or do you need time to think about this?"

"Oh, no," she clutched his hand, "I will not let you change your mine. The answer is definitely yes. Oh, Logan, I am so excited!"

"Show me how pleased you are," he commanded softly. "Stand up, put your arms around my neck, and kiss me."

He was impressed with her ability to follow his orders. Apparently, Gillian had no intention of sealing their betrothal with a demure kiss. With a newly discovered enthusiasm, she stood on her toes, pulled his head down to her mouth, and mimicked all that he had taught her about kissing. Now it was his turn to pant and want much more.

"Gillian, I cannot wait to teach you the rest."

Not until she had floated out of the house a short while later, did Logan Hammond remember that Gillian had not told him why she called on him in the first place.

With the wheels inexorably set in motion, Logan shrugged aside any doubts about the complications of such a marriage. Somehow he would manage to keep Gillian unaware of his espionage activities, and he certainly would keep her at arm's length from any mistress. For it never occurred to Logan that he would remain faithful to his wife.

The news of the Marlowe-Hammond betrothal became the talk of London. Within a matter of hours, the word had spread that Lord Logan Hammond, the future Earl of Stanton, would no longer be available. Women were shocked that the most eligible, handsome rake not only decided to settle down, but with, of all the women, the almost-spinster Gillian Marlowe.

Some of the gentlemen at White's mourned the loss of another bachelor, while others placed wagers that Hammond would eventually find some way to back off.

Logan cared not, for he was soon to depart. But he had to settle one other matter.

Three nights after Gillian's morning visit, Logan left White's early to keep another appointment.

Hiring a hack, he rode to the East End of London to a public house not far from the old Port of London. Since many a London dandy was known to cavort along the Radcliffe Highway in Shadwell, Logan made a point of selecting a place frequented by sailors and merchants associated with the East India Company. It was unlikely that he would be recognized by anyone here.

He had deliberately dressed simply. No cane, silk beaver hat, expensively tailored coat, trousers or boots—but plain dark wool trousers, jacket over a faded blue shirt, and old black leather boots.

His companion looked even less conspicuous. Short, stocky, slightly balding beneath a rumpled cap, Harold looked more like a stevedore than the leader of the American espionage network in England. Logan knew less about Harold than he did about his own servants. Judging from the balding hair and wrinkles about the eyes and mouth, Logan thought the man to be in his late forties. He wasn't sure that "Harold" was his real Christian name, and his last name was never mentioned. Yet there was something about Harold that Logan trusted. Perhaps it was his merry grin and calm attitude about this dangerous way of life.

"So, lad, what are you going to tell me about first? Your personal news or the political machinations of your friends in government." Harold lit a cigar that must have been lit three times previously. It was cheap and smelly, but Harold loved those cigars.

"Remind me one day to send you a box of imported Spanish cigars."

"I like these just fine. Besides, you're importing the tobacco from my side of the world, remember?" Logan heard the humor underneath the gruff reply. "Do you intend to answer me, or are we doomed to spend the rest of the evening in this charming place? Goodness, Logan, I never saw so many drunks, prostitutes, and thieves under one roof. Speaking of roofs," Harold dubiously looked up at the dark wood ceiling, "I do not believe that will hold up much longer."

"Come now, Harold, you have seen worse. Besides, I think this public house has its own charm." Logan signaled to the serving wench for drinks. "The whiskey is watered down, you know."

"I am not surprised. Well? Tell me about politics first, since you will not tell me about Lady Marlowe."

Not bothering to ask how he knew about Gillian, Logan told him about the events of the last week. "I am most troubled about Althorp. I believe his scheme to send or recruit agitators to the southern states is finding support with Canning. The Americans won't know until it's too late to stop them."

"Always the pessimist, lad. I will take care of informing our government about this latest development. But it would be helpful if you could come up with names and financial backers. Including those in Italy and France."

"I don't understand why the French would be involved in this." Logan tried to ignore the loud argument erupting at the table behind theirs, but it was becoming difficult to hear Harold or himself.

"I don't think the French government is backing this. They have enough problems with Spain and her American colonies. But there are a number of influential and wealthy men in France who would like nothing better than to weaken the growing American economy. The know how to deal with the British. The Americans are too unique. Say, Logan," Harold leaned forward, the smelly cigar smoke wafting into Logan's face, "can you hear me? Are you quite sure we are safe here?"

"Yes," he laughed. "These sailors won't harm you, unless you blow that infernal smoke in their noses. Even they have better taste than you."

"I'm hungry. Do you think we can acquire normal food here? On second thought," Harold looked around at the tables that were stained with food and drink, "I think I'll wait until later."

"How long do you think I'll be on the Continent?"

"This little assignment interferes with your wedding, does it?"

"Harold, if this is your way of asking for an invitation, there is no need to fret. You are not invited."

"Ah, well, I suppose I must wait until you bring your wife here."

"Logan tried to swallow his drink before choking.

"Here? Gillian? She would faint from the putrid smells of the docks while still in her carriage."

"Do you love her?"

The whiskey went into his nose. Only when Logan stopped coughing did he ask Harold to repeat the question.

"Listen, lad. I think it a good idea to marry and settle down. You need to become a member of the old guard. That's the only way to get accurate information. Marriage helps. It provides a certain entrée that dandies have been denied."

"My father would be pleased to know you feel this way. And I am delighted that you approve," Logan drily commented.

"Now don't take offense. I know you aren't asking my permission. What you do with your personal life is your business. However," he rubbed one stubby finger along his jaw, "if you become emotionally attached to this Lady Marlowe, it could cause you as lot of trouble later on."

"You have no cause to worry about that. I don't love her, but I do not deny that I am fond of her."

"Logan, what happens if you must make a choice?" Harold leaned forward again to make sure Logan heard his every word.

"I don't understand."

"I think you do. Having a wife is a fine cover. It might restrict your travels, but I suppose we can work around that. What I mean, however, is what will you do if you are forced to choose between your wife and your country? You are an American in my book, and a damn good agent. I don't ever want you to become careless because of some preoccupation with love and family. It can be an emotional strain. I've seen men die because of it. I would hate to see that happen to you."

"It won't," Logan firmly said. "Besides, I can and always do take care of myself. Gillian has nothing to do with this. She's an ornament, that's all." It annoyed Logan to think Harold could misjudge him.

"Don't let her get to you, lad. My wife doesn't."

Harold's aplomb amazed Logan. So the little man was married. "I wonder what she sees in you."

"Money. It's not that bad, though. I like having someone to take care of me when I am home."

"Does she know what you do?"

Harold shook his head. "She thinks I'm establishing another business, which makes her happy, because she can spend more of my money."

"If Gillian ever found out what I was doing with such a troublemaker like you she'd shoot me. My fiancée is a devout Tory. She likes Canning, and she even likes that slime Althorp."

"Careful, lad. Althorp won't forgive you for taking his girl."

"You knew? Ah," he slapped the wood table, "why do I ask such stupid questions. Do you know when I plan to marry?"

"Not yet. Because you don't."

"That hasn't stopped you before."

"Logan, if we don't leave this friendly place, I may get deaf and sick. Come on." Harold rose after laying too many bills on the table. "Next time, let me select a meeting place."

The two incongruous-looking men—one so tall he had to lean down to hear the words of the much shorter, chubbier one—walked out into the foggy night. But they had walked no more than one street when Logan threw Harold into a doorway.

"Stay put," he growled.

Whirling about, Harold didn't see the gleaming knife deftly removed from the waistband of Logan's trousers.

"Hey what are ya doin', fella? Ya ain't from aroun' here. Are ya and ya little friend lost?" The two young sailors were confident of the outcome of this mismatch.

"I'm not lost. Thank you for your concern." Logan remained in place. Heart pumping with anticipation and excitement, Logan waited until the burlier sailor stepped forward before he made a move.

"I wouldn't come any closer if I were you. Why don't you leave my friend and me alone."

"Got any money?" The fat one kept moving.

"None for you."

"Wanna bet?" Turning to his companion, the man said, "I'll see to this one. He's too sure of himself. You take the other one."

"Watch out Mikey!" the other shouted.

But it was too late, for Logan was already on top of the fellow, his knife blade held up to the sailor's throat. "Make one more move, and I promise you, it's your last."

The sailor laughed, his stale breath making Logan wince. "You're not too smart. Look around, dandy. Some of my friends are behind you."

"He's right, Logan," Harold called from the darkness of a doorway. "Take it easy."

"Don't get up on my account, mate," a new voice called. "We have lots of time."

"So do I." Logan's smile would have warned a more rational man to leave.

With one swift kick to the sailor's groin, Logan spun around to the two new thieves.

But they descended on him like a pack of hungry wolves. Keeping his wits and strength, Logan disarmed one by kicking the knife out of his hand. Another raised a pistol and tried to crack Logan's head open, but Logan was still too fast. He quickly ducked and punched the man in his gut.

With only two thugs left, Harold, against Logan's command, stepped forward with pistol in hand.

"I'm a very poor shot. I could aim for your leg, and who knows where the bullet will strike."

Catching a sharp right to his chin, Logan reeled backward, but kept the knife firmly in hand. Feeling a sharp sting to his left arm, Logan didn't need to look to know he had been cut.

"I'm gonna kill ya." The burly sailor was standing in front of Logan.

Charging once more, this time with a knife aimed at Logan's heart, the sailor did not stop until Harold's loud pistol shot pierced his side.

"Had enough, Logan?" Harold called.

"Yes." He felt another blow to his stomach but remained in place and sliced the forearm of his attacker.

The two remaining sailors fled before Logan turned to face them.

"Let's go home, Harold." He took the arm of the man he would forever call his friend. "I have a need for some fresh air and a good meal."

"At last you agree with me."

Chapter Eleven

Gillian could not recall ever feeling so wonderful. Each day she awoke with a smile and a dreamy expression wondering, thinking, and planning what her life would be like after her marriage to Logan. That he was going away in a matter of days did not penetrate her ebullient haze—at least not yet.

Nothing satisfied her as much as entering a room on Logan's arm, smiling smugly to herself at the forlorn faces of the women. Particularly, Lady Hartshorn. Caroline had barely greeted them, and when her husband pulled her along to congratulate the couple, Gillian had to be blind not to see the intense hatred that marred the woman's even features.

Logan cared not a whit. Enjoying their social life through the eyes of his betrothed was a new and not an unpleasant experience.

Tonight, however, was going to be difficult, for Gillian and her parents were to dine at the Earl of Stanton's home. It was a test she had to pass. No matter what she and Logan felt for each other, Gillian wanted his family's approval of their marriage.

Because Logan had spoken so little of his father and stepmother, Gillian could not understand his true relationship with them. From her parents, Gillian knew that the Hammonds were very well-respected and well-suited to each other. Perhaps a love match, she had thought more than once, but for some reason was afraid to ask Logan anything about any member of his family unless he mentioned it first. It was different with his little sister Luisa. Logan spoke of her often, usually while laughing when mentioning her antics.

Dressed as demurely as fashion allowed, Gillian descended the long staircase of her home to see her father waiting at the base of the stairs.

"My my, you look ravishing," he said, beaming at his daughter's unmistakable beauty. "I dare say that the prospect of marriage agrees with you. We should have done this thing sooner."

"Only if it were Logan Hammond." She gracefully accepted his arm. "And you, Father, would never had considered selecting Logan for me. But," she twisted slightly to kiss his cheek, "I am so glad you accepted him."

"Mayhap it's love after all."

"Perhaps," she coyly smiled. "But after his family sees me, it may all be for naught."

Charles led his daughter into the library to await Helena's arrival. "Your mother is never on time. Why, she is worse than you. Men do not appreciate tardiness, you know. Bah," he grunted and helped himself to a glass of port. "Now then, whatever you are thinking about his family is utter nonsense. I know his father. Richard Hammond is a trifle younger than I and belongs to a different club, but we have seen each other in the House of Lords and at various functions. Why, when you were a little miss,

105

we all spent some time together at Euston Hall in Cheveley. His first wife Judith was still alive. She was an American, you know, from Charleston, South Carolina."

"We have relatives there, too, don't we?"

"Yes, on your mother's side. Don't you remember your cousins Julia and Theodore Grayson? They visited us about six years ago. Nice people." Charles was talking more to himself than Gillian now. "I cannot fathom why they chose to live in the Colonies. Theodore was a member of the peerage, but they gave it all up for the wilderness."

"The Graysons must know Logan's relatives."

"Oh, I am certain they do. Charleston is not like London. In a small town like that, the upper classes must know each other and socialize quite often."

"Sounds charming," she commented drily. "I find it difficult enough in London with those snobs. I can just imagine what it must be like in a small, provincial town." Concentrating on the tiny figurines on the end table, Gillian forgot the immediate conversation and returned to what was uppermost on her mind.

"What do you know about Logan's father?" She needed her father's knowledge, no matter how old or meager the descriptions were. If Richard Hammond were anything like her father, well, it could be difficult. Gillian was too easily intimidated by opinionated men.

"You have naught to fear." Charles tweaked her flushed cheek. "The Earl of Stanton is an amiable chap. Goodness, child, if you can hold a conversation with none other than our Foreign Secretary George Canning, you can surely handle a lesser man."

"Father, is that a compliment?" She was pleasantly surprised by his voice of confidence in her.

"Why, of course." His voice sounded more gruff than usual. "Now, I hear your mother, let's greet her and be off."

Logan knew she would look lovely. With a little more help from him, Gillian was destined to be a fine beauty. The pale green satin gown complimented her azure eyes. Wearing only a small diamond heart at her throat for adornment, he admired the modest square-neckline of her dress. It enhanced her smooth, long neck. Her hair, bound loosely in dozens of soft curls, was begging to have him remove the pins.

There was, he decided, something unique about a woman in love. He remembered the special looks between his parents when he was a boy. Even his father and Charlotte shared a glance or two.

There was no doubt in his mind that Gillian was falling in love with him. Logan should have done something to prevent it, but somehow forgot each time she looked up at him. He hated to kill that delightful gleam in her rounded blue eyes or the becoming flush to her cheeks.

There was a chance they could be happy with each other. As long as she never found out about his work with the American government. More importantly, as long as he never had to choose between Gillian and America.

Refusing to acknowledge the possibilities, Logan hurried to greet his fiancée and her parents.

"You look enchanting," he whispered in her small ear. "I wish we were alone."

"I hope your parents agree with you."

"Oh, I doubt they'd want us to be alone. Not with the elaborate meal Charlotte has planned for this evening. Come," he took her gloved hand in his, "let me take you up to the drawing room. Charlotte was thoughtful. She wanted me to greet you first, to put you at ease."

Gillian felt her knees start to shake, but Logan continued to chatter amiably with her parents about nothing she could later remember.

Upon entering the tastefully decorated sitting room, Gillian immediately noticed the little girl in a small white upholstered chair. It was obvious she could barely restrain herself. Long, pale blond curls that someone must have taken great pains to put in order sprang to life as soon as the child jumped out of the chair to greet her brother and his fiancée. Pink satin ribbons almost became undone.

"You must be Gillian," she breathlessly said, "I've heard much about you. Logan likes you." Her dark brown eyes sparkled.

"Luisa," her mother admonished, "where are your manners?"

"Oh," she curtsied perfectly and beamed with pleasure at accomplishing the feat. "Mother taught me yesterday."

"Luisa, dear sprite," Logan took her hands, "I want to formally introduce you to the Lady Gillian Marlowe and her parents." His sister's behavior clearly amused Logan.

"I am a lady, too." The child wore a long white dress that was the exact style of her mother's. Delighted with this creature, Gillian slowly lost her bout with nerves. Bending down to Luisa, she whispered for her ears alone, "I would wager you have the largest doll collection in all of London. Perhaps all of England. Will you show them to me later?"

"How did you know?" she asked, wide-eyed with wonder.

"Because every pretty girl has some dolls. I have quite a few, too, you know. But I am positive that your collection is a grand one." Gillian's eyes strayed to the porcelain doll abandoned in Luisa's chair.

"Logan," the child looked up to her brother, "I like her, too."

"I am delighted. For if you could not approve, I wouldn't marry." Logan kissed the tip of his sister's pert, freckled nose.

The introductions to the rest of the family were not as simple, but Gillian managed to smile and say a few pleasantries. As long as her father was in the room, one did not have to worry about conversation.

Logan's father and stepmother seemed nice. Although their paths should have crossed many times before, at numerous social functions during the London season, Gillian did not recall ever meeting them. Logan once commented that the Hammonds cared little for socializing with the ton, preferring the company of each other and occasional close friends.

Lord Hammond, the Earl of Stanton, looked much younger than her father. Tall and slim like his son, Richard Hammond appeared almost as fit as Logan. Lady Charlotte Hammond, much shorter than Gillian and not so slim, immediately took Gillian into her arms and kissed both cheeks.

"I am thrilled to welcome you to our family. Logan has made a wonderful choice and I only hope you feel the same." Her blond curls bounced just like Luisa's and Gillian could not help but instantly like the woman.

The two families managed to get along quite well. Since the exact date of the wedding was temporarily set for the following November, there was little need to discuss details. And as long as Luisa Hammond was in the room, it was difficult to discuss any serious topic.

From his corner on the far side of the room, Logan watched the families mingle. He knew Gillian had completely won over Luisa and was grateful that she would want to try—if for no other reason than to please him. No one had ever pleased him this way. Gillian Marlowe was not such a poor choice as a mate after all. She would be good to him and his family. Hopefully, she would remain loyal to him for the first few years. He did not know if he could expect more than that. Logan had heard and seen enough to know about the fidelity of many ton wives.

The hour was late so Luisa would not be dining with the family tonight. Begging her brother and Gillian to visit with her before bedtime, Luisa promised to show Gillian all of her dolls.

Mindless of the state of her satin gown, Gillian sat on the side of the bed with Luisa, listening to the names and origins of the fine dolls.

"Your room is lovely. Much like mine when I was your age. I, too, had pink-and-white striped wallpaper, a lace canopy over my bed, and lace-curtained windows. All my dolls stayed in the room with me

110

on a small white shelf. And do you see your white table?" She pointed to the small table in the middle of the room, strewn with tea cups and various pieces of china. "My table was painted pale yellow. I still have it."

"May I see it?"

"Of course. I am sure your brother will bring you over to my home soon."

"Will you, Logan?" She bounced the curls to face him.

"I will as long as you go to sleep now so I may escort Gillian to dinner."

"I will, but Logan?" she leaned on her knees, pulling him close to her face, "will you read me *Aesop's Fables?*"

"Only a few pages, all right?"

Gillian remained in the room while Logan's voice took on the nuances of each character. She was as enthralled as Luisa, who lay quietly under the pink-and-white-checked coverlet. Her deep brown eyes never left Logan's face.

When Logan and Gillian finally left the child's room, they walked arm in arm down the long corridor.

"We are to join them in the dining room, but Gillian," Logan turned her to face him, "have I told you how much I would like to kiss you?"

Not needing a reply, he pulled her into a soft embrace. The kiss began as a tender touch, but within seconds, he found he could not pull himself away. Oh to pull her into another room and have her all to himself. He found himself intoxicated by her jasmine scent; even her hair smelled as sweet as the neck he was now kissing.

111

"Mmm, I have a hunger for you, Gillian. I don't know if I can wait until I return from my trip."

"Then let's not," she breathlessly replied. "I want you, too."

He pulled back. "Gillian," he looked deeply into her eyes, "do you know what you are saying?" His hands roamed along the curve of her neck and down her soft shoulders.

"Yes," she leaned her head back to see his face. Touching his cheek, she said, "I wish I could go with you. But I realize now you are not changing your mind or asking me to travel with you—not that I could, of course. You've told me a number of times that you want to be alone with me. "Well," her fingertips seductively moved to his lips, "I want that, too. I don't want to wait until November, Logan, I couldn't stand it. I am no innocent little girl." At his look of shock, she laughed and continued quickly. "No, I do not mean what you are thinking. But I am not that young not to know about love. And," she added in a much lower tone, "lovemaking."

"I am not sure it would be a wise thing for us to do." Logan could not believe the words came from his own traitorous mouth.

"Come now, Logan, I am not that naive. You will not be faithful to me while we are apart, but I want you to have something very special to remember about me—about us. I know what I am saying."

"Very well," he kissed her ear, "I am convinced. But I do not think tonight is a very good time. Agreed?"

"Well then soon, tomorrow or the day after. I am confident that you have been in similar situations before. I shall leave the planning to you."

"Gillian, you amaze me."

"I am pleased to hear you say that. Now, shall we join the others, or must I spend the night in this dark corridor in your warm, loving embrace?"

The rest of that evening Logan could barely remember even parts of conversation. Preoccupied with calculating and planning the time alone with Gillian, he answered every question put to him, but afterward could not recall what was asked.

Only Gillian seemed to understand. More than once that evening, she raised a glass of champagne while looking into the confused gaze of her fiancé and smiled. Logan recognized that smile. It was both flirtatous and seductive. This time there was a specific meaning in that look. Thinking of the moments alone with her, his blood raced through his heated body.

Chapter Twelve

"Logan, you couldn't have planned a more lovely afternoon."

Seated in the library of Logan's townhouse, Gillian appeared calm. Wearing an ice-blue lawn dress with a matching satin ribbon woven through her upswept hair and another around her slender neck, Gillian looked almost too innocent, and it made him nervous to think of this premeditated afternoon. "It is not too late to change your mind," he addressed her, with trepidation, standing beside the unlit marble fireplace.

"Ever the gentleman, aren't you? No, my mind is made up. One thing about me you should know, Logan, is that I rarely change my mind. My father attributes this to a stubborn streak that runs through his family tree. Mother says it's because I'm the younger child.

"Your plan is quite brilliant and I know Adeline will never breathe a word. Everyone thinks she and I are spending the day together shopping and dining. Oh, Logan, it's so clever!" She looked him squarely in the eye and said in a voice full of wonder, "You really do have quite a bit of experience arranging these matters."

"I do not. You must realize my reputation has become mythical. For all the wrong reasons, I might add." He wished for a much stronger drink than brewed tea, but in deference to Gillian, refrained for the moment. Besides, it was not lunchtime yet.

Pulling on his cravat, he cursed himself for dressing so formally. It wasn't necessary to wear a perfectly tied cravat over a new white shirt, but he thought Gillian would appreciate the formality. Yet the room seemed stuffy and the wool jacket and cravat were making him perspire.

"Your servants? What will they say?"

"Absolutely nothing. No one but Webster is here today. I gave the others the day off."

"Oh. I should have known." She smile tremulously. "Logan? Do you suppose we could, ah, I mean would you think it very unladylike if I asked for a glass of wine before lunch?"

"I think I will not let you imbibe alone." It took a few seconds to serve the needed drinks. The library was not only well-stocked with fine leather-bound books along the paneled walls, but a lovely enameled liquor cabinet in the corner of the room held an ample supply of wines and whiskey.

"This room is lovely. No," she shook her curls, "I do not mean lovely, that's too feminine, I mean it is tastefully decorated. I like the cherrywood panels. And I love velvet. This sofa is divine." She patted the deep blue velvet. "Are those family portraits over there?" She pointed to the opposite end of the room. There was one outstanding portrait of a dark-haired woman dressed in yellow, with a small child comfortably settled in her lap. The woman's expression was serene and content. She had known love, Gillian decided. "That is your mother," she stated.

Logan walked over to the portrait. "Yes. I was only

three when my father commissioned it. My parents were devoted to each other." He stared at his mother's secretive smile. "She was probably looking right at him while the artist was painting us."

"Did you decorate the townhouse yourself?"

"Mostly. I had some assistance from my stepmother. She loves decorating. But I am quite pleased. Of all the rooms, I prefer this and my bedchambers." He hadn't meant to remind her of the suite of rooms upstairs and stammered over his words.

When Gillian quickly drained the first glass of wine and asked for another, Logan decided to set a limit of four glasses. If they were going to follow through with their plans, he did not want her to be blinded by drink and have no memory of the day.

Logan had no doubt about his abilities to seduce a woman. Once he had spent days planning the seduction of a lovely French countess. But there was something different about this woman. He was going to marry her.

Gillian, too, was apprehensive about numerous things, among them, what if Logan did not like their lovemaking? What if he did not find her attractive or her performance satisfactory? Would he change his mind about marrying her? Without thinking, she blurted the questions to him.

"Gillian, my love, you must be jesting." He rushed to her side, kneeling before her. "I have never been so heartless to a woman. Besides, I know all I need to know about us."

"You do?" She gazed into his golden-brown eyes, crinkled in amusement, so like the woman's in the portrait. He looked so kind and understanding.

"Here, let me prove it to you." With ease born of practice and strength, he put her drink down on the Chinese table, then pulled her into his arms for a short yet breathtaking kiss. When she opened her eyes, she was met by his wide grin. "How do you feel?"

"A little lightheaded," she answered honestly.

"I know. Me, too."

"Really?"

"Absolutely. Gillian, I don't know how this has happened. But I find you more attractive than any other woman. And from this moment on," his hand traced the contour of her small ear, then inched down along the sides of her face, "I want you to think of nothing else but us. There is no one else."

"Oh, I quite agree. Logan?"

"Yes, love."

"Kiss me again."

"With pleasure."

The kiss deepened and Gillian felt a strange, quivering sensation in the pit of her belly. All too quickly, she forgot that they were standing in the middle of the large library, on Logan's fine Persian carpet. His tongue slowly insinuated itself into her mouth, instructing her on how to kiss and be kissed.

When it became difficult for Gillian to breathe and stand, he ended the enthralling kiss.

"We have all afternoon together, my love. Why don't we enjoy our time alone, shall we?" His eyes darkened.

"Mmm." Gillian reached for her wineglass and had no idea how shaky her hands were until she spilled the contents over her dress.

"Oh, Lord," she jumped back in disbelief. "How can I be so clumsy!" She stared stupidly at the growing stain. "Oh, Logan, I cannot got home looking like this."

"You won't need to. I'll have Webster clean it. Contrary to popular belief, I do not keep a supply of

117

ladies' clothes in my house. But I am sure we can find you something to wear in the meantime. Wait here," he gently commanded.

Logan wasted no time in locating substitute clothing. Before Gillian had the chance to sit again on the sofa, he had returned with a black silk garment over his arm.

"Here, I'm afraid this was the only item I could find that looked decent." Logan held it out for her.

"It's a robe!"

"Well, yes. But it is certainly long enough to hide any maidenly modesty you may feel."

She giggled. "You aren't serious. 'Maidenly modesty,' you say. I am alone in your townhouse. I've come specifically for an assignation. I am clumsy enough to spill wine all over the gown that will surely be removed later on—at some point, I mean." She blushed, then laughed again. "And I am supposed to be concerned with modesty?"

"I admit it odd." Logan laughed with her. "You are a mite clumsy. Here," he handed her the robe. "Stand behind the Chinese screens over there and hand me the soiled dress. Unless you prefer I leave."

"Logan?"

"Yes?"

"You aren't wearing your jacket."

"Under the present, uh, circumstances, I thought I might be overdressed." The lighthearted banter was infectious.

"I must agree. Please, stay while I change."

When she reemerged from behind the screens, he sucked in his breath at the delightful picture she presented. The robe fell to her ankles, but he could see she still wore silk stockings and satin undergarments beneath it. The sleeves were far too long. The sash tied loosley around her waist could have been

118

wrapped around her three more times. Gillian tried her hardest to keep the plunging neckline closed, but without a pin, it was hopeless.

"May I be of assistance?"

"How gallant of you," she sweetly replied.

"First the sleeves." He deftly rolled the sleeves into neat cuffs below her elbows. As for the exposed neckline, he removed the stickpin in his cravat to secure the errant ends of the robe. Standing so close, Gillian inhaled his spicy scent. Logan had to reach into the robe, his fingers gently brushing her chest. "I don't want to stick you. I've never done this before, you know."

"I wonder."

"There." He beamed. "A fine job, I must say. You look," he paused, searching for the proper words and shrugged when none sufficed, "interesting and different. Go look." He pointed to the mirror above the mantelplace.

"I shall never forget this day." She marched over to the mirror, twirling to get a better view of herself.

Logan could not resist peeking at her exposed shapely legs. "I think we have started a new fashion craze."

"I believe you are right. However, I shall not be the one to model this ensemble at Almack's."

"Stuffy lot, aren't they?"

"Well," she sighed, "now what?"

"I think we should lunch now. I'll tell you what. Since you are obviously not dressed appropriately for a formal luncheon, why don't I arrange for our lunch to be brought in here?" The more he thought of it, the better he liked the idea and the intimacy of this room. "I will help Webster bring everything here. You, my lady," he bowed, "need only wait for my return."

For lack of anything else better to do, Gillian perused the collection of leather-bound books on the walnut bookshelves, which took up one end of the room. She couldn't imagine Logan taking the time to read some of the lengthy tomes. He didn't seem the kind of man to sit patiently and read about life in Ancient Greece and Rome or novels about present-day England. Deciding the collection must be more cosmetic than purposeful, she reached for a red leather-bound book and was surprised to find small pieces of paper interspersed between pages. Some of the papers, she noted, had hand-written notes on them. Looking at the title, Gillian wondered how interesting a book called, *The Peloponnisian Wars* by Thucydides could be to anyone, let along Logan Hammond.

"That, my lady, is my favorite book. How did you know?"

Embarrassed, she moved too quickly to face Logan, unaware of the view she gave him. He was in danger of toppling the heavy silver tray, laden with hot food and china. Her upper thighs flashed before him and he wished he could see much more.

"I am sorry. I wasn't prying."

"I know. I gave you permission to make yourself comfortable, did I not?"

"Logan," she carefully replaced the book, "how many of these books have you read?"

"If you promise not to tell anyone," she nodded solemnly, "then I confess to having read most. But no one must know, for my reputation as a rake would be shattered."

"Why don't you want anyone to know? With whom do you share your knowledge? Logan," she couldn't mask her irritation, "why do you go on letting people think you are an empty-headed dandy? Would it be so dreadful if the fellows at White's knew there was a well-read man among their illustrious peers?"

"Gillian, calm yourself."

She backed away. "You are wasting your life!"

"I am what?"

"You are wasting your life. I would love to have this collection of books and have the time to read and understand what I am reading and be able to discuss these books with someone who knows more than I. Oh, it would be delightful." Her eyes lifted to his amused face.

"It will be my pleasure."

"I beg your pardon?" She focused her attention on his hands.

"I will be pleased to share this information with you. In fact, the best thing I can offer you while I am on holiday is the exclusive use of this library. In exchange, I expect to engage in witty, intelligent conversation with you for the remainder of our married lives. But not," he moved closer to cup her defiant chin, "not on our wedding night. Agreed?"

"Yes," she whispered. "Just tell me where to begin."

"You begin by putting your arms around my neck."

She did his bidding.

"Very good. Now, let's see how good a pupil you are today. I want you to kiss me. Like this." His lips barely touched hers as he placed featherlight kisses on her mouth.

"Mmm, I think I can do that." She forgot to open her eyes. When she perfectly mimicked his kiss, she was pleased to hear his response.

"Not bad for a novice."

"Logan, you don't intend to grade me every step of the way, do you?" She looked into his half-closed eyes.

"Just let me kiss you now."

The kiss started as the other, but before she could catch her breath, his arms tightened around her back, while his tongue explored the inner recesses of her mouth.

"You taste sweet. No, no, leave your arms around my neck. Let me kiss you again."

While his tongue tantalized her, his hands ever so slowly lowered down the silk-clad back. It seemed so odd to enjoy the feel of his black silk garment on a woman's body. It took less than half a minute to unravel the sash. The robe fell open, much to Gillian's amazement, but she was too lost in the kiss to utter any words. Only a soft moan emanated from deep within her throat.

Experience taught him to unpeel the robe, allowing it to swirl around her feet. Clad only in a white satin chemise and stockings, Gillian felt a soft rush of cool air on her bare shoulders. But she felt his hands, the slightly roughened fingertips that ran along the sides of her arms, and reveled in the new sensations that began between her thighs.

One thin satin shoulder strap hung below her shoulder, the other immediately following. "Do you like this, Gillian?" he whispered huskily against her mouth.

"Oh, yes."

"Gillian, you are lovely. Your body was molded for loving." When Logan pulled her arms away to admire the disheveled woman before his eyes, she flinched.

"What's this?" He looked into her eyes. There was an irrepressible smile on his handsome face. "You are ashamed of the truth?"

"No, not really," she stammered. "I have never heard anyone say such wonderful words to me."

"Let be the first. Shall I tell you what pleases me?"

She could only nod once.

"I love the outline of your breasts against the chemise. High, firm breasts, waiting to be touched." Almost on cue, he noticed the small nipples protruding against the material. "Begging to be touched." His eyes never left her face as he massaged each breast, softly at first, but increasing the pressure.

Taking one rounded bud in his fingers he rolled the satin-clad nipple, enjoying the sensation of it swelling and her surprised moan of delight. Repeating the motion with the other nipple, he kept his eyes on her face. She was ready for another lesson.

Pulling her to him once again, he captured her mouth in another mindless kiss, while his hands continued to discover her body. Gillian wanted to force his hands to remain on her breasts, but dared not speak, and quickly changed her mind as soon as she felt those lovely hands against her waist then lowering to her derriere. Pulled into him, she knew at last he was enjoying his sensual assault on her senses — for his desire was as obvious as hers. Tempted to test her prowess, she moved against his lower body and heard his soft groan.

"You are getting ahead of me, my love. I was just about to teach you that."

"No need. Go on." She nuzzled his neck.

"Impatient little vixen." He nibbled her ear all the while his hands made circular motions from waist to derriere, then around and under the chemise.

"Logan," she gasped.

"Not now. Your skin is so smooth." His hands remained on her fine skin, inching up to cup one breast, caressing, then kneading, only to abandon it and pay attention to the other.

She fell into him, her knees no longer able to withstand this sensual assault.

"Gillian," he whispered against her neck, "do you want me to make love to you here or will you allow me to carry you upstairs?"

He could have asked her to make love out in the street and still she would have nodded in agreement. Clearly the decision was his to make.

In one swift yet firm move, he effortlessly lifted her into his arms, managed to open the library door, and carried her up the two dozen stairs.

Chapter Thirteen

Gillian would never remember how she came to be in his bed suite, lying in the middle of his huge bed with Logan poised above her.

"Now, where was I?" he murmured.

"Logan," she lifted heavy-lidded eyes to his, "are you going to remain dressed?"

His subdued laugh gave her chills. "No. I had no idea you were such an impatient minx."

"I just wanted to feel your skin."

"So you shall, my dear."

"Let me unbutton your shirt."

Thank goodness he had removed the knotted cravat moments earlier, for her shaky fingers had difficulty with the pearl buttons. But he did not assist. Instead, he leaned against the cherrywood headboard, enjoying the little fingers on his chest. Her lips pursed in concentration, he laughed with Gillian when she triumphantly accomplished her task. Her hands tunneled through dark chest hairs.

"My trousers, too?"

"Oh, no," she blushed hotly. "I think you should."

"I will, if you do something for me first."

"Of course," she said without hesitation, but not able to keep the excitement out of her voice. She trusted him and could barely wait for him to teach her the secrets of lovemaking.

"Take off the chemise. Over there," he pointed to the center of the room, "where I can enjoy the view from a distance."

"I don't know if I can move."

He pulled her face closer to his to offer another mindless kiss. "Please?"

In a thrice, she stood where directed. Her slender arms raised above her head, she slowly removed the satin chemise. Her first impulse was to cover her bare breasts, but Logan anticipated the modest action and said, "Now let your hair down. Slowly remove the ribbon, then the pins. But leave the ribbon around your neck."

It was just as he had imagined, and he felt his temperature rise as all those strawberry curls fell down her back and over her high breasts. He didn't know how much longer he could refrain from taking her on the floor. But that would not do. Not for Gillian's initiation.

He stood before her now, playing with the silky strands of hair, running them over his hands and her breasts. "Ravishing" was all he said before crushing her against his chest.

Soft hairs rubbing against her chest, while his firm lips enclosed hers, Gillian wondered why anyone ever thought there was pain in lovemaking.

She almost recoiled, however, when his fingers lowered to the red-gold hairs between her still silken-clad thighs. "I am going to touch you. I want to show you how much you need me. How much you want my body and my touch. See, you are moist there," his fingers dallied with her, continuing the sweet torture until she moaned aloud. "Tell me you like this."

"Oh, God, Logan. Nothing ever felt so good."

"There is more, love. I promise."

Continuing the motion with one hand, his mouth lowered to capture one nipple, licking and nibbling it with his tongue and mouth.

The pressure built deep within her, but she could neither identify nor speak of this burning need for more of Logan. His hands and mouth worked magically on her body, as if he had known every inch of her well before this day. Her body did not belong to her but to him.

"Let me love you now."

Back in the middle of the bed, her hair spread out before them like a gossamer curtain blending into the burgundy counterpane, Logan revered the beautiful, vulnerable woman before him.

"Now the silk stockings." First the right leg experienced the touch of his fingers as he deliberately took his time unrolling the silken hose while his mouth followed the same path. By the time he was finished with her left leg, Gillian grabbed his tousled brown hair to urge him up to her mouth.

Half leaning across her body, she felt the fine wool of his trousers against her side. The thought of her lying naked before him while he was still half-clad was more erotic than if he were naked. He could view every inch of her, while his body was yet to be explored.

Turning to face him, she deliberately rubbed her body against his. The effect was stimulating for both. Logan's hands were everywhere—her hair, face, neck, then lower to the moistness, until one finger was expertly inserted, moving in and out, then in again. She nearly screamed with delight, but his mouth was on hers again, his tongue increasing the motion against her tongue, sucking it.

"Logan, I want . . ."

"What, sweetheart, what do you want? You don't know yet, but you will."

One hand left her to unbutton his trousers. When he pulled them away to remove them, Gillian leaned on her elbows to delight and take fright in what she saw.

He was enormous. His swollen manhood begged for her touch. When he took her hand, she eagerly allowed him to place it over him. "Like this, Gillian." He showed her how to stimulate him—almost to the point where he had to pull her hand away—albeit reluctantly.

"If I let you continue, I may never make love to you."

Having no idea what he meant, Gillian protested softly when he pulled her arms around his neck and half lowered his body over hers. Nudging her thighs apart with his legs, he tantalized her with his probing member. Involuntarily moving up to him, she closed her eyes.

"No, please look at me," he whispered before kissing her again. "I want you to know how much I need you, too. How much I want to bury myself deep within you. It will only hurt once. I promise you. After that . . ."

He said no more. In one quick thrust, he entered her. The pain lasted only a few seconds, but he murmured encouraging words against her ear while rotating his hips against her.

Lost in the powerful sensations, Gillian heard nothing but the sweet cadence of his voice.

Moving slowly at first, she instinctively followed his motions until it was no longer clear who was the initiator.

"Wrap your arms tighter around me," he commanded gently.

His hands moved to touch her breasts, rubbing them, pulling the nipples before capturing them in his mouth.

"Logan," she moaned.

"Gillian, you are mine now. Forever you will be mine. Never will you forget our first passionate moment together."

The sensual assault continued. His hands lowered to cup her buttocks, pulling her up against his hip bones. She felt every motion. When he rolled over with her, she was amazed to find herself positioned above him.

Looking deeply into his molten-gold eyes, she wondered if anything in life could ever feel as wonderful or as powerful.

"Like this." He showed her with his hands how to move. Her panting increased with each movement against him.

Suddenly Logan could no longer bear the strain. Turning her quickly beneath him, he increased the rhythm of his hips until she gasped with pleasure. "There is still more," he said. "Come with me, Gillian, let yourself go." The tempo was harder against her body, but she cared not. She wanted much more.

A powerful throbbing was building deep within. Not knowing what was happening to her, she opened her eyes in panic.

"Let yourself go," he repeated, unsure if he could restrain his own climax.

As if on cue, her eyes misted and her nails raked down his back. She cried aloud in awe of the never-before-known ecstasy that wracked her body.

Logan saw it and cried out, too. "Take me," he groaned before burying his head into her shoulder.

Something made her nose itch. When at last she could no longer ignore it, she scratched her nose and tried to reclaim the comfortable position and warmth of the person beside her.

Then it finally dawned on her that she was not alone, not in her own bedroom, and not dressed. So it hadn't been a wonderful dream after all. Initially, she felt the panic and guilt over what she had deliberately allowed—had even helped Logan plan. Afraid to turn her head to see him, Gillian stared straight ahead. There were deep shadows against the brocade print curtain, a sure sign that it was afternoon. Soon she must leave to spend the night alone in her bed and the next few weeks alone without Logan.

Perhaps it had been a mistake to learn of this pleasure today instead of waiting until their wedding. For now she pondered how she would live knowing all the nights and days she would miss being held in his strong embrace, allowing him to do those wonderful things to her body. This day, Tuesday the twenty-seventh of May would never be forgotten. Logan had made her his woman this day.

"Feeling sore?" came the hoarse but now familiar whisper beside her.

"A little." There was no need to be dishonest.

"It won't always be like that. Any remorse, Gillian?"

"One." She slowly turned to face him. Her lightly freckled nose barely touching the tip of his. She saw his look of dismay and immediately guessed what he was thinking. "It's not that, Logan. I am not going to deny anything or blame you for taking me against my better judgment." She giggled when he sighed in relief. "I am sorry, that's all."

"I do not understand." He pulled the cover over them.

"I am going to miss you. Very much." She couldn't look at him but only at the satin sheet covering them. "I don't recall getting under these, do you?"

"I moved you after you fell asleep. You sleep deeply, my lady. Nothing bothers you." He smiled.

Impulsively, she kissed him. He was so handsome, and at the moment, so boyish, that she felt the urge to protect him.

"I shall miss you, too, Gillian. I will do whatever I can to shorten my trip. But you must understand, I cannot and will not change my plans."

He said the words so quietly and with such kindness, she could not be angered. "I know. It's just that I don't know how I can live like a virgin again." She twisted the corner of the sheet in her hands and was surprised when he pulled her to him.

"You must and you had better! Goodness, woman, are you planning to cuckold me before our wedding?"

"Are you jealous?"

"Indeed I am." And it surprised him, for it was true. Thinking of the fire this woman unleashed and the many lessons in love yet to learn, he realized he could cheerfully strangle Gillian and any man she dared to look at.

"I meant, Logan, that I will be thinking of you and longing for you each night and day you are gone." She stroked his tousled hair. "I miss you already."

"No need." He pulled her into his embrace. "I seem to recall a little unfinished business."

"Unfinished?"

"Well not exactly that." He nuzzled her neck, slowly removing the last vestige of clothing. The blue satin ribbon swirled to the floor. "I am curious, that's all. I wonder if you will display such a wildly passionate response to me each time I make love to you."

"I cannot say, my lord." She hid her face behind the

131

long tangles of her strawberry hair.

"Let's see, shall we? Are you cold?"

"A little."

"I shall remedy that instantly." He pulled the sheet higher over their shoulders, then allowed his hands to roam over her long slender torso and legs.

"More," she murmured throatily. "I cannot believe what you do to me."

"Lie back," he said tenderly. "And no matter what, keep your arms on your sides." Leaning on one elbow, raised above her supine body, he continued the exploration with his eyes and hands.

Her eyes were also trained on him. But aside from the intense physical delight his hands elicited, her satisfaction was twofold: from watching the darkening gleam in his golden eyes and the perspiration on his brow.

"When can I touch you?" She wanted to run her nails lightly across his hair-covered chest.

"Later, love. This moment is mine." Taunting the pink nipples to hardness, he alternated sucking and rubbing her breasts that seemed to reach up to him for more.

Inching his mouth lower to her belly, his tongue flicked along her stomach, pausing a few delicious moments at her belly button before continuing the journey.

When her hands gripped his shoulders, he playfully scolded her. "Uh uh, what did I say?" He took her arms, pinning them to her sides.

"I want to give you pleasure. I want you to remember these moments while we are separated. I want you to close your eyes while you are lying *alone*, my lady," he emphasized the words, "in your big girl's frilly bed and think of us, like this."

"I shall perish of loneliness." She looked into his

eyes.

"No you shan't, but you will eagerly embrace me when I return."

His hands cupping her buttocks now, his mouth descended to the one area Gillian could not believe was permissible to kiss.

"Oh, no, Logan. You cannot." She struggled to rise, but his tongue began kissing and licking and she suddenly saw a number of shooting stars above her head.

Raising his head briefly, his mouth damp from the taste of her, he said, "Nothing is wrong when two people enjoy making love. There is no such thing as prudity with me, sweetheart, and there won't be with you. You can be as wanton as you like."

"But that's not proper," she demurred.

"There is no such thing as 'proper' behavior, just uninhibited passion, my love." Without seeking permission, he resumed loving her with his mouth.

Her head fell against the pillow as she gave into the powerful sensations he unleased. It felt as if Logan's hands and mouth were everywhere, that her body was no longer her own, but his. Like a finely tuned instrument, he taught her body to respond to him, to love and be loved. That was her last rational thought before she felt the world darken, her body trembling uncontrollably as an all-consuming quake in her very soul made her toes tingle while she screamed his name in abject joy.

"Now, you can touch me." He moved up to take her mouth. Aroused by the taste of her on his mouth, she did not realize that she pulled him against her before running fingers through his hair, along the sharp contours of his face. When he pulled away to look at her, there were tears in her eyes.

"Gillian," he looked troubled, "did I hurt you?"

133

"Oh, no, Logan. It was just something I could never describe. Will our lives together be as glorious as this moment?"

Telling her only what she needed to hear, he smiled broadly. "It shall be as you wish."

"Can we, ah, meet again like this before you leave?"

"Every day that's left, if you wish." His body rotated against her hip. "I think there is a bit more time left of our late-afternoon tryst. Let me show you something else."

He moved on top of her. Before she could utter a sigh of pleasure, he was deep inside her moist body. The tempo alternated. First he was the gentle, solicitous lover, but as her excitement grew, Logan could not contain his and thrust harder. Gathering the back of her knees over his forearms, he looked directly into her pale blue eyes, plunging deeper. Her response surprised him. Grabbing his buttocks, she pulled him deeper and they moved as one. Gillian matched every movement until it was she who led the dance of passion.

"Ah, Gillian," he groaned aloud, "you are truly an enchantress."

"I am your lover now," she answered simply.

"Then turn around, on your knees." He did not know if he could leave her, but the desire to explore another position with her was too tantalizing.

"Put your hands here," he demanded, showing her what he wanted. Reaching for her quivering breasts, he entered her.

She tried to look behind her to gauge his reaction, but after two quick thrusts, she could barely concentrate on anything but the new storm building within. His hands continued to stroke her breasts and moved lower to pull her against him. Both on their knees,

Gillian leaned into him, exulting in the stimulation of his thrusting body.

"Let me hold you, Logan," she pleaded.

Quickly, he pulled her around to enter her yet again from their original position.

"Do you want more, my love?"

She thought he spoke, but was too weak to answer. Only when he seemed to leave her did she cry in protest.

"Do you want all of me?" he teased, and she loved it.

"Oh, yes, Logan, I want to feel you deep inside me. Like this." Clutching his buttocks again, she impaled herself against him.

It was more than he could stand. His stamina could not remain in check, not as long as this witch held him and looked at him with those sultry eyes and mouth. She was a firebrand and she was his.

"Take me," he called. She gladly reveled in the new-found power over him and suddenly all became one explosion of light and sound as they clung to each other, calling out to each other, not letting go of each other as they rode the tidal wave together.

Chapter Fourteen

The succeeding days flew past so rapidly that Gillian was surprised when Logan announced he was leaving the following morning.

They had spent nearly every daylight hour together—in Logan's bed—except for the one Tuesday afternoon when Logan had driven them to a small inn just outside London. Since the inn was far removed from the traditional route of the daily day coaches that routinely traveled to and from London, Logan had not been concerned about anyone recognizing them.

That day had been perfect in every way, from the picnic lunch Webster had packed for the two-hour journey to the small but elegantly appointed room on the top floor of the inn. They had forgotten about the food until much later when they were inside their cozy room. Somehow lunch had become dinner when Logan insisted on feeding Gillian while she soaked in a large brass tub. Afterward, they had laughed uproariously when Gillian noted that she would never think of duck liver pâté in the same way ever again.

Lady Helena was not ignorant. Gillian's mother noticed the particular glow on her daughter's face and her lack of comprehension about the simplest issues. It was also odd that Gillian claimed to be spending so much time with her friend Adeline Barrish when Logan was soon to depart. Blessedly, her mother did not say one word.

But Gillian's world was coming to an end, for Logan was leaving. This was to be their last tryst. Logan had offered her a number of choices for their last day together: a return visit to the inn; a day of shopping and the theater; a long ride into the country. She chose none. All that mattered was spending as much time as possible alone with Logan — in his naked embrace under the black satin sheets. So they had remained in his townhouse.

"I feel wretched," she proclaimed. Hunched on her knees in the middle of his huge four-poster bed, she watched as he gathered some last-minute toiletries into a leather bag.

"I know. But . . ."

"No, no there is no need to say it again. I know there is nothing you can do about this."

He turned to face her. Damn but she was the most enchanting creature he had ever bedded. Thinking he would become bored with her after their physical encounters, Logan was astonished to realize he wanted more of her. It was an addiction he had only heard of, but, fortunately, never experienced. Until now. It had never occurred to him that he would miss her.

More important, this was the first time in all the years he had been working for Harold that Logan Hammond regretted leaving on assignment. It was not a pleasant realization.

"Will you write me as soon as you reach Paris?"

"Yes, I promise. But you know I am not staying in France. I must be in Rome by the end of the week." How he would send a letter postmarked Rome would be another, albeit minor, problem. She was asking a lot of innocent questions, and Logan hoped he wouldn't forget his answers — especially when writing to her about his travels.

"Will you take me to Venice someday? Perhaps we can honeymoon there."

"If that would make you happy." Recognizing the sadness in her small voice, he added, "Why don't you plan our honeymoon trip while I am away. Whatever you want is fine with me, sweetheart. Just make sure you find us rooms with extra large beds." He winked.

"And privacy."

"Absolutely. And do not plan too much touring in one day. I have some touring of my own to do." He strutted over to fondle her breast and kiss the top of her head.

A soft knocking at the door interrupted what Logan had wanted to do with the willing girl.

"Damn you, Webster, go away!"

"A letter. It is important, my lord. The man who delivered it said it was to be given to you immediately."

Gillian ducked under the sheet while Logan opened the door for Webster's hand to fit through with the missive.

It was from Harold. Logan had to meet him tonight — alone. How the devil was he supposed to get away from Gillian on their last night together? Since there was no way of contacting Harold, Logan sighed deeply and quickly conjured up some answers for the inevitable questions.

"Is it a problem, Logan?"

"Yes and no." He crumpled the note and flung it into the fireplace. Fortunately it was lit, despite the time of year. Since the day was unusually damp and chilly, Gillian had insisted on a romantic fire. Logan wistfully looked at the thick white bearskin rug. Gillian had taken the initiative that time.

"Well?"

"Sorry, I was just thinking of that white rug. You know," he grinned, "for someone who was a virgin a couple of weeks past, you certainly learn very quickly."

"You had everything to do with it." She did not blush this time. "But if you don't put something around your magnificent naked body, I will be forced to attack you yet again and never learn about the note."

"Oh, well, it seems I must meet with a business acquaintance of my father's this evening. There are some contracts I must sign. Gillian," he lifted a long curl, "we must end our day a little earlier."

She was going to cry and Logan did not think he could bear it. "Oh. Well, what am I supposed to say?"

"Say you understand." He took her arms, pulling her into his lap.

"Perhaps I can see you afterward?"

"I think not. These things can take hours. How could you explain that to your parents? I can't imagine they aren't suspicious by now."

"My mother is. My father is preoccupied with his health. I doubt he notices my absences." Looking up into his amber eyes, she could only think of Logan and their time apart. Determined to spend every last minute together, she boldly declared, "Why can't I spend the night with you?"

Her stubborn chin was set, her thick red-blond eyebrows folded, and he knew this could be trouble.

"I don't think it wise."

"Who cares what is wise now, Logan. You are leaving tomorrow! I want to be with you. If you must have that silly meeting, so be it. But, Logan, please,

please let me spend the night with you." She pulled his arm, tears welling in her eyes.

"No. I will not jeopardize your reputation."

"Hah! Now you worry about my reputation?" Angrily, she pulled out of his embrace and scurried to the other side of the bed.

"Yes. I think it unwise. I don't know when I am coming back. I may be out most of the night and I must be on the coach by 6 A.M. You know that, Gillian." He remained seated on the bed, his arms resting on his raised knees.

Naked or not, Logan Hammond had the casual grace of a panther and it upset Gillian to see him so unperturbed by the change in their plans.

"If I did not know better I would think you planned all of this, Logan." Now she was standing on the other end of the room, reaching for the black silk robe that had become hers after their first time together.

"Don't be daft, Gillian." He started to rise.

"No, don't move." She shielded his advance with her hand. "I don't want you near me. I remember what you said about goodbyes. You said you hated them, especially if they were protracted and sentimental. In fact, those were your exact words."

"Keep your voice down. You are beginning to whine."

"And you, my lord, are beginning to upset me." She stood arms akimbo, waiting for another verbal encounter.

"This is absurd." He stood up.

"Stay right there, Logan," she warned. "Stay away from me."

Heedless of her warning, he crossed the room in two long strides. Grabbing her arm, he forgot his strength and roughly pulled her to him.

"Ouch, you are hurting me!"

"Calm down. This is idiotic. You are behaving like a silly schoolgirl."

"I said let go of me." She wrenched her arm free and heard the sound of a ripped seam.

"Not until you've calmed yourself."

She was losing control and knew it. Her anger reached new proportions. All she knew was that Logan was leaving sooner than they had planned and he did not seem to mind.

"I want to go home. Now, Logan." Her hair almost whipped his face as she impatiently turned around looking for her long-ago discarded clothes.

"You don't mean that." He had never tried to calm an outraged woman before. He had never cared, but it bothered him to see Gillian so upset. Short of not meeting Harold, there was nothing else Logan could do. He could not, would not, accede to her demands.

She was, without a doubt, in love with him, even if she was too naive or unwilling to recognize what he knew to be obvious.

"Yes I do. Now will you take me home or not?"

"No. I want you to stay with me longer."

"You don't mean that and we both know it. You're probably eager to get away from me. Now that you've taken my virginity, there is nothing left to conquer, is there?"

Tempted to slap her back to sanity, he felt his hand rise, but immediately checked the impulse.

"Touch me and I will scream the house down," she snarled.

"Gillian, love, please listen to me. You are being unreasonable. I want you to . . ."

"If you won't take me home, I will go myself. There are plenty of coaches for hire this time of day."

She was not listening. "All right. Let me dress. And

141

you can use a little time to make yourself presentable, too." His voice was low and controlled.

Knowing she would regret her actions later, he decided to escort her home and keep his meeting with Harold. If it was possible to end it at an early hour, he'd visit her home and accept her apology.

They rode to the Marlowe house in silence. Too angry and hurt to care about anything but her misery, Gillian did not think of the consequences of her behavior. With her cloak pulled tight and the hood covering her messy hair, she sat stiffly on the farthest end of the tufted leather seat, refusing to look at Logan. Staring blankly at the leather interior and brass lanterns on the vehicle, she tried to ignore him. It wasn't possible.

She could feel his presence and without looking at him, she knew he casually leaned against the seat, calmly taking in the sights they passed. The sky was almost dark now, and only a few gaslights illuminated the path ahead. When she heard the distinct sound of his cigar being lit, she angrily turned to him. "Have you no manners? How can you smoke that thing in this enclosed carriage? Did you ever think I might choke?"

"It never bothered you before. I thought you rather liked it."

"Well, I don't!" she snapped. "And you could remember your breeding, just this once."

He should have put the cigar out, but Logan, too, had a stubborn streak and a blind desire to strike back at Gillian. Raising the expensive cigar to his lips, he looked directly at her haughty expression and took one long, deliberate draw.

"This is unbelievable. Will you blow that thing into my face, too?"

He exhaled out the window.

142

"I can't wait until I am home," she muttered aloud.

"I think you will be very sorry. I am leaving tomorrow. You do recall?" There was a hint of amusement in his voice.

"How can I not? But you have more important things to do this evening than spend your time with me. I will try to remember that after we are wed."

"So you are still marrying me?" he chuckled.

"Well . . ." she hesitated. "I don't want to talk about it." It finally occurred to her that she would not see Logan after this ride. Angry as she was, did she want to end their betrothal? Of course not, she knew. So shouldn't she tell him? But Gillian didn't know how and said not a word as they turned into the street of her house. Biting her lip in consternation, she hoped that Logan would bring the subject up just once more. But he seemed to be enjoying himself and that awful cigar.

"Shall I escort you inside?"

"No thank you." As the carriage stopped, she grabbed the handle to let herself out. With the hood covering her teary face, she had no desire to let him know that she would easily relent if he said the right words.

"Look at me," he said, placing one hand on her shoulder.

"I must go." She didn't turn.

"I shall miss you. And I will write you first thing tomorrow night upon my arrival." His hand found the satin edge of the hood.

"That would be nice. Now can I leave?"

"Will you kiss me goodbye?"

"I cannot, Logan. My parents must be looking out the window, wondering what this coach is doing in front of their home this long."

"Is that the only reason?" He pulled back the

hood. "I want to see your lovely face and red-blonde curls once more, my love. Don't deny me one small pleasure."

That hypnotic tone worked. With some effort she rotated to meet his smiling countenance. Damn, he made her feel so wretched.

"I wish you a safe journey," she whispered.

"Thank you." He captured one errant curl in his fingers. "I shall think of you all the time. And I shall remember these last two weeks every night."

Logan leaned closer to kiss a tear-stained cheek lightly.

She did not want to relent, not here, not now. Acknowledging the tender kiss, she bravely smiled and exited the coach, offering her hand to the waiting footman.

Gillian knew he was watching as she slowly ascended the stone steps. She could have turned to wave or run back into his waiting arms, but pride made her behave differently. Looking ahead, Gillian saw her mother waiting in the vestibule. It was too dark to see her face, but Gillian knew Helena must have guessed that something was not right. Only when the door closed behind her did she finally run into her mother's waiting arms.

Chapter Fifteen

"I behaved like such a fool. I cannot believe he will ever want to speak with me after my childish behavior! My God," she placed her palms to her throbbing temples, "I will not see him anymore. Not after today. And he's leaving tomorrow!"

Gillian continued ranting and wailing over her behavior, having decided she had lost him forever. He could not possibly condone such infantile behavior.

Lady Helena patiently sat on the edge of Gillian's bed, trying her best to listen to her daughter's words and cries of despair. When at last the cries subsided and all that remained was an occasional hiccup, Lady Helena decided to speak.

"I understand your pain, Gillian," she began.

"No you don't!" She whirled on her mother, forgetting to keep her secrets intact. "How could you? I ruined it. Don't you see? Oh," she slapped her forehead, "you cannot understand what I have done."

"I can and I do. Gillian," her mother rose to stand in the path of her daughter's furious pacing, "I know precisely what you have done. And you better pray that not only will Lord Hammond come home quickly, he will come home to you. I know, Gillian, that no other man will marry you."

Frozen in place, Gillian stared wide-eyed at her mother. "You know? But . . ."

"Gillian dear, I am no fool. And I was young once, too," her mother smiled tenderly. "I cannot and will not condone what you have done. But I will not lecture you, either. You are not a silly child fresh out of the schoolroom. You knew what you were doing, did you not?"

Afraid to look at her mother's sympathetic face, she concentrated on the white carpet. "I did. I have no regrets. I am sorry if I have shamed you by my behavior."

"You love him." It was a statement.

"More than anything, and now," the tears welled again, "I have turned him away. I may never see him again."

Helena placed a comforting hand on Gillian's shoulder. She did understand. What Gillian did was wrong—she would be condemned and ostracized among the ton if anyone were to learn of her actions. Her reputation would be in tatters, not to mention Charles's reaction to such an act.

But Helena was not concerned with that right now. Her only daughter was in love and she was in pain. Helena wanted to help. She wanted to give her daughter what she herself had never received from anyone—particularly her own mother. Helena wanted to ease her pain and, if possible, be her confidante.

"Does Adeline know what is going on between you and Logan?"

"Yes. But I know she would never tell anyone, if that is what you want to know?"

"Does anyone else know?"

"Know that the Lady Gillian Marlowe had been compromised? Or that she is a stupid fool for forcing the man of her dreams out of her arms?"

146

Helena smiled. Whenever she smiled she looked much younger than her forty-one years. Gillian suddenly realized that she hadn't seen her mother smile like that in such a long time. Too concerned with herself, Gillian did not notice her mother's unhappiness.

"I mean the former. And no, I am not about to lecture you about morality. Your father must never know."

"I certainly will not tell him."

"Gillian, sit with me on the bed and tell me what has happened."

Glad to have her mother's arms around her, Gillian explained how she wanted and planned to be with Logan. The details would forever remain private, but hopefully her mother would understand that her daughter was not a loose or careless woman.

"I know he feels something for me, Mother. I don't know if it will ever be love, but I know that he cares. And I believe he has—or *had* before today—every intention of marrying me. But, Mother, do you know something? It did not matter. I didn't give myself to him because we would marry eventually. I did it because I wanted to know how it felt to love a real man. And to be loved in return. Logan made me feel that much and more."

"I cannot approve."

"I realize that." Gillian's shiny eyes lifted to her mother's pale face. "I am so glad you are willing to listen. I," she choked back a sob, "I couldn't think of anyone else I would rather have to hold me while I cry."

Ten minutes later, Gillian made a decision. "I must see him. Tonight. I shall wait for his return, no matter how late it is."

"I cannot let you go alone. Nor can I go with you."

Gillian's face fell. "I have a suggestion. You can go, and somehow I will make up some story to tell your father, if you promise to take my maid Alice and one of the footmen with you. You must have some protection."

Alice had been with the family for more than twenty years, and as long as someone else had to know Gillian's secret, Alice was better than anyone. So thoroughly devoted to Helena, Alice would never say or do anything her mother would not want.

"All right. As long as Father never finds out." Flinging her arms about Helena, Gillian kissed the woman's cheek and flashed a brief smile. "Perhaps everything will work out. Whatever the cost, at least I will know that I sought Logan to apologize." Her red-rimmed eyes rolled. "I only hope he's not with another woman."

Logan had no intention of spending the entire rainy night with Harold. Positive that Gillian would be wallowing in remorse, he tried everything possible to end the meeting before nine.

Harold would have none of it. "Logan, there is more you need to know."

They had been sitting in a crowded public house, not far from Logan's house in Regent's Park.

"Harold," Logan had been staring at his gold timepiece, "I must leave."

"Is it the Lady Gillian who is waiting in your warm bed?" Harold favored Logan with one of his rare smiles.

"That is none of your concern," he replied coldly.

"Now now, lad, no need to be touchy. But I did warn you about choosing between your country and your woman."

"That has nothing to do with this, Harold," Logan snapped. "I want to say goodbye to her, that's all. I shall be happy to meet you again later this evening, if you feel I have not already absorbed enough information. We have gone over everything twice. I have it all memorized. What more do we need to review?" Logan consumed three glasses of claret without thinking.

"You cannot appreciate fine wine that way, lad."

"Harold," he warned, "I think I may slit your throat."

"Oh, all right. I simply want to be certain you know who you are to contact and who you are to look out for. This fellow can be very dangerous. And every contact in Florence indicates he is waiting for you."

"This chap has no idea who I am."

"You cannot be certain. Remember, one of our agents was forced to speak while he was ruthlessly tortured. It is not safe for any of us. I may be forced to return to Washington myself."

"Come now, Harold. Nothing frightens you. If you are sailing home, it's because of another, more important reason. A special assignment perhaps?" He grinned. "Or your wife's summons?" Logan found a little pleasure when Harold grunted. "Besides, we know who was responsible for that death. Althorp." His lip curled in contempt of the man who was too involved with Gillian and her family. Logan did not need Harold's confirmation.

"Just be careful, lad. I've taken a strong liking to you." The little man spoke clearly.

Surprised to hear anything other than assignments and codes from Harold, Logan was pleasantly surprised.

"I appreciate that, Harold. Now if you don't mind, do you think I can allow my fiancée to apologize this evening?"

"Are you going directly to her home?'"

"No. Gillian cannot abide the smell of cheap cigar smoke and whisky, and if she smelled this vile stuff on me she would never believe I had a business meeting at the club. I'd better go home first."

"Splendid. Then let me escort you home and test your knowledge of Charleston and the British loyalists living in the surrounding areas."

"Why? Harold," Logan looked suspiciously at the man, "you are not planning another assignment for me when I return, are you?"

"Don't tell me you are worried about your fiancée again."

"I most certainly am. I am going to be married. You do recall that petty detail," he drawled.

"Yes, I do. And no, I am not sending you to Charleston, yet. I am sending two others. They should arrive in Charelston within the month."

"Do I know them?"

"One of them you will remember. He's been with us quite a while. Peter Harris. A good man."

"Yes he is. And the other chap?"

"I never said 'chap' my boy. She is rather new."

"A woman? How intriguing." The carriage stopped in front of the townhouse. "Harold, why don't you come inside. No one will recognize you. No one would be stupid enough to be walking the streets on this damp night."

He was wrong. No sooner had Logan jumped out of the carriage than a familiar voice called his name.

"Logan," she rushed up to him, heedless of the other man with Logan or the two companions left sitting in her carriage, "I came to apologize." She touched his arm. "I don't know what came over me. Will you please forgive me? I was such a . . ."

"Sweetheart, calm yourself." He firmly took her arm. "I would have come to you. As soon as my meeting was over."

"Over?" Gillian noticed the little man wearing a round black hat, smoking a funny-smelling cigar. "Oh, forgive me," she placed a gloved hand to her mouth, "I am afraid I did it again."

"Yes you did." Fortunately, Logan saw some humor in the situation. Gillian was impulsive and it made her that much more endearing to him.

"May I present my father's associate, Harold, ah, Porter?" It was the first name that entered his brain. "This is my fiancée, Mr. Porter. Lady Gillian Marlowe."

Harold shot Logan a knowing glance. "I am pleased to meet you, miss."

"You are American?" She hadn't missed the funny accent or the way he referred to her as 'miss' instead of the proper title.

"Yes, I am and proud of it, too. I must say I miss my home."

"Excuse me, but shall we go inside? I am certain it is too damp for you, darling. Why don't you tell your servants to go around to the kitchen for a cup of tea?"

If Logan was taken by surprise, he gave no indication of his discomfort. Ushering both Gillian and Harold inside, he began a discussion about the weather and his voyage.

The little group failed to notice that another waited and watched. Standing in the shadows of the townhouse to the left of Logan's was Brian Althorp.

Hat worn high on his head, his hands stuffed into the pockets of his dark brown overcoat, Brian remained rooted to the spot. He could not believe that Gillian would leave her home—virtually alone, so late at night—but when she ended up at Hammond's home, Brian wanted to grab her by the collar and spank her silly behind. When she ran into the bastard's arms, Brian wanted to strangle her. Gillian was lost to him. For now.

Seeing Hammond's companion redirected Althorp's thoughts. There was something naggingly familiar about the short, stocky American. He had seen him before. Brian smiled into the darkness. He never forgot a face. It would be interesting to learn what Hammond was doing with this uncouth American at this hour.

"I will get you, Hammond. Never fear," he whispered to no one before disappearing into the park and the foggy night.

In the meantime, Gillian sat primly on a Chippendale settee in Logan's sitting room. It was not her favorite room in the house, perhaps because it lacked warmth and color. The walls were a stark white and there were no carpets or comfortable sofas — most of the chairs lacked thick cushions.

"This room was decorated by a former lady friend," he had told her once. She had needed no other reason for disliking the room and its contents.

Within minutes, a staid-looking butler — not Webster — emerged with a silver tray filled with delicate china tea cups and pot.

There was an awkward silence while Gillian pretended to look about the room. "I apologize again, gentlemen."

"No need. I must leave."

"Please, not on my account, Logan," she stood, "let me freshen up a minute and give you and Mr. Porter a chance to conclude your business in private."

"Delightful young woman, Logan," Harold commented as soon as the door closed behind Gillian. "You are a lucky man. Lovely."

"Yes, I know." Logan suppressed a smile. "She's

152

not stupid, either, Harold."

"Well, as long as she does not find you out. Now, before I forget, let me tell you about Peter and Lily. They are married."

"Really?"

"Well, not exactly, but for the purpose of this assignment they are. I wanted them to have the names of your friends and relatives. Especially those who are well connected socially."

"No problem." Logan strode over to the sideboard and poured them ample glasses of whiskey. "Here, drink this. This is from the finest stock in Britain. Not like the watered-down drinks you are used to. This is guaranteed to make your eyes tear while it smoothly floats down your throat."

"I have no time to savor such fine liquor. From the looks of your fiancée, I gather you two have something to discuss."

Harold collected his hat and coat. "Please extend my apologies for leaving without waiting for her to return. Have a good trip, lad." Harold took Logan's extended hand. "Remember, be careful. I want you in one piece. By the way," he called over his shoulder, "the name is Robinson."

"I appreciate your concern. I think," Logan grinned. "I can take excellent care of myself. Just watch your own back," he warned. "I don't want to report to anyone other than you. I expect to see you in London upon my return."

When Gillian reappeared ten minutes later, she was grateful that the little man had left. "I am so sorry . . ." she began.

"No need. You seem to be saying those words often tonight."

"I should." She walked over to him. Looking around the room, she asked, "Can we go to the library? I like the memories we've shared in that room."

"How long can you stay?"

"As long as you want me to." She wrapped one arm around his waist. It was an intimate and pleasant gesture.

Kissing the top of her head he allowed her to lead them into the other room. "May I kiss you?" he asked after the double doors closed.

"Never ask me that question." She stood on her toes to receive his gentle kiss. "I want you to forgive me for such boorish, childish behavior."

"I was never angry with you, Gillian. I am pleased that you came here to apologize. I would have gone to your home, regardless of the hour."

He took her into his arms. "I realize that you care about me and it pleases me to know that you will be here waiting for my return. I shall hurry home."

His deep kiss sealed the vow he earnestly believed. It would be nice, he thought, as his fingers pulled the pins out of her hair, to have a warm, loving, and inventive bed partner waiting for him.

Chapter Sixteen

"20th May, 1825

My Darling Logan,

Today is Sunday, only two days after your departure, and I feel as if you have been gone two months. I miss you so. I cannot tell you how difficult it is knowing I cannot be with you today or any other day for the coming weeks.

Our last night together was memorable. I know there is no need to apologize again, but I feel terrible whenever I think of the extra hours we could have shared.

Fear not, Alice is as loyal to me as she is to my mother. And when you return, I must tell you all about the part my mother has played in keeping us together. I never fully realized the extent of her love and devotion. She knows a great deal about us — mercifully not *all* — and she only wants what I want.

That, my love, is you. You have become the most important person in my life. Thinking of the rest of our lives together provides some solace for the weeks ahead.

I am looking forward to your letters and your descriptions of your travels. Please, please tell me everything, no matter how trivial you think the information may be. I cannot think of a better way to enjoy the time away from you than reading and sharing your thoughts and feelings about your travels abroad.

I know it is not ladylike to tell you this, but, Logan, I love you. I never meant to let you know. I never meant for this to happen. But if one must fall in love, I daresay there is no one better than you to love and be made love to.

Logan, if you show these letters to anyone I fear I shall be mortified. Forgive my boldness. I have learned so much from you. I cannot wait to receive your letters. Think of me, as I do of you, each night and each morning. Let me be the first and last thought of your day. Until the day I can fly into your waiting arms, I remain, faithfully and forever yours,

Gillian"

"25th May, 1825
Rome

Dearest Gillian,

I apologize for this scrawled and brief letter. The journey was swift and uneventful. Travel by coach, ship, coach, and so on, no matter how luxurious it is — after twenty consecutive hours is painful.

You have been on my mind constantly. No matter where I am or who I am with — I see your lovely face, your silky strawberry hair cascading over my hands as I undo the numerous pins, your adorable smile, and I cannot concentrate.

I have other thoughts as well, but I am not sure to whom you are showing this letter and if heaven forbid this ship that carries the mail packet sinks, well . . . I am only trying to protect your reputation.

I am staying at the home of a friend, and have every convenience. But I see your smile and think how long the nights are in Italy and wonder if they are equally long in London.

Enclosed is the name and address of my solicitor. Since my travel plans are still in flux, I cannot be certain where I will be when your next letter arrives. Signor Castelli will forward the letters.

I will write soon.

Faithfully,
Logan"

"15th June, 1825

Dearest Logan,

I cannot tell you how thrilled I was to receive your letter. I had no idea your handwriting was that difficult to decipher, but I managed and have committed your letter to memory.

I have been spending the last few days at my aunt's estate in Stratford. It has been a pleasant stay, but I do not recall much. I keep thinking of your letter and hoping you are having a miserable time.

I expect to see you bounding up the stairs to our townhouse. Mother thought I was acting strangely by sitting in the front parlor on the window seat for two days in succession. That explains this trip. Mother thought I might benefit from a little country air.

You have missed nothing in London. The social life is at a peak, but I cannot tell you any gossip because I have no desire to listen to anyone about anything.

We will be traveling again soon to the family

home in Hamptonshire. Father thinks Foreign Secretary Canning will join us for a few days. Perhaps his political talk will keep my mind from wandering — but I have my doubts.

Mother is calling me. I promised to ride with her today.

Logan, my love, I miss you terribly. I have strange dreams, if you know what I mean.

I will write again in a few days. I hope to receive your letters soon.

All my love,
Gillian"

"7th July, 1825

Dear Logan,

I cannot understand why I haven't received another letter, and assume our letters have crossed. As you requested, I am sending this letter to your solicitor in Rome, hoping he knows where it should be forwarded.

I hope you are enjoying your trip. Mother and I have been making plans for the wedding. Before we left for our Hamptonshire country house, I invited your stepmother and sister to lunch. Luisa is charming and thoroughly convinced there could never be any boy as smart, handsome, and, to paraphrase her, as marvelous a horseman and marksman as you. Since I have been denied the pleasure of seeing those skills, I must assume Luisa is correct.

They, too, are concerned over not hearing from you these past weeks.

The weather has been awful. It rains most of the time, which makes me feel tired and oftentimes depressed. Mother says I am lovesick.

Please write soon.

Love,
Gillian"

"23rd July, 1825
Venice

Dear Gillian,

Forgive me yet again. I only received your letter three days past. I have been kept quite busy with my father's business associates and have met some interesting gentlemen — French and American — interested in establishing a private concern with me. I know my father will agree it is in my best interest to establish my own business relationships.

Unfortunately, this may delay my return. I pray you understand. I miss you, too, and think of you all the time.

I will be in Paris in a few weeks and hope I can settle these matters with dispatch and rush across the Channel — even if I have to swim — to your waiting arms.

Faithfully,
Logan"

"31st July, 1825

Logan,

I need you. There is something we must discuss and I cannot put my thoughts and feelings to paper. Moreover, I simply do not trust this solicitor who is supposed to be forwarding my letters.

Your last letter was postmarked Venice, but there was no address or forwarding address, so again this letter is sent to you via Rome.

I do not know how much longer I can go on not seeing you. I am lonely. I find myself crying over silly things more often than I care to admit.

Brian was sweet enough to drive all this way to Hamptonshire to spend an evening with us. He tried to cheer me up, but nothing is the same without you here.

Please, please hurry home.

Love,
Gillian"

"15th August, 1825

Logan,

I have written more letters to you than I care to write to anyone for the rest of my life. Where are you? No one has heard from you in weeks. I pray you are not in trouble. I also pray you have not found another woman or women to keep you entertained while I am in misery.

I do not know how much longer I can wait to hear from you. I must speak to you and you alone. You are the only one who can help.

Each day Mother asks me why I am so pale and teary. I do not know what to say anymore. She is afraid I am making myself ill over your infrequent letters. It is not that.

Where are you?

Gillian"

"20th August, 1825
Paris

Dear Lady Marlowe

I am writing to you at the request of your betrothed. I am a business associate and friend of

160

Lord Hammond. Unfortunately, he has been taken ill. It stems from the result of a wager, which is no longer amusing.

Logan took a terrible spill from his horse during a steeplechase, suffering a broken arm, and a fever resulted from complications. He is out of danger but was not able to write in his own hand.

Logan wanted me to tell you how much he misses you and hopes to be sailing for London within a fortnight.

I am sending a similar letter to his family and hope all your fears have been allayed.

Your servant,
Frederick Gibson"

"7th September, 1825

Dear Logan,

I hope this letter finds you completely recovered from your illness. We have been worried and prayed constantly for your well being.

Son, I know no other way of telling you this. Lady Gillian seems to have disappeared! I have written to her family on numerous occasions and received only one rather curt reply from Lord Marlowe telling me his daughter and wife have decided to go on holiday. I have no idea where they have gone or when they are planning to return.

If my sources at the club are to be taken a fraction seriously, I have heard that the Lady Gillian has been the subject of some malicious and unfair gossip — most of which concerns you and your extended holiday.

This does not bode well. Come home quickly.

Your Father"

"2nd September, 1825
Calais

Gillian,

I am writing a hurried letter and sending it on the first and fastest ship I can find. I hope this letter reaches you before I. I am boarding another ship for London tomorrow and expect to be at your door within one day.

Except for my arm, I am mostly recovered. I promise to explain everything when I am home. The wedding can be set for any day you desire. Just make it as soon as possible, for I long to be alone with you, rediscovering you for weeks on end.

Faithfully,
Logan"

"9th September 1825

Lord Hammond,

I have been instructed by my daughter to inform you she no longer wishes to become your wife. Lady Gillian did not know how to reach you and since you obviously did not want to be reached — or for that matter want to come home to her — we all felt it was in Gillian's best interest to break the betrothal immediately.

She has departed for an extended holiday and has left explicit instructions that you are not to contact her. She never wants to hear your name again. You, sir, are a despicable man and if you care to call me out, I welcome the opportunity to put a bullet in your heart.

The Earl of Dalton,
Lord Charles Marlowe"

Part Two

CHARLESTON, SOUTH CAROLINA, 1826–1827

Chapter Seventeen

November 1826

The streets were deserted. Although it was only 9 P.M., no one was foolish enough to walk about in the downpour unless it was absolutely necessary and unavoidable. The rhythm of the steadily falling rain and the occasional sounds of a horse's brisk trot along the cobblestone street were punctuated by the clanging of a buoy and a ship's horn.

The nocturnal noises did not penetrate the ears of the lone woman who leisurely strolled along the Battery as if it were a sunny afternoon. Huddled underneath a man's bright yellow rain slick, her strawberry-blond hair tightly coiled around her head and covered by a long hood, she was unrecognizable.

She liked these walks, making a point to stroll up and down the high sea walls of the Battery each night regardless of the weather or time. Unlike the daytime when the Battery was crowded with people taking advantage of the cool weather and sea breezes, the nights—particularly the inclement weather nights—were reserved for the more adventurous or foolish individuals.

The lone lady relished these minutes of solitude.

She could think, walk, and even talk to herself. Sometimes the words emitted were full of hostility. All were directed at one man.

Lady Gillian Marlowe was pregnant. "Enceinte" was the more delicate way to phrase it, but the word could not change the condition or the situation. She was not married. As far as she was concerned, the father of her child had chosen his holiday over her love. There had been no letters from Logan after August 15th. Therefore, she had angrily concluded he had wanted nothing to do with her and now refused to have any communication with the father of the babe or his family. Logan had eventually returned to England, but for Gillian it was too late. She had been forced to flee her native England to the United States where, it was assumed, no one would be the wiser about the circumstances surrounding her condition.

Most people were aware of Gillian's condition— although she was hardly showing. "Condition," she muttered aloud, feeling the slight swell of her abdomen. "In a few weeks one would have to be blind not to notice."

It did not matter now, for there was a master plan she and her mother had devised on the journey across the Atlantic that was fine-tuned with the assistance of their cousin and hostess, Julia Grayson. Gillian never realized how clever and resourceful her mother could be.

Thank God for her mother. Lady Helena Marlowe would not hear of her daughter traveling without her. Throughout those long bouts of combined morning sickness and seasickness on their voyage across the sea, she had stroked Gillian's aching head and held her hand. When everything appeared bleak and hopeless, she had tried to humor her daughter. She had dried Gillian's tears and listened to her curses.

166

Telling her mother had been the most difficult decision, but once Logan had deserted her and she knew her condition was soon to be obvious, she was left with little choice. She had waited until her mother noticed the first signs of Gillian's discomfort.

Helena had considered the consequences of Gillian's liaison with London's notorious rake, but had believed Logan Hammond wanted to marry her only daughter. Once the truth became obvious, Helena had seen no reason to argue with or reprimand her daughter for her indiscretions. It was too late for that. Helena had questioned Gillian delicately and then everything after the confession, including the decision to leave England, was relatively simple.

Of course Lord Marlowe had been another obstacle. With her mother standing at her side, Gillian had explained what she could of her doomed relationship with Logan. It was not the lust of a wanton that led to her predicament, but the deep, trusting love of a naive woman who believed in the word of a so-called "gentleman." Charles had been greatly upset and angry with Gillian, but, surprisingly, it did not last long. He had soon switched his fury to Logan Hammond.

Her father had wanted to track Logan down and force him to marry his daughter as soon as possible. But Gillian had been adamant about never seeing him again.

"He does not want me. He never cared for me. And I have no intention of letting him see me suffer. You were correct, Father. Logan Hammond will never face his responsibilities."

Gillian had been convinced that Logan's abandonment was deliberate. Perhaps a wager at White's or Logan's warped sense of humor had accounted for the seduction. But why had he forced her to fall in love with him? Why had he led her to believe he

167

wanted to marry her?

"It was all part of his game," she said aloud. Noticing that she was walking too close to the wharves, Gillian realized she would have to turn around soon and go back to her cousin's house.

Her mother and cousins had finally accepted her eccentric behavior, but it hadn't been so easy when they arrived in Charleston four weeks ago.

Gillian had been impressed by the beautiful, romantic city. Although its history was not as long as London's, she found Charleston and its people hospitable and charming. This was not, as she originally thought, a backwater town. There was a definite English influence on the city which blended with a unique southern but patriotic American culture.

Almost immediately upon their arrival, the ladies had found themselves thrust into Charleston society. It was not a very large group, but it controlled the city and the social life.

Twisting the thin gold band around her finger, Gillian cynically laughed at the mockery her life had become.

She was now known as Lady Gillian Marston. Helena, ever so practical and rational, had decided the initials must remain the same as her given names. It was also easy to remember and stumble over the first syllable of the last name before it emerged.

Alas, according to their plan, Gillian had not been destined to remain a loving wife too long. The mysterious, fictitious husband, "Viscount Gerald Marston," a diplomat for His Majesty, of course, had been on special assignment in Egypt and India. Unfortunately, the husband had met an untimely death while in India — all in the line of duty for His Majesty's government.

The widow had been inconsolable — especially since

she was expecting their first child. The widow's family had decided it best to leave England and the awful reminders of their happy life together; thus their extended visit to relatives in the Low Country.

The announcement of the bogus Gerald's death had appeared in the London papers—Charles had thought of that idea. By the time the ladies had arrived in Charleston—Gillian suitably dressed in widow's black—the trauma over Gerald's death had subsided.

Gillian had received a number of condolences among the Charlestonians. It had made her uncomfortable—and she had felt some regret for acting like such a hypocrite. But her mother and cousin Julia told her it had to be done this way. Once again, even in Charleston, one's reputation and social standing had to be protected.

The ultimate irony was that Gillian and Helena had fled to the one city in the United States where Logan Hammond had once lived, and where his American family was very much part of Charleston society.

He was well known among the populace although they hadn't seen him in four years. His grandfather spent most of his days now on the Raveneau family plantation outside Charleston on the Ashley River. Like most wealthy planters in Charleston, Logan's aunt and uncle divided their time between Charleston and the plantation. There were a number of other relatives, cousins, great-aunts, and uncles in and around South Carolina. The Raveneaus were greatly admired and respected as one of the oldest, wealthiest families in Charleston and the United States.

Each night, as Gillian meandered along the sea-wall walk, she would pass the newly constructed planter's-style home that belonged to Logan's grandfather. It was well known that the Reaveneaus owned more than one large house in Charleston, three plantations along the Ashley and Santee rivers, and summer cottages in the Blue Ridge Mountains of North Carolina. Among their vast holdings, the family was involved in shipping, banking, and other commercial concerns.

The sound of her feet sloshing through the puddles reminded Gillian of her soggy state. She had a responsibility to another human being now, and catching pneumonia could be fatal to an unborn babe. Despite her heartache, she fiercely wanted this child—her child. She would protect it with her life.

The Grayson home on Meeting Street was not far from the Battery. By the time she climbed up the stone steps to the imposing front door of the Grayson home, her maid, mother, and cousin were standing in the doorway with towels.

"Gillian, you cannot continue these solitary walks. Why, it isn't safe! Someone must accompany you," her mother admonished.

"Nonsense," she removed the slick and accepted a fluffy white towel, "I am fine. The babe is fine. I am quite convinced she or he enjoys these walks as much as I."

Julia Grayson smiled indulgently at her cousin. "I think Charleston agrees with you. But not even the most intrepid gentleman would casually stroll along the Battery in this weather."

"It reminds me of London." Gillian blotted her face and neck.

"It will not for long. You will see. As soon as the weather improves in the early spring, the flowers begin to bloom and you will forget all about dirty London."

"Cousin Julia! When was the last time you visited London?"

170

The petite dark-haired woman shrugged off the question. "I know what I know, darling. And you must take better care of yourself. After all . . ."

"Yes, yes," Gillian sighed loudly. "After all, I must think of the babe." She finished her cousin's sentence.

"Come, I have prepared English tea for you. You can use something hot."

"If you don't mind, I think I'd prefer some of your hot cocoa."

The older ladies smiled at each other.

"Gillian, change your clothes first and join us in the morning room." Helena led her daughter to the stairs.

By the time Gillian returned in an old comfortable, dark blue dress, the women were waiting in the brightly lit room.

"You must be tired, dear," Helena said.

"Quite the contrary, I feel refreshed and wide-awake." Her damp reddish hair curling around the sides of her face made Gillian look more like a young schoolgirl than a pregnant unwed woman.

"There are a few matters we should discuss, if you are feeling up to it," Helena announced. Gillian wondered why her mother had to be separated from her father in order to become independent and competent in handling their lives.

Everything about her mother, including her regal posture, bespoke a woman of confidence. More than once, Helena had commented about this new life in Charleston, marveling at the city and the easy life. She hardly spoke of England—or of Charles.

Sitting on a comfortable settee beside the large window, Gillian waited for the discussion to start. These talks were generally about her pregnancy, which agreed-upon story they'd tell to society about

171

the "dead husband," and whether to accept the many invitations to leave Charleston and spend Christmas at a plantation.

Helena removed something from her pocket. "I received this letter today. It was sent to your father, who forwarded it along with his letter."

Gillian recognized the bold handwriting. "I am not interested in any of his letters," she coldly replied. "It is too late for Logan Hammond."

"Gillian, how do you know what he has to say? Perhaps he wants to marry you. He does not know about your condition." Helena held out the letter, but Gillian ignored the paper. "Look at the postmark. This letter originated in Paris. Perhaps Logan tried to contact you." Since Gillian's hands remained clasped in her lap, Helena set aside the letter for the time being.

"Whether he tried or not is irrelevant. I am no longer interested in Logan Hammond. I am a respectable widow and I shall live that way until this babe is born. Afterward," she shrugged, "well, afterward we shall see."

"Gillian, dear. Logan suspects you are in America. He told your father that much."

"Oh?" Gillian seemed engrossed in her hot cocoa. "What else did he tell Father?" She did not look at her mother's knowing expression.

"Your father neglected to mention all the details in his letter. From what I gather, they met quite by accident—at White's. Logan approached your father first. I think Charles would have challenged him on the spot if it weren't for Brian's intervention." Helena laughed gently. She would have loved to have seen Charles bluster and rant—especially if he had done so in front of all the other gentlemen at White's. As long as she wasn't the recipient of Charles's anger, it would have been a pleasure to see her husband vent his fury on one as deserving as Logan.

"Now Brian is involved?"

"Not exactly, dear. But Brian has been pestering your father with many questions. All concerning your whereabouts."

"I do not want Brian to know. He was once a dear friend and it would be hard to explain the truth to someone like him. He would never understand, and I still value his friendship."

"He would have married you—even knowing the truth."

"I think not." Gillian was certain that Brian would never consider marrying a "soiled" woman. Moreover, Brian made his dislike of Logan quite clear.

"You'll never know. However, Brian told your father he wants to ask for your hand when you return."

"Really? And did Father tell him I was already married?"

"Not exactly." Helena smiled. "Your father merely hinted that you were seriously involved with a diplomat in His Majesty's Service."

Gillian lifted one hand to her dry curls. "Say no more. Brian wanted, no, *demanded* to know who the gentleman was so he could personally investigate the man's worthiness."

"Precisely. Your father politely refused."

"Ladies," Julia interrupted at last. "Aren't you forgetting the story about Logan Hammond?"

Helena might have become sidetracked by this bit of information concerning Brian, but Gillian had not. She had no intention of asking about Logan. If her mother remembered the rest of the story, she would politely listen.

"Oh, of course. How foolish of me." Helena straightened in the chair, warming to the subject.

"According to your father, Logan came up to him as if nothing were amiss. He asked about everyone's health and wanted to know when you were returning from your holiday. That was when your father wanted to challenge him, but was restrained by Brian."

Long before they had left London, the rumors and gossip surrounding the broken betrothal had spread rapidly through the clubs, theaters, and balls in the city. Gillian could just imagine Logan's casual inquiry about her whereabouts. Nothing mattered to him. He must have thought it necessary to approach her father and ask a polite question, as if a broken betrothal were a common occurrence.

"Your father told him we were thinking of extending our holiday." Helena smiled broadly. "He mentioned something about Russia."

"He didn't." Julia laughed.

"Oh, Charles will say anything if he's angry." Helena sounded wistful. How could she possibly miss him, she wondered to herself. "Nevertheless," she dismissed the queer emotion, "Logan did not seem amused. He told your father he believed you had sailed for America. Then he asked if he could send a letter to you."

"Charles, of course, refused. Then Logan asked if your father would include a letter in his mail to us."

"Since your father was not inclined to answer one way or another, Logan took it as a yes and had a letter hand-delivered the very next day." Helena withdrew another envelope from the folds of her gown. "This is for you, too."

"Take them," Julia advised. "If you destroy these letters without ever reading them, you will never know what he said. Do you want to spend the rest of your life wondering what might have been?"

"She is right, Gillian." Helena placed the letters in

174

her daughter's lap. "Read them when you feel like it. But read them."

Gillian nonchalantly glanced at the letters in her lap, hesitant to touch them. Accepting a small pastry from her aunt, Gillian almost missed the beginning of the conversation that followed.

"I met Liza Raveneau Fenwick today."

Gillian swallowed the tasty morsel before inquiring, "Did she ask about me again?"

"Liza is a very lovely, gracious woman, even though that fool is her nephew. She belongs to my ladies' group. You know, my weekly meeting with the Ladies Society. Someday you must accompany me. The discussions are very interesting. Mostly about preserving our history."

"Liza Fenwick attends this group?" Helena asked.

"Yes, whenever she is in town. Anyway," Julia waited for Gillian to look her way, "she told me about a letter from her nephew in London. Liza was more surprised than you appear to be to receive a letter from Logan. She hasn't heard from him in two years. You can imagine her reaction."

"You don't think she will tell him about me?" Gillian finally betrayed her calm facade. She did not want Logan to find her, not ever if it could be helped. But certainly not before the baby's birth. Anger and growing hatred for him were welcome emotions, for she disliked remembering those few months with him. Anything was better than feeling hurt and ashamed of loving someone who did not return that emotion. She could not soften her heart for him ever again regardless of his honeyed words and abject apologies, whether in print, or, heaven forbid, in person.

"Liza asked me how well you knew each other. I, of course, repeated what you've instructed me to say, that yes, you knew him and did not like him and

175

would rather not talk about someone you did not think well of. Although sooner or later she will learn of the betrothal."

"It shall be later," Gillian replied coldly. "I am tired of being the subject of everyone's gossip and speculation. Surely, Julia, you and Mother can understand why I do not want him to know I am here. I do not want his relatives to know how well I know him," she wryly added. "I need time to adjust to being a widow and a mother. I need more time." With her sad, downcast eyes and soft words, she implored them to understand.

"I don't know how much time you will have." Julia glanced nervously at Helena, waiting for her signal to proceed.

"What do you mean?" Gillian stared at the two women who obviously knew much more than they were saying. "Don't make me pry it out of you two. Say it and be done with it." Gillian braced herself for the coming words, but nothing could have prepared her for what she was about to hear.

"Logan Hammond may come to Charleston."

Chapter Eighteen

"When?" She could manage to utter only one word. Gillian jumped out of the sofa, pacing nervously about the room.

"Liza did not say."

"Well, how do we know it's true? Why would Logan consider traveling to America when he hasn't been here in four years?"

"I cannot answer these questions, dear." Helena remained seated, trying to affect as calm a posture as the situation permitted.

"Well, what am I supposed to do now?" Gillian threw her hands in the air. "Am I supposed to pack up, yet again, and flee like a thief in the middle of the night? Am I supposed to wait and count the days until Logan arrives — *if* he arrives — then wait until he discovers his former fiancée is living here?"

Gillian caught her breath, then continued ranting. "And then what do I do? Must I tell him the truth? Why should I tell him anything at all? Let him think I am carrying someone else's child."

"Gillian!" Helena gasped. "How could you?"

Gillian swung about to face her mother. In a deceptively calm voice, she answered, "Very easily, Mother. Logan has forfeited all rights to this child. I see no reason why I can't tell him anything I damn well please. However, that will never happen, for I never intend to see him again."

"There is no point in discussing this subject further. For all we known Logan may never arrive in Charleston." Julia tried to sound practical but doubted her own words.

"Yes," Gillian laughed wickedly, "maybe his ship will sink."

Delighted to change the subject, Helena turned to a favorite topic. "Dear, perhaps you should go to bed now. You must be exhausted, and we did not intend to upset you. Tomorrow we will go to Julia's dressmaker and select some appropriate dresses. How long must she wear drab colors?"

"I do not think it matters. I am certain people will understand that she cannot wear black and gray for the duration of her pregnancy. It will be warmer in a few months, and it wouldn't do for Gillian to be in the sun wearing such dark colors. Even a short walk in the Charleston sun can burn your face and bake your body."

It became obvious to Gillian that her presence was no longer necessary. Her mother and Julia would spend a few more minutes planning her life whether Gillian participated in the conversation or not.

"When is Cousin Theodore due to arrive?"

"Oh, yes, Theo," Julia twittered. "I seem to have forgotten all about my husband. He is scheduled to arrive in a few days, I believe. Theo hates to go up North, but he must."

"At least he will not spend all his time talking about my," she rolled her eyes, "my condition."

178

Gillian marched off to her room, unaware of the amused glances her mother and cousin shared.

"She still cares for him."

"I know."

"Do you think Liza Fenwick will tell Logan that Gillian and I are in Charleston?"

"If she answers him at all, I am certain she will mention it. I think she has a special fondness for her scoundrel nephew. Besides, everyone knows one another in Charleston. Liza knows it's not that much different in London."

"I wonder what Logan's reaction will be when he discovers his fiancée is hiding in the town where he has spent much of his youth."

"Helena, I remember Logan as a charming but reckless, sometimes hot-tempered young man."

"He hasn't changed all that much."

"I hope Gillian is as strong as she appears."

She read the two letters. Even before undressing for the night, Gillian ripped open the letters, not knowing what to expect from Logan or which sweet phrases he would use to lure her back into his web of deceit.

The first letter, postmarked Paris, was not very different from the earlier ones she had received. The opening sounded very much like the one he had written after he left London. But towards the end the tone varied.

"I miss you, sweet Gillian, and I count the days and long dreary nights that I must wait to hold you in my arms. I want to taste your soft, luscious mouth and whisper sweet, intoxicating words of passion for your ears alone."

She almost cried, then remembered that he must have written the letter before receiving any of hers. He hadn't known she left London.

The other, however, made her simultaneously furious and miserable. He had received two of her later letters and expressed concern for her. But some dreadful accident had kept him in bed and unable to communicate with her. Gillian accepted the fact that he was abed, but doubted the seriousness of his injuries or that he was alone.

The letter explained that he was back in London and wanted to find her. Lord Marlowe refused to assist Logan.

"I cannot tell you how sorry I am that I could not be with you when you needed me. I needed you, too, Gillian. I thought of you all the time and fantasized more than once about my joyous homecoming to your arms. Imagine my distress and dismay upon learning you have deserted me and broken our betrothal."

He asked her to write him. He asked her if there was anything he could do for her now. He asked her to reconsider their broken engagement. She memorized that letter and wondered if it might have been different for her if she had waited for his return. That was when the dreams began, of Logan holding her in his arms, kissing her tears, and lovingly caressing the softly rounded stomach.

But, mercifully, dreams fade, and at the beginning of each new day, Gillian felt rejuvenated. And ravenous.

"Goodness, I had no idea one's waist could disappear so quickly," she commented to her mother.

"That's not all that is expanding. In case you haven't noticed, the bodice of that dress is a trifle, um, how shall I say it . . ."

"It's tight, Mother, I know. But I love this pink dress. It's one of few that still," she raised a skeptical brow, "well, almost still fits."

"Not much longer."

Gillian set aside the silver spoon. "This grapefruit is delicious. I love all the fresh fruits."

Helena watched as her daughter resumed eating. Gillian had never been especially interested in food until now.

"Julia would love it if we joined her at one of her ladies' meetings this afternoon. There is going to be a speaker today. The subject, I believe, is India. It might be interesting, don't you agree? Do you feel well enough to attend?"

"Mother, I feel fine. Nothing bothers me now that the queasiness has left. I would like to go today. Besides, people think I know so much about India because of my 'marriage.' What's his name died there, didn't he?"

"Gerald, dear. His name was Gerald."

Attacking another sweet roll, Gillian could only nod. After she swallowed, she asked, "Who attends these little get-togethers, Julia?"

"Most of my friends. Liza Fenwick will probably

be there today."

"I like her. It's unfortunate that she is related to," she swallowed the chunk of bread, "him."

Since there was a hint of rain in the cool air, the three ladies rode the short distance to King Street in their enclosed carriage. Gillian wore a long white cape over her lilac dress. Unlike London society, the Charleston matrons seemed to understand Gillian's dilemma and applauded her spirit. No one questioned her story or doubted her sadness that the father would never know the baby. Privately, a few ladies thought it best that Gillian remarry quickly, for the sake of the child. With that thought in mind, Hattie Mathews had insisted upon inviting Lady Gillian Marston and her mother to the meeting. Known as one of Charleston's best hostesses, Hattie wanted to extend her hospitality to the English ladies.

As soon as the three women entered the crowded drawing room, Gillian immediately sensed the warmth and friendliness of the ladies in the room. There were concerned questions about her health, family recipes for healthy eating, and hints as to how to avoid queasiness.

"Gillian, dear," their hostess claimed her arm, "I would like to present another newcomer to Charleston. Lillian has been here less than one year. Hattie signaled to a young woman, beckoning her to join them. Although shorter and slightly older than Gillian, the young woman's ready smile and sparkling gray eyes delighted Gillian.

"It's so good to meet another non-native. I must say everyone has been most gracious to Peter and myself. I rarely feel homesick. But it is pleasant to meet another who does not know a cousin twice removed now living up North or some other relative now deceased who fought bravely in the Revolutionary War."

"Lillian's husband Peter bought the Wells's old plantation, Thistle Hall, on the Ashley River. Such a sad story." Hattie clucked her tongue while one hand still rested on Gillian's lilac muslin sleeve. "The house and land were in such disrepair after Linton lost it all in a card game. Can you believe that? Wagering one's home and ancestry in a card game? That house was in the family for over fifty years."

"The fellow who won the home never bothered to see his prize and allowed the land and house to rot," Julia added.

"Well, not any longer. I hear your husband is doing wonders with that property now."

Lillian smiled, glad to have the opportunity to speak at last. "Yes, Peter has fallen in love with the land and hopes our first rice crop will yield something next season. Considering how little we knew of rice planting and plantation life in general, I think we have learned quite a bit in the last six months." Lillian's dark curls swiveled as she proudly spoke of her husband, Peter Harris.

"Where are you originally from?" Gillian inquired. The petite Lillian interested her.

"Baltimore. Maryland," she added in case Gillian was not yet familiar with American geography. "It's still the South, of course, but being closer to the northern states, well, let's say life is different up there."

"They have done very well for themselves since

183

their arrival. Everyone admires what the Harrises have done to preserve the Wells plantation and its environs. I'm pleased to have them as my neighbors." Hattie hurriedly excused herself upon seeing the arrival of another guest.

"She knows everyone and everything about Charleston," Lillian commented. "She has been so kind to us. I did not know anyone when I arrived, and Hattie made it her business to befriend me. I don't know what I would have done if it weren't for her generous spirit."

"Mrs. Harris, do you like Charleston?"

"Please call me Lily. And yes, I love it here. We are renting a charming little house on Tradd Street. Life is more leisurely here than in Baltimore. I would imagine it's a lot slower for you coming from such a large city."

"I like it here as well. Nothing seems to really upset anyone in Charleston."

"Except the threat of a hurricane or fire."

Gillian laughed. "Oh, I know, they don't appreciate bad weather, do they?"

"With good reason, I suppose. The last hurricane in 1804 caused so much destruction. The city government was finally persuaded to build the stone wall along the East Battery. Why, I heard that ships were blown into the streets? Can you imagine?"

"I would hate to be caught in such a storm, but I admit I love walking in the rain. Sometimes I feel as if that sea wall was my private garden wall."

"Reminds you of home?"

"A bit. The air is much fresher here, however." There was more than one meaning to her sentence.

She was free from censure in Charleston, and free from Logan Hammond's presence.

"I understand." Lily met Gillian's direct gaze, and for a brief second, Gillian thought the woman had known exactly what she was thinking.

For the next twenty minutes, the ladies chatted amiably about a variety of subjects. Gillian found herself interested in Mrs. Lily Harris and hoped the two could become better acquainted. She missed Adeline Barrish, and although no one could ever be as close to her as Adeline had been, Gillian felt she needed a friend or two while in Charleston. Lily was not much older than she—Gillian guessed she was in her late twenties. It would be nice to have someone other than her mother or cousin for a companion.

Before the afternoon gathering had ended, the two ladies agreed to meet again for tea at the end of the week.

It was turning out to be a pleasant outing after all, Gillian thought during the long but informative lecture about the mysteries of India. Looking about the room, Gillian recognized a number of women—most of whom were acquaintances of Julia's. Seated next to her mother and Lily, she realized that the ages of the ladies varied—some were younger than she, but most were older. yet all had the same serene look and all were dressed in the latest fashions. Life in Charleston agrees with them, she decided, hoping she, too, could acquire that look of peace and contentment.

By 6 P.M., the meeting began to break up. Some ladies lingered to question the guest speaker, others waited for their husbands or fiancés to arrive.

Feeling a bit fatigued, Gillian took a seat in the far

corner of the room, near a huge potted plant. It afforded her a view of the arriving men. Silently, she congratulated herself for correctly pairing a number of ladies with their mates. Yet Gillian was surprised to see a stocky gentleman of medium height approach Lillian. He gently, almost reverently, lowered his head to kiss Lillian's cheek. Gillian did not miss the downcast eyes and shy smile Lily gave him in return. It was odd, and she wanted to study the Harrises further but became interested in yet another scene on the opposite end of the drawing room.

If she had never set eyes on Logan Hammond, she would have thought that the man entering the room was the most handsome fellow she had seen. Perhaps it was the blue military uniform contrasting against his dark red hair that was so appealing. Pausing in the doorway, he looked for and eventually found someone.

The woman he sought was without a doubt beautiful. Gillian had seen her before and had been introduced to her twice, yet Eve Carlton did not appear like the other ladies. She neither seemed friendly nor interested in the others. While she would nod her head in recognition to a few women, Eve Carlton did not engage anyone in conversation unless she was addressed first. During the lecture Mrs. Carlton sat in the last seat of the last row. Clearly, she was not approachable.

Trying to remember her cousin's gossip, Gillian recalled that Mrs. Carlton was widowed more than two years ago. Young, childless, beautiful, and very wealthy, she had a fair share of suitors but not one serious beau. Originally from New Orleans, her dark hair and dusky skin suggested to some that she was of Creole descent — but Gillian did not remember what that meant. Making a mental note to check with Julia, she continued to stare at the handsome couple.

It wasn't until she had reached into her recticule for a scented handkerchief that Gillian realized someone was staring back at her. It was that man and he was heading straight for her with her cousin Julia in tow.

Trying to appear nonchalant, Gillian slowly looked up and smiled politely.

"Good afternoon, Lady Marston. I insisted your cousin do me the honor of presenting myself to you." His voice was deep and melodic with more than a trace of southern accent.

"Gillian dear, may I introduce Richard Paxton. Captain Paxton," she amended. "He is an old family friend. Otherwise I never would have allowed him such liberties." Julia actually blushed like a young girl. "I knew him as a charming little red-haired boy and now look at him."

Gillian did, and liked what she saw. Tall, with wavy auburn hair and large, dark green eyes, there was nothing lacking in the gentleman's appearance. Dressed impeccably in his starched dark blue uniform, Richard Paxton stood erect as he bowed from the waist to kiss Gillian's hand. Gillian remembered two things about that moment, his light musk scent that drifted through her nostrils and the gentle touch of his large hand.

"I hope I have changed a little in your eyes, dearest Julia," he drawled. "I would hate to give your cousin the wrong impression. I am, dear lady," he looked straight in Gillian's face, "a trifle older than Julia recalls. Moreover, I have spent most of my adult life abroad, so I think I have become better mannered — if not more aware of what to say when a beautiful creature like yourself sits alone in a room full of gossiping women." He reluctantly released her hand.

"Really?" Her voice lightened. "And what is that?"

"May I call on you tomorrow for tea?"

Gillian contained her laughter, but her eyes lit up and her fingers playfully pulled at the lace hanky. "Sir, I think you are unaware of who I am and why I am in Charleston."

"You are a widow. So is my cousin Eve. You are recently arrived in Charleston and, as I have just learned, you are expecting an addition to your small family."

"Doesn't that concern you?"

"Why, no. I think you are the most beautiful woman I have seen in a very long time. I would like to talk with you about Europe. I miss being there."

"Then why are you in Charleston and the American Army?"

"Family tradition. The Paxton family served with Washington's army. I am the second son, you see. Since I am not about to inherit the family's property, I chose to uphold the family's military obligation. Besides, I like the adventure and I like serving my country. As for still being in Charleston, I am conveniently stationed at Fort Moultrie." His dark green eyes crinkled in the corners with his wide smile as he asked, "Have I answered all your questions?"

"Forgive me," she had the good sense to blush, "but you just said you miss Europe."

"Yes, I do. I plan to return in a few years. Hopefully, after another promotion and some successful business ventures. I dislike poverty."

Completely charmed by his directness and broad grin, Gillian was almost reluctant to leave. But their driver had arrived and Lady Helena wasted no time in appearing alongside her daughter. Eager to meet and evaluate the man who made her daughter laugh like the carefree girl she once was, Helena decided Richard Paxton was the perfect antidote to a broken heart.

There was a lighter bounce to Gillian's step as she walked along the Battery that night.

Chapter Nineteen

The Charleston season was coming to an end. As the weather became cooler with the approach of winter and the number of rainy days increased, the social events began to diminish. It was time for the planters to return to their large plantations and oversee their crops. A new social season was about to begin along the banks of the Ashley, Cooper, and Santee rivers—hunts, festive balls, picnics, and day-long parties were commonplace. Many of the families had already left. The number of boats, barges, and sailboats multiplied as they sat in the harbor awaiting the outgoing tide as well as those families and their servants who traveled the two hours or more up the rivers to their huge homes. They usually did not return to Charleston until the beginning of May.

Gillian was unaffected by these changes. The streets were less crowded, the social obligations were fewer than before, and people seemed to settle into a quiet daily routine. It wasn't as if the Graysons and their cousins couldn't afford to leave Charleston—Theodore's bank was very successful—they simply chose to remain in the city and the home they adored. Nor were they lacking for invitations to visit those friends and relatives who moved to the country. They were considering a short visit for the Christmas holiday as long as Gillian's health permitted a trip.

In the last few weeks, Gillian acquired three new companions—much to her delight. Lily Harris saw Gillian most often—sometimes Peter was with her. Gillian did not mind that she was unaccompanied by a beau for the Harrises did their utmost to make her feel welcome and her company eagerly desired. The threesome often attended the City Theater on Broad Street and appeared at a few socials. Mostly they dined together in the Harrises rented house on Tradd Street. They were a nice couple, but Gillian still thought their relationship a bit odd.

There was a lack of intimacy between the Harrises, sometimes even actual formality. They were unfailingly polite to each other and rarely touched or shared private thoughts or gestures. Gillian was tempted to ask Lily about her husband, but would not dare, knowing prying questions could be asked of her.

Sometimes, Gillian found it difficult to answer the most simple questions about her "husband." She never brought up the subject. At first Lily asked polite questions about Gillian's husband, but upon seeing Gillian's hesitation, stopped the inquiries. Between the women, there was an unwritten understanding not to discuss their marriages. If and when Lily wanted to talk, Gillian would be there to listen.

Towards the end of November, another person

was admitted to the little group. Captain Richard Paxton would not accept Gillian's repeated but polite rejections. From the moment they met, Richard sent letters and appeared at her doorstep with dozens of flowers and notes begging her to see him.

It was hard to accept that a man—particularly one as sought after by the ladies as Richard—could be interested in her. A widow who was five months pregnant was not considered eligible. Richard could have his pick from among the dozens of young belles waiting for him to acknowledge their existence. It was not uncommon for a second son to marry a woman whose dowry far exceeded one's wildest dreams. The delighted fathers were extremely generous, and a number of young men who married fortunes increased their wealth by investing wisely. Richard could have his pick of wealthy heiresses. Instead he focused his attentions on Gillian.

After spending an exhausting day shopping with her mother and cousin, Gillian found herself unable to muster the energy to join Richard and the Harrises for dinner. Richard, of course, would not accept the no and joined the Graysons for a light supper.

"Gillian, did you know that although Richard was educated abroad, he trained at West Point?"

"Mrs. Grayson, I sincerely doubt that Gillian, I mean Lady Marston," he bowed his dark red hair in apology, "knows or, for that matter, wants to know about American military life."

"Oh, quite the contrary, Captain. I am quite interested. In England, my father continuously scolded me for showing an interest in unladylike topics such as politics and the military." Gillian paused to swallow another mouthful of rice pilaf. "This is delicious, Julia. I can eat this every night."

"You have, Gillian," Lady Helena commented. "It is a miracle that you still look so slim."

"I think she looks wonderful. Don't you agree, Richard?" Theodore Grayson had taken note of Richard's keen interest in Gillian and sought to stimulate the flourishing friendship. Neither Julia nor Helena discouraged him.

"I want to hear about West Point."

Richard briefly outlined his military education. "I have made some lasting friendships. Although it was not easy at first. Coming from such diverse backgrounds and all."

"Yes, it is odd. Your states are very much like separate countries. From what I've been told, the customs and cultural life vary."

"That's geography, I suppose. And politics in America, as well as in your country, can be influenced by geography and culture."

"And power. But of course it is easier for us to unite because we have a monarchy to protect. It is the English common cause. Although why anyone would want to protect King George is beyond me."

"Gillian, really. You mustn't say such things."

Smiling mischievously at Richard, Gillian lifted her wineglass to take a long sip. "It is true, Mother. I am quite sure there are strong political differences in this country, too. Why, Richard, didn't you tell me about the feud between your

President Adams and oh, what's his name?" Pausing to tap her head for the answer, she waited for Richard to supply the name.

"General Andrew Jackson."

"Yes that's it. A general, you say? Have you met him? Did he attend West Point?"

Richard laughed. "No to both your questions, and if you ever saw the man you would understand."

"I find it difficult to understand your system. Not that our parliamentary process is easy to grasp."

"Certainly not for a woman." Theodore realized his mistake as soon as the three women glared at him.

"If you think Jackson's feud is difficult to understand, wait until I tell you about our vice president."

"Where is he from?"

"Why, South Carolina, of course," Richard proudly said. "And I have yet to meet a man who is a better orator than John C. Calhoun. I consider myself his friend."

"A popular fellow." Gillian wanted to learn more, but upon noticing her mother's third politely stifled yawn, decided to ask Richard about the vice president another time.

"I hope to meet him someday."

"You will. He comes to Charleston quite often. And I hope you will travel to Washington."

"Not for a while," she answered, fondly patting her rounded tummy.

"Well, I shall tell you everything you need to

194

know and describe things in such accurate detail, you will feel as if you have traveled to Washington."

"And New York. I would like to see New York."

That very moment, Richard swore to himself that he would be the one to take Gillian wherever she wanted to go. As long as she did not shut him out of her life, he believed he had a chance to court her. It was most unconventional, but Richard Paxton never considered himself to be a devotee of customs. He was a man who followed his instincts and his heart. His father often warned him to be more practical, less impulsive, but Richard dismissed that notion. His elder brother would need to be concerned about such mundane matters, not he.

Later, Gillian invited Richard to walk along the Battery with her. The moon faded in and out between the thick night clouds. The night was cool, but Gillian was protected from the strong breezes by a pale blue woolen cape and hood.

"I don't think you can see much this time of night, but out there," Richard stood very close to Gillian, inhaling her jasmine scent, "out there is Fort Moultrie." As he extended an arm to point out the fort, he wrapped the other around her shoulders. It was more than he could hope for. Being close to Gillian was a gift.

"I should like to see it."

"You can someday. Sullivan's Island is a lovely place, you know. A number of summer cottages have been built."

"I can imagine the joy of the young ladies who

195

live on an island where soldiers are stationed."

"And the chagrin of the proud papas."

Feeling more lighthearted than before, Gillian did not realize until later that she was flirting with Captain Paxton.

"Do any of the papas object to your presence?" She smiled coyly.

Just as the moonlight appeared, Richard caught the radiant look on her face. She could not help but notice his sharp intake of breath and deep glint of his green eyes.

"I want to kiss you, Gillian." All traces of humor were gone from his voice. "I want to taste your sweet lips."

"Richard," she hesitated slightly, "I don't know."

"I don't care about anything but wanting to kiss you. Please," he implored gently.

Giving her mouth up to his sent a small shiver of anticipation along her spine. It had been so long, she thought to herself as his mouth took hers in a short but oh so comforting kiss.

"Gillian," he still held her shoulders, "I love the sound of your name. Sometimes I repeat it to myself before I go to sleep. You are an enchantress, for I confess that I have never felt this way about a woman before."

"Particularly one you have known less than one month."

"No, I am serious." He looked into her smiling face and without asking for permission, kissed her again, a kiss full of promise and longing.

"I will be spending the Christmas holidays with my family at Bolton Plantation. Say you will come for a visit."

"Richard, I can't." She tore away from him to stare out into the harbor. "I do not think your family would appreciate your association with me."

"Why? Are you a leper? They will adore you."

"Richard, in case you haven't noticed, I am expecting another man's child." At the moment she felt two things, remorse for not knowing Richard first, and a strong kick from the babe, who was probably reminding her of the name of his father. Damn you, Logan, she swore to herself.

"Gillian, Gillian, it matters not." Gently taking one arm, he turned her about to face him. Misinterpreting the sad smile, he said, "I know you must be thinking of your husband at a time like this. I suppose you loved him, but time changes everything. I ask for nothing more than a chance to open your heart, ever so slightly, for another man. One who would protect you and the babe with his life."

She hadn't meant to cry, and blamed her condition for that, but his soothing words and soft pleas tugged at her heart. Here was someone who wanted her. Someone who wanted the baby. Enfolded in his arms, she wept softly on his dark blue wool jacket.

"Oh, I am sorry," she sniffed. "I did not mean to soil your uniform."

"I could care less. Gillian," he cupped her chin, "will you give me a chance to court you?"

"I don't know. Richard, I don't think I should consider anything until after the baby is born. Surely you understand."

"No, I do not." His voice rose petulantly. "Doesn't it matter that your child bears his dead father's name? Shouldn't he be born with the name of the father who intends to raise him as his own?"

Lord, he made sense, and the temptation was great to give in to everything Richard asked and let him take care of her forever. She would not need to make another decision, to spend another sleepless night wondering what would happen to her and the baby when they returned to England.

"Give me some time. Please." She took his strong arm. "The last few months have been like a tornado. Sometimes I cannot think."

"I understand." He lightly kissed the tip of her nose. "I will be here for you, Gillian. I swear it." The serious tone gave way to an amused one. "Tell you what. Don't think about the Christmas holidays yet. If you do not want to stay with my family, I am certain you can visit with the Draytons or the Middletons. Didn't the Ashtons invite your family?"

"I admit we are not lacking for invitations. Mother and I figure we could travel from plantation to plantation and be away until May. But I think I would like the babe to be born right here in Charleston. Not in some stranger's home."

"It does not need to be the home of a stranger, but," he smiled, "I almost forgot. I shall not bring up the subject of fatherhood for another week."

"Richard, I swear you have the touch of the blarney in you."

"I do. Scottish and Irish. One set of grandparents is from Ireland and the other is from Scotland. Hence the color hair."

She playfully tugged at a long curl. "I am partial to red hair."

"There must have been a touch of the Scottish in your family, too."

"Indeed."

He took her arm. "Perhaps your son will have red hair and everyone will think he is mine after all."

No, she thought to herself, much later while abed. This child will have brown hair shot through with gold and golden eyes to match. Just like his father.

Chapter Twenty

"Mother, I am feeling fine," Gillian repeated for the third time. "I think it would be a nice treat to spend the holidays at Ashton Hall."

"From what I understand, there will be numerous balls, soirees, teas. It all sounds too much." Helena noticed the recent dark circles under Gillian's eyes and worried about her health. Sitting in the upstairs drawing room, the ladies leisurely took a late-morning breakfast.

"I can manage. I am not a fool. If I feel unwell, I shall stay in my room. Really, Mother," Gillian leaned over to touch her shoulder, "There is no need to worry."

"Richard Paxton invited us to Bolton Plantation for a few nights. I think he would prefer a few weeks." Helena knew of Richard's feelings for her daughter. It was plain to see. From the moment Gillian entered a room, Richard could not take his eyes off her. That look bespoke of love and desire.

"I know. His mother sent a lovely note the other day. She said Richard would be heartbroken if we did not visit. And since he has to be in Washington for a couple of weeks, it would be a nice surprise if we were at Bolton Hall to greet him when he returned. It is upriver from Ashley Hall."

"I am impressed that his mother does not mind Richard's interest in you."

"Why should she? I am 'Lady Marston' and our blue-blooded ties trace back hundreds of years." Gillian's nose wrinkled in mock disgust. "Mrs. Paxton is quite impressed with my lineage."

"And wealth."

"Oh, yes. Do not forget wealth. Lord, it does seem to be a common occurrence here. Marriage for money, power, connections, and strong alliances." She blew into her cup of hot cocoa. "Reminds me of home, Mother. Doesn't it?"

"You forget that many of these southerners retain strong ties to England. There is a very strong English influence here."

"So I have noticed. I suppose that's one of the reasons why I feel so comfortable here in Charleston."

"Is Captain Paxton another?" Helena met Gillian's gaze.

"I am not certain," she honestly replied. "He is awfully nice, and of course, handsome, charming, and sweet. I find it so hard to understand why he would want to court me. Especially now. My title means nothing to him. And although my money must be appealing, I am not half as wealthy as some of the other eligible young women of Charleston seem to be."

"Did you ever think he finds you attractive because you are a beautiful, intelligent woman?" Helena's voice softened. "Despite those dark circles under your fetching blue eyes, being enceinte agrees with you, dear. Your skin glows, your hair is thick and shiny, even your, um, breasts have swelled."

"Mother!"

"What I mean is that you are lovely, pregnancy and all."

"I don't know what to think. I am quite flattered by Richard's attention. It makes me forget."

Judging from Gillian's melancholy expression, Helena knew of whom her daughter was thinking. "Someday you will forget him."

"I don't think so. This is his child. How can I forget my baby's father?"

"In time, that is all Logan will ever be—the baby's father. Not the man you loved."

"The baby should have a father."

"I know."

"Richard does not mind."

"I am certain a number of your suitors would not mind."

"There aren't that many suitors," she forced a small smile.

"At least three. I should know, dear, for you have left me with them each time you've retired early from dinner."

Folding the linen napkin and placing it on the round cherrywood table, Gillian stood up. Her rounded tummy was carefully concealed beneath the folds of her pale peach dress. "You know, Mother, I think a trip to the country might be appealing."

They were packed and ready to depart before the end of the week. The weather in Charleston was cool, and as the rainy season began in earnest, the Marlowe women and Julia Grayson were eager to spend some time in the warmer, hopefully drier climate.

Their trip along the Ashley River took almost three hours. Considering how much longer it would have taken by coach, Gillian valiantly ignored the rocking of the little boat, concentrating instead on the festivities to come.

Charleston Harbor was crowded, but once they rounded a turn, the winding Ashley River was a sight to behold. With only a few other boats slowly sailing along with the tide, Gillian was again enthralled by the beauty around her.

Huge homes dotted the banks of the river. But it was the flora, the vibrant colors of the plants, bright green grassy banks, and long, willowy live oak trees covered with Spanish moss that nearly took her breath away.

"No wonder why people move to the country," she sighed in awe. "It's lovelier than the grandest English country estate."

"Just wait," Julia knowingly smiled. "This is only the beginning."

As their boat was deftly navigated onto the Ashton Hall property, Gillian's eyes rounded in wonder and for the first time in a while, she was speechless.

Surely it was like a palace. A large English manor house stood at the end of a long grassy path. On either side were carefully manicured shrubs, trees, blossoming plants. Inhaling, Gillian thought she was in the forest, surrounded by the scent of fresh earth after a rainstorm. The air sweetly fragranced with blooming red and violet azaleas and other aromatic flowering shrubs such as wintersweet and hanging blue wisteria. White and pink camellia trees were beautifully alternated with chrysanthemums along their paths.

"Goodness," Helena sighed, "can you imagine

what this looks like in the early spring?"

"I think we should stay and see," Gillian laughed.

Greeted by their hosts, descendents of the original builder and owner, John Ashton, Gillian understood the meaning of southern hospitality and generosity. The brick house, built in 1730, was, according to their hosts, a fine example of the symmetry and grace of Georgian design. Two flanking buildings added in 1753 — served as the coach house and stable for the fine Thoroughbreds that were raced during the winter season.

The Ashtons quietly informed their guests that the entire house as well as the gardens were equally accessible, and if there was anything anyone wanted, one of the house slaves would immediately accommodate them.

"The parties and balls are already in full swing. I hope you have not missed too much of the festive season, but I can assure you, there are more soirees planned," Cora Ashton informed them as she led the ladies up the double stone steps to a large hallway on the first floor. Barely given time to assimilate the beauty and elegance of the brightly decorated house, the ladies were swiftly led up another double stairway to their rooms on the second floor.

"Your home is magnificent." Gillian was still reeling from the splendor of Ashton Hall.

"If you are interested I would be delighted to give you a guided tour any morning you desire."

Too exhausted to think about tours and parties, Gillian used the wooden steps to climb up and gratefully sink into the four-poster bed against the stenciled wall of the guestroom and, within seconds, fell asleep. For the first time in weeks, her dreams were not punctuated with the image of the tall, laughing man with golden eyes and the tiny cleft in his chin.

By the next morning invitations had arrived for three hunts, four balls that preceded Christmas, and another to usher in the New Year. Two days later on a bright and warm Thursday, the ladies spent most of their time preparing for a large ball at a neighboring plantation.

Excited to be part of this festive atmosphere, Gillian carefully chose a gown of shimmering turquoise watered silk. The modestly cut neckline outlined her full breasts whereas the high waist, unadorned with ribbons, disguised her growing middle. Gillian deliberately chose to wear a sleeveless gown, despite the slight night breeze. The long lace gloves and matching shawl gave her added warmth, in case she needed it.

"Thank goodness for these fashions. I feel like a beached whale as it is, but at least I don't always look like one. I only hope no one can see through this material, for I couldn't bear wearing anything other than a chemise. Everything else is too restricting. I never cared for corsets and laces. After such freedom, I may never wear them again." She inhaled deeply to demonstrate how easily one can manage without whalebones.

"Darling, you have some time yet. Believe me, you get rounder and fuller."

"Now I understand why the so-called 'delicate ladies' choose extended confinements. It's to hide their large bodies. It does not matter," she dismissed the notion with a wave of a jeweled hand, "I shall not hide. I enjoy the outdoors too much."

"Just don't enjoy champagne too much. And stay away from the Madeira. You know how fond

205

everyone here is of that wine. It makes you sick."

"I know," she giggled. "The baby does not like it, either. Why, the last time I drank, I did not feel it kick for quite some time. I tell you, Mother, it made me nervous."

"Richard will be here soon. Since his arrival, he's been eager to see you. His note said he wanted to talk to me before we left for Drayton Hall. Gillian, I think I know what he wants to discuss." Dressed in pale pink satin trimmed with silk roses at the bodice and hem, with tiny diamonds woven through her blond hair, Helena Marlowe looked like Gillian's older sister.

"He asked me to marry him yesterday."

"What did you say? Goodness, what am I supposed to say? This is something for your father, not me."

"Richard is only being excessively polite. I told him I wanted to wait until Christmas. I promised him an answer then."

Careful not to crinkle the silk dress, Gillian slowly eased herself onto the end of the high bed. "He is a wonderful man. And very persistent. I'm beginning to think there is no reason to wait until after the baby is born to marry. I enjoy his company."

Gillian also enjoyed his kisses and soft words of endearment. She felt comfortable in his arms. She hadn't felt that way since . . . Quickly she swept the unbidden image of Logan Hammond from her mind. Richard was nothing like Logan. That was why she liked him so much.

"Gillian, you haven't had enough time. Do you love him?"

"I could." Gillian looked around the papered room, unable to meet Helena's direct gaze. "I think that is enough."

"I hope it is." Helena stood in front of her daughter. "Come here," she opened her arms, "I haven't given you a hug in a while."

"It will mess your hair." Her voice lightened in childish delight.

"To hell with my hair." Helena took her daughter in her arms wanting desperately to protect her from heartache and despair. "I only want your happiness and a healthy grandchild."

While Helena met with Richard in the formal parlor on the first floor, Gillian's maid added the finishing touches to her long hair. "My hair has lightened, I think. It must be this strong sun. And the lemon rinses." Forgoing the diamond studs in her hair and ears, Gillian instructed the maid to weave turquoise ribbon through her thick curls. In her ears were matching large, square-cut turquoise stones set in gold that were large and square cut. A thin gold chain around her throat with a delicate gold heart-shaped locket in the middle was the only other accessory. Richard had insisted she accept this one small present, telling her it had nothing to do with betrothal.

"I knew it would look splendid on you," he announced when she descended the stairs to greet him. "You look enchanting, from the tip of your turquoise-accented hair to the matching slippers. I am," he bowed low at her waist, "at your service."

"I think I like men in uniform. Especially dress uniforms."

"Then I shall remain in the Army forever." Standing tall and erect, Richard Paxton looked like a man whose pride and happiness were directly linked to the woman at his side.

Feeling especially lighthearted, Gillian allowed

Richard to kiss her in front of her mother. Helping with her ivory lace shawl, Richard whispered in her ear, "I am proud to have you by my side."

"Thank you." And damn those little tears for blurring her vision.

Drayton Hall was only three miles downriver. Comfortably ensconced in the schooner and navigated by a slave using long poles that silently slipped in and out of the Ashley River, their journey was pleasant and romantic. Since Helena, Julia, and the Ashtons chose to follow, Richard and Gillian sat closely to each other and watched the smooth motions of the schooner as it sliced through the river.

Plantations along the way were brightly lit, while the shimmering stars overhead directed their path downriver.

It was a beautiful night, a night for love and happiness, Gillian thought seconds before Richard gently turned her face up to his. One short sweet kiss became the prelude to a deep burning one that made her stomach quiver. Sliding his hand under the lace shawl, Richard needed to feel the smooth white skin beneath his palm, and needed to hear her acquiescent sigh.

Thinking to herself, how long it had been since she felt anything like this, Gillian allowed his hands to roam leisurely up and down her neck, pausing to finger the gold heart and lower to touch one rounded breast.

She forgot about their destination, forgot there was someone else in the schooner with them. "I love you, Gillian," he whispered in her hear, his tongue outlining its delicate shape. "I want you."

Was it possible he could want her in this condition? Apparently the baby didn't think so, for just as his hand threatened to explore beneath the top of the silk gown, the baby kicked. Hard. Hard enough for Gillian to mutter, "Oh," and hard enough for Richard to feel the stubborn kick against his chest.

"You must forgive me." He sharply pulled away. "I didn't think," he stammered. "I forgot."

"I know. So did I. It matters not now, for we are here."

Before them loomed the gracious, huge Drayton Hall. There was nothing to do but collect themselves and wait until the other schooners departed before being assisted out of their boat and onto land.

It had been so long since Gillian had felt any passion, and she was shaken.

Judging from the slight tremble of his hands against her back, so was Richard.

Chapter Twenty-one

For the second time in one week, Gillian was overwhelmed by the sights, sounds, and grandeur of a plantation. Drayton Hall was, according to Julia, the most palatial residence on the Ashley and Cooper rivers. Nothing compared to its classic Georgian design.

A glowing path of Chinese lanterns held by dozens of immaculately uniformed slaves led to the house. But first, three footmen standing in their most formal dress — somewhat overdressed, she thought — offered chilled glasses of champagne. The gardens on either side of the path were illuminated, too. After Richard's passionate kiss and now this splendor before her, Gillian felt lightheaded and giddy.

"Oh, I am so glad we decided to visit the Ashtons. Just think, Richard, I would have missed so much." She turned sea-blue adoring eyes up to his beaming face.

Thinking that Gillian was his at last, Richard placed a very protective arm around her expanding waist and kissed the top of her jasmine-scented head. "There is much more," he whispered.

As they approached the massive palladian portico—two stories high—and slowly walked up one of the double stone steps, Gillian heard the delightful sounds of what could only be an orchestra. Nothing was done in small measure here, she thought.

Inside, they were greeted by their hosts and a number of formidable South Carolinians. It wasn't until Richard saluted smartly before grasping the hand of the tall, thin gentleman before him that Gillian remembered the man's name.

"Gillian, dear, I am proud to introduce you to our distinguished Vice President, John C. Calhoun."

The man's dark brown eyes ignited with a quiet intensity that gave contrast to his thick chestnut hair. For a man who, if she could remember correctly, was only in his late forties, John C. Calhoun looked as if he had lived a lifetime of experiences.

"Mr. Vice President, it is an honor to see you again." Richard's awe was obvious.

"Captain Paxton, I am delighted to be here. I hope we can share a moment later to catch up on some politics." Mr. Calhoun turned his attention to Gillian. "Lady Marston, I hope you are feeling well enough to provide this old man with one turn around the ballroom floor."

His voice deep and commanding, Gillian understood some of Richard's respect for the man.

They were forced to move on past the entrance into the great hall. Gillian's first impression was if all the tallest men in the room stood side by side and if three more stood on each other's shoulders

211

like circus performers, there would still be room inside the massive marble fireplace.

The great hall, painted in shades of cream trimmed in tan and beige, easily accommodated the one hundred invited guests. Looking around as quickly as she could, Gillian immediately noticed the exquisite detail that must have gone into building this mansion. The intricately carved ceiling, mantels, painted wood panels, and doorways demonstrated the craftsmanship and artistry of the builders and planners.

"Richard, I am impressed," she breathed.

"I knew you would be pleased. Now don't think that every plantation in South Carolina looks like this one. Ours does not. Each home has a distinct style. This is by far the grandest of them all—to date."

"To date?" she quoted him.

"I hear the Raveneaus are planning to build again. So are the Fenwicks and Pinckneys."

Swept up in a social whirl, Gillian did not have time either to finish any conversation with Richard or leisurely stroll around the house to carefully examine her surroundings.

Making their way up the double matching mahogany stairs, Gillian glanced out the large palladian window. From this landing, she had an unobstructed view of the garden path leading to the Ashley River. A number of boats were still lined up along the shore. Gillian noticed the Fenwicks disembarking. So that was Henri Raveneau, she thought. An elderly gentleman shrugged off the proffered arm of his daughter, Liza

Fenwick, to agilely hop out of the schooner. Old? she thought again. He stood erect and looked up. Gillian thought he was looking at her, then realized that could not be possible. There was something eerily familiar about the old man's posture, a haughty air that reminded her of someone else.

"Gillian, darling, are you feeling well? Do you need to rest before climbing up the stairs?" Richard's concern made her flush with guilt.

"Oh, no. I am fine." She took his arm. "I am so looking forward to a fun evening." She sounded breathless.

The grand ballroom on the second floor was the entertainment center of Drayton Hall. The large windows were wide open to allow the cross breezes to cool the house. Two large doors opened onto the second-story portico where one could see the back of the house and much—but not all—of the land surrounding it.

Off to the right of the room was the ten-piece orchestra. The four rooms leading off the ballroom were duplicates of the ones on the floor below.

"Has anyone lectured you yet on the unique architecture of this region?" Richard offered her another glass of cold champagne.

"I know a little, and I find it all so interesting."

"This house is typical of the Georgian style. In Charleston, they call it the 'double house' because there are four rooms to a floor. The rooms are separated by an entranceway, or hallway on the first floor, and usually a drawing room, or in this case," he made a sweeping gesture, "a ballroom. What truly complicates matters is that, architecturally, all rooms must be symmetrical. If the fireplace is in the center of the room, and there is one door to the left, there must be another door—whether it is functional or not—on the right. They call these fake doors 'shams.' Are you still interested?" Richard looked down at her furrowed brow.

"Yes, do go on. I knew about those fake doors, but I still think they're ingenious designs. Julia's home is a double house."

"Then you also know about the 'single houses'?"

Her strawberry curls bobbed. "I've seen the new ones along the Battery. They look grand."

"That is the most popular style in Charleston. It is also the most practical. It's taken from the West Indian plantations and is quite clever. The homes are designed to accommodate the warm weather and catch the breezes. They are reasonably cool in the hot weather. The large piazzas run the length of the house, usually on both floors, facing the south and west fronts of the house. The house is only one-room wide, two rooms on each floor. One end is turned to the street to catch the prevailing breeze. It's the same idea with the plantations."

"I gather the different styles borrow from one another. I've noticed piazzas on double houses and the careful attention given to keep homes cool."

"It is imperative in this part of the country. The heat in the summer can be brutal. Not everyone can afford to go North."

"So I have heard. Mother and I thought we might travel North this summer, after . . ." It must have been the champagne that loosened her tongue. Richard looked so crestfallen that Gillian turned to grab his arm.

"Oh, Richard, forgive me. I did not mean that I am not considering your offer."

"It is not just an offer, as you put it. I am not offering your hand simply because I feel some sympathy for the Widow Marston. I am offering you my love and devotion."

"I know," she whispered.

"You have no idea how much that means to me," he answered enthusiastically, and more than one head turned to overhear his fervent voice.

There was no point in discussing such a serious topic in the middle of a grand ballroom. Dancers swirled past to the delightful strains of a brisk waltz.

"May I?" He bowed low and kissed her hand in a familiar gesture. A number of heads turned to see how smitten Captain Paxton was with the widowed Lady Marston.

"He is going to ask for her hand. I know it," one lady whispered enviously behind her lace fan to Eve Carlton. A small group of women stood on the far end of the room seemingly enjoying the sights and sounds around them.

Eve Carlton was sumptuously dressed in a low-cut, gold silk net, or maline, dress. Her tightly laced corset pushed her ample breasts up and almost out and when she moved, the tiny crystal beads around the high waistband, hem, and sleeves quivered. The gown clung seductively to her curves with little material to spare. With a Chinese silk fan covering her mouth and nose, only her dark eyes could be seen, which were now narrowed sus-

215

piciously at Gillian.

"My cousin can take care of himself" was the enigmatic reply. "I do not believe he would marry her." The French-accented voice was cool.

"I think she is a lovely and charming young woman." Liza Fenwick hadn't missed Eve's comments or the dour look. It seemed that Eve did not like Lady Marston.

"Would you want your son or nephew to marry her?" She raised her nose above the fan.

"Of course."

"And raise another man's child as his own?"

"Eve, what difference would that make? When two people are deeply in love, I believe they can overcome any obstacles." Liza's eyes were trained on the dancing couple and Gillian's merry laugh reached her ears.

"I think it is in poor taste that a woman in her condition should parade around the dance floor like a young girl," another matron sneered.

"Come, come, ladies. This is the 1820's. What would you have her do? Stay home, dressed in black, locked in the house until the baby is born? Isn't that a bit harsh? Besides, why should she be punished for her husband's demise or for being in that condition?" Liza always lost her patience when the women chose to unleash their malicious tongues on someone she liked.

Although there hadn't been many opportunities for Liza to chat privately with Lady Marston, she knew that the young woman was pleasant and gracious. Moreover, she was not a gossip. Gillian appeared a bit reserved, but as soon as someone

216

spoke to her, she smiled brightly and willingly talked about a number of subjects. Except her dead husband. Gillian Marston's face paled whenever his name was brought up.

Too bad, Liza thought more than once, a woman like Gillian would not be considered suitable for her nephew. Logan did not like such decent women. Well, it wasn't her problem anymore. He was a grown man and far away from Charleston. Let his father worry about him.

"Here they come," whispered another. "Smile."

Richard had seen his cousin and Liza Fenwick along the side of the room. Thinking it appropriate to pay his respects now and ask Eve for one dance, Richard placed a possessive hand on Gillian's back and guided her to his cousin.

"Lady Marston, you look lovely." Liza spoke first.

"Please call me Gillian. There is no need for such formality any longer," she smiled sincerely. "You look lovely, too. I admired your dress from across the room. That is a lovely shade of rose." The dress accented Liza's dark brown eyes and chestnut hair. Looking closer, Gillian noticed a tiny cleft in her strong chin. There was a strong resemblance to Logan, but there was no point in staying away from Liza simply because she had a dreadful relative. Liza Fenwick was a true lady. She was generous, soft-spoken, a gracious hostess, not at all like those bitter-tongued women standing alongside.

"I hope you can visit our home. It is only a few miles upriver from the Ashtons. Do you enjoy needlework?"

217

"Actuallly, no. I am clumsy."

"Splendid." Liza smiled. "I loathe it. But I love gardening, and we raise the best thoroughbreds at Raveneau Hall."

"It sounds appealing, thank you."

"But first she must visit Bolton Hall," Richard joined the conversation. "There is so much I would like to show Gillian." He smiled into her eyes, and the remaining women standing nearby, eager to hear snatches of the conversation, knew there was much left unsaid.

"It would be most difficult in her condition," Eve snapped. She addressed Richard as if Gillian were across the room.

"I shall let Gillian decide." He glanced meaningfully at his cousin, but Eve ignored him.

"When do you begin your lying-in, dear?" Eve did not look at Gillian, but at her rounded tummy.

"Not for a while. Thank you for asking." Gillian wanted to snap her fan on Eve's upturned nose. She could be as frosty as this one, perhaps more so thanks to her English upbringing.

Recognizing the sign of anger, Richard quickly claimed Eve for one dance. Promising to bring Gillian a cold glass of water, he kissed Gillian's hand and winked.

"Forgive my manners, dears." Liza indicated a tall, thin young woman in their group. "Gillian, I do not believe you have met Hattie Mathew's niece, Anabelle Blacton. She has come to visit for a few months."

"We've met in London." Her voice was so low, Gillian had to step closer to listen.

218

"Have we?" she asked, wondering if anyone noticed her sudden alarm. If Anabelle knew of Gillian or any member of the ton, then she would certainly know Logan and about the engagement.

"Yes, it was almost a year ago at a ball given by my parents. I've been on an extended tour, you see," she smiled. "Alas, no husband."

Judging from the woman's looks, Gillian could not understand why she hadn't met her match. Anabelle was not beautiful, but her thick blond hair and light gray eyes were appealing and she certainly seemed pleasant enough.

A cool breeze wafted across her face and Gillian wanted to feel the soft wind on her cheeks. Pregnancy did come in handy, she decided. "Would you ladies mind if I excused myself. I could use some fresh air. Perhaps we can chat again soon, Anabelle." She looked directly at Eve's back, then dismissed her with one wave of her hand. "Liza, would you ask Richard to join me on the portico with my water?"

"Certainly, dear. If there is anything else you need. . . ? Would you like some company?"

"No, thank you. I will be fine." Gillian wanted to be outside. She wasn't in the mood for Eve Carlton's waspish tongue tonight.

It was lovely on the portico. The breeze ruffled her hair and pinkened her cheeks. Gillian could see the lit torches illuminating the long path with overhanging trees that led to the river road. Voices rose and fell from the kitchens below. On the far right of the house, she could see the slave quarters.

Looking up, Gillian saw hundreds of tiny stars,

sparkling way above the treetops. From her vantage point, she noticed the young couples leisurely strolling along the grounds, some disappearing behind the grove of trees near the pond. How nice to be in love, she sighed to herself. How nice not to have a care in the world.

But tonight there were no regrets, no tears, and no more self-pity. She could be happy in Charleston. She could be happy with Richard Paxton.

Hearing a pair of booted feet graze the concrete and thinking them to be Richard's, Gillian kept her gaze focused on the stars as the chilled crystal water glass was handed to her.

"Thank you, darling," she said, unaware of the endearment.

"You're most welcome, sweetheart," came the familiar reply.

"It cannot be," she groaned aloud.

"Is this how you greet your long-lost fiancé?"

Tiny pieces of crystal shattered around her feet.

Chapter Twenty-two

"Get out of my life, Logan." Although her answer was fiercely spoken, she refused to turn and face him.

"I have come for you."

Damn that seductive voice, she thought. She wasn't going to look or listen. She would pretend this was all one nasty nightmare.

He touched her arm and she pulled it away as if burned.

"I am dreaming."

"As I have dreamt of you. Often. But this is real, sweetheart." Logan guided her arm making her reluctant body follow suit.

It was impossible to determine who was more shocked: Gillian at seeing that handsome face and rakish smile frozen in place or Logan, who could not take his eyes off her stomach.

"Why didn't you tell me?" The grip tightened.

There was no point in feigning she did not know what he was talking about. "I tried. My letters. You do remember the dozens of letters I sent to you. I did mention once or twice about an imminent problem." She tried to pull away, but Logan would have none of it.

Choosing to ignore her bitter tone, he responded in the most primitive way he could. All he wanted was Gillian's mouth on his and, forgetting everything else, his arms wrapped around her back. He forced her to accept his lips and tongue in a kiss that was filled with anger, hurt, and passion.

For one tiny second, Gillian felt as if she had returned to her cocoon, and she allowed the familiar passion to swell and answer his. Then she remembered and just as quickly pulled away and with as much strength as she could muster, sharply slapped his face.

"You arrogant bastard! What makes you think you can march back into my life?" Now the anger took control and she forgot where she was, unmindful of the voices of the guests around her.

The little scene had not been lost on the people nearest the open doors. Eve Carlton, Liza Fenwick and some friends had arrived soon enough. Although their voices were hushed, it was obvious that Lady Marston was furious and equally obvious that those two knew each other.

Still holding a glass of water in one hand, Richard approached the ladies only to discover that Gillian was not among them, that they were engrossed in something outside on the portico.

"Richard, dear, I think you should assist Lady Marston. She seems, ah, in need of something." Eve smiled in anticipation of the scene to come.

Alarmed that Gillian should be unwell, he rushed outside, not looking at anyone or anything around him. He stopped short upon seeing Logan Ham-

222

mond, of all people, holding Gillian with one hand while the other patted his stinging cheek.

"What is the meaning of this?"

Both Logan and Gillian turned to glare at the intrusion.

"Oh, my God, Richard." She twisted out of Logan's grasp and rushed to Richard's side.

"Richard, is it? Don't tell me you have gained another champion and in that condition." Logan's contemptuous reply was not lost on Gillian or Richard.

"Logan Hammond, under ordinary circumstances I would have said it's good to see you again. What are you doing in Charleston? And what are you doing with my fiancée?"

Either he killed Paxton on the spot or he tried to collect himself and find out what was going on. Never predictable in behavior or temperament, Logan looked at all the faces around him, threw his head back, and laughed. It was ludicrous. For the second time in his short relationship with Gillian, another man had marched up on them claiming her as his fiancée.

"Not again." He wiped the moisture in his eyes. "Gillian, dear, haven't we played this little scene before?" Logan's eyes darkened as she stared at Paxton's arm familiarly wrapped around her thickened waist.

"You know each other?" She did not know what else to say. Desperately wishing for Logan to disappear, her eyes scanned the crowded ballroom. Too many faces were turned in their direction.

It was precisely the question Richard was about to ask Gillian.

"You forget, my sweet, that I spent many summers in America. Paxton and I grew up on neighboring plantations. Under normal circumstances, Richard, I would have been happy to see you, too." Logan reached into the inside pocket of his dove-gray jacket. "Mind if I smoke?" He did not wait for affirmation and lit the cigar. "Where was I? Oh, yes," he exhaled slowly, unmindful of the smoke that wafted under her nose, "Gillian, does he know?"

"Logan, for heaven's sake, what are you talking about? You show up out of nowhere. I find you alone with my fiancée — arguing in a most familiar way."

Leaning against one white column, Logan casually crossed one booted foot over the other ankle. "So she hasn't told you."

"Told me what, dammit!"

"Now, now, Richard, you do not want to cause a scene."

"Logan," Gillian warned, "keep out of this." Feeling brave as long as Richard protectively held her, Gillian's mind wondered which weapon she would use to kill Logan, for if he ruined her life yet again, she would gleefully kill him.

"That is quite impossible, Gillian, and you can well understand. Shall I tell him?"

"This has gone far enough." Richard's arm slipped from her side as he took one menacing step towards Logan. "You tell me."

A tiny smile formed as Logan's eyes remained on Gillian's horrified face. She deserved this and much more. "She cannot possibly be your fiancée, Richard, since she is mine, or was until September

224

ACCEPT YOUR FREE GIFT AND EXPERIENCE MORE OF THE PASSION AND ADVENTURE YOU LIKE IN A HISTORICAL ROMANCE

Zebra Romances are the finest novels of their kind and are written with the adult woman in mind. All of our books are written by authors who really know how to weave tales of romantic adventure in the historical settings you love.

Because our readers tell us these books sell out very fast in the stores, Zebra has made arrangements for you to receive at home the four newest titles published each month. You'll never miss a title and home delivery is so convenient. With your first shipment we'll even send you a FREE Zebra Historical Romance as our gift just for trying our home subscription service. No obligation.

BIG SAVINGS AND FREE HOME DELIVERY

Each month, the Zebra Home Subscription Service will send you the four newest titles as soon as they are published. (We ship these books to our subscribers even before we send them to the stores.) You may preview them *Free* for 10 days. If you like them as much as we think you will, you'll pay just $3.50 each and *save $1.80 each month* off the cover price. *AND you'll also get FREE HOME DELIVERY.* There is never a charge for shipping, handling or postage and there is no minimum you must buy. If you decide not to keep any shipment, simply return it within 10 days, no questions asked, and owe nothing.

past."

"But your husband?" Richard stuttered, and turned to Gillian for denial.

"Damn you, Logan," she hissed.

"Answer him, Gillian. What about your so-called husband? I am equally curious." Logan's casual stance did not alter. Outwardly, he appeared calm and in absolute control of the situation. Yet his insides were churning with anger and if he were completely honest with himself—jealousy.

"There was no husband, Richard." Taking a step forward to touch Richard's arm in a comforting gesture, she glared at Logan before choosing her words. "I would have told you, but not like this. Leave it to this swine to interfere in my life once again."

Understanding dawned on him like a splash of cold water. "His," he accused.

Shame engulfed her. "Yes," she whispered. "Perhaps you can understand."

"Not here, and not now. Gillian, love, I think it is time we returned to the party. Don't you agree, Captain? For the lady's sake." Flinging the cigar below, Logan took Gillian's arm. "I shall not say anything tonight. I will give you two time to work things out. Now, I suggest you smile, dear, and you, too, Captain. A number of people would give their last diamond to overhear our friendly chat."

The moment Gillian's slippered foot stepped over the threshold, the noises from the ballroom seemed to have hushed. People were staring, not at her, although many would speculate about Lady Marston's friendship with Hammond later. They were staring at Lord Logan Hammond, grandson of one of the wealthiest men in all of South Carolina.

It was like a scene out of a painting. People remained frozen, scrutinizing the two men on either side of the woman.

"Logan, my goodness, you're back!" Liza Fenwick raced forward to embrace her nephew.

Logan grabbed his aunt, kissing her cheeks and laughing. "I had no idea I would receive such a greeting."

"The return of the prodigal son," she laughed. Liza had seen enough on the portico to know all was not well with her nephew and the Englishwoman. But there would be time for that later. At the moment, they were the center of attention in the Draytons' overflowing ballroom. So many tongues had gossiped about Logan Raveneau Hammond so many times over the years. Tonight was for pleasantries and family solidarity.

"Where is Grandfather?"

"Downstairs, I think, sharing a drink and politics with Vice President Calhoun."

"Do you think he could stand a surprise?" Of all the reasons for returning to America, his grandfather was one of the higher priorities. Yet somehow, Logan had to ensure that Gillian would not leave, not until he had had his say. That, he ruefully smiled, could take days.

"What is so funny, dear?" Liza's innocence struck another amusing chord.

"Liza, be a dear and show Lady Gillian around the grounds. I am certain she would be delighted with the gardens. Like England, you know."

"I think I should rest. Richard," she tried to concentrate on his solid presence, "would you mind escorting me to my mother?"

"Ah, the Lady Marlowe is here as well. Splendid. I must have a word with her as well."

"Stay away, Logan," Gillian cautioned. "She has no desire to renew acquaintances."

"We shall see. I insist on reviewing your dance card, Gillian. I hope you will save one dance for me."

His audacity was almost laughable if she weren't so furious with him. And frightened, too. For now that Logan was actually here, Gillian had no idea how she could repair the damage he had caused in a few short minutes.

"Goodbye, Lord Hammond." It was said loudly and meaningfully.

"Until later, Lady Gillian." He bowed low and maintained a cool smile until she disappeared with Paxton alongside.

Lady Helena had seen enough. Rushing to her daughter's side, Helena insisted Gillian spend some minutes alone. Their hostess had graciously set some rooms for ladies to withdraw to and Helena could not help but notice the tiny white lines around Gillian's suddenly drawn face.

But Gillian would have none of it. "I must speak with Richard, Mother. It is important."

"Gillian, it can wait. Your health and that of the baby's is more important." His solicitous voice made her want to cry. How could he be so considerate at a time like this.

"I think it best we talk now."

Ignoring the stares and whispers, Gillian and Richard proudly left the room. Outside, a delightful river breeze rustled through the trees.

"Do you want to talk or sit?" He pointed to a joggling board behind the trees.

"I think it best I don't rock. I have never been too steady on those boards. It reminds me too much of my father's knee. Always bouncing." She forced a laugh, then lost it all in a sob.

"Gillian, tell me what you can. Was there ever a Lord Marston?"

When she miserably shook her head, he did not know how much more he had a right to ask.

Gillian decided to make it easy for him. He did not deserve any more lies. Slowly, through tears and hiccups, she explained, within reason, her sordid relationship with Logan.

"There are no excuses for my behavior. I should have known better," she concluded much later. "I knew all about his reputation with women. I blindly believed that he cared enough to marry me. Of all his miserable tricks, Logan had never become betrothed. I thought he was sincere this time."

"So you ran away from him. Why? It appears to me as if he was willing to marry you."

"I was angry. I am still angry. I will never know his motives, Richard. I do not care to know. That part of my life is over. I want to make a new life for myself here in America. In Charleston." She raised teary eyes to him.

"With me?" Richard took her cold hands in his.

"If you still want me." Gillian leaned on his shoulder. She only wanted to blot that other face out of her mind—forever. How dare he barge in here looking as gorgeous as ever and acting as if nothing could be wrong. She would not let him back into her life no matter what the cost.

"He has a right to see the child." Richard echoed her unconscious thoughts.

"He relinquished those rights when he refused to come back for me." She spoke with conviction and anger. Later, she would remember these words, for Gillian knew she would cry herself to sleep tonight and every night hereafter.

"Richard, do you mind if I stay outside alone for a while. I cannot go back inside looking like this." She dabbed at her eyes again. "I must look awful. I do not want anyone to know about Logan and me."

"I understand. Do you think he will say anything? I could speak to him . . . " he began.

"No. This is my responsibility. Even if I have to shoot him through his metal heart." She indelicately blew her nose into his borrowed handkerchief. "I will be fine," she assured him, hoping he would believe what she did not.

After he quietly left, Gillian strode towards the slave quarters. There was music and song. The night was echoed in music and song, she thought. So why did she feel so utterly alone and miserable.

She should have recognized the scent. The pungent but familiar mixture of lime and spice mingling with the faintest odor of cigar smoke.

He did not touch her, merely stood behind her. "Now it is my turn, Gillian."

Chapter Twenty-three

"I have nothing to say to you." Gillian's attempted haughty reply was betrayed by a lone tear tracking down her flushed cheek.

"I disagree. Mind if I join you?" He sat on the joggling board, causing it to jump with the added weight. "Ah, how I've missed this thing. When I was a boy, I used to stand up and perform tricks that made my mother's hair turn gray. Yes," he sighed heavily, "those were wonderful days."

"Of course. You did not have a responsibility in the world. Everyone else took care of things for you," she bitterly replied.

"I am fully aware of my abilities, thank you."

"Oh, really? I think you somewhat shortsighted, Logan."

"Gillian, I had every intention of coming home to you and fulfilling my promise to marry you." Since Gillian stared stonily ahead, Logan was afforded her profile, which, despite her pursed lips and angry snorts, was as lovely as ever. The pert nose that he had so often tweaked during playful encounters and those full lips that so invitingly begged to be kissed and nibbled. Seeing her again made her more desirable than ever, despite her condition.

"You did not come home. Not until I was about to become the laughingstock of all London, of all England. I was desperate, Logan, do you have any idea of what that feels like?" Turning at last to look into his golden gaze, she answered her own question. "No, I don't think you've ever had a desperate moment in your life. How could you when absolutely nothing matters to you? You have no feelings, how could you? You have no heart."

Now that her anger took control she continued the tirade. "Have you ever felt pain, Logan? Pain from betrayal? From trusting someone so completely, then discovering that the whole thing was a cruel hoax? And that you were the butt of the joke?" She panted.

"Gillian, why won't you listen to me?" Logan's voice was controlled. If she weren't so upset and engrossed in self-pity, Gillian would have noticed he was *too* calm, as if each word spoken slowly and clearly was forced between his lips.

"Because I don't want to feel anything other than hatred for you, Logan Hammond." She stood to face him. Her face was too close to his, her fists leaning against her hips.

Logan reacted instinctively. In a thrice he was standing and enfolded her in his strong, caring embrace, sobbing on his shoulder. Tenderly, he brushed loose tendrils of hair away from her face. At the same time, he began to kiss the top of her fragrant hair. Without understanding or thinking clearly about the consequences, Logan's tender kisses found her forehead, her wet eyes, and still

231

his mouth lowered to her tear-stained cheeks. Finally, he found her mouth and gently, reverently kissed her sweet lips.

Not until the moment he enfolded her in his arms and delicately kissed her face did Gillian begin to realize how much she missed and needed him. "Oh, Logan, why did you abandon me?" She sobbed without thinking.

"I did not abandon you, I swear it. I want to explain what I can to you. I want you to give me a chance again." He took her shoulders and looked into the glimmering hazel eyes.

"You asked me before why I am here and didn't like my answer. The truth is I came for you. I knew you were in Charleston and came after you. Isn't that enough proof of my devotion to you? I want you to marry me, Gillian. Now more than ever. I want to claim my child."

"Our child."

"You know what I mean." He smiled, revealing a glimpse of the Hammond charm. The shock of seeing him was too much for her. Her strained look and twisted handkerchief reminded him he had better treat her gently now, or lose her yet again.

"Care for a dance?" The delightful strains of a Strauss waltz drifted through the night wind. That would take her mind off killing him. "I think we could use a reprieve."

"Inside there?" She looked horrified. "Logan, I must look like a wreck. Besides, I am not sure I want to be seen with you." It was the wrong thing to say, and she knew it the moment the words left her mouth.

"Why? Would your fiancé be insulted?"

"No, not that I think. Logan, I do not want people to know how intimately we know each other. I do not want to jeopardize the baby's reputation."

"What difference would it make once we are wed?" He was falling into the trap he thought to avoid.

"*If* we are wed." She corrected, poised for a renewed battle.

"Gillian, I will not argue with you tonight. I've caused enough stress with my surprising appearance. I only want to dance with you. Besides, you look," he grinned, "well, you look ravishing, tear-stained, pregnancy, and all. I would have you no other way."

She had no idea how she fell back into his seductive, charming trap, but within minutes, with Logan's able assistance, Gillian had repaired her face and hair, allowing him to escort her inside.

The whispers began in earnest as soon as they entered the room. Logan proudly stood beside her, his eyes scanning the room defying anyone to challenge his right to be with her.

Joining the twirling couples and expertly leading her around the dance floor, Logan's smile was only for her. People moved out of their path, watching, speculating on the mysterious reappearance of Logan Hammond and his friendship with the Widow Marston.

"Richard, you are not going to stand for this," Eve hissed into his ear.

"Why? Because Logan hasn't noticed you yet?

233

He will. I am certain you will see to it." Without looking at her pale countenance, Richard knew he had hit his mark. Her sudden indrawn breath was sufficient evidence.

Richard's attention was centered on the whirling couple who moved so well together, too well, as if they had done this many times before. A quick stab of jealousy and hatred pierced his heart. When Hammond pulled her a little too closely, Richard was ready to interfere, but the sudden appearance of Lady Helena tempered the action.

"Don't, Richard. It will only make matters worse." She took his arm, her face full of understanding and compassion.

"She loves him."

"She once did."

"She was betrothed to him." He miserably restated the fact, unaware that Eve was still at his side.

"Things change, Richard. Don't give up on Gillian yet. Just be patient."

"Richard, dear," Eve's throaty voice interrupted his misery, "why don't you ask Anabelle Blacton to dance. She's been dying for an invitation".

Logan's eyes were trained on Gillian. Whatever Eve Carlton thought of her past "friendship" with him was certainly not on Logan's mind this evening. No one else was in the room — only Gillian. Only the lovely creature who fit so perfectly in his arms. He wanted Gillian. His possessive grip tightened around her thick waist, making her glance sharply at him. Smiling in apology, he quickly picked up the pace and looked over her head of curls as he told himself yet again that no matter what it cost or who he had to destroy, he would have her. And his child.

The rest of the evening became one awful blur. Gillian despairingly prayed for the clock to strike twelve so she could plead fatigue and escape.

A number of people in the room were aware of her discomfort. Richard wondered how and when he would see her alone. Eve Carlton couldn't wait for her to leave so she could pry Logan's eyes away from that woman—whom Eve now knew was certainly no lady. And Lady Helena was painfully aware of daughter's misery and felt utterly helpless. Perhaps later this evening, or tomorrow morning, they could sort out this mess.

Logan thought he would crawl out of his skin, if the evening did not end quickly. There was too much to do tonight. He had to talk with his grandfather, something that was always an enervating experience. The old man insisted on knowing every detail of Logan's life, and if the answers did not satisfy him, Henri would not quit badgering his favorite grandson.

If the trial with his grandfather weren't difficult enough, Logan still had to keep his appointed rendezvous with Harold at dawn. Jesus, he thought, so much could happen between now and dawn. If only he could spend the night with Gillian, with her safely sheltered in his arms, where she belonged.

Life had been hell since his return to London. Logan did not know how the little chit had gotten to him. She wasn't classically beautiful. Certainly not an accomplished lover, although her instincts were nothing to scoff at. She was a trifle tall, a trifle too thin—or was before the pregnancy—and her nose too small, her chin too stubborn, and her lips too full.

But damn if the image of the wanton angel did not haunt his dreams each night since their separation: naked, her pale skin glowing in the moonlight, her long red-gold curls cascading down her back and over her upturned breasts. She would always smile at him, a secret, knowing smile, that remained until the instant her lips found his. He would reach up for more of this elusive beauty and discover his emptiness.

She had become a part of him. If this was love, he hated it. But he would not let her go until he was certain of his feelings. Or tired of her. The child would have his name.

Feeling claustrophobic, Logan exited Drayton Hall to wander along the river road. The beauty and serenity of this night was lost on him. His thoughts were jumbled. Gillian Marlowe was inevitably in the eye of his storm.

Lighting a cheroot and holding a bottle of bourbon, Logan thought back on the last four months. Leaving Gillian had been difficult, but once he arrived in Paris, his focus had turned to his assignment, for the sooner he identified the European contacts involved in the "separation conspiracy," the faster he would be free to return to England.

He had marveled at how smoothly he had been able to identify the French conspirators—the names were quickly dispatched to Harold. Italy had been difficult, and it was there in Italy that Logan was left for dead.

It had not been an accident. One night, after returning from a Venetian ball, he had almost reached his guest quarters when he had been attacked. There had been four of them—three, after Logan shot one. Evidently their assignment had been to severely injure, not kill him. Enough, he later surmised, to scare him. He had been badly beaten, and stabbed twice in his chest and left side. His right arm had been broken.

When he had regained consciousness five days later, Harold, of all people, had been at his bedside. But Logan had been unable to identify the attackers. Harold had coaxed him back to fair health, insisting that the assignment could wait.

"You called for the girl a number of times, Logan," Harold had told him, in between bites of his late-afternoon lunch. "I cannot believe you could feel that way for a woman. Perhaps you took my suggestion to settle down with a nice, docile girl a bit too seriously, eh, lad?"

Docile, he had learned, was not a proper term of reference for Gillian Marlowe. As soon as he felt able, Logan had instructed a friend to write her, making up that ludicrous story about a riding accident and wager. But he knew now that he had underestimated Gillian's wrath and the dire situation he had placed her in.

After returning to England, Logan had immediately sought her, only to discover Lord Charles Marlowe's letter. Why had Gillian left him? That Lord Hammond's name was involved in yet another

237

juicy scandal in London had not bothered him. Lord Charles had thought differently about the malicious gossip concerning his daughter and Logan.

"I never should have trusted you, Hammond. If it wouldn't add to my daughter's misery and shame, I would call you out now." Charles had threatened to call him out at least six more times after that.

After learning of Gillian's departure, London had seemed uneventful, even boring. Logan found himself involved in but not enjoying his old pastimes. Gambling, parties, balls, hunts, drinking, had left a sour taste in his mouth. As usual, he had not been lacking female companions, but the desire was no longer there. He did not care about bedding anyone, except for one, and she had left him, had insisted he not find her. She had refused to accept his letters.

Once he had realized that she was not returning in the immediate future, Logan craved adventure, had begged Harold for new assignments, but Harold had insisted that the time was not right. Logan had almost been killed. Someone knew his identity as an American agent. It was not safe for him to remain in England.

Gillian's father had refused to provide information as to his daughter's whereabouts. His impotent frustration had begun to get the better of him. Once, he had come very close to killing Brian Althorp in front of dozens of witnesses at his club. Only the timely intervention of his friend Arthur had prevented the slaughter. Althorp had taken perverse pleasure in reminding Logan that Gillian had left him. The only satisfaction Logan had received was in knowing that Althorp had no idea of her whereabouts, either.

And then he had received his aunt's letter. Liza's letters were usually chatty and contained a bit of gossip about Charleston. Logan had almost skipped over the passage concerning the recent arrival of two London ladies. In a fit of boredom he had forced himself to finish reading the letter over three glasses of port. The contents of the glass fell to the fine Aubusson rug, the red stain saturating one spot. Logan cared for nothing at the moment but the beautiful but sad "Lady Marston" and her mother, who only recently had arrived in Charleston.

Logan could have kicked himself for forgetting that Gillian, too, had family in Charleston. Seconds after shredding the letter, he had decided to return to America.

Even Harold thought it a brilliant idea, but had insisted on modifying the assignment against Logan's wishes.

"Logan, my boy, someone knows who you are and wants you dead. There is no point in putting your handsome face directly in front of a loaded pistol." Harold had thought his words amusing, but Logan did not. "No more arguments, this is a new order. I want you to identify the names of the people planted by the British to foment strife among the southerners."

Logan hadn't thought it very different from the original assignment until Harold had added, "But only in Charleston and Savannah. No further, do you understand?"

"Why?" Logan had been disappointed.

"We have enough people working on this now. Since timing is important, I have reassigned a few of your coworkers to the other states. Lily and Peter will remain in Charleston to work with you. Henry Clay only wants the names. He intends to present the list to Foreign Minister Canning on his next trip to London. That should embarrass the foreign minister I should think."

"Threaten a worldwide scandal?"

"Something like that. Perhaps Mr. Canning might be more amenable to negotiating a new West Indian treaty with us after we present him with this new information."

"And the British agents in America?"

"Sent home in disgrace, of course."

So here he was, home again, given the two biggest chances in his life. One to halt a disastrous evil, and the other, to pick up the pieces of his personal life.

All that mattered was reclaiming Gillian, force her to listen to his explanations, and then win her over again. The temptress had made a permanent space in his heart.

Logan was afraid he was in love.

Chapter Twenty-four

"Grandfather, I thought you would have been pleased to see me."

"Of course I am, Logan, but I can never understand why you enjoy surprise visits. What would you have done if I left the city for the mountains? How would you have found me then?" The old man's golden eyes lit with anger.

"I would have found you, no matter what. Besides, you are not fooling me. I know you love to argue. With anyone about anything," he added with a wide grin. Bless this man, he thought, he never seems to look and act any older than the memory of the gray-haired man Logan always fondly held with him.

"Well," Henri harrumphed, "I was surprised to see you come at me yesterday. At a private ball no less. I could have had an attack on the spot in front of all those people, including the vice president!"

"You would never give anyone the satisfaction of seeing you ill, Grandfather." Logan moved to the large palladian window. Unaware of his actions, he rubbed the back of his sore neck. The crisp white lawn shirt was open at the neck and the sleeves rolled neatly above his elbows. Since his return a short while ago, Logan had little chance to do anything other than wash and change his clothes. His unshaven face reminded him of how unkempt he must appear to the old man.

"Long night, was it? I know you did not return until an hour ago. So no more excuses, lad." Henri remained seated behind a massive cherrywood desk. "Should I offer you a hot drink, or another bourbon? It should make little difference to you that it is 8 A.M. You have not stopped drinking this stuff since your arrival." Despite his words, Henri handed Logan a glass of bourbon.

"Joining me?" Logan accepted the drink with a laugh. "You always could drink me under the table."

"Still can. But even I recognize that it's a bit early in the day for me." The old man drank the strong black coffee instead. "I'll leave this nearby, in case you ever feel the need to sober up."

"I am perfectly sober. Just tired," he sighed heavily. "It's been a long night."

"Can you tell me about it?" Henri had long ago suspected his favorite grandson's involvement with the American government. Wisely, he kept all suspicions to himself. When and if Logan could talk about it, he would. His grandson always came to him.

"No. Not yet."

"What about the girl?"

The question was so startling that Logan forgot to keep his features impassive. "Wh-what do you mean?" he stammered.

Henri Raveneau rose dramatically. Leaning large fists against the desk, he raised his white bushy eyebrows to just the right height that never failed to remind Logan he was about to be reprimanded. "I saw her. I saw her with you. I saw her cry. And I saw you imbibe this potent stuff the moment you set eyes on her."

Logan pretended to study the bookshelves lined with leather-bound books in various languages. This was his favorite room in the house, the one refuge from the noise and bustle of a busy household. As a young man, he spent hours secluded in this room, reading or thinking. No one bothered him once the wide oak doors closed behind him, except his grandfather.

"You cannot fool me," his grandfather's deep voice interrupted his quiet musings. "I will not let you leave this room until you tell me about her."

"Must I remind you that I am no longer a boy of fourteen?"

"I am waiting."

Knowing that Henri would never be satisfied unless he knew the truth—something he would probably discover within a few days anyhow—Logan decided to talk.

Turning from the window, he took a place by the marble fireplace, leaning one arm against the mantel. "Her name is Gillian."

"I know that!" Henri snapped.

"If you will let me speak without interrupting me you might discover there are some things you do not know." Logan met his grandfather's stony gaze with one of his own. "She is Lady Gillian

Marlowe." His hand lifted to silence another interruption. "I said Marlowe, not Marston. She was my fiancée. Until August, that is, when she saw fit to break our engagement. With good cause, I think."

"The baby?"

"Is mine."

"Good God, lad, you've got to do something!" he exploded, pounding one fist on the desk, scattering papers across it. "We cannot allow one of my heirs to be born illegitimately."

"She's going to marry Richard Paxton."

"That's absurd! You cannot permit such a travesty."

"It is not entirely my decision, you understand."

"Stop talking to me as if it doesn't matter. I know it does and unless I am a poor judge of character, you care about the girl. She probably cares about you." Henri ignored Logan's cough. "She's just angry, that's all. You have to mollify her."

"How do you suggest I go about accomplishing such an impossible task?"

"Court her, lad. Start courting her today. Tonight. There is nothing more important than getting her to marry you. That child must be born on Raveneau land, a legitimate heir, do you hear me?"

"I think you're arguing with the wrong person. I wonder what you'll think of Gillian after you delicately describe the virtues of marriage to your grandson. You seem to think you can be more persuasive than I. Go ahead."

"Give me a chance. I don't mind trying. I have

plenty of charm left in this sixty-two-year-old body. I could not fare any worse than you."

Paying no attention to Henri's new verbal assault, Logan bent his tousled head. Pretending to concentrate on the tips of his black leather boots, he wondered if Henri was right. Perhaps he should court Gillian. Outcharm Paxton. Win over her mother and cousin and anyone else remotely close to Gillian who could influence her.

"You will have to devote all your time to this endeavor, Logan."

Suddenly reminded of his other, equally important responsibilities, Logan rose, shoved his hands in his pockets, and paced around the room. "I cannot devote as much time as you would like. There are certain matters that need my attention."

"Forget them for now. They will have to wait unless someone can handle them for you." Henri was tempted to ask the questions now, but Logan's scowl halted the inquiry. "You must decide what is more important to you," he wisely warned. "The girl, or your other involvements, no matter how noble they may seem."

"I know. I know. I suppose I could manage both," he grinned mischievously. "That old Hammond charm and all. Must have inherited it from you."

"When is the child due?"

"Christ," he sobered, trying to think. "I am not sure."

"Well, just make sure you marry Miss Marlowe *before* the child is born. Think you can see to that?"

"With your assistance, how can I lose?"

Slightly mollified by the compliment, Henri realized that Logan exited the room without revealing any of his plans. With or without Logan's encouragement, Miss Marlowe and he might get better acquainted.

Gillian would not have felt any better knowing that she was the topic of conversation at Raveneau Plantation. Nervously pacing around the gardens, she did not hear her mother's soft approach and questioning voice. "Gillian?"

Whirling to face the intruder, Gillian's stern features softened. "Mother you frightened me."

"I thought you could use company now. Did you sleep well?"

Gillian couldn't help but laugh. "You mean did I sleep?"

"You must speak to him again."

"I know."

Briefly, Gillian explained the conversation with Logan from the previous night. "I will not marry him," she concluded in a determined voice.

Helena suspected there was much more her daughter left unspoken. "He wants to see you. He deserves an explanation."

"Why? Did he explain anything to me when he forgot to write?"

"But his injury . . ."

"I know what he told me. I don't necessarily have to believe him, do I?"

That was the problem. Believing him. Accepting

Logan's honeyed words and falling prey to his graceful charm. Acting as if nothing had happened. Abandoning the carefully constructed story about her widowhood. And leaving the security of Richard Paxton's arms for another wild ride with Logan Hammond.

"I am too tired," she said aloud. "I no longer think Logan is the man for me. I could never be certain he would be there for me when I need him, when the baby needs him. Why should I take any more chances, when Richard offers me much more than Logan?"

"Such as?"

"Love. Richard told me he loves me. Logan tells me nothing. Oh," she almost smiled, "he used to tell me how much he desired me. That was before I looked like this."

"Soon you will have to choose."

"I suppose. But not yet. I would much rather think of this lovely day, the warm sun on my face and a chance to take a long, undisturbed nap." Gillian absently pinned up her hair, then placed a damp cool cloth on her neck.

A lounge chaise and net had been set up for her underneath a huge live oak tree. Shaded from the sun, with only the rustling of the leaves and the soothing breeze against her flushed skin, she finally dozed.

When her eyes finally fluttered open, she felt disoriented. Looking up into the cloudy sky, it took her a full five minutes to come fully awake. When she turned her head, she saw Richard calmly sitting on the grass, cross-legged, smiling at her confusion.

"I hope I did not wake you." His deep voice softened as he noticed the slight blush on her cheeks. "I think the sun has kissed your cheeks, despite the shade from this old tree."

"How long have you been here?"

"Long enough to ensure that no one dare disturb you. It was your mother's orders, and as a good soldier I know how to follow orders."

"Why aren't you in uniform?" Dressed in fawn trousers and white linen shirt, his hair looked brighter in the sun and his smile as loving as always. He was so handsome, she noted, and so sweet.

Unconsciously, her mind made the immediate comparison between Richard and Logan. They were almost the same height, Logan only an inch or two taller. While Logan appeared leaner than Richard, she suspected both men were of equal strength. Richard's grin was far more ready and sincere, yet Logan's rakish one could melt her heart. Richard's green eyes were warm, crinkling in the corners when he grinned. Logan's golden eyes turned dark with passion whenever he was about to kiss her.

"What are you staring at, sweetheart? Have you never seen a man dressed as a country squire?"

"Yes, but not you." She started to straighten her legs to stand, but his hand stayed the action.

"I've come to enjoy the remainder of the afternoon with the woman I hope wants to marry me."

"You still want me?" Since her mind was still groggy, there was no artlessness with Richard.

"Why, of course."

248

"I doubt your parents will agree."

"No one knows about our conversation with Logan. And I am not worried about him. I've known him a long time. He'll be gone soon. He always leaves."

"Does he always leave a string of broken hearts?"

"Eve thinks so."

She straightened. "Eve? Was she involved with Logan?"

"It was a long time ago. She thought they would marry. Then he left, of course, and Eve married shortly thereafter, although I always wondered if she saw Logan the last time he visited. Her husband was away at the time . . ." His voice trailed off, suddenly unsure of how much he should tell Gillian of Logan's numerous, often trivial encounters.

"I see . . ." She considered his words. Logan acted no differently in the Low Country than he did in England. Once a rake, always a rake. And an insufferable brute as well, she angrily concluded.

"Anyway, you asked me a question about my state of dress. I am temporarily relieved of duty in Charleston."

"Oh? Is something wrong?"

"Not at all," he grinned. "I have been given a wonderful assignment, although," his smile vanished, "it will take me away from you for a few weeks."

A sudden state of panic engulfed her. Richard must have seen her crestfallen expression and promptly misinterpreted her reaction. "Darling,

249

darling," he rose to her side, taking her cold hand in his warm one, "I shan't be away long. Only a few weeks at most. I will come back to you."

She was certain he would return. Unlike Logan, Richard was a man of his word. That was not her concern. Without Richard's protection, Gillian would be vulnerable to Logan's assault. She needed a barrier. Richard did not realize the desperate state she would be in without him at her side, keeping Logan at bay.

"Vice President Calhoun asked me to accompany him as his military escort while he tours the southern states. It's a wonderful opportunity." His voice filled with awe at the mention of Calhoun's name. "Who knows? Calhoun has not given up his quest for the presidency. I would enjoy living in Washington, wouldn't you?"

"I am not certain." She shyly met his earnest gaze.

"As my wife, of course, Gillian. Always together. After we are married, I promise to keep you by my side."

Those were words she wanted to hear. Unfortunately, she needed him at her side now, tomorrow and each day she would be forced to face Logan Hammond.

Taking her in his arms, he kissed her temple and cheeks. Gillian stared at the billowy clouds above, wondering why they reminded her of a fierce lion circling his prey.

Chapter Twenty-five

Richard's departure created mixed feelings in Gillian. She was to spend Christmas and the New Year without his companionship, his ready smile, compliments, conversation, and proposals of marriage. Gillian knew she was going to miss him, needing him to keep Logan away. Then again, she decided, it would be a small relief to have time to herself again. She would not be pressed into thinking about marriage and whose surname her unborn child should have.

Yet moments after Richard's tender goodbye kiss, Gillian felt lonely and something worse—vulnerable, exposed to Logan Hammond's charming assault. As if on cue, Richard's sloop had just made the turn around the Ashley River at the precise moment Logan rode up on a large black stallion.

Leave it to Logan, she thought, to not only know the exact moment Richard left her side, but to gallop up the dirt road, not an easy route since the old Indian trails used as roads were muddy, narrow, and cluttered with obstacles. Hardly anyone traveled by road, unless absolutely necessary. Not even the treks to church were by road, but by the more comfortable river routes. Logan, of course, had to be different.

It was perfect for him, she grimly decided. The roads paralleled Logan's peculiar personality.

The dust kicked up by the stallion temporarily blinded her and made her sneeze. Within seconds, he stood before her.

"I apologize." His deep voice sounded amused. "I did not mean to cause you harm. Here," he offered her his linen handkerchief that smelled of his cologne, "let me help."

"No, please, I am quite all right." She tried to look up, but her left eye continued to tear in irritation.

"Let me," he repeated tenderly, leaning over, gently pulling her head back so he could see the particle in her eye. "Hold still," he commanded.

His breath was warm on her face. There was no trace of liquor or wine this day, which seemed unusual for him considering the lateness of the afternoon. No, he smelled of . . . She thought, then laughed delightedly. ". . . Strawberries?"

"What about them?" he absently inquired. "I said hold still, woman, do you want me to get dirt out of your eye or not?"

"You smell like strawberries." She tried to contain the rising giggle in her throat.

"I love to eat them. Is that a problem, too?"

"You do not seem the kind of man who could nurse a passion for anything other than women and liquor. I am not positive of the order."

"There!" He appeared to ignore her perceptive statement. "It's out. Feel better?" He stared down at her, and she childishly wished she could kick him in his booted shins.

"Why are you here?" She pulled away from his gentle grasp, noticing that, unlike most southern men, he was not wearing a hat. Looking tanned and fit, it annoyed her to realize that Logan was impervious to the strong sun and any other physical discomfort that affected most people.

"To see your mother, of course." His laughter boomed across the back lawn well before she opened her mouth with outrage. "No, no. I am only jesting, sweeting. I've come to see you. I want you to come to Raveneau Plantation tomorrow. My grandfather insists on meeting you."

"Why?" she asked suspiciously. "What have you told him?"

"Nothing he does not already know." The evasive answer did not mollify her.

"I will not be humiliated by any member of your family."

"Stop being so indignant. I am merely extending my family's hospitality. If you do not feel well enough to join us, I am certain he will understand. My aunt Liza thinks you are lovely and quiet. Lovely, yes, but I think she does not know you very well to think you are quiet."

He was mocking her and damn well knew it. Nevertheless, she rose to the bait. "What time?"

"I will come for you before lunch. Around eleven. It will give me another opportunity to steal a private moment with you."

Looking resplendent in a pale blue shirt, and deerskin breeches that clung to his muscular thighs, Gillian wondered how any woman would resist Logan Hammond. She was trying, but damn it was

253

not going to be easy.

"Gillian, did you hear me? You seem engrossed in the sky."

"I, ah, I am sorry, I did not mean to be rude. What did you ask?"

"I asked if I could visit with your mother. She is here, isn't she?"

"I think so," she stammered. "I haven't seen her since Rich — I mean I have not seen her this afternoon.

"Paxton gone, I see. My luck, isn't it?"

"I do not think that is any of your business, nor do I think I want to hold any conversation with you about my suitors, especially not here in the blazing sun. I feel red all over."

To Logan she looked like a delicate rosebud, all reddish pink and full of promise, just before it opened to reveal its hidden glory and sweet scent.

"The sun has never agreed with me. But being this way and all, I cannot tolerate much heat." She tried to modify her hostile tone. Unwilling to acknowledge his amused smile, she studied the fine lawn material of her pale pink dress. Blessedly, she had no idea that the material was almost gossamer in the afternoon sunlight. Logan saw the outline of her breasts, her dark nipples clearly pressing against the bodice. There were no silk undergarments beneath the dress. Even her long, shapely legs were outlined, something he had noticed well before dismounting the stallion.

"I think you look lovely. No," he saw her about to protest, "I mean it. You've filled out in all the right places." Without seeking permission, his hand was on her bare arm, leading her to the house.

"Let me get you a cold drink."

Briefly, Gillian thought she was in his home. "I appreciate your concern, but as I've already told you, I do not need your assistance."

"Don't play the high-and-mighty lady with me, Gillian. You need me more than ever. And you will marry me." He did not break stride as they climbed the stone steps.

"Logan," she tried to stop but his grip was firm, "I do not want to discuss anything with you today, or any day for that matter. Richard has just left. I feel a bit sad. I am not good company at the moment."

"Gillian, I grew up with Paxton. We played together, shared the same tutor, even the same pranks with girls. I know he is not the man for you."

"Richard loves me."

Logan did not answer the unasked question. "A cold lemonade, please," he called to the servant by the door.

"Logan, you are the guest, remember?"

"I've been at Ashton House more times than I can recall. I practically grew up in these fields. I know the house better than you. I am not the guest. Come this way." He led her into the morning room. "This room is cool late in the day."

"Logan," she warned.

"I am not going to harm you. I want another word with you, that's all."

She sat on the most comfortable piece of furniture in the room. The white brocade sofa was thickly cushioned and offered her back support. Above her head was a large gilt-framed mirror, which in the morning reflected and magnified the sun's rays. A black lacquered English tea table, surrounded by two Chippendale chairs, stood in the center of the room.

Logan, of course, remained standing, towering above her. The windows were wide open, to catch the cross breeze of the river, which made the billowy sleeves of his blue shirt flutter. No matter where she looked or what she thought, the focus of attention drifted back to Logan.

Forcing herself to concentrate on the bright patterns of the upholstered chairs, Aubusson rug, and cheery paintings, she finally admitted that nothing could alter her glum frame of mind.

"What do you want now?" She did not bother hiding her irritation in front of the servant who walked in with their drinks.

"Why are you always so suspicious of my motives, love? I only want to protect our child. So tell me . . ." he paused to take a sip and wrinkled his nose at the tart taste. "I should have asked for a Madeira," he muttered. "Tell me what story you have concocted for society. I must be aware of what is expected of me."

He sounded like the old Logan, Lord Hammond, son of the Earl of Stanton. Yet he had to know, or forever ruin her reputation. As concisely as possible, she outlined the story of her marriage and widowhood. Not daring to hope he would assist her, she prayed he would simply keep quiet or leave Charleston.

"How do you know someone won't reveal the truth? What about this Anabelle Blacton?"

"Do you know her?"

"I met her years ago. She was not a member of

my circle, but I am certain she knows many of our acquaintances. How can you be certain she won't know the truth?"

"I cannot," she sighed heavily. "But as I've told you before, I have no intention of leaving Charleston." Anger renewed her courage. "How long are you staying?"

"At Raveneau Plantation?" he countered, knowing exactly what she meant but delighting in her frustration.

Pressing the cool drink to her hot cheeks, she was sorely tempted to launch the lemonade in his grinning but oh so handsome face. "I have a right to know, too, Logan. I want to get on with my life."

"So you shall." He inclined his head. "Gillian, would you tell me something?" There was no mockery in his hesitant smile. "You do want our child, don't you?"

"Yes," she conceded, "despite everything you have put me through, I want this child." Her eyes began to shimmer. "How can I explain the changes that are taking place in my body? What I feel?"

Without asking permission, Logan lowered to one knee, before her, taking her hands in his. "Tell me. I want to know. Please?"

It must have been the first time she had ever heard him speak this way, humbly asking something of her. It moved her more than anything else he had ever done. If this was some devious technique to win her favors, then Logan Hammond was a much better actor than she thought.

"I, I don't know what . . ." she stammered.

"Gillian, talk to me." He stroked her hand. His

wrinkled brow and luminescent eyes somehow convinced her that he was sincere.

"I think it's a boy," she laughed shakily. "I don't think a girl could be this active so early in one's pregnancy. And look at me, why I'm huge!" In a now familiar gesture, she looked down at her rounded tummy, as if it were growing before her startled eyes.

"I think you're lovely," he whispered huskily. "Gillian, may I touch you, I mean your stomach?"

He was awkward and nervous. This was one experience Logan had never known. If there were another child of his out there in the world, he could not be certain. But this one he did know. It was his. And oh how he wanted to be a part of this miracle. Tentatively, he raised his hand, but did not know what to do with it. Plop it on her stomach. What would happen if he hurt the baby?

"Well, perhaps I shouldn't," he demurred.

Suddenly Gillian found her strength. "Here," she took his large hand, "let me." Gently placing his hand on her stomach, she nervously laughed as his fingers slowly spread, trying to encompass her width. His eyes widened in pleasure and he laughed out loud. It was the laugh of a little boy.

"My God, I think it moved!" His voice was filled with wonder.

"It's happening more often. Mother says that by the seventh and eighth months, I will be fortunate if my ribs aren't bruised."

Fortunately his head was bent as he studied her new form. He could not see Gillian's tender smile or her hand poised midway in the air, tempted to touch his hair and neck.

When he looked up once more, she valiantly tried to compose her features, but he knew. He felt the moment, too, and without thinking, pulled her into his soft embrace. "I want to be there when he's born. I want to know my child."

"Don't," she choked. "I cannot think. Richard's just left and now you barge into my life again. I want time, Logan. I must have some time to myself."

The late-afternoon sun cast long shadows along the manicured lawn. The room was darkening with the departing sun.

Realizing this was not the time to press his suit, Logan kissed the top of her head. "You smell like freshly cut flowers. Lilacs, I think."

A soft knock on the door severed the tranquil moment.

"Gillian, I heard Logan is here," her mother called through the door. "Are you together?"

"You will come tomorrow?" he whispered urgently as he rose to his full height.

"Yes. I have nothing to lose."

You're wrong, he told himself. You have your heart to lose. "I only want a chance. The same chance you are giving Paxton."

Chapter Twenty-six

Logan arrived early the following morning, which did nothing to assauge Gillian's nerves. She was late. It was one of those rare evenings when her dreams had remained undisturbed, peaceful. There were no images of Richard asking her hand in marriage. There were no images of Logan bestowing a mocking smile as he walked off with Eve Carlton. The last image Gillian remembered before falling asleep was of Logan kneeling before her with one hand resting gingerly on her swollen abdomen.

"Gillian, you must hurry," her cousin Julia chirped, bustling into the room.

Standing before a large mirror, Gillian grimaced at her appearance. "I hate mirrors. All mirrors. They do not do justice to a pregnant woman."

Scattered about the room were four dresses made of pale green muslin, violet and yellow cotton, and a peach confection of linen and lace.

"I have no idea what is appropriate. What did you say Henri Ravenueau was like?" Gillian asked for the third time.

"Gruff, I admit, but he can be charming. If he likes you, Gillian, I assure you he will let you know."

"Wonderful." She bit her lip in dismay. "If he does not like me, how quickly can I come back here?"

Julia assisted Gillian with the pale green dress. It modestly revealed a little neckline, and the short, capped sleeves did not constrict the blood flow in her upper arms like many of her dresses did of late.

"It's so plain." She stared sullenly in the mirror.

"It is simple and lovely. Goodness, Gillian, why should you be so nervous? It's Logan who should be quaking in his boots. Whatever the Raveneaus think of you is irrelevant. Or at least," Julia smiled keenly, "that is what you have said."

"I know, I know. But it does not make me feel any better at the moment. I don't know why I accepted this silly invitation."

"Because your curiosity has bested you. Admit it, child, you want to know what Logan's home and family are really like. Now, let's fix your hair and be off with you."

"Don't bother. It will only fall down as soon as we sail. I'll wear it down now. Hand me that ribbon, will you?" She motioned for the matching green satin ribbon and lifted her hair off her shoulders to tie the bow underneath her neck.

"I look like a child, but this body says otherwise." She curtsied to her image, then quickly found her bonnet and reticule to dash down the stairs to her doomed meeting with Logan's relatives.

Seated in the morning room with Helena, Logan

261

had wasted no time in explaining his intentions.

"I want her to marry me. As I've told you yesterday, Lady Marlowe, I seek to undo the wrong I've caused Gillian. I hope you have thought it over, too. You must realize that I am the right man for her. Not Paxton or anyone else." Logan sounded more like a barrister than an ardent suitor.

"I cannot force Gillian to do anything, Logan. You must understand that better than I."

"I'm only asking that you try to guide her. You haven't told me what you think, Lady Marlowe. Do you think she would be happy with anyone else? Do you agree that I should give her my name?"

"I suppose so. But, Logan," Helena looked deeply into his golden brown eyes, "I have not heard you tell me that you love my daughter. Richard has."

"If wanting someone more than anything else in the world is love, then I do love her. I also want to protect her and our child." Logan would have said more if he had not seen Gillian slowly descend the mahogany stairs.

Gillian, he thought, what a contradiction. She was intelligent but naive. She was all passion—just thinking of their rapturous moments together reminded him of his present celibacy. Yet this demure woman walking down the stairs looked as innocent as a child.

"Logan," she blurted before reaching the door, "I don't know if I can do this."

She was also honest and guileless.

"Come sweetheart." He ignored Helena's presence by choosing such an endearment. "I appreciate your cooperation. My family will adore you. They always seem to know what is good for me and enjoy conspiring against me."

"Do they ever succeed?" Dressed as casually as yesterday, in a crisp white shirt but with dark blue pants, he looked less like the London rake and more like the southern gentleman. He'd probably look just as handsome dressed as a farmer or a stablehand.

"Sometimes," he winked.

"Mother, if I am not home tonight, it will be because I chose to end my life in a convent."

"Have a wonderful day, Gillian. I am certain Logan will know how to take care of you," she blithely replied.

Logan, of course, had to do things in a different fashion. The little schooner waiting by the Ashton landing was unmanned. "I saw no reason to have someone else along for our sail. Besides, I enjoy navigation."

"Don't tell me you were once a naval officer." She accepted his hand as he effortlessly assisted her into the schooner.

"Never. Father wouldn't hear of it. And whose navy would I serve? The British or the Americans?" It was the closest he ever came to revealing his true self.

"Why, the British, of course," she answered for him. "Don't tell me you would take up arms against England?"

She looked aghast at such a notion and he decided this was not the moment to launch into a political discussion. He had already spoken too much. Thankfully Gillian was too engrossed in her nerves to realize what he had just said about loyalty.

"Gillian, let me tell you about Grandfather before we arrive. I think you would like to hear about him."

He hastily rolled up his shirtsleeves as he stood before her, dredging a long bamboo pole in and out of the Ashley River. Gillian forgot everything but the sight of his muscled arms, effortlessly guiding them up the river to Raveneau Plantation. Since he faced the sun, Logan could not see her face. It would have bolstered his confidence if he had seen the desire in her eyes and the way she absently licked her suddenly dry lips.

"Grandfather is a tough fellow, but fair. Mother and Liza were his only children, and you would think that a man who sired girls would care less for them. Not Grandfather. He taught them all he knew about planting. When that wasn't enough, he brought them to his office and taught them about shipping. Grandmother put her foot down when he began on banking." Logan's delight was evident in his wide grin and carefree laugh.

"He still runs the family and the businesses, mostly from the plantation nowadays. He'd rather spend his days near his crops, he says, than in Charleston. Likes the smells better, he says."

"He must have been devastated by your mother's death," she quietly said.

"Oh, he was. I never knew he could hurt so much. It was strange, Gillian," Logan looked at her, surprised to confess something so personal, "I thought he would die, too. Mother was buried in England. Grandfather was furious. He wanted her on this land. But it wasn't possible. Grandfather, Liza, and Uncle Joseph stayed with us at Stanton Park during Mother's illness. We knew she was dying, you see."

"It must have been awful," she whispered.

But Logan did not hear her. He was reliving the painful memories. "They left two weeks after the funeral. Grandfather swore he'd never set foot in England again. That was seventeen years ago."

Logan ducked to avoid the extended branch of a live oak tree. "We're almost there," he cheerfully changed the subject. Just as they rounded a bend in the river, the beginning of Raveneau property appeared before her. "Grandfather's passion, you can see, is gardens."

What she saw was a splendid array of colors, tall trees, blooming flowers, and, off to the side, well-manicured hedges. And this was only the beginning of the property.

"I never knew Americans lived so well."

"This is an interesting country, you know. Most Englishmen languish under the notion that America is a backward, uncivilized country. It is far from the truth."

"I admit I was one of those prejudiced Englishmen. Not anymore, Logan. I like what I have seen, although my exposure to this country has been quite limited."

"You will have other opportunities, I hope."

Wisely, she did not say that Richard had told her the very same thing. Today, she needed Logan's help. There was no need to bring up the subject of her relationship with Richard Paxton.

A number of slaves greeted their little schooner upon their arrival, but Logan impatiently waved off any assistance offered to Gillian. It was his hand that reached down for hers, gently but firmly pulling her up and out of the boat.

It was not easy for Gillian to remain graceful under the best of circumstances, but climbing out of a small schooner was no easy feat. She promptly lost her balance, falling against Logan's shoulder.

"I'm so sorry, Logan." For a few seconds her head was buried in his soft shirt.

Bending to kiss the top of her head, he could not help but chuckle. "I don't mind at all. I was hoping to carry you into the house. You have given me the reason."

To her absolute mortification, he easily lifted her into his arms and carried her up the long flower-lined path to the house.

"Logan, this is ridiculous. I don't need to be treated like a helpless child. I hope no one is looking," she mumbled into his shoulder.

"They are all looking."

Not only were they looking, they were standing in the large reception hall, smiling indulgently as Logan carried her up the stone steps, reluctantly setting her down two feet away from Henri Raveneau.

"Oh, my God," she whispered.

Logan took her hand and laughed. It was the infuriating sound of a child who delighted in allowing a sibling to take the blame for something he had done.

"Grandfather, this is Gillian, I mean Lady Gillian Marlowe," he paused meaningfully, "uh, Marston."

"Delighted, my dear." The old man bowed low, taking her shaking hand in his large one. "Don't let this rapscallion unnerve you. I was hoping to have the pleasure myself."

Gillian looked up sharply and could not be certain if Henri Raveneau was serious. Only when he coughed into a handkerchief did she realize the truth.

"You two have much in common." She smiled in return.

Deciding it was time to take charge of the situation, Liza Fenwick took Gillian's hand, insisting she freshen up in her bedroom.

"Don't worry, gentlemen, I shall bring her back immediately. You will have to think of some horror to perpetrate on our guest. Gillian," Liza led her out of the grand hallway towards the cherrywood staircase, "you must understand why it is difficult to invite guests over when both my nephew and father are present. They tend to bring out the worst in each other."

Flustered, but aware that the situation could not worsen Gillian looked bemusedly at Liza. "Is it always like this?"

"No. Only when they want to impress an important guest. Father knows that you are important to Logan. You see, Logan has never brought any woman here for us to meet."

Those remarks did not ease her nerves. "Liza,

you do plan on staying around today?" Gillian raised hopeful eyes to the only understanding person in the house.

"Of course, dear. But they are harmless."

"So is a bear until you take interest in her cub."

Liza insisted on showing Gillian about the magnificent house. There was nothing unplanned about Raveneau Plantation. Certainly not the houseplants and flowers. Every room, depending on its color scheme, had a lovely porcelain vase full of flowers from the gardens.

Each room was lovelier than the other. The large house was built in the late eighteenth century. Its style, although similar to most of the large plantation homes in the Low Country, was unique because it was one of the first great houses built on the Ashley River. Liza explained that more than twenty-five years ago a wing was added—primarily to accommodate the growing Raveneau family.

"Father wanted both families to live here. How could he know that Judith would move to England, and I, well, my husband insisted we build our own home—albeit not far from here. Logan uses the wing for himself now. Father insisted Logan be given a private entrance."

Of course, Gillian mused, Logan could come and go as he pleased. Henri Raveneau would be none the wiser, yet Gillian couldn't imagine the old man not knowing what was going on in his home.

There were, by her count, at least twelve rooms in the main house. The design was similar to the Georgian style of the other homes along the river. The house was symmetrical in appearance, the same number of rooms per floor all the same width. The rooms were large, airy, and the walls were either painted white or covered with imported French paper. Double doors abounded, and intricate wood-carved ceilings, doorways, and mantels, although subtle in appearance, attracted one's immediate attention.

Liza explained that the third floor looked almost the same, but since those were primarily the nursery rooms and there were no youngsters about, it was seldom used. Gillian looked the other way as Logan spoke about children and how empty the house seemed without the sounds of young ones.

Clearly, this was a house built out of love. According to Liza, the exterior was given a fresh coat of paint each year.

She wanted to gawk, to explore the rooms with their porcelain figurines, crystal chandeliers, imported and Charleston-made furniture, but it would have been inappropriate.

Sensing Gillian's desire to linger, Liza tactfully said, "Perhaps we can extricate ourselves from the men later. The house is lovely, and I would love showing you around."

The gentlemen were waiting in the library for Liza and Gillian. To Logan, Gillian looked a bit confused and flushed. He solicitously took her arm, leading her to the cherrywood Empire settee, then handed her a chilled glass of lemonade. The action was not lost on the occupants of the room. Henri sent Liza an "I-told-you-so look," then hurriedly looked away when Gillian complimented him on his home.

"I hope you have a chance to spend time with us. That is, if my grandson here knows how to properly court a properly bred young woman."

Looking at Logan, Gillian did not think he minded his grandfather's cutting but unerring observation. With his long legs crossed, Logan slouched in an armchair, grinning.

"You will get used to him, Gillian. He speaks like a crusty old sailor, but underneath is a heart of gold. You just have to wait a while to see my grandfather's true nature."

Luncheon was served with the minimum of formality. By the time dessert was brought, an assortment of fruit cakes, puddings, and an interesting sweetmeat that Gillian loved called "peach leather," she felt comfortable. Even Logan's humor was appealing.

It was wrong, but she felt as if she belonged to this happy group. They obviously adored Logan, and although aware of his reputation in London, seemed to forgive his many transgressions.

"My grandson is bit high-strung, Gillian — I can call you Gillian by now," he stated without waiting for her permission, "but he is a fine young man. He knows about farming, if he ever chooses to follow in my footsteps and he has a keen business sense."

"Also from you, Grandfather," Logan added cheerfully. "Gillian, I think you've heard enough about my virtues. If that sweetmeat you are eating doesn't make you ill, Grandfather's words about me will. May I show you around the gardens?"

Apparently not waiting for an answer was a

Raveneau trait. Logan was up and beside her chair in seconds offering his arm for the late-afternoon stroll. Just as Gillian stood, a small boy came running into the room and screamed the one word that struck terror in the hearts of every occupant of the room.

"Fire!"

Chapter Twenty-seven

"Where? Tell me?" Logan grabbed the boy's arm, propelling them out of the room.

"In the slave quarters!"

"How many cabins?"

"Dunno," he breathlessly said. "Theys tol me to get ya."

One second Logan was holding her arm, charmingly smiling down at her face, and the next he was out of the room running towards the back of the house, his grim face a reminder of the possible devastation.

"Father, you must stay." Liza tried to call to Henri's retreating back. Her husband was not far behind. Gillian, too, was ready to run when Liza clutched her arm.

"No, you must stay here. There is no telling the extent of the fire."

But there was. Gillian looked out of the palladian window. The once-blue sky was filling with large black spirals. The clean air that once smelled of azaleas and roses now smelled of burning wood. The sounds of birds chirping and people humming were replaced with screams.

Fear gripped her heart. Not for herself, but for him.

"Logan!" She pulled away from Liza. "I must see if he needs me. I must help. Liza, we cannot stand here and do nothing!"

Swinging about, Gillian ran out of the house, taking the steps two at a time as she raced down the freshly cut, green grassy path towards the fire. Discovering her slippers a hindrance, Gillian paused long enough to fling them aside as she ran barefoot. The pale green ribbon had been lost as soon as she left the house. She could have run faster if it weren't for her dress.

"Logan . . ." She repeated his name aloud, hoping it would bring her comfort, but it only multiplied her fear.

Everywhere she looked, people were running, some screaming, some helping the injured. A crowd gathered close to one of the cabins.

Bending over an injured child, Logan did not notice her arrival. He looked over to his left, shouting orders to three slaves. To the overseer he shouted, "Get anyone who can hold a bucket over to the well. Start the line. Hurry, man!"

Then he saw her. His face was smudged with soot and grime. His white shirt had been removed and used as a bandage for the injured.

"Get out of here, Gillian. Now! I have no time . . ."

"But I'm here to help," she shouted back and it was obvious he did not hear her, for Logan rose to run towards the sounds of the trapped, screaming horses.

"The stables have caught fire!" someone yelled.

Logan became a blur.

Henri was nowhere to be found. Praying the old man would be all right, Gillian bent down to assist the slave women with the burned victims. There was no thought to her actions, only instinctive reactions.

A little boy lay very still, afraid to moan or cry, but she knew he was in great pain. His entire left side, from scalp to knee, was blistered. Gillian put his head in her lap, uttering nonsensical but soothing words. She knew enough not to touch his raw skin or allow anyone who was unclean to touch the boy. Liza, who had finally caught up with Gillian, yelled that a doctor was on his way. So was help from neighboring plantations.

Fighting the nausea and fear, Gillian steadfastly cradled the child. She could feel the heat of the still-burning fire against her face.

At last Liza appeared by her side. "Gillian, there is nothing you can do for him now. He's in God's hands. Gillian, do you hear me?"

She knew, but could not let go. A child was dead. How many more innocent people would die? Why couldn't she help them? Her face smudged, her hair now in wild tangles around her face, Gillian lifted mournful eyes to Liza. "He was only a child. Why him? What did he do?"

A slave woman appeared out of nowhere, screaming at the sight of her dead son, railing at God for not taking her instead of her child.

"Oh, God," Gillian cried with the woman, understanding, realizing that she, too, would protect her child with her very life.

Finally, Liza was able to pull her away. "The house is safe. For now. As long as the wind remains mild, the fire can be contained."

It seemed so odd that Gillian could clearly visualize those beautiful flowers, the huge trees with Spanish moss hanging languidly to the ground. She only wanted to lose herself in Henri's English garden. Just before the terrible announcement, Logan had insisted Gillian accompany him for a private walk in his grandfather's gardens.

She had to help the Raveneaus protect their heritage. After all, it was her child's heritage, too. Shaking her head of the pristine image, she focused on the carnage around her. Somehow she prayed Logan, Henri and Joseph would get this chaos under control. Turning to Liza, she said, "I'll be fine. I want to help. Tell me what to do."

"Let's go back to the house. Dr. Phillips will need our help. He'll need clean bandages, water, ointments. We need to make room in the house for the injured."

Of course Liza was right. Gillian hurriedly turned towards the house. There was much to be done and she would not remain frozen and incoherent when so many people needed her. She would have made it up the dozen stone steps, too, until a thunderous crash halted any movement.

"What's that?" she demanded of Liza.

"I . . . I don't know," she stammered.

Looking in the direction of the calamity, both women stood open-mouthed in horror. The stable's

275

roof had collapsed. For a few seconds, there was nothing but silence, then suddenly a myriad of sounds erupted at once. More screams, human and animal. God, how would she ever be able to forget the sounds of people in agony — wagons racing across the land, shouts for assistance, lumber falling, dogs barking. And she could have sworn she heard some birds — no, that was ridiculous, she told herself. And she was about to tell Liza when Henri came running out of the carnage.

"I need bandages, *now.* And water and a litter and anything . . ." He was babbling and both women ran towards the old man, thinking he needed medical attention.

"It's Logan," he shouted. "He's hurt."

The words echoed sharply in her mind, first as a whisper, then building in crescendo until Gillian had to hold her ears.

"No!" she screamed, remembering the feeling of the dead child's head in her lap. "Not him, too."

Blindly she ran towards the wreckage, holding her dress high above her knees. What was left of the building was still smoldering. That was not what captured her attention. It was the small group of men standing solemnly around a pile of rubble.

"Logan," she whimpered, "be alive." It was one of the few moments in her life when she did not know if she should run over to the crowd or walk slowly with the clipped precision of a condemned criminal.

"Over here!" Joseph shouted to the slaves carrying the litter. "He's in there."

That was all Gillian needed to propel her reluctant legs forward. "Joseph." She grabbed his arm. "What's wrong? Where is he? Is he . . ." She could not say the word.

"He's alive. But barely conscious. The roof caved in. He's caught under that pile." Joseph pointed to the left side of the rubble.

Then she saw what she feared most. His arm. Flung outside of the smoldering wood pile. One strong muscular arm, the sleeve ripped off. There was blood, dirt, and scratches. She could not imagine what the rest of him looked like.

She wanted to vomit, but she also wanted to see him. She wanted him to know she was here.

"Logan!" she called in a surprisingly strong voice. "Can you hear me?"

His fingers moved.

"I'm here. We're going to get you out in a few minutes." Gillian bent on the filthy ground, unmindful of the group of men surrounding them. She wondered why they couldn't work faster, then saw the reason. Another dominolike pile of lumber lay precariously close to Logan. If anything or anyone should upset the layers, Logan was sure to suffocate or burn to death.

"Logan, I'm not going to leave you. Not ever. I want you to see all of us again. I want you to be with me for the birth of our child. Logan, do you hear me? Our child needs you."

If Joseph, Henri, or Liza heard, they did not seem surprised by her clearly spoken words. For what seemed like hours, she knelt on the ground, touching, stroking his hand, talking to a now-wet pile of wood. Blessedly the fire was out. Looking

277

wildly around the plantation, Gillian noticed that the fire was out there, too. Just smoke. The kind that robbed breath from one's lungs, permeated everything and anything that ever smelled sweet and fresh. The smell that as long as she lived Gillian could never forget and would always fear.

As the lumber pile methodically diminished, more of Logan was revealed. His legs were trapped but mercifully the top of his head appeared. At last she saw his face, what she could see of it. His gold hair was black with grime and blood, his shirt almost ripped from his upper torso. And his beautiful eyes were tightly closed against what could only be tremendous pain.

"Logan," she shouted above the din. "You are going to be fine," she lied. "I know it. We will see to it." She wanted to crawl on top of the pile and cradle his head, but was afraid she'd bring on more agony if any bones were broken. His left arm was folded in a peculiar angle. Gillian did not have to be a physician to know the diagnosis. It was, she dimly recalled, the same arm that he said had been broken in his accident in Europe.

At long last, his legs were freed. They did not appear mangled. Perhaps, she thought, that was a good sign.

As he was carefully lifted out of the rubble, under the supervision of Dr. Phillips, Gillian cringed when she heard his anguished cry. She could not help herself as she ran to the bushes and emptied her stomach. Seeing Logan in pain was more than she could bear. Yet she had to be near him, she had to hold his good hand. She had to hold his head and tell him how much she wanted him to live for her and their child.

It looked like a bedraggled funeral procession that inched its way along the graveled path to the house. On Liza's orders, the guestroom on the first floor had been cleared for the patient.

When Dr. Phillips ordered everyone out of the room, she wanted to cry in protest, but Henri took her shoulders and compassionately said, "He'll need you later. Let's get you cleaned up. Rest a while. Then come back and stay at his side."

Looking up into his weary, lined face, she reacted on impulse, flinging herself into his arms. "I don't want him to be hurt. I never wanted . . . I only want him to be laughing again." She sobbed and hiccuped. "I want him to know . . ."

"Please, child." He patted her tangled hair. "He'll get well. I swear it. But you and my great-grandson must stay strong and healthy. Go on . . ." He led Gillian into Liza's hands, kissing her cheek.

Exhaustion finally claimed her remaining strength and Gillian collapsed onto the high, canopied bed, unmindful of her filthy state.

"Here," Liza handed her a cool glass of water, "let me help you."

Gillian could not speak as Liza and a maid assisted her out of the soiled clothes, washing her face and hands. Aware of nothing but Logan lying or possibly dying in bed, Gillian protested again that she must be with him.

"Just rest for a few minutes. That's all I ask." Liza's voice sounded far away. Once Gillian was asleep, Liza instructed the maid to stay while she fought off her own exhaustion to be with the men downstairs.

It was a restless sleep filled with images and smells. Tossing and moaning, Gillian could not forget the faces of the dead boy in her arms or Logan's so contorted by pain. She must have screamed, for a soothing hand and voice patted her head, telling her everything would be fine. She even heard a light, lilting song, which lulled her into a deep sleep.

Hours or minutes later, she heard loud voices. She could hear Logan's voice, she swore. She could hear his laughter. He was running up the stairs to take her into his arms, to tell her that this had only been a terrible nightmare.

She wouldn't wait for him to tell her that he loved her. She wouldn't wait for him to ask her again to marry him. No, Gillian would rush off the bed, into his arms. She would run her hands through his hair, kiss his eyelids, and every inch of his beautiful face.

"I love you, Logan. I want to be your wife. I want to be with you, always."

And he would laugh and kiss her face and wipe away her tears, telling her how much he wanted to make love to her. And how much he loved her. They would fall onto the bed together, and she would feel his strong hands, both hands, run riot over her body, exploring her as if for the first time. Then he would kiss her, and it would be a wondrous kiss. They'd laugh together, amazed at how happy they could feel with each other.

"No!" A loud painful shriek pierced her numb

280

mind. "No!" There it was again, coming from downstairs. She suddenly bolted upright in bed. It was no dream. The nightmare was real and she was still living it.

Chapter Twenty-eight

Within three heartbeats Gillian was running down the long staircase adjusting whatever she had thrown over her head.

"Gillian!"

As soon as she heard his anguished cry for her, Gillian began sobbing. "I'm here, I'm coming," she yelled.

Once inside the room, Gillian was terrified by the sight that greeted her. Logan, thrashing about in the bed in the throes of some private, pain-racked agony; Henri, the doctor, and Joseph stand-ing around the bed, trying in vain to keep him still.

"He'll injure himself further if we can't keep him still," Dr. Phillips warned.

"Dammit, help me!" Logan shouted to no one. "The fire!"

She shoved Joseph aside and leaned on the bed. "Logan," her voice was much firmer than her nerves, "Logan, darling. I want you to listen. Can you listen?" Not knowing which part of his body did not hurt, she gently smoothed the hair off his bandaged forehead. "Logan, you are safe. You are in your home. We are all here. You need to rest, sweetheart. Just rest. Everything will be fine," she crooned. "I promise."

"The babe?" he croaked.

"Here, feel your child." She struggled to the other side of the bed, took his right hand, and placed it over her stomach. "Can you feel him?" A slight thump responded to his touch. "See?" She smiled through the blur of tears. "We're both fine, but we need *you,* Logan."

He quieted almost immediately after hearing her voice.

The doctor handed her a glass. "Get him to drink this, it's laudanum."

Leaning over his prone, battered body, she looked up at the doctor waiting for the nod of approval before lifting Logan's head. "Logan, love. This will ease the pain. Please, darling, drink this. Let me help you."

Like an obedient child, Logan followed her instructions. Seconds before he eased into a deep, hopefully painless sleep, she thought she saw the formation of a tiny smile.

Still sitting on the bed, next to him but not too close to jostle him, Gillian kept his hand in hers. "I want to stay with him." She looked at the doctor, daring him to deny her wish.

"Of course you will," Henri answered. "I've already sent a message to your family at Ashton Hall. They're sending some clothes."

It suddenly occurred to her that she had no idea what time of day it was. Looking around the room, the ornate gold-and-lapis French mantel

283

clock silently ticked. It was past 10 P.M. Her mother would have been frantic if Henri hadn't thought to contact Helena.

"I forgot" was all she said. Logan sighed deeply. Lovingly she stroked his forehead. "Tell me, how bad are his injuries."

Henri was afraid to catalogue all of them, but realized she was no fool. Gillian was the only one who could keep his grandson calm. She would have to know how to nurse him. Nodding to the doctor, Henri moved to Gillian's side and placed a reassuring hand on her shoulder.

Dr. Phillips cleared his throat. "At the moment, the most serious injury is the one to his head. Normally, we keep a patient awake, but it wasn't possible in this case. Logan was in too much pain. We have to wait. The next day or two is crucial. If he falls into a deep coma, there is no telling how long it could last and if there is permanent damage to the brain."

She swallowed the rising bile. "Go on."

"His arm is broken again. In almost the exact spot as his previous injury from what I can see. I," Dr. Phillips shrugged his shoulders, "I cannot guarantee he will have full mobility of his arm. Then there are the burns to his chest and legs. I think we cleaned them as best as we could. I don't think there will be any infection. But they are painful. The bandages need to be cleaned twice a day. The skin needs air. But only if Logan cooperates."

"He'll cooperate." Gillian touched his good arm. "I'll make him cooperate."

Henri grinned. He hadn't needed further reassur-

284

ance that this was the woman for his grandson.

"I want to look at you, Lady Marston. It's been a difficult day for you and the babe."

"I feel fine, truly."

No one else seemed convinced. Liza ushered the men out of the room so Dr. Phillips could quickly examine Gillian. "For someone as thin as you appear, you seem to be quite strong and that child as resilient as his parents." Gillian forgot to blush at the reminder of her unwedded state. Nothing mattered any longer except Logan.

"If you insist on staying with Logan, you must get fresh air and, above all, rest and food. Is that understood?"

She looked at the elderly doctor and smiled. "Thank you for saving his life."

"I'll be back tomorrow morning to check on both of you."

Only much later did she leave the room to change her clothes and share a light meal with the family. It was then that she learned the extent of the damage to the plantation.

"At least six cabins were destroyed. And you know about the stables. Four people died." She remembered the face of the little boy. "They were buried earlier." Henri was not a man devoid of emotion. He had to clear his throat more than once while he spoke.

"We lost some horses, too. But we are going to rebuild everything. We start tomorrow." Joseph Fenwick tried to brighten the somber mood. "At least we can rebuild."

Insisting that she had to sleep in Logan's room,

Gillian relented when Liza insisted a bed be moved into the room for her. "No cot for you."

It was near dawn when Gillian finally fell asleep. She didn't know how long she had stood over his bed, staring at the man whom she prayed she would see laugh again. He was so damn still that it terrified her to think of the consequences of a prolonged illness. Logan never awaken? That was preposterous, she told herself over and over. He'd fight this. He'd live.

Through the long night, she sat by his side, telling him how much she loved him, then telling him nonsense. She needed the reassurance of his hand in hers. Curling up beside him on the bed, Gillian was tempted to sleep as close to him as possible. That, she rationally realized, would not help Logan.

As the sky began to brighten, she heard the morning call of the birds who delighted in the beginning of a new day. Would this be a new day for Logan? Or would he never know a sunrise again? Tempting fate, she silently opened the shutters. Perhaps Logan could feel the sun's brightness on his face.

Trained now for every sound or movement he made, Gillian was delighted when he stirred. But after ten long minutes when nothing else happened, she decided she must have been imagining things and reluctantly settled into her bed. Her last thoughts were the silent prayers she sent to God. "Let him live."

It was the sound of clinking glass that awakened her. Wanting to forget the previous events, Gillian tried in vain to go back to sleep. But she had to look at Logan. She had to see if he was still breathing. As long as he breathed, Gillian would hope.

Sweeping the tangled hair from her eyes, Gillian sat up to discover Henri standing over his prone grandson.

"I did not mean to disturb you, Gillian," he began, having long ago abandoned the formalities of titles. "I wanted to see him."

"I know," she rose to stand alongside Henri, "I had to see if he was breathing, too."

"He's my life," the old man whispered brokenly.

It must have cost him dearly to crumble in front of Gillian. "Mine too." She took his arm. "I pray I have the chance to tell him."

They stood that way for a long while. When Liza walked into the room, she froze, dare she disturb the touching scene before her. Henri's arm was wrapped around Gillian's thin shoulders, her head leaning on his shoulder. Dressed in borrowed night clothes, with long hair streaming down her back, she looked like a little girl, not the pregnant woman who was carrying her nephew's child.

Henri must have known Liza was near, for he bade her to come forward and not hang about like an errant child. "We've got to get some food into this girl. I don't like feeling her bones."

The only way the Raveneaus could get Gillian to leave the room was to threaten her. She had to eat, bathe, and maintain her strength. When Logan awakened, he was going to be an impossible patient, and she would need every ounce of energy, they warned.

By the time tea was served, it was obvious that Logan was not emerging from his deep sleep, and Gillian agreed to accompany Henri on a stroll around the gardens. Since her clothes had arrived earlier, she had run out of excuses for remaining inside the house.

In deference to Logan's condition, there was little activity near the house. They silently walked out the river entrance, down the grassy path that followed the Ashley River. Henri's garden, separated from the rest of the beautiful fauna by hedges and a gate, was a glorious refuge. They walked towards a stone bench facing the river.

"Careful of those 'cypress knees,' " he warned.

"These?" she pointed to the huge roots that jutted out of the ground.

"Interesting, aren't they," he smiled.

"I've never seen anything like this before. In fact," she sat on the bench, "I've never seen such beauty."

"It's more lush in the summer." He tilted back the brim of his white straw hat. His crisp white jacket and trousers gave the impression that this was a man who never got near the soil. One had to look closely to see the dirt under his fingernails and the telltale green smudge on one knee.

Gillian could not imagine anything more beautiful than these winding paths, perfectly manicured hedges, the profusion of spring flowers. It was all carefully, lovingly arranged.

"I never appreciated gardening."

"This is an art. I'll teach you."

288

"You are far too kind to me as it is," she said, alluding to the topic that had to be discussed.

"Logan told me all, you know."

She nodded. "Certainly whatever he didn't say before yesterday, I must have announced to everyone within five miles."

"You'll marry." It wasn't a question.

"I won't leave him again."

"You're good for him." Henri handed her a plucked rose.

"You don't know me."

"I do. I also know my grandson. I think fatherhood will stabilize him."

Staring out at a passing barge, Gillian wondered if there was any point to this discussion.

"He's strong."

She laughed. "If he's anything like you, sir, I have nothing to fear."

"I want the child born on Raveneau land." Henri busied himself pruning an azalea bush. "I'd prefer this house, but if you must reside in Charleston I'll understand. When is the babe arriving?"

She couldn't catch her breath quickly enough to answer any of his statements and questions. "March. Goodness, I haven't given much thought to my reputation."

"Harrumph, such nonsense. Who gives a damn? I'd kill anyone who dared slander my great-grandson or his family."

She looked at his reddened face. "I believe you would. Yet I have my family's name to protect as well."

"Leave it to me. By the time Logan is up and

about, you will be married, the child will have its rightful name, and no one will think about your 'dead husband.' By then some other drivel will take up everyone's time. You'll be forgotten."

It sounded so simple. Aware of society's rules and scandals, Gillian had little doubt that the rumors swirling over her head about the true parentage of her child would die down. Eventually. It was true that scandal was superceded by a more glorious scandal.

"I see that skeptical brow, missy, and I do not like it. I give you my word as a gentleman. No one will every breathe a false word about the Raveneaus."

Settling into a more lighthearted discussion about planting while continuing their late-afternoon stroll, the two did not notice the arrival of a large boat.

Gillian and Henri were nearing the main entrance to the house when they realized that Liza's stiff posture in the doorway boded ill.

"What is it?" Gillian was alarmed as she ran up the steps with Henri not far behind. "What is wrong with Logan?"

"He's the same, I'm afraid. That's not our problem."

Henri noticed the word 'our' and immediately looked farther into the main hallway. "Who is here?"

"We have guests, Father. Gillian," Liza nodded to Gillian's casual attire, "perhaps you would like to freshen up before joining us for tea."

"Is it Mother?"

"I wish it were," she mumbled under her breath and could say no more when the unmistakable sounds of another female voice filled the hall. "It's Eve Carlton."

Chapter Twenty-nine

"I simply had to see how Logan was doing. Why, hello, Lady Marston. You are still using that name, are you not?" Eve Carlton, cooly dressed in white muslin, sauntered up to Gillian, as if she were the mistress of Raveneau Plantation.

Thinking it best not to answer, lest she scratch out the woman's dark eyes, Gillian bestowed Eve with her haughtiest look.

"Gillian is our guest, Eve." Liza wisely stepped between the two adversaries.

"I find that odd, considering she is almost betrothed to Captain Paxton. Unless, of course, it is true that the bastard she is carrying is Logan's. Is it?" she purred.

This time Gillian forgot about restraint and decorum and almost lunged at Eve's smug face. "You seem to know so much about all the men in Charleston, dear. I gather you speak from experience." And before Eve had a chance to close her mouth, Gillian sweetly smiled at Henri who stood silently watching the scene unfold. "I am somewhat fatigued. If you don't mind, I would like to go up to *my*," she emphasized the word, "room."

Almost completely up the stairs, Gillian's back

stiffened when Eve's unmistakable words rose to her. "I never doubted for a minute that she was a harlot. I wonder if the child really is Logan's or is she only trying to force him to marry her. *That* would be the only way she could snare a man like Logan."

She made it up the stairs and out of everyone's line of vision before she ran into her room and threw herself on the bed. "That bitch." She pounded the pillow before dissolving into tears.

An hour had passed before a soft knock awakened Gillian.

Liza entered the room carrying a pitcher of cold lemonade. "Thought you could use some sustenance."

"I'd rather have Madeira. But I don't think the baby cares for it." She tried to smile, but Liza was not blind to the red-rimmed puffy eyes.

"She's gone."

"Probably gone to tell everyone in the Low Country about me. As if I didn't have enough heartache I have to worry about the scandal that little tramp will spread about me." Gillian struggled to sit up. "How is Logan?"

"The same, I'm afraid. Eve wanted to see him, but Father was adamant. He almost threw her out of the house after her nasty comment."

"Someone should throw her in the river," she sniffed.

"Well, I think Father would be the first candidate and Logan a close second."

"Liza," Gillian put the cool glass to her flushed cheeks, "I know this is none of my business, but,

293

well, did Eve and Logan . . ." She could not finish the sentence. Richard had told her they were once lovers, but Gillian wanted to know if Logan ever considered marrying her.

"I think they were once involved, if that is what you mean. That was many years ago, and to my knowledge Logan never gave her any reason to think he was considering marriage."

"Oh." She stared at the bruised pillow.

"Logan, well, you understand. He's cut quite a wide path with the ladies on this side of the ocean, too."

"Has anyone, well, I mean has any woman ever claimed he was the father of her child?"

"Once. But it was so obviously untrue. Logan had been away for months before she claimed she was pregnant. And when he returned he swore he hadn't been with her for six months." Liza sat on the bed next to Gillian. "My nephew is a lot of things, but I've never known him to be a liar or a man who shirks his responsibilities."

Gillian snorted.

"Besides, you only have to ask his grandfather to know the truth. He knows more about Logan than he cares to tell any one of us. Sometimes I think he's had Logan followed."

"Henri loves him and must make excuses for him."

"You should know my father better than that. Logan would have been disinherited long ago if Father believed he was a ne'er-do-well."

"It's really none of my business." Gillian thought it best to change the subject. It was too painful to think of Logan's past and all the women in it. For all she knew, she was probably just another one in the long list of fools who have fallen hopelessly in love with Lord Hammond.

"Father told Eve something else before he suggested she leave early."

"Oh?" Gillian wished she could have heard Henri's cutting remarks.

"Yes, he told Eve that Logan intended to marry you all along, that Logan followed you to Charleston from London." Liza's golden eyes sparkled. "He told Liza that you and Logan were to be married the day of the accident. Logan's last conscious wish was that the minister be here to marry you two the moment he's awake."

"She believed that?" Gillian gasped.

"Every word. I thought I saw her sniff into her lace hanky as she hurried off. She left soon after that, you see." Liza laughed. "Eve said she had forgotten an appointment."

Gillian burst into a combination of laughter and tears. "Wait until Logan hears this, if he ever awakens. He'll want to throttle your father and me for putting him up to such tricks."

Liza waved her hand. "Again you're wrong, dear. I know Logan wants to marry you. He announced his intentions to the family."

"When . . . how?"

"It seems so long ago, but it was yesterday. Right after your arrival, I escorted you upstairs. He told Joseph and Father while we were gone."

"There is no point in discussing this now." Gillian abruptly stood up. "He may not live to make

295

an honest woman out of me." She burst into a fresh round of tears and soundly cursed herself for being so weak. "No matter what, Liza, I am not leaving until I know he is well."

After four more days with no sign of improvement in Logan, Gillian was near collapse and despair. He remained in a coma. Broth and other liquids were force-fed into him. Usually Gillian held his head while Liza patiently eased the drops into his slack mouth.

Each morning, Henri insisted Logan be freshly shaved and someone be with him all the time. It was Gillian who decided to talk to him about anything, including her upbringing in Suffolk. When she grew tired of her ramblings, she read to him.

Since Gillian spent the nights in his room, the early morning was her time to collapse in her own room. She'd often fall into a deep, dreamless sleep until noon. She'd return to Logan's bedside in the early afternoon, then walk in the gardens with Henri before dinner.

She liked the old man. He was strong, and although often cantankerous, he was a good man and devoted to his family. Helena Marlowe arrived on the third day of Logan's illness. Armed with fresh clothes, toiletries, and letters from home, she accepted the Raveneaus' invitation to stay at the plantation with her daughter.

"I'm worried about her," she confided to Liza one night. "I know she is strong, but if anything should happen to Logan now," she shrugged, "I don't know how much more stress she and the baby can take."

"I know. She won't leave him, though. And it's better for her to be here rather than someplace else. She thinks Logan can hear her voice."

"I know. She swears she saw him smile this morning."

The two families seemed to become one as the days slowly passed. Helena and Liza became instant friends. Even Cousin Julia visited a few times.

As soon as the news spread about the fire and Logan's accident, a number of people paid visits. Some were genuinely concerned. Others, like the gossips, wanted to know if Logan Hammond was going to die. It was hard for Gillian to smile and pretend not to notice the curious stares people gave her. Why, they wondered, did she have a special place in this house. Apparently Eve Carlton had not spread her malicious gossip yet.

On day five, Gillian felt Logan squeeze her hand. Although weak, she did not imagine his fingers curling around her palm. She giggled, kissed his cool forehead, and restrained herself from throwing herself into his good arm.

Dr. Phillips was skeptical at first, but witnessed the very same thing later on that day.

"It's a good sign," he pronounced to the expectant faces before him.

The cherrywood grandfather clock in the hallway chimed four. Even in her half-asleep state, Gillian listened to and came to welcome the distant chimes, for it meant another hour that Logan lived.

She found sitting on the windowseat more comfortable than lying in bed. The baby kicked more than once. Rubbing her hand in circular motion around her stomach, she began to croon a long forgotten lullaby.

"It's beautiful," a voice croaked.

"Oh, thank God," she cried, abandoning her seat and rushing to the bed. "I better not be dreaming."

"You're not."

Leaning over him, Gillian's copious tears made it difficult for her to see his still-handsome, albeit withdrawn face. "You've given us all a terrible fright." She stroked his head in a gesture now familiar to both of them. "I must tell your family." She started to rise, but Logan's hand stayed her. "No, wait. I want to know if I've been dreaming about your presence." His breaths were labored.

Gillian handed him a glass of water, holding his head as he sipped. "I've been here." She was suddenly embarrassed to tell him about her vigils.

"It was your voice I heard." He was pleased with himself.

"You've been a model patient thus far."

"I've been unconscious. What day is it?"

"Thursday, the twenty-third of December." She couldn't stop smiling. "Let me light the candles. I want to get a good look at you." He was pale and probably still in pain, yet his eyes were clear and his boyish smile reminded her of happier days together.

"How's the babe?"

"Couldn't be better."

"You look tired. I don't like those circles under your eyes."

"You have the same circles. How's your head?"

"Hurts like hell. And my arm, well . . . Gillian?" His eyes became heavy and he felt a sudden wave of fatigue.

"Yes, love?"

"Are you going to marry me?"

"Absolutely." She kissed his cheek.

Logan was sound asleep before she could say more. But what did it matter? He was alive. He wanted to marry her and she would not be foolish enough to deny herself her most fervent wish—to be with the only man she could ever love.

The household was awakened by her shouts. "He's going to be fine. I know it. He spoke to me and smiled." Oblivious to her state of undress and that of everyone else, Gillian related most of their conversation.

She did not want to sleep yet, but knowing that he would awaken in the morning, she wanted to feel refreshed. Henri insisted that he remain in the room with Logan, shooing Gillian into her own room.

It was late morning by the time Gillian bounded down the stairs, dressed in bright pink, heading straight for Logan's room.

She nearly fainted when she found the room empty, the windows wide open, and all traces of a sick man's chamber gone. In her panic she ran past Liza, screaming Logan's name. "It wasn't a dream. He's better."

"Of course he is." Liza caught up with Gillian. "But you know Logan. He was wide-awake by dawn, insisting he be brought to his own rooms in the adjoining wing. He wanted a bath, too, but finally agreed to Father's demands that he wait until Dr. Phillips's arrival. The doctor has come and gone. He's fine, Gillian. Except for some headaches and an immobile arm, he'll be fine."

"He's upstairs?" she stupidly asked.

"Probably strapped to the bed if I know Logan and my father." Liza's smile faded.

"What is it?" Gillian recognized something was not all right.

"Well, it's Logan's arm. Dr. Phillips thinks it will take a long time to heal. Logan doesn't know that yet. And . . ."

"And what?" she demanded.

"The doctor is not certain Logan will gain full mobility."

It was not good news, but Gillian did not want to think about problems. Not yet. Not when it was time to celebrate life.

"Dr. Phillips said that already. Don't fret, Liza. Logan will defy the odds and regain all his strength. I know it."

Liza did not want to cause further alarm. Temporarily setting her fears aside, she ushered Gillian into the dining room for breakfast.

"You will have to look your finest today, my dear."

"I beg you pardon?" She swallowed the cocoa, but stared at Liza's peculiar smile. "Is there something wrong with my appearance?" She looked down at her attire, which was in the latest fashion.

"Oh, no. Logan insisted we invite a guest to stay the night."

Praying it wasn't some young beautiful and thin woman, she hesitated before asking, "Who?"

"Reverend Peters. He'll be here this afternoon. According to Logan, the wedding will be tonight."

Chapter Thirty

Having decided that it was best not to interfere with Logan's wishes, Gillian spent most of the afternoon preparing for the event of her life.

It wasn't her idea of a romantic wedding ceremony. Against his wishes, for Logan wanted to walk, he was carried across the hall and placed in the music room. It was a cheery room, made more so by the mirrors and white lace curtains with which Liza and Helena had quickly decorated it. Flowers from Henri's gardens filled the room, hyacinths, lilacs, wisteria, and even out-of-season magnolias were produced to add a variety of color.

To make everything appear brighter, Liza used "illuminators" or crystal bowls filled with water with lit candles behind them. The light reflected off the mirrors creating a radiance that was unmatched by the largest crystal chandeliers.

Gillian almost panicked when she scoured through her meager dress collection. She decided there was nothing appropriate for a pregnant woman to wear to her first wedding. Helena persuaded her to wear the peach-and-lace dress.

"This is ridiculous," she announced. Her hair was swept up into a dozen curls. Liza produced a

302

magnificent diamond choker and diamond studs that were threaded through her hair.

"You look like a princess," Liza sighed.

"I doubt that." Gillian's gaze was riveted on her stomach.

A bouquet of fresh-cut camellias was presented. Deciding to hold them over her belly, she slowly sauntered out of her room to Logan. It was Logan she wanted to see, and *Logan,* standing tall, proud, and miraculously fit, smiled in welcome at his bride. She forgot to be nervous when he extended his right hand for hers.

Considering his health, he looked refreshed in dark blue trousers, maroon jacket, and a white linen shirt with an expertly tied cravat that would have made old Beau Brummel proud. His only concession to the warm weather was a pair of shiny black shoes instead of his Hessian boots.

His left arm remained confined in a awkward-looking splint. The thick head bandage had been removed earlier in the morning. There was a deep gash in his forehead, but it did not detract from his physical presence. Afraid that everyone could read the burst of desire in her hazel eyes, Gillian had to quickly lower her gaze. Logan seemed to know, for his grin widened, and when she looked up, he winked!

Reverend Peters stood by the open window. A telltale breeze from the Ashley River fluttered against the curtains. Gillian waited expectantly for the words that would forever bind her to the man by her side. After so much pain and worry, she marveled at the overwhelming happiness that threatened to make her giggle and cry.

Lost in her private world of bliss, she did not notice when the minister turned to address her. "Do you, Gillian Marlowe Marston, take Logan Raveneau Hammond . . ."

"It's Gillian Marlowe, not Marston," she supplied, suddenly fearful that the marriage would not be legal if the minister used her phony name.

The man looked surprised, but merely adjusted his spectacles when Logan instructed him to continue the service.

A ring was produced. "It was my grandmother's," Logan whispered.

Turning to Henri, she smiled her thanks. It was a noble and generous gesture, one that would forever endear the old man to her heart.

"I shall cherish it," she quietly replied. Lifting her dewy eyes to his, she waited until the minister pronounced them man and wife. Logan's right arm snaked around her waist and he kissed her deeply. "I have dreamt of kissing you thus and much more," he huskily whispered against her mouth. "So much more."

Someone cleared a throat and Joseph clapped. The ladies dabbed hankies on their eyes.

"Damn, but I'm going to cry again." Gillian could not control the desire to weep.

"Be my guest, Mrs. Hammond. Here, use mine." He handed her a red silk handkerchief.

"Oh, Logan, I am so happy."

"We shall be a family. It's what I've wanted for so long."

It wasn't until much later, when they were finally undressing and alone in Logan's huge bedsuite in the other wing, that Gillian realized she hadn't told him of her love. Nor did he tell her of his.

Did he love her? she wondered. Or did he want to ensure that his child not be branded a bastard?

The question gnawed at her until Logan finally noticed the way she was fidgeting with a crystal goblet and spoke up.

"Are you upset about something?" Then he said the most obvious thing that came to his mind, given his state of physical abstinence. "Are you concerned that Dr. Phillips said our marriage could not be consummated?" He was sitting in a large white sofa by the side of the bed.

"No." She decided to pace across the room.

"I asked him about you."

"Asked him what?" she asked distractedly.

"I asked him if it were safe for the baby if we make love." Logan was his usual forthright self.

"I know. I asked him, too."

"Are you suddenly feeling a little modest? That's a bit silly under the circumstances. Don't you agree? Gillian, will you please stop wearing tracks in the carpet and come over here? I'd like to join you, but for once in my life I fear you would exhaust me. And I want to save my strength." He suggestively reminded her of his agenda.

"I haven't finished undressing."

"I can see that, and neither have I. Now, come here," he commanded impatiently.

When she did, he put his good arm around her stiff shoulders, began to nuzzle her bare neck, and

305

seeing no response, he asked her again why she was upset.

"Logan Hammond, are you truly happy we are wed?"

What a stupid question, and he was about to say as much when he noticed the determined look on her face. Deciding it was another of her notions induced by the pregnancy, he answered, "Of course. Aren't you?"

"Yes, but I had a specific reason for marrying you."

"I am pleased to hear it," he chuckled. "So did I."

"Was it to give the baby the Hammond name?"

"Yes."

She was up and almost heading out the door when he yelled for her to stop. "Gillian, you are not exactly fully clothed. The chemise is lovely but not the rage at the dining room table. Will you tell me what you want?"

"What I want? What do you think? I want to know if you love me. You've never said it. Not since the day we became betrothed in London. I've never heard you tell me anything about your feelings, other than your physical desire."

The words came out so fast, he thought she would burst. Restraining himself from shaking her around that slender but silly neck, Logan ordered her to sit down.

"You don't know me very well, do you? Perhaps it's my fault. You've obviously accepted all those ridiculous rumors you've heard about me in London and here. If you really knew me, Gillian, you

would now that I want you as my wife first, then
as the mother of my child. I want to spend days
with you in this bed," he gestured to the mammoth mahogany four-poster in the center of the
room. "I want to be with you when the baby arrives. I want to hold you in my arms and shield
you from all the pain in this world."

Her head fell on his shoulder.

"Is that love? Tell me?" he asked gently.

"Yes."

"Then I love you."

"Oh, Logan," she sobbed. "I love you more than
anything. I want us to feel the same things, to
share the same thoughts. I want to be by your side
forever."

"To my knowledge you are still betrothed to another," he grimly reminded her.

"Oh, Richard."

"Yes, you do remember your other fiancée?"

"My God! I have some explaining to do. But
another time, Logan." She looked up into his
amused face. "I want to hear you tell me you love
me again and again."

"I want to tell you, and with your permission,
and uh," he tried to move his left arm, "assistance, I'd like to show you."

They remained on the white sofa. For the moment, Logan wanted nothing more than to kiss her
ripe lips. He heard her surrender when she sighed
into his mouth and ran her fingers through his
hair. He had thought of this moment often. Now
she was in his arms and she was his — forever.

Over the white silk chemise, his hand found her

full breasts and he gently fondled them. "Please tell me if I am hurting you or the baby. I want you so badly, I don't know if I can resist taking you right here on the sofa." His breath was warm in her ear.

"Logan? Just keep kissing me, if you can, that is. And hold me. For so long I've thought of being held in your arms—I mean arm."

"Did you dream of me?" He nuzzled a path between her delicate ear and her slender neck.

"Too much." Taking a bold step, she moved a little out of his embrace to watch his face as she slowly unbuttoned his shirt. "I think you might like some assistance."

"As long as you're removing my clothes, you can assist me anytime. Oh, Gillian, that feels so good." Her hand was inside his shirt fanning his chest and lightly pinching his nipples.

His good hand continued a restrained but leisurely exploration of her breasts, then lowered to her exposed thighs. "You have such long legs. I can't tell you now about the dream I had about those legs. I fear we could not duplicate it until well after the child's birth."

Gillian knew he was experiencing pain from his arm. He was also trying very hard to maintain control of his desire. He was doing this for her, and she loved him all the more.

"Let me take this off." She reached for the chemise.

"What makes you think I cannot?" His wicked smile made her heart thump. Somehow he neatly and efficiently managed to remove the garment with his right hand, tossing it to the floor. "I like you better naked."

This was the first time he would see her un-clothed pregnant body. "I'm not such a pretty sight."

"Said who?" His eyes rounded in wonder at her beautifully rounded tummy. "I think you're exqui-site. I want to kiss our child. May I?" He knelt before her, his hand resting lightly on her knees, while he trailed tiny kisses along her stomach.

The tender gesture threatened to undo her, but then his hand began another journey. Modesty soon became an afterthought. How long had she wanted Logan to touch her there? So soft, so ex-pert in fanning the flames of passion. She was moist and ready for him, but still he continued to torture her when his mouth replaced his hand. "You taste sweet," he murmured as he stole a glance upward.

Her head was thrown back against the sofa. Her eyes were closed in rapture and her mouth opened to emit tiny moans that became loud as his tongue teased and stroked her inner flesh.

Only when the intensity of her release lessened, did Logan stand up, suggesting they continue their mutual exploration on the large bed.

He moved to lift her and Gillian came to her senses long enough to realize that was not possi-ble. "Come here," she offered her hand, "I'll lead you."

Climbing up the two steps to the bed, she in-sisted he stand before her. Kneeling on her haunches, she placed her arms around his neck and kissed his moist mouth. She tasted herself and found it erotic to share so much of herself with him. "Now it's my turn," she whispered.

Before he could utter a sound, Gillian's hands were quickly unbuttoning his trousers. Guiding them down over his taut buttocks, she let him step out of them while her eyes focused on his proud member. "I want to taste you." Her tongue circled around the tip, but it was not enough for him. Logan thrust himself into her mouth and groaned aloud when she began a rhythm of her own.

His hand locked on her head, while he allowed her to lead him to a new level of bliss. "I can't wait," he moaned.

"Don't. Logan, I want all of you. Let me taste you."

And she did. It intensified his pleasure just knowing she wanted to give him the ultimate satisfaction.

"You are a vixen, my lovely wife. I wonder how many other pleasures we can invent."

"Once I get bigger, we'll have to become very creative."

He lay beside her on the bed. She was naked and he had yet to remove his shirt. "This is unfair," she removed the garment, flinging it off the bed, "although I think it will fit me perfectly."

For five minutes they snuggled, at her request, before he again sought her mouth with his own. "I don't think I can get enough of you tonight. I wonder how long we can remain thus."

"Only until your child tells me it's time for food." She leaned over him. Feeling wondrously free and wicked, and slowly removed the diamond pins from her hair.

"Oh, no. I know what you're going to do and I want to be the one to do it." Unpinning the last two pins, his golden eyes darkened as her hair slowly uncoiled down her neck, over her shoulders, and into his face.

"Gillian, you're beautiful. I am amazed that pregnancy can make an already beautiful woman more enchanting."

"If that's your way of telling me you want dozens of children, darling, I beg to differ." But she was smiling despite her words.

"You know, I've never paid much attention to pregnant women before."

"And I've never paid any attention to babies or children. I think we're both in for some surprises."

"You did the right thing." Captivated by the long, thick red-gold curls, he playfully moved some strands around her breasts.

"I did? What was that?"

"Marrying me. I will take care of you." He glanced up to her radiant face.

"Just love me, Logan." She nearly fell on top of him to wrap him in a fierce hug.

"I will. I swear I will." Finding words a sudden chore, he decided to show her.

Chapter Thirty-one

Marriage, Gillian decided, was wonderful. After almost one month of wedded bliss, Gillian was more in love with Logan than ever before. His recuperation was much swifter than Dr. Phillips initially thought and by the first week of January, Logan was able to walk about the plantation without tiring.

The Christmas and New Year celebrations were particularly joyous, but remained private family affairs. Logan did not feel like entertaining the well-wishers and gossips, and Gillian had no desire to be the object of the malicious slander that Eve had undoubtedly been spreading. Liza had already heard some of those rumors just this afternoon while attending tea at a neighboring plantation.

"Never married," they had whispered.

"The child's Logan's. He'll never marry her. Richard Paxton wouldn't consider a woman breeding another's bastard."

Liza had heard plenty but waited for the most propitious moment to make her announcement. With Eve Carlton seated by her side, Liza watched Eve's complacent expression as she cheerfully called for everyone's attention.

"My nephew is going to be fine. Thank you all for asking. His recovery is rapid, and with his new wife by his side, I see no reason why they cannot move to Charleston within the month."

"Wife?" Eve stammered. "Don't tell me." She had looked horrified.

"Why, yes, of course, dear. What did you think?" Liza had looked at the open-mouthed stares, reveling in the new gossip she would undoubtedly create.

"Logan followed Gillian to Charleston. It's a long and very complicated story—I wouldn't want to bore you all with the details. But Logan and Gillian were betrothed in London and became separated. She left for Charleston, unaware of his family connection. But as soon as Logan discovered her whereabouts, he chartered a ship to bring him here."

"How romantic," an old lady had whispered.

"How preposterous," Eve had scoffed.

"Well, they are very much married and in love. I am delighted to tell all my friends." She hadn't looked at Eve or Richard's mother. Liza hadn't cared one whit about Eve, but felt sorry for Edith Paxton.

When Liza had related the story to Gillian, she was reminded of her duty to Richard.

"I must write him, Logan. I do not want him to find out from Eve."

That very night, Gillian remained alone in the library, writing, rewriting dozens of letters. Saddened and tired, she finally emerged to find Logan seated in the hallway, trying—with success—to

313

shuffle a deck of cards with one hand.

"Finished?"

"I think so," she whispered. "Can we have someone post this for us tomorrow?" She handed him a
thick envelope.

"Of course. Now, would you like a game of
whist?"

"I never win."

"Perhaps your luck will change tonight." He
dragged her upstairs to their private suite. "You
don't need me to tell you that you did the right
thing. By marrying me, of course," he grinned,
trying to add a little levity. "It had to be this way."

"I know. He is such a nice, dear man."

Suppressing his jealousy, Logan said, "I've
known Richard a long time. We were once friends.
He is a strong man. He will survive."

One day after her letter to Richard was posted,
Gillian received one from him. It was full of awe
for Vice President Calhoun, joy at the possibility
of being reunited with Gillian by February, and
again a request that she set the date for their marriage.

That afternoon, she cried. Logan could not
offer comfort, not this time. He could not understand her feelings no matter how many times she
tried to explain. Richard had not deserved her
harsh treatment. And he certainly deserved a
woman who would return his love tenfold. Gillian
had hurt him, and knowing what it felt like to be
abandoned and hurt, she hated herself for inflict-
ing pain.

It was Henri who tried to put the situation into

perspective. Finding her on the stone bench in the garden, he quietly waited until the last sniff before approaching her.

"Mind if I sit?"

"Oh, forgive me, Henri. I know this is your favorite spot."

"And yours, I am glad to see."

"I love the view of the trees, flowers, and the river. It's so peaceful here. It's as if I am all alone with the beauty and the sweet smells."

"I know. But I hate to see your tears. Logan does not know what to do for you."

"There is nothing he can do now. It's my problem."

"Gillian? Have you ever known or seen unhappily married couples?"

Her parents, she decided immediately. Although they seemed to have managed with their arrangement, like many other members of the ton. "Quite a few," she answered.

"I thought so. And of those people, do you think they would have lived their lives differently if given a choice?"

"Yes," she quietly answered.

"You and Logan are very fortunate to have found each other before it was too late. And Richard. Do you think he deserves a life with a woman who loves another?"

A small tear trickled down her right cheek. "I know."

"He'll thank you for this someday. Believe me."

"I hope so." She accepted the handkerchief he offered.

"Now dry your eyes. You have a young man pacing the confines of the house trying to please you. Be happy, Gillian. You deserve it. And, Gillian?" he waited for her to look up. "I would greatly appreciate it if you called me Grandfather." The lines around his eyes softened with his smile.

"I would be honored, Grandfather." She kissed his cheek.

That night Logan showed Gillian another way to make love. She reveled in his attention and care, but more than that, she loved falling asleep in his arm, nestled under his shoulder, protected from the world.

"I have to go to Charleston," he announced two days later. Feeling fit and looking healthy once more, Logan was chafing to resume his assignment. Harold had contacted him twice already and wanted to know what, if any, progress was made. Harold needed to see both Logan and Peter Harris, and requested they meet him in Charleston.

"I'll come with you. I'd love to see your house." Her enthusiasm was tangible. Gillian was going to be a problem, he realized.

"I don't think you should leave here, not until after the baby's born. Any trip can be dangerous in your condition. I'd rather not take the chance," he said, those concerns genuine ones.

"But you cannot travel alone. You'll need my help. Besides, I'm not having the baby in the next month, you know. I told you . . ."

316

"I know, I know it's March. But I thought you wanted the child born here at Raveneau? How can you take any chances with our son's health? Besides, I am not an invalid. See?" he moved his arm that was now stiffly binded, but without the cumbersome splint.

"Logan, please." She stomped across the Persian rug in their bedroom. "This is ridiculous. I'm in perfectly good health. There is no reason why I cannot go with you."

"There is. I forbid it." He remained seated in the armchair beside the fire. He did not want to look at her crestfallen expression. She'd been so happy lately, and he felt like a damn heel for causing friction by lying to her. "Gillian, I can make better time without you. I can be back here within three days. Isn't that better than spending weeks in Charleston? And what would happen if we were stuck there? Then what? Would you want to have the baby alone in a house that is barely completed, let alone fully furnished? Why, we haven't hired the help yet."

"You're moving slaves from one house to another," she snorted. "And I wanted to decorate the house while I have the time. After the baby's birth, well, I don't know how much time there will be for those things."

"You wanted to hire a housekeeper, did you not? And an English nanny for the child?" One eyebrow arched.

"I'm not so certain anymore. Grandfather thinks it a silly notion. There is someone here at Raveneau."

"Oh? And if my grandfather thinks something is silly, that's acceptable, but if I think it silly, you scoff at me!" His annoyance with himself made the anger directed at her.

"Oh, do what you want," she conceded at last. "I only wanted to be with you." She pouted prettily. "But I hope you look up Peter and Lily Harris. I have no idea why they rushed back to Charleston before meeting you."

He did not blink as he commented, "Perhaps they had enough common sense not to bother us, unlike a host of other idiots. They sent us a lovely note and gift. That Sèvres vase cost quite a tidy sum."

"I know, it's beautiful. Well," she shrugged, "I hope you have the opportunity to meet them. Since I assume," she archly looked at him, "you've made no plans for the evenings, you can take them out to dine. Or if you are fortunate enough to have our household staff in place, invite them."

"Come here." He extended his right arm, eager to change the subject. "I want to kiss you all over. I promise I will return quickly. Look what I have to rush home to." He kissed her lips and patted her belly. "I can't wait to see him."

"Don't be so certain it's a him."

"I'll love all our children equally, regardless of sex. You should know that by now." He stroked her long, thick hair and inhaled her fresh flowery scent.

"There are many things about you I do not know."

He looked beyond her to the roaring fire in the

318

hearth. "Such as?"

"Why you feel the need to rush out of here so soon after our marriage. What it is you really do that occupies your time and thoughts when you're not thinking of me, of course. I know you're not a farmer. What does interest you?" She squirmed out of his arms to look at his face but found no expression, save a gleam in his eyes.

"Someday, my love, I shall tell you all about the other Logan Hammond." His voice deepened in mock horror.

"Will I love him as much as you?

"I hope so." He sobered, but Gillian was unaware of the true meaning of his words.

"When are you leaving?"

"The day after tomorrow. I'll be home before Sunday church service."

The first thing he did upon arriving in Charleston was to send a brief note to Peter and Lily Harris. Gillian would be pleased, he told himself.

The house on the East Battery was mostly completed. By the time Gillian and the baby moved in, it would be furnished. The finer touches would be left for Gillian. Knowing he would be deceiving Gillian for a long time and feeling some shame, Logan was inspired to decorate the nursery. She would appreciate his effort, he decided. The baby would have a furnished, handsome room to welcome him in his new home.

Logan had been introduced to Peter three years ago in Vienna, but he had never met Lily Harris.

Having no idea of what her true surname was, he decided to think of them as the married couple Gillian knew and liked. So when the petite, dark-haired woman entered the house that evening, Logan was not surprised by her age or attractiveness.

There were no servants to eavesdrop this evening. His faithful manservant, Webster, would be arriving in Charleston at the end of the month.

Leading his guests into the freshly painted drawing room on the second floor, Logan had nothing to offer except bourbon and Madeira. Long before they settled down to discuss the true nature of their meeting, Logan had asked Lily to help him decorate the baby's nursery.

"You know what Gillian likes. I'm not certain she approves of my taste yet."

"You cannot be the Logan Hammond of whom I've heard such extraordinary stories," Lily chided. "You're not at all fierce or heartless."

"It must be marriage and impending fatherhood," Peter joined in the fun.

Logan, however, was not amused. "I can assure you both, I am quite capable of handling any assignment given to me. Married or not." He abruptly stood to stare moodily out of the shuttered window.

Lily quickly realized this was not a subject to pursue. "I would be honored to assist you. Besides, this gives us a better reason for being seen together in public in the next few days."

Mollified, Logan asked Peter to update him on their progress thus far.

"It has been easy identifying the English spies.

Before coming to Charleston Lily and I spent quite a bit of time in Washington. Since our arrival last year, we've managed to travel around the state and have made excellent contacts. I believe most of our work is complete, except for Charleston and Savannah."

"You can help us. I know time is important now, with the signing of a new trade treaty with England, but we've yet to find the person or persons Harold has been seeking." Lily explained that although a number of newcomers had settled in Charleston, they had yet to find the one responsible for establishing the British network in South Carolina.

"I've made my politics known. We've been scorned by a number of old families who would never think of allying with the British no matter how dire the circumstances." Peter added.

"Charleston did not fare that well in the War of 1812," Logan reminded him.

"I understand, Logan. But you would think that someone would have picked up my hints by now. There has been a lot of talk about states' rights, thanks to the vice president, but not talk of treason. I wonder," he sighed heavily, "if Harold is on the right track this time." Peter sat back in the armchair. "It's been damn frustrating, Logan."

Logan noticed the sidelong glance Lily gave her "husband," and wondered how much these two really shared with each other. "What about Captain Paxton? Second sons are often an unhappy lot."

"We've checked and rechecked his assignments, friends, and acquaintances. He's not involved as far as we can tell. He is devoted to Calhoun, though, and who knows what, if any, trouble that could bring."

"He's scheduled to return to Fort Moultrie tomorrow," Lily quietly added, wondering how Logan felt about his rival.

"Good, I'll follow him myself."

"Logan, I do not think Gillian would appreciate . . ." She never finished, for again he was out of the chair.

"That's her problem," he coldly replied. "I have an assignment to finish. And I don't want any interference from anyone. Understand?"

That man with the inscrutable expression and cold voice, Peter decided later, was the infamous Logan Hammond. He would do his job well regardless of the consequences to his personal life.

Poor Gillian, Lily thought.

Chapter Thirty-two

Something was happening to him. If he had been in a more rational mood, Logan would have recognized the change the moment Lily had mentioned the item about his being soft on Gillian, which in his mind meant he could not fully devote himself to his assignment. Too many people were counting on him. Lives were at stake. How many times had Harold told him he was one of the best agents in America.

And, another more insistent voice added, how many times had Harold told him that once love got in the way, a man would be forced to choose between his woman and his profession. The danger was too great to combine the two, and no woman could ever understand what he was doing and why he felt the need to take such extraordinary risks with his life.

As soon as the Harrises departed, Logan wandered through the empty house. Gillian had cast a seductive spell over him. True, he had been desperately ill for a while and reliant on her assistance. But that was over. He was here in Charleston. She was miles upriver, ensconced in the bosom of the Raveneau family. They could take better care of her than he.

Throughout the long, lonely night, Logan thought about his wife. Only yesterday, before he had left her, he felt tempted to tell her the truth about himself. He had thought she might want to know, would even understand. How could she? He then realized. She was a loyal citizen of the Crown. She liked Foreign Secretary Canning. Worse than that, she liked Brian Althorp.

Logan must have walked along the piazza at least a dozen times that night. Too keyed up and frustrated, he had abandonded the notion of sleep hours ago. Now seated on a white wicker rocker, he stared morosely at the harbor. The cool night was clear and silent. Thousands of stars contrasted against the dark sky. The half moon provided little light. Only one small boat drifted out into the starry night. The ships docked along the wharves bobbed up and down against the mild wind and lapping waves. Water slapped against the hulls, and that was the only sound he heard.

He had forgotten to think about his future, about his double commitment to his country and wife. Gillian would make demands. She had a right to ask questions. She had a right to want him by her side. Moreover, he wanted to be a good father, an attentive and loving father to his child. But was that possible?

Fearful that she would marry Paxton, Logan could think of little else save getting her to marry him before the birth of their child. Now she was his. What was he going to do?

"Damn it all," he said aloud. "I'm going to make

her unhappy." He knew it, and he could do nothing about it.

Gillian was surprised when she received his letter the next afternoon. There was too much business—whatever that was!—left unattended during his illness. He would be staying another week, possibly two in Charleston. He told her not to worry about his health, his arm was vastly improved.

Resigning herself to her husband's eccentric nature, Gillian spent the next week concentrating on the baby's clothes. She was fairly adept with a needle, but not nearly as good as her mother and Liza. Sitting with the women, listening to their talk of children and homes, Gillian felt contentment such as she had never known.

But it lasted only two weeks. Logan sent yet another letter, saying he'd been delayed once again. He could not tell her when he would return.

That night she found out why.

It was her own cousin Theodore who innocently started the trouble. Deciding to join his wife for a short visit, Theodore and Julia accepted an invitation to dine with the Raveneaus.

Excited to see her cousin, but, more important, anxious for any information about her husband, Gillian wasted no time asking questions.

"Oh, he's fine. His arm is a bit stiff. I saw him at one of the social clubs the other night. Seemed to be in his cups."

Gillian stiffened. Thinking him buried under paperwork, overworked and tired, she almost felt some sympathy for him. Now she wondered just how busy he was.

"He's been with the Harrises a few times. Nice couple. Logan's been banking with us, you know. I think I have you to thank, Gillian."

Well, she thought, at least Lily would keep her eyes on her husband. "Mrs. Harris had to go to Baltimore for a few days. Someone sick in her family."

Damn my luck, she thought.

"Well, I hope he's all right in that house. I have no idea if he's hired the staff. I cannot imagine Logan cooking a meal for himself," Liza added.

"Oh, he can take care of himself," Gillian supplied. "He's probably talked himself into a number of dinner invitations."

"Indeed he has. I saw him just the other night at a dinner party. He seemed to enjoy reminiscing about London life with that English girl."

"What English girl?" Liza and Helena saved Gillian the trouble of asking.

"Anabelle Blacton. Charming young lady. And quite witty, too, I might add."

"She charmed you, too, Theo?" Julia wanted to stuff more food into his mouth just to keep him quiet.

Gillian lost her appetite and retired early to her room.

But at least Theo had prepared her. The next day another guest arrived, a so-called friend of Liza's, who wasted no time in relating some of the stories circulating in Charleston about Logan's wild behavior with more than one young lady.

While Mrs. Waterson eagerly related the gossip, she was unaware that Gillian was sitting quietly on the portico above the morning room and could hear every word.

"We all thought marriage would tame him, but I guess a man like Logan cannot change. Isn't that right, dear? But to be seen in public with Eve Carlton again when everyone knew about their affair! I think it's a shame. His poor wife must be heartbroken."

Gillian was ill, then furious. Logan could not be content to cheat on her with one woman, now he had to add that bitch.

"Oh, I think Eve would love to have him, married or not. And Anabelle Blacton seems to be enjoying herself in his company as well. I tell you, everyone is talking about it, Liza. You must do something."

Gillian did not wait to hear what Liza had to say, for her mind had been made up the moment Mrs. Waterson opened her big mouth.

She stormed out of the portico, through the drawing room, and across to her suite of rooms. Throwing as many clothes as she could grab into one large portmanteau, she was just about to lift if off the bed when her mother quietly entered the room.

"You heard?"

"Every word. I'm going to kill him when I find him."

"I'm going with you," Helena resolutely said.

"No. This is my problem, and I'll handle it my way. Besides, Mother," her voice softened, "it's time

I dealt with things by myself. I am going alone."

There was fire in her eyes, and Gillian doubted if she could ever think of the man she now called "husband" without wanting to slap his face.

Informed that she could leave with the changing tide of the Ashley by dawn of the following morning, Gillian knew there was yet another night without sleep.

Sitting between Anabelle Blacton and Eve Carlton made Logan feel like a fox whose scent had become an intoxicating challenge to the hounds. Before the evening was over, Logan firmly decided that the most adept diplomat could not have managed this situation with as much skill and finesse as he.

Eve, exuding sultry looks, innuendos, and outright gestures—her hand accidentally found his knee twice, for one!—wanted him in her bed this night. And he was tempted. With Eve, Logan would not have to think of satisfying her, of being gentle, of kissing and holding her while she peacefully slept in his arms. He remembered how lusty and passionate she could be, but the thought of waking with any woman other than his wife beside him did not appeal to Logan Hammond.

Anabelle was a different problem. She was drawn to him, and if Eve were not rubbing her leg against his, Logan might have succumbed to her witty conversation and astute observations about the differences between American and British societies. Not only was she an attractive young woman, but judging from her anecdotes about life abroad, Anabelle was an experienced one. They had traveled in the same social circles in London but had never previously met. It was odd, he decided, but not enough to discourage her friendly overtures.

"Logan, be a dear. I would so very much like to see Fort Moultrie. I've heard so much about the military life." She fanned her pink cheeks. "There must be a number of women who find Sullivan's Island an interesting place to live. Perhaps I should convince my uncle to buy me a home there."

"That depends on how eager you are to live the life of a soldier's wife."

Her tinkling laugh intrigued him. "Who said anything about being a wife? Goodness, Logan, just because I am interested in widening my circle of, ah, acquaintances, does not mean I want to marry each man I get to know. I like variety," she winked over the fan. "What I mean is that I enjoy different kinds of company. It's quite stimulating, you know."

Oh, he knew. Anabelle Blacton might prove to be a very entertaining acquaintance. Her dark green eyes glittered from too much champagne and her flirtatious smile sent an invitation that he knew well.

He found it hard to concentrate on the dinner conversation with the two ladies vying for his undivided attention. Neither woman mentioned Gillian, and before the end of supper each presumed Logan would be in her bed that night.

The assembled guests had moved into the drawing room for musical entertainment. He had almost decided to accept Eve's invitation to escort her home when a harried butler informed the hostess that another guest had just arrived.

"Darling," Gillian swept past everyone in the room, ignoring the open-mouthed stares and sudden titters, "you did not have to beg me to come to Charleston, I was planning to surprise you within a week. Just think how pleased I was to receive your letters and messages. Why, I told Grandfather I would not think of leaving you alone any longer than necessary."

She fiercely hugged him then kissed him firmly on the mouth. No one saw her bite his lip or step on his toe. "I am going to kill you," she whispered for his ears alone.

He should have been embarrassed. He should have shrugged her off, demanding to know what she was doing in Charleston without his permission. He should have looked at the astonished expressions on Eve and Annabelle's faces.

Logan hugged Gillian, claiming her mouth once more in a far more passionate kiss that was not meant for the public. Then he laughed and said, "I am thrilled you responded so quickly, dearest. Though I feared forcing you to travel so late in your condition."

Gillian knew the matrons would talk among themselves after their departure. After all, she should be "lying-in," and if Logan could not faithfully remain by her side, then the least he could do was not appear publicly with two women fawning over him. Gillian knew they would fuel parlor gossip for weeks—and did not care.

The Hammonds remained a while longer, but most of the assembled guests were reluctant to approach them.

Gillian dropped all pretense the moment the large front door of their hostess's house closed behind them. They rode home in silence, and, once there, she majestically paraded up the curved staircase to the room she assumed was theirs without giving Logan a backward glance. Her belongings, though, were strewn about the large master bedroom, and Logan's could not be found.

"I assumed you would be sleeping in the guestroom." She spoke to the pink-and-gold broacade coverlet. "By the way, I am delighted to see you using your arm."

Logan vainly tried to wipe the silly grin off his face. "I think you should at least listen to what I have to say." At the moment, however, he could not find anything appropriate to say. If she hadn't walked into the party when she did, Logan might have been in Eve Carlton's house.

"You, sir, are a cad. And a bastard. I've come to claim my rights." Calmly walking over to the dressing table near the window, Gillian placed her silverbacked hairbrush on a mirrored tray. "I would like to undress now."

"Go ahead," he remained leaning against the large bedpost, his arms folded, "I have no place to go."

"I am certain Eve would still want you." She rigidly sat in the chair, unpinning the heavy mass of hair.

He remembered and cherished those movements,

eagerly anticipating the waves of strawberry-blonde hair unwinding down her slender back. There was something missing in her gesture.

"Where is the ring I gave you?" Logan moved away from his position, preparing to do battle.

"Oh, that. I had to take it off." Gillian caught the glint in his eye and was pleased by his show of anger. "It's not what you think," her voice softened, and she almost sounded like the loving Gillian. "Although I have every right to fling it in your face for what you have done to me yet again. My fingers have swelled from the heat and all. The ring became uncomfortable."

Since this was not the moment for levity, she decided not to tell him how difficult it had been to remove.

"I'm sorry, Gillian." He stood behind her now. His hands threatened to reach for her stiff shoulders, but remained at his sides. She looked into the mirror and saw his eyes. Was that remorse? Or was she seeing things again.

"Gillian, I've been a bachelor too long. I've lived the way I pleased, often acting on whims. I'm not used to sharing." This time both hands found her shoulders as he bent lower to kiss her neck. "I did not mean to hurt you. It's hard for me. And damn, this is the longest speech I've ever had to make, and I wish you wouldn't stare at me like a cornered doe."

"You frighten me, Logan," she whispered. "I cannot be at your side, reminding you of your marriage vows. Your business takes you elsewhere, and eventually," she looked down at her ever-growing belly, "there is another to protect. I will not leave the babe with a nurse or nanny while I chase you around the world reminding you of your marriage vows. I was not meant to be a gadfly or a leech."

Her words were clearly spoken and with enough conviction to conjure an alien emotion within his chest. Fear. It suddenly occurred to him that he didn't know what he would do if Gillian left him. He did not want to be alone.

Damn if he wasn't in love with his wife.

Chapter Thirty-three

In the days following Gillian's arrival, Logan felt another strange temptation to confide in her. It was damn hard making up excuses for leaving the house and harder still to spend a night away from her.

As she entered the last stages of her pregnancy, Gillian needed him more. She needed his reassurance that she was still attractive. Although their lovemaking was less frequent, there was not a night when she did not curl up in his arms, her rounded belly often nestling against his back. Logan sometimes felt the babe's kick in the night. Although it disturbed Gillian's sleep, he took it as a sign of reassurance that all was well with the baby. It had become their private communication.

Gillian's days were filled with the house. She loved the planter's-style single house and delighted in furnishing the nursery and redecorating their bedsuite. Logan did not mind and whenever he was about allowed Gillian to drag him about Charleston. Upon learning that Thomas Elfe, one of the most famous American cabinetmakers, resided in town, Gillian spent hours selecting desks, cabinets, sideboards, armoires, and two desks. She took particular pleasure in the selection of an unusual triple chest-on-chest for the first-floor drawing room. All of Thomas Elfe's designs were unique, with intricate and painstakingly carved patterns in the finished pieces.

One cloudy Thursday morning, Gillian persuaded Logan to join her on a shopping excursion to King Street. Surprisingly he obliged and, against her better wishes, insisted they select an unusual silver candelabra for the music room and the pianoforte that he wanted designed.

"It's for our child, Gillian," he happily dismissed her protests.

"Logan, you're either far more wealthy than I ever imagined or you love to squander money that is not yours. I do not want to be in the house when the bill collectors arrive *en masse*."

"Now, darling," he took her gloved hand, "I could have said the same of you when you decided we had to have the only triple chest-on-chest in all of South Carolina, or the States, I think you said."

"Mmm, well, I appreciate fine workmanship."

He cast an appraising eye on her upturned nose and winsome smile. "So do I, my love."

The afternoon would have passed without a blemish if they had not run into Anabelle and Eve. The ladies were strolling together down King Street and, upon seeing the Hammonds linked arm in arm before a bookshop, decided to approach the couple.

"Why, hello, Logan," Anabelle smiled broadly. "And Gillian, dear, you are looking, ah," she deliberately let her gaze drop to Gillian's large middle, "well, you are looking robust."

Gillian turned a delicate shade of crimson under her straw bonnet. Fortunately, the brim was wide enough to shield her flushed face.

"Yes, dear. It is unusual that you roam freely about town in your condition. Isn't it, Logan?" Eve's voice dropped an octave lower when mentioning his name. It as obvious that her dark eyes were riveted on Logan's handsome profile. She could not help but ache with desire each time she set eyes on him. To separate him from that huge wife of his was proving a most interesting challenge. It was taking much longer than she had thought.

"I think my wife is more than beautiful each day. Don't you agree, ladies?" Logan's molten gold eyes were fixed on Gillian. He would have dearly loved to strike Eve, but Gillian being a lady would be greatly offended.

"Logan, I do love to see you dressed all in white." Eve admired his white linen jacket and trousers. "It's so becoming on a tall, muscular man."

"I know," Gillian chimed in at last. "I insisted he have this suit of clothing made." Her arm tightened around his. "But you must know that Logan looks wonderful no matter what he does and doesn't wear." Her voice and smile were so sweet that the ladies almost forgot to listen to her words.

Logan did and nearly choked. "Ah, sweetheart, I think it's too warm for you to remain outdoors.

336

Please excuse us, ladies." He bowed at the waist. "My wife needs my attention."

Grateful that he had dampened the obvious desire of both harlots, Gillian did not care if he meant the words or not. He had stood by her side and protected her, that was enough for now.

"What is Anabelle doing with Eve? And if you dare say they share a mutual interest, I may strike you in public."

"I cannot say, nor do I care," he replied calmly. But he did think it odd and made a mental note of asking Lily about this budding relationship.

The Harrises were the only couple to visit the new Hammond home frequently. Lily delighted in Gillian's joy and only late at night, when she was alone in bed, did she envy her friend's life.

Somehow, the Harrises and Logan arranged not to travel outside of Charleston at the same time, as Gillian's suspicions would have been aroused. And they would have managed to keep her in the dark if it weren't for the strange late-night appearance of Logan's friend Harold Carter or "Porter."

Gillian was too fatigued to remain in the music room with the Harrises and Logan. By 10 P.M. she was climbing up into the huge four-poster bed and was asleep within minutes.

Some time later, realizing that Logan was still not abed and that she was suddenly interested in a chilled lemonade, Gillian donned Logan's large black silk robe and tiptoed past the music room and down the stairs. Harold, Peter, and Lily were standing at the main entrance of the house with Logan nearby.

"Why, Mr. Porter, isn't it?" She did not fail to notice the urgent, low tones Peter directed at Harold. If they had not known each other before this evening, they surely seemed to have made each other's acquaintance quickly.

"Oh, hello Mrs., I mean Lady Hammond. Good to see you again." Harold stepped forward, much to Logan's relief, for he had no idea what to do.

"I heard you were in residence, and when Logan invited me to visit anytime, I took him on his word this night. I was hoping for a good meal and drink. I'm a bit tired of the inn, you see."

"Are you in Charleston to do business with Logan?" she innocently inquired.

"Yes, indeed. It seems your husband is a man of many talents." The others seemed to hold their breaths as Harold warmed to his subject. "I'm interested in purchasing race horses and I understand that the plantations around the Low Country raise some of the finest stock. Logan and his friend Peter promised to direct me to the most promising horses."

"I did not realize, Logan, that you knew about horses." Realizing yet again that there was not much about her husband she did know, Gillian felt awkward. Why did they know more than she?

"Ah, yes, my love. I had no idea that you liked horse breeding as well." Logan put his arm around her shoulders. "There seems to be much I do not know about my wife. Tell me, dearest," there was mischief in his eyes, "do you enjoy needlework?"

Forgetting the others, Gillian burst into loud laughter. "I loathe it."

338

"You see, Harold, how much about your wife do you really know?"

"Very little. And I think I prefer it that way. Now," he seemed to back out the door, "if you will excuse me, I shall come back another time." He doffed his round brown hat.

"Please join us for dinner soon." She did not mind being gracious to one of Logan's friends. Besides, the pudgy fellow looked tired and lonely.

The Harrises offered to give Harold a ride in their coach, and within minutes the house was again empty.

"Logan, I feel funny." Gillian had a peculiar expression.

He did not miss the grimace.

"My stomach must be upset. I wanted lemonade, but perhaps I'd better not have anything but water."

Now Logan's expression became sickly. "Gillian, there is no one in this house but the two of us. Not even Webster, who is scheduled to arrive tomorrow, and I doubt he knows anything about births."

"No, it cannot be the baby. It's too early. We have another month. Perhaps I've caught a chill."

He wanted to say not in this heat, but refrained from saying anything lest he alarm her. They planned on staffing the house before the end of the week. Maintaining that she loved the silence and privacy of their new home, the house was only filled during the day with craftsmen and household slaves. Logan knew that he had to travel yet again, and until her mother arrived in

Charleston, Logan did not want to leave her alone.

"Tomorrow I want your mother here. I'm sending for her in the morning."

"Oh, but Logan," she started to protest, but her queasy stomach arrested the words. "Oh, all right."

"Gillian, I do not want you alone here. And I must leave in two days. Please, sweeting," he kissed her warm brow, "it would make me feel a hell of a lot better."

But the weather that Friday was terrible. Not only was Webster's ship delayed, but it was impossible for Helena to travel from Ashton Hall to Charleston. The high winds and erratic downpour made any travel impossible.

Gillian was not feeling much better the next morning. Insisting that it was not the baby, but some other upset, she protested when Logan ran out of the house to find a physician.

Returning two hours later with a young, bespectacled man in tow, Logan ushered the fellow to the bedchamber.

Gillian was leaning over the chamber pot, her hair streaming about her face and neck.

"Sweetheart, what's wrong?" He rushed to her side, forgetting briefly about the doctor.

Still wearing his silk robe, Gillian raised her head and groaned, "Oh, please, I look a fright. Logan, go away."

Ignoring her soft plea, he dropped to his knees and held her head. "Just try to relax, love. I'm staying with you."

340

As soon as the episode ended, the doctor spoke up. "Mrs. Hammond, my name is Clayton Warren. I'm a doctor." He hadn't spoken those words often enough to exude confidence.

Looking at the young, pale-haired man before her, Gillian's first thought was that he was too young to shave. "I don't need a doctor."

"I've sent for a midwife, too. She'll be here in a flash, I hope." Logan assisted Gillian to the bed and sat down beside her, never letting go of her clammy hand.

"I'm telling you it is not the baby. It's too soon. I simply have a minor stomach upset."

"Well, as long as your husband dragged me out of bed threatening me at gunpoint, may I please see for myself?"

She could have laughed at the lunacy of the situation but felt another stomach cramp. "Do it fast. I fear I am not destined to remain seated."

Dr. Warren's examination was brief but thorough.

"Mrs. Hammond, despite your denials, I believe you are about to have your child."

"It can't be," she gasped. "I know when I conceived," she meaningfully looked at Logan, "and I assure you my calculations are correct. I have at least six more weeks."

"Tell that to your son, Gillian." Logan tried to smile, but failed.

"The midwife will arrive soon, I hope. Unless I have studied the wrong profession, those stomach pains you are experiencing are early signs of labor. Now," he noticed the terror on both faces, "if you

341

are absolutely certain about your calculations . . ."

"She is," Logan said.

"Then perhaps we can find a way to delay your child's insistent arrival."

"How?" they asked in unison.

"Mrs. Hammond, you must remain in bed. I mean not move. Not even to scoot over there . . ." He glanced at the necessary chair behind a screen. "No bath, no meals downstairs, no combing of your hair, nowhere but this bed."

"For how long?"

"I don't know. It depends on your child. I've seen a few babies born early and survive." Dr. Warren could have bitten his tongue for such tactlessness. "I do not have a great deal of experience. Forgive me. I did not mean it to sound that way." He actually flushed. "I've also heard of an unorthodox method of keeping labor at bay, for a short while, that is."

"Anything." Gillian was frightened, but upon seeing Logan's pale face, decided to remain silent.

"Whiskey. Preferably vodka."

"I don't understand." She looked to Logan for some clarification and saw he was smiling.

"I think, love, he means that whiskey can have the same effect on your, ah, labor pains as it does on one's brain. What I mean is that it can slow things down."

"I hate whiskey, especially vodka."

"I have some excellent vodka. Private stock of the Czar of Russia."

"Logan, I am not a connoisseur of fine wines, whiskey, or anything of the sort. I don't care."

342

"You will, although after a few glasses you may not know which city you are in."

"Leave it to you to find humor in this," she snapped.

"If it will make you feel any better, I will join you."

"So will I," Dr. Warren added.

"I wish my mother were here after all." She waited for Logan to prop the large pillows behind her back.

"If Dr. Warren's method is a success, perhaps she will join us, too."

Chapter Thirty-four

"Logan, thish ish ridic . . . ricid, I mean dumb."

Logan grinned conspiratorially at Clayton Warren. It was nearly dawn. They had been imbibing for three hours and Gillian had not experienced any pain. Long ago the trio had abandoned formalities with one another.

"How long can she remain like this?"

"I don't know. I never got that far. I've only read about these matters, you see. I've never seen it."

"Well, it seems to be working." Logan lifted the glass to his lips. "I may not be able to taste anything for weeks."

There was no description for Gillian's state. Her blue eyes looked brighter but drooped from fatigue and too much liquor. She had finally allowed Logan to remove his borrowed black robe, replacing it with her peach muslin nightgown and matching robe. Insisting that she wanted to feel pretty, she allowed Logan to comb her hair then tie it behind her with a ribbon.

He washed her face, hands, and neck, and, before long, Gillian drifted into a restful slumber.

"Tell me, Clayton, what could happen if . . ."

"The baby can live. But in some cases, the lungs may not be fully developed. Remember, it will be small and more susceptible to infection."

"Not this one. Not the way he kicks her at night." He remembered the thumps in his lower back.

"I suggest we sleep, too. I don't know what happened to that midwife."

"I should have threatened her at knifepoint. You rest, Clayton, I'll stay with her a while."

The rain pounded against the windows while the world seemed asleep, and Logan stood guard over his wife. "You'll both be fine. I know it. I swear it." His repeated whispers were for his ears alone. "I won't let anything happen to either of you. Ever." Then he walked over to the window, spread the blue-and-gold damask curtain aside and looked up into the heavens. "Please, God," he choked on a tear. "Please."

By early morning the rain had stopped, the sky brightened, and the weather turned cool.

The first thing Gillian noticed upon awakening was her pounding headache and Logan's rumpled light brown hair. He was sleeping in an uncomfortable position, his lower torso in a chair while his head rested on his arms on top of the bed. His face was averted, facing the window, and he was breathing deeply enough to echo through her dull brain.

"Oh," she moaned softly.

"What is it?" His head shot up to stare at her

bloodshot eyes. "You look hung over."

"I feel it. By the way," she noted his crumpled white shirt and creased fawn trousers, "you don't look much better." Despite her alcoholic haze, Gillian wondered if she could ever love him more than she did at this moment. He cared for her, that was obvious now. He might even love her. Given the state of his dishevelment, he had not left her side.

"My mouth feels like I swallowed cotton."

"Wash it down with this." He handed her a glass of clear liquid. She took three large gulps before realizing her error.

"Not that vile stuff again! Logan, I tell you I don't know if I will ever look at a glass of water without sniffing it."

"How are the pains?" He straightened the pillows behind her.

Gillian inhaled his fragrance. Stale smoke, vodka, and some essence of lime. Her husband. "Not as frequent as last night. A little pang here and there."

"Well, Clayton said that each day we delay the stronger the baby will be."

"He's a nice chap."

"Not bad. I fear I frightened him." He grinned. "I hope he stays with us."

"You can't expect him to drop everything. With luck, my mother will arrive today. So will Webster and with some more luck, the midwife will, too."

"I've taken care of that. I've sent for the midwife at Raveneau. She's had far more experience than anyone I know. She's not a voodoo lady or unkind. I've known Hilda most of my life."

"Ah, Logan." She squirmed against the bedcovers.

"I'll remedy that immediately." He understood her discomfort and carried her over to the necessary chair.

"I feel embarrassed."

He lovingly looked at his wife. Despite last night's travails, she still looked lovely. This was love. Caring and helping. Holding her hand when she needed his presence. He would have it no other way.

"There is never anything to feel ashamed of with me, Gillian. I am your husband. I want to be here with you. I will do anything for you and our child." Somehow the rest of the words would not come.

"Logan, do you have to go away tomorrow?"

Damn, he forgot about this next assignment for Harold. He had to be in Savannah by Sunday. There was no way he could abandon her now. Yet what would he tell Harold?

"I won't leave you." She did not see his frown.

He stayed. Sending a brief missive to Harold, Logan brooded over his reaction. Never had he willfully declined an assignment or request.

By early the following morning, Harold sent a reply. "I understand. Someone else is on the way," was all it said. It did not assuage his guilt. Someone else had to take his place. How many more times would this happen.

There was little time to sulk. Gillian, still in a semi-alcoholic daze, lost track of time. She ate little, slept much more, complained often. Yet whenever she needed Logan, he was there to assist all her needs.

"Lord, I hope I don't have to wash your hair, madame. Being a ladies' maid is not my forte." His white sleeves were rolled up under both elbows, exposing hairy arms. Both hands worked at trying to comb and style Gillian's long hair.

"I always thought you enjoyed helping ladies in their boudoirs." There was little humor in her voice. "Oh, damn, I cannot stand being like this." She slapped the pillow. "I feel like an invalid. I keep looking at these walls. I think the first thing I will do after the baby is born is change the paper. I see these gold-and-blue stenciled stripes in my dreams. They're making me dizzy. I think I want pink. Or yellow. Oh, Logan," her large eyes beseeched his, "how much longer?"

"You heard what Clayton said."

She did. Clayton Warren visited her at least twice a day. Pleased that the pains were no worse, he insisted she follow the same routine. Gillian thought she would lose her mind.

Deciding it best to occupy her mind, Gillian took up, then discarded, a dozen books. She could not concentrate. If she wasn't worried about the baby's well-being, she fretted about Logan's restless pacing about the room.

By late Saturday afternoon, the midwife Hilda appeared. Ushering the woman into his bedroom, he bid a hasty retreat as soon as the corpulent Hilda began issuing orders. Wearing a colorful scarf around her short, wiry black hair, her dark skin glistened from the exertion of running up and down the stairs. The woman was more like a drill sergeant than a slave. But Logan would have none other than this woman deliver his child.

By evening, Gillian's hair was freshly washed, her face pink from Hilda's delightful ministrations with her hands.

"Logan, I have no objection to Hilda giving you a massage. It feels wonderful. I hope you can teach him to do this to me."

"I's taught that boy enough," she snorted. "Better watch out for him or you'll be with child for the rest of your childbearing years." Her ample bosom vibrated with laughter.

That night, as with each night since her confinement, Logan shared dinner with Gillian. He was in the middle of savoring Hilda's delicious chicken when he heard a carriage speed through the gates before screeching to a halt.

Then he heard the all-too-familiar voice of his manservant Webster. It was such a pleasure to have someone pamper him for a change that Logan gave Webster the run of the house. Even Gillian seemed pleased to see the little man with the missing bottom tooth.

"Does she know about ye yet, your lordship?"

"No! Is that clear? I am counting on you to remain your usual discreet self. Understand?"

"Is Mr. Harold in Charleston?"

"He was but had to go to Washington. Remember, Webster," Logan frowned, "it's a long way back to England, especially in the cargo hold."

"I've kept all your secrets for years, my lord.

What makes you think your lovely wife can get anything out of me?"

"Just an uneasy feeling, that's all." But he was glad that Webster was here. With Gillian ensconced in her room, and Hilda standing guard, perhaps he decided to escape for a short time and pursue the information Peter sent in his letter.

Gillian did not sleep well that night. Despite the amount of vodka consumed and Hilda's neck rubs, Gillian's discomfort increased. Having refused Hilda's orders to leave Gillian alone in bed at night, Logan, too, was kept awake by her tosses and murmurs.

He took her in his arms, soothing her brow and hair, but to no avail.

"I heard you return," she stated. "I'm sorry if I've driven you out of your house."

The all-too-familiar feeling of shame overwhelmed him. God but she had the knack for making him feel like a heel. He hadn't been with another woman, not really, that is, and still she knew how to make him wish he had never left the house.

"You did nothing of the sort. I only needed a chance to be alone. I still had some business to tend to, and as long as Hilda was with you, I thought you would not mind."

"But you came home so late . . ."

"I stayed for a drink with some other associates. That is not the problem now, is it?" He noticed her wince again. "You're in more pain, aren't you?" His hair fell into his eyes as he bent over her.

"I don't know if I can sleep. I'll understand if you want to sleep in another room." She plucked at the edge of the sheet. "It's just that I feel so warm, the room is so dark, and I keep wishing the dawn would come. I hear noises, I look up at the clock, but it's still late at night. I feel stronger during the day, I suppose."

Remembering a number of uncomfortable nights when he prayed he would live to see the dawn, he told her he understood and tried to soothe her back to sleep. Lighting every candle in the room, he told her to pretend it was morning, while he hopped naked out of their bed and reached for a book. "Isn't this your favorite?" He displayed the book. "The novel by Samuel Richardson?"

"Oh, you would read *Clarissa* to me?" She giggled. "I love that book. So romantic. And I could use a little romance tonight."

He read like an actor. Seated in the familiar blue brocade armchair that he left near her side of the bed, he read each part as if he were each character.

By dawn, Gillian was dozing in bed with Logan staring at her from the armchair. He had no idea whose circles under the eyes were darker, his or hers. He also had no idea how much longer she could go on. He never really thought of her as a strong woman, but in the last few days she had shown him her tenacity. He wondered how long she — or anyone — could bear such discomfort and again he felt shamed for putting her in this physical condition.

Gratefully, Lady Helena bustled into the house

Sunday afternoon. Upon seeing her mother, Gillian cried. She even wished her father were here.

By late afternoon the pains returned. Again Logan galloped through the streets for Clayton Warren.

Dr. Warren was smart enough to confer with Hilda, and within five minutes both decided to take the chance. No more vodka. It was in God's hands, they decided. If this child were strong, it would emerge healthy in a matter of hours.

As soon as the pains intensified, Gillian begged Logan to leave the room. He would have none of it. She was frightened, and the least he could do was remain by her side, with her hand firmly held in his.

She yelled at him, even cursed him twice, and still he remained. Her long nails clawed his palms and upper forearms, and Logan kissed her wet brow.

"You can do it, Gillian. I know you can." He tried to keep the fear out of his voice. There was little else for him to do but offer loud encouragements while she panted and raged. But she heard him, and she smiled into his worried eyes.

"You don't have to stay." She heaved the words.

"I'm not leaving you." He smiled broadly, then wondered if the uneasy feeling in his stomach would disappear. He wondered how much more it would hurt both physically and emotionally with each of Gillian's loud groans.

Everyone was encouraging her, but she tried to focus on Logan. Her husband, who kept cool cloths on her head, wiped the strands of hair out

352

of her face and valiantly smiled while her clenched fists nearly pounded his chest.

"I see the head," Hilda yelled.

"Come on, Gillian, push harder," Clayton yelled. Logan could not look anywhere but into her grimacing face. "I love you, Gillian," he said clearly. "I love you." He felt his eyes sting, but could not imagine what was wrong.

It was frantic. Loud voices faded in and out as she panted and exerted all her energy to at last hear the tiniest whimper bellowing above the other voices.

"She's got some pair of lungs," Clayton said to no one.

"You hear dat, Masta Logan? It's a girl!"

All he saw was a bald head more in the shape of an egg than rounded as he supposed it should be. But he heard her cry of life, and nothing else in the world mattered but the woman laughing and crying in the bed and the baby announcing to the world that the newest Hammond had arrived.

Chapter Thirty-five

Nothing in the world could compare to the euphoric state Gillian and Logan shared after the birth of their daughter. It was decided they would name her Judith Rose Hammond, after Logan's mother. Although born nearly six weeks prematurely, Judith was by no means a scrawny, unhealthy child. According to Hilda, she was as large as any baby born in the ninth month and judging by her lusty screams at mealtime, her lungs seemed fully developed.

"Gillian, just look at this," Logan called her from the dressing room. "She's smiling, I swear she is smiling at me. And just look at the way she's clutching my finger," he marveled.

Peeking from the other room, Gillian watched her husband dance around their bedroom with the baby nestled securely in his large hands. Singing some little sea ditty, Logan had no idea he was being observed and probably would not care.

"Are you disappointed?"

"What do you mean?" He continued to sashay across the carpet.

"Having a girl. That's all you talked about, you know. Wanting a son, wanting to continue the

354

Hammond name. I even recall some mention of the title he would inherit."

Logan stopped short in front of her. "Look at this beautiful, healthy child, love. I could not love a son any more. You have no idea how grateful I am that she is alive and well and smiling." Shifting Judith into one arm, he lifted Gillian's chin. "And you, too. I don't know what I would have done if anything happened to you or Judith. You're all that matters." He kissed her pert mouth.

"I'll never tire of hearing you tell me those things."

"Every day, if you like." Savoring the taste of his wife's lips, like a glass of rare wine, Logan was suddenly reminded of another hunger.

"Ah, Gillian, when did Clayton say, ah, when can we . . ." He actually flushed.

"A few more weeks, that's all. Can you wait that long?"

"Do I have a choice?"

"I think I would murder you if you did." The smile did not seem to reach her eyes.

"Fear not. I am a happily married man."

And he meant it, too. He had never felt this sort of contentment. At last he understood what his parents had shared, what his father now shared with Charlotte. All his years of wandering, the periods of extreme boredom, the hours wasted playing cards, making outlandish wagers, taking chances with his life were, he now realized, a childish way of marking time. What mattered was these two females. The urge to protect and shield them from pain and discomfort was now the driving force of

355

his life. So when Harold Carter sent a note a few days later, Logan had almost discarded it before realizing that he still had other obligations in his life.

They met in an ale house near the wharves. It was another cold, rainy afternoon, yet Logan chose to walk the short distance. That was something that Gillian liked to do, too, he recalled, but there was no time for sentiment now, not with Harold sitting in a dark corner, drumming his stubby fingers against the small, square table.

"I am not here to lecture you. I shall say it once. I told you so. I see that look on your face, Hammond, and I know exactly what it means."

Logan wanted to say something in his defense, but Harold raised his hand. "Not now, I'm not here, lad, to chastise you. I understand." His light eyes looked into Logan's confused face. "It happens to the best agents. Love."

"Jesus, is it written all over my face?"

"Yes. But don't be ashamed. You deserve some real happiness, you know. I'm grateful I got as many years out of you as I have. And you have done a great service for your country, you must know that now."

"Harold," Logan leaned across the table, "what are you telling me?"

"I'm telling you that I don't think you should continue. I have other things you can do. Far less dangerous, yet just as valuable. If you decide to settle in America, that is."

"We haven't given it much thought."

"I know. But I also know that I cannot allow

you to work in your former capacity. For more than one reason."

"Such as?" He tried to sound casual, but Harold knew better.

"You have to protect your family. Your wife, if she ever discovered your profession, would undoubtedly object. No, no," he saw Logan's mouth open to interrupt, "she has a right to want her husband alive."

"It's my decision," he bristled.

"Wait. There is more. It seems that whoever wanted to kill you in Venice knows much more about you than you think. Your identity is no longer secret to the British."

"Althorp," he whispered, conjuring up the name and face of his nemesis and another of Gillian's admirers.

"He's crafty, lad. Since he could not kill you, he will see to it that you are caught and hung."

"First they'd have to give me a fair trial."

"If you live past Althorp's inquisition."

"I'm not afraid." Logan's cold voice had an edge of steel to it.

"I am certain you aren't. But tell me, what would you do if he threatened your family? Your wife and daughter?"

"I'd cheerfully strangle him."

"I doubt you'd be given the chance. Don't you see, Logan, Althorp would give his arms to trap you. If you return to England and dare to resume your activities, he'll snare you and," he smiled ruefully, "I hate rhymes, but he will not spare you."

"He hates me, I'm aware of that."

"You stole his woman."

"A number of men think that."

"None are as dangerous or powerful as Althorp. Logan, you do not have a choice. I will not give you any more assignments in London."

"What about this one?"

"We're close, very close."

"I'll finish this," he declared. "It's my responsibility, and I want to see it through."

"What about Gillian?" Harold accepted a second glass of Madeira.

"What about her? There is no need for her to know. I'm very close, as you well know, to discovering the leader of the Charleston–Savannah network. With luck, I'll be finished within two months, maybe less. Didn't you say that Henry Clay wants this information before he sails for London?"

"He's scheduled to leave in April."

"He'll have the names. I give you my word." Logan was determined to finish this assignment. If it was going to be his last, he'd like to retire with a perfect record.

"I'd give anything to settle the score with Althorp."

"I'm delighted you said that." Harold offered Logan a cigar, then waited until Logan lit it. "I just received word that Althorp is scheduled to dock within a fortnight."

"He's coming here!" Logan was incredulous. "The man never leaves England. I gather it's not a social visit. He wants my skin."

"Your heart will suffice. Althorp's network is far

more sophisticated than ours. I'd wager he knew about your marriage long before your letters ever reached your father. You've been watched for a long time."

Logan's fist pounded against the table, splashing his tankard of ale. "I will kill him if he harms them," he swore.

"I don't think he wants to harm Gillian or the child. Making her a widow is more likely his goal."

"I'll not give him the opportunity. I'm enjoying fatherhood far too much."

"Logan, my boy, we've been quite close over the years. I would like to give you some fatherly advice, if I may."

Logan rarely appreciated anyone's advice, but today he was willing to make the exception. "Go on," he nodded.

"It's about your wife." Harold saw Logan's head snap up in wary attention. "No, no, I do not have any dark secrets about her or her family to reveal. I told you this is personal. Remember the story I told you about *my* wife?" Logan's furrowed brow told him no. "Well, I once told you that she did not know about my activities for the American government. That wasn't true. Not only does she know, she actively supports them. She's had to lie for me on more than one occasion. She's even been dragged into some things against my better judgment."

"I had no idea you would confide in anyone, particularly your wife."

"I had to. You see, son," Harold paused to flick his cigar, "that was the only way to keep her. For so long Alice suspected I was keeping a mistress that when I finally revealed the truth, she was actually relieved!" He laughed, then quickly sobered. "What I am trying to tell you is that sooner or later your wife will find out about your activities. Better it come from you."

Appalled by such a suggestion, Logan could only sneer. "You must be daft. I could never tell Gillian that I used her, her family, betrayed the country that she believes we both love. Your Alice may be forgiving, but I know Gillian would never forgive."

"I've told you my experience. Just think about it."

He did. All the way home to the house on the East Battery. There was some merit to Harold's suggestion. But not now. Not when their shaky marriage was first beginning to settle. In time, when she was secure in the knowledge that he was a loving and devoted husband and father, he would tell her. They would laugh about it in bed, seconds before he made love to her. Then after, she would lie in his arms, and he would explain everything.

Yes, he decided, telling her could wait. First, he liked the idea of getting her in bed. God, he couldn't wait for that moment.

Running up the steps two at a time, Logan almost banged the door wide open, then quickly caught it lest he awaken Judith. Dashing up the other flight of stairs, he was halted by Gillian's voice coming from the morning room.

"Logan, we have a guest." She sounded agitated.

Certain that Althorp was the uninvited guest, he almost jumped down the steps to join his wife in the morning room. Relieved that the intruder was not Althorp, Logan extended his hand in a friendly greeting to Captain Richard Paxton.

"Welcome back, Richard. How is Calhoun faring?"

Gillian hung back against the papered wall. Logan was behaving as if Richard and he were still old friends. He seemed to have forgotten she had accepted Richard's proposal of marriage.

"My trip was most interesting and enlightening, but not nearly as much as my discovery that you and Gillian are wed. Congratulations on the birth of your daughter." He stood stiffly near the window, refusing to accept Logan's outstretched hand. The gold buttons on his dark blue uniform caught the afternoon sun, shining brightly in an otherwise somber atmosphere.

Looking for Gillian, Logan saw her misery. She still cared for him, he thought jealously.

· "Logan," her voice was husky, as if she were holding back tears, "I think Richard was unprepared for our marriage."

"So was I," he laughed, but no one joined him. "Uh, Richard, shall we go for a walk?"

"I think not. I came to offer my congratulations. I hope Gillian finds her happiness. I hope you will be the one to give it to her." Glancing over to the lovely, sad-eyed woman across the room, he continued. "It was always you, I should have known that. But I want you both to know," his green-eyed glance sharpened on Logan, "Gillian will always have my friendship. So treat her well."

Logan had a number of choices at the moment.

He could punch that noble smile off Paxton's face, he could argue with Paxton before punching him, or he could be a good chap and accept the man's kindness to his wife.

"I assure you I will take good care of my own. However, I thank you for your concern," he replied coolly.

"We were once friends, Logan. Maybe someday . . ." His voice trailed.

"I hope you find what you want, Richard."

"I did," he looked at Gillian again, "but I shall endeavor to start again."

When he left, Gillian walked him outside to his horse. Taking his cold hand in hers, she paused to collect her thoughts. "I have not been fair to you, Richard. Nor was I the perfect woman you wanted me to be. You should have a woman who is far better than I can ever be. Logan and I, well, I think we deserve each other."

"While I was away, I thought a great deal about us, about him." Richard gestured to the man staring at them from the window. "I believe there is a saying about destiny and people being made for each other. I do not believe I could have made you happy. Not as long as Logan walked the earth. I want you to be happy, I do." He took her hand. "Your daughter looks just like you, you know."

She could not stop the silent tears streaking down her cheeks. "I'm so sorry, Richard. I don't expect your forgiveness, just a kind thought now and then."

"I will always be your loyal friend." He smiled bravely. "I just need some time to myself. I'm not

362

used to being turned down, I suppose." He forced a laugh.

Impulsively she kissed his freshly shaved cheek. "Be well."

She waited for him to mount the horse and slowly trot down the Battery before turning to go inside. Logan stood by the door. He opened his arms and she ran crying into his secure embrace.

Chapter Thirty-six

The Hammonds decided Judith was too young to travel to Raveneau Plantation and chose to remain in Charleston for the next couple of months. The season would begin again in May, and although neither Logan nor Gillian felt like being a part of a mad social whirl, it was reassuring to know that friends and family would return to Charleston. Even Henri Raveneau, who made his distaste of the city clear, wrote that he would come to visit his great-granddaughter.

It also became obvious that the Hammonds would remain in the United States for a while. Gillian had no idea that Logan could not return to England lest he face arrest. Instead, believing that Judith should not travel overseas until she was much older, and that Logan had much too much work to complete in the States, Gillian accepted their temporary residence in Charleston.

"I hope we can return home eventually," she had told Logan after making the decision.

"Eventually," he had repeated, grateful for small miracles.

Love and contentment did wonderful things to people. Gillian blossomed under Logan's loving attention and her daughter's dependence. She carried her tall frame with pride now. Her strawberry hair, now streaked with golden highlights from the strong South Carolina sun, enhanced the contours of her face. Now that her shapely figure had returned, Gillian wondered if she could attract men—but only one mattered.

Dr. Warren had pronounced her physically fit this morning. With Judith safely ensconced in the third-floor nursery with Hilda, who had eagerly agreed to remain with the baby, Gillian had to admit that she, too, could not wait to resume her intimate relationship with Logan. During the last stages of pregnancy, she had felt that she was holding back, for fear of hurting the baby. But now, ah, now she had nothing to worry over. Nothing except the nagging fear that her husband no longer found her appealing.

How could she know that Logan dreamt about making love to her? Fearful that it was too early to resume their physical relationship, Logan kept his dreams to himself, much to his chagrin. Some mornings, he awoke in painful anticipation, wanting her, watching her offer her full breasts to their daughter as long curls fell enchantingly down her bare shoulders. Her porcelain profile reminded him of a Michelangelo statue, finely developed and ethereal. But when she smiled, her lifelike qualities became apparent. She was his woman, but he could not have her—yet.

Some nights he deliberately waited until she was abed, under the sheets, her lacy satin nightgown out of view. If he watched one more night of Gillian seated in front of her dressing table combing her hair, her ripe breasts outlined against the fine lawn material rising and falling with each brush-stroke as she hummed some lullaby, oblivious to the world around her, he might go mad from wanting her. Afraid that he could not trust his carnal instincts, Logan waited in his study down-stairs. But that rarely did him any good, for his imagination was as good as his eyesight.

Tonight, he slowly walked up the mahogany stairs, almost wishing she was asleep, the sheet wrapped up and under her chin. He did not think he could say another word to her without revealing his true emotions. And he no longer knew if Gil-lian wanted him. Sometimes she was so preoccu-pied with Judith that Logan wondered if she knew he was around—watching her face and body, studying her every move. He did not have the courage to discuss his feelings with anyone, and so Logan Hammond, once known as London's most infamous rake and lover, became an insecure, hopeful suitor, longing for his wife's attention.

His sky-blue shirt was half unbuttoned as he reached the first landing. When he noticed the candlelight peeking out beneath their bedroom door, he almost decided to turn back down the stairs. Cursing his cowardliness, Logan forced his booted feet up the wooden steps.

Old habits die hard, so when he slowly opened the bedroom door, his eyes naturally roamed to the dressing table. But she was not there.

"Logan?" she called from the bathing room. "I'm in here. Would you hand me a towel? I forgot again to place it beside the tub."

Like a doomed man sentenced to die, he did as he was bid, but dreaded looking at the beguiling creature in the porcelain tub. The walls were damp from steam. Moisture bubbled on his nose and forehead. The room smelled of lavender and attar of roses. He had to leave or make a fool of himself.

"Oh, I love this tub. I'm so pleased you had it made. Why, it's so large and roomy," she splashed gaily, "there's room for two."

He knew that, of course. That was his reason for ordering it. Keeping his golden-brown eyes averted, he focused on the fluffy white towel that would wrap around her luscious body.

"Ah, Gillian, I think I left a lit cigar downstairs. I'd better see." He almost turned to run out of the room, but her lilting voice stayed him.

"You never forget such things, Logan. Here," she splashed some more, and he knew she was going to stand, "hold the towel for me, will you?"

He gulped. Trapped with this naked vision before him, Logan could not dare touch the glistening white skin lest his passion erupt. "Here." He almost threw the towel at her.

"I can't. Oops, I dropped it."

Left with no choice but to reach for the towel, his eyes slowly traveled up her bare legs, those long shapely legs that could drape around his body, traveling higher to her now-flat tummy and higher still to the rounded, firm breasts that begged to be touched.

"Gillian, please." His aching whisper gave her

courage.

"Logan, would you look at me?" Her slender arm touched his shoulder. "I have something to tell you."

"It's all right, Gillian, I'm leaving. I won't touch you." The words jumped out of his mouth.

"But, Logan, I want you to touch me."

His eyes shot up to hers. "This is not the time to jest, woman. You are playing with fire," he growled.

"I know." She smiled devilishly. "But it's all right now. Clayton said so."

Like a child whose fondest wish had been answered, he threw the towel on the floor as he wrapped himself around her wet, naked body.

"You'll get drenched."

"Who gives a damn." He took her lips. "Gillian," he said after one breathtaking kiss, "you have no idea how much I have longed for you."

"I was afraid," she whispered into his damp neck.

"Afraid of what?"

"Afraid you wouldn't want me."

Her confession made him guffaw with glee. Gillian was tempted to smack his face.

"I think I should tell you about my dreams. In detail. But now I want to experience them. Each one, all night." He lifted her out of the tub, pressing her body against his chest. "You have no idea how long I have waited for this moment." He kissed her eyelids. "I've never stopped wanting you, thinking of you, craving your skin, your hands, on my body. And I've never stopped thinking about all the sensual things I would do to you."

"I'd like to hear about these dreams. I wonder if I've had the same ones." She nuzzled his neck. "I'd like to take your shirt off now." She reached down to unbutton the remaining buttons, then laughed when it was obvious he could not take his clothes off as long as she remained in his arms.

"Logan, would you like me to bathe you?"

It was a glorious inspiration, but Logan did not think he could wait. "Later. That's another dream I wanted to tell you about. But first . . ." he put her down to remove the shirt, "first I want to kiss these." He lifted her heavy breasts. "Just as I thought." A drop of warm liquid dripped into his mouth. "Mmm, I envy our daughter."

The rising heat in the pit of her stomach made her forget to blush. "Oh, Logan," she stood on her toes to kiss his mouth, "I can't wait and yet, yet in some way I feel like a virgin. It's been so long."

"I've never wanted anyone as much as I want you now. It's like a sickness," he paused to kiss her neck and ears, "I cannot get enough of you. I think of your body, of your passionate little moans, of your sighs of pleasure to the point of obsession."

She lifted her chin to gaze into his face. "I love you."

"Gillian, I love you, too. And I need you." He took her hand, lowering it to the swollen manhood trapped beneath his skintight trousers.

Never before did her hands so nimbly unbuttoned the material that separated his skin from her

369

heated touch. They were both liquid fire, groping, stroking, aching for a fulfillment that only the other could provide.

They never made it out of the bathchamber, for Logan lowered her to the white carpet while she tore at his shirt. And without further preamble he found her heated center and moaned as his release sent thousands of shattering stars around him.

"Oh, my God. Gillian, I'm sorry," he was still deep inside her, rhythmically moving against her heated flesh, "I feel like a schoolboy who has lost control."

"Logan, I need more," she whispered in his ear, aching for her own release.

"With pleasure, madame." He adjusted his weight, rolling over onto his back with her now seated astride. "Now, sweetheart, tell me exactly what you would like me to do."

Stretching like a feline, her head thrown back in anticipation of the delights ahead, she laughed throatily. "No, darling, you don't have to move. I know you are spent," she looked into his eyes, "it's my turn to do all the work."

He loved watching her face. Their eyes met, and she smiled, first in pleasure, then in ecstasy. Her mouth curled almost as if in pain as her body moved along his, setting the pace, as she kept striving for the starry sky.

But he wanted to increase her pleasure. Cupping his hands over her rounded buttocks, he told her to do the same. Her nails dug into him as they pressed so close it was not possible to distinguish whose body set the rhythmic pace. They moved in unison, Gillian panting in his ear, begging for more while Logan rotated his hips to accommodate her wish.

"I want more," she pleaded. Placing her hands on his shoulders, she lifted her head to take his mouth and tongue into hers. Sucking lightly on his tongue, she began to moan, as his hands dug deeper into her buttocks, pressing her against his bones, not giving her the opportunity to separate their bodies for an instant.

"Feel me, Gillian." He spoke against her swollen lips. "Feel how much I want you. Do you want me?" He pressed harder against her hips.

"Oh, Logan, I cannot get enough."

Somehow she was on her back, with his handsome, perspiring face above hers. "Let me help you, love." His seductive smile heated her soul. Placing his muscular arms on both sides of her face, he leaned, letting his lower body pound into her warm, wet core. "Can you feel me now?" He pounded. "No? Not yet? How about now?" He saw her eyes glaze in ecstasy.

Instinctively she bit her lower lip. "No, Gillian. Don't hold back. Let me hear your passion." His voice filled her ears, and all she heard was his deep voice encouraging her to soar to the heavens with him alongside. Briefly, everything around her was black, so she held onto him as if they were truly flying through turbulent clouds.

"Oh, Logan," she moaned aloud.

"Feel me, love. Feel our love. Gillian . . ." He repeated her name, and she could not think of anything but the overwhelming desire and love for

371

the man who held her heart and soul in his powerful hands.

When at last they settled back to the world around them, Logan decided it would be fun if they finally used the large tub for its intended purpose. Scooping up his laughing wife in his arms, he settled himself in the tepid water, then none too gently lowered her on top of him.

"I must compliment the fellow who built this to my specifications. I think he did an excellent job."

"I hope you have two more made, for London, and for the plantation."

This could have been the time to tell her about his other life in England, he thought fleetingly. But with Gillian laughing as she rubbed her perfumed soap into his chest, he quickly abandoned the idea. There would always be another time.

The large gold French mantel clock struck three times when she begged him to let her sleep. "Just a few minutes, love. Thank goodness Judith no longer requires a 2 A.M. feeding. She could have starved!"

"I have a delightful method for sleeping," he grinned, leaning above her. He was starving for her body. "Have I ever shown you this way?" As they lay entwined, he gently slipped into her wet and willing body. "Don't move," he whispered against her tangled hair. "Just sleep."

She giggled, but he insisted. "No, I mean it. Just sleep this way."

It lasted five minutes before they invented yet another way of making love off the bed.

Near dawn, when exhaustion claimed them, Logan thought he had found peace at last. Nothing could change their feelings for each other.

He had made a costly error in judgment.

Chapter Thirty-seven

April 1827

As long as Gillian and Logan remained cloistered in their single-style house on the East Battery, their private world of love had a chance of remaining intact. But outside forces were working against them, most notably two people. And one was about to make himself known.

On a bright and sunny Friday morning during the first week of April, Viscount Brian Althorp arrived in Charleston.

The other mysterious person was the English agent still hard at work in Charleston and Savannah.

According to Harold and Peter, this person and his associates were doing a proper job of fomenting strife and doubt among many prominent southerners. It had even been rumored that Vice President Calhoun's intensified interest in the issue of states' rights, the right of the individual state to make its own laws and declare what is constitutional, was due to a number of individuals whispering in his ears.

Not all were British agents or sympathizers. But

the right chord had been struck in the hearts of many unhappy southerners who continued to blame the North for the South's economic woes.

Harold was desperate for Logan's assistance and told him again during one of their weekly meetings at the same dockside tavern. Leaving Gillian for a few hours was not a problem, but Logan was reluctant to leave his wife's side—even overnight—and now Harold needed Logan to spend a week in Washington.

"This should be the last time, I hope. We've arrested two individuals in New York and another in Boston. We are close, Logan. With luck we'll have the names of the others. But I want you to talk to them. I want you to be Lord Logan Hammond again, the famous London rake who, while visiting America, learned about his two compatriots. Make them believe that you are outraged by the Americans' boorish behavior and plan to intervene on behalf of His Majesty's government. Make them confide in you, man."

He could not say no. Not this time. Logan could not think of a time when Harold sounded and appeared visibly upset. Knowing that Henry Clay was leaving in a fortnight for Paris made the assignment more urgent. At least they had extra time, for Clay's plans had changed. He'd stay in Paris three weeks before leaving for London. That left them five weeks. Considering the time they needed to get a message to Clay in Paris, they only had three weeks to break this firmly entrenched English network.

"Logan, the sooner this matter is settled, the

375

sooner we can all go back to living normal lives," Harold confided. "Even Peter and Lily are anxious to solve this."

"I know. They've become less comfortable with each other." Privately Logan speculated as to why the Harrises' behavior seemed more formal than before. He knew the signs. He could see a man who was falling in love against his better judgment. He could see the conflict in a man who had a responsibility to serve his government but suddenly discovered his dreams were filled with one woman's laughing face.

And if he weren't mistaken, Lily Burke Harris was showing the same symptoms. Even Gillian had noticed the secret glances she stole at Peter when he wasn't looking.

Logan smiled nostalgically while remembering his peculiar courtship with Gillian. "I think they'll need some friendly assistance. As soon as this matter is finished once and for all, I think I'll have a long chat with Peter. It might be a challenge, trying one's hand at matchmaking."

"Just because you're so disgustingly in love does not mean every other man in the world should share your feelings," Harold scolded gently. "Besides, I have some grim news for you."

Suddenly, Logan recalled a conversation with Harold less than one month ago. He sat rigidly in his chair, his face a sudden mask of stone. "When did Althorp arrive?"

"Yesterday."

"I see." At last Althorp was here. Logan no longer had to think about when and if he would arrive. Was he here for Gillian or for His Majesty? Or did King George know nothing, while Canning continued to mastermind British foreign policy. Or was it possible Althorp was acting alone?

"He left the city this morning. He's on his way to Savannah. My sources believe he'll be there for at least a fortnight. You could be to Washington and back before Althorp's return. No one knows about the agents we arrested. They've simply disappeared. Once he finds out about his people, there is no telling what he might do."

"Althorp has been known to have a loose fuse. He must know we are here."

"He knows Gillian is not leaving. He must be as anxious as we to finish what he started. I think he wanted to pull his agents out of the country before it gets too difficult to cover his tracks."

"I wish Gillian and Judith would go to Raveneau Plantation. I'd feel better with Grandfather standing guard, but I cannot alarm Gillian. She still thinks of Althorp as her dear childhood friend."

"You said your grandfather was planning to visit shortly. Convince him to stay with Gillian while you're away."

Logan considered the suggestion, then flashed a devilish grin. "I think that's just what Grandfather wants. Another opportunity to take charge of our lives. While I'm away he'll most likely harangue Gillian about my wayward life and the need to settle permanently in Charleston. Harold, it just might work. I think I'll tell him the truth. It's about time he learned a trifle more about me."

"I don't mind. Your grandfather is a loyal supporter of Henry Clay. Do as you think best. And Gillian?"

Logan knew precisely what he meant, but decided to avoid the question by shrugging noncommittally.

Before returning home, Logan stopped at the South Carolina Society Hall on Meeting Street. It was too early in the evening for any of the club members to bother him, and using the club's stationery, he dispatched a missive to his grandfather. "Come immediately, we need you. No one is ill or in danger . . . yet." The rest Logan would explain personally, but the note was enough to get Henri on the private schooner with the next outgoing tide.

Logan briskly walked down Meeting Street, then cut onto Tradd Street towards his house. Gillian was probably feeding Judith by now, a scene he regretted missing.

The sun's descent caught his eye. The glare, magnified against the Ashley and Cooper rivers, temporarily blinded him. It was enough to disorient him and enough for one man to jump out from one of the private alleys on Tradd Street. With a gleaming knife in hand, the burly seaman's eyes and hand were directed at Logan's stretched neck.

"See ya, matey." His cockney accent was obvious.

Instinct and strength prevailed. No longer off guard, Logan jammed his elbow in the man's ribs. It was enough to lessen the lethal grip around his neck. Whirling, his fists found the sailor's face and stomach, the staccato motion felling his opponent in two minutes. The knife sliced through his coat sleeve before clattering to the cobblestone street.

Three flower ladies, their wares still in hand, passed by, then screamed at the gruesome sight before their eyes. "He's dead!' one yelled.

"Get help!" screamed another.

Logan grabbed the man by his neckerchief, twisting the filthy cloth enough to make him choke. "Who paid you?"

"Dunno" was the raspy reply that deepened as Logan's feral smile forewarned the man's fate. Effortlessly, he lifted one knee to the man's groin. "Can you recall now?"

"I dunno his name. An Englishman, that's all. Sailed on my ship. Arrived Friday."

"Tell Althorp I'm sorry he forgot my reputation as one of London's most formidable pugilists. Can you remember the words, man?"

The scarf twisted again and the man gurgled his reply. "Good, for the next time I see you, I'll waste no time in sparring with you. I'll kill you." His mouth curved in a vicious smile. "And I think I'll enjoy it."

The sailor dropped to the ground like a fallen tree after a hurricane. Logan straightened his cravat and jacket, grateful that the sleeves were wide enough to deflect the knife's intended path.

The ladies still screamed as Logan looked straight ahead, resuming the quick pace that would take him home to his family.

She was at the door.

"Logan? What happened to you. Goodness, you look like you've been in a fight." She scurried over to inspect his face before settling on the damaged coat sleeve.

"Its nothing. Some drunken sailor mistook me for the rich planter who stole his girl. I wonder who it is." He forced a light tone. "I'd like to see this woman."

"Are you hurt?" Her hands roamed along his arms.

"I'm fine. I swear it."

"And the sailor?"

"He'll live."

"Logan, my goodness, he could have killed you." The import of her words took seconds to irritate her raw nerves. Gillian started to babble nervously. "This is absurd. I thought America was civilized. How can anyone walk through the streets without fearing for his life? And to think I walk along the Battery late at night. My goodness . . ."

"Whoa, darling." Logan gently grasped her shoulders. "It was an accident, nothing more. Walk with me into the library. I wouldn't mind a glass of Madeira. Will you join me?"

Gillian made him repeat the story three more times before finally relaxing. Logan decided it was best to hit her with his news now.

"Gillian, sit next to me." He patted the red-and-gold brocade settee. "I must go to Washington." A little truth would be good, he decided as he took to his story. "I must meet two business acquaintances there. One of them is a Senator from Massachusetts." He prayed she wouldn't remember names later. "Since Congress is still in session, it's best I go there."

"What for?"

His mind whirled, searching, rejecting, then finally settling on a plausible story. "I want to buy some more land. In the North. I'm interested in one of the new factories in a place called Fall River." God, he better remember what he was saying later on when she asked him how his trip went.

He rattled on about diversifying one's business interests and his grandfather's desire to accumulate more property in the North. Whatever he said, Gillian seemed to accept it was important to the Raveneaus and Hammonds. "Uncle Joseph cannot go. I must do it alone. I don't really mind. I can travel faster unencumbered by anyone. I promise to be back in one week." He nestled her hand in his. "I will not leave you again after this."

"Oh, I doubt it, Logan. But I understand, especially if you promise to stay away from any and all females." She tweaked his nose.

He hugged her tightly, forcibly expelling his breath slowly. "I promise."

Three days later, as Logan prepared to leave, the front door of the house banged open.

"Logan! Gillian?" a gruff voice bellowed. "What's going on here? Where the deuce are you?"

From that day on, Logan decided there must be a God or some heavenly angel watching over him. Gillian was not home. She and her mother had gone to the dressmaker's and milliner's shops.

"Hello, Grandfather." Logan sauntered over to the imposing figure in the doorway.

381

"Speak to me, lad, and quickly. What kind of trouble have you gotten yourself and your family into now?"

Henri doffed his hat, coat, and silver-tipped cane, then led the way to the library.

"I thought you've never been here before?"

"I lied." The old man agilely settled himself in a large armchair, leaning his hands against the cane. "Speak."

Logan told him everything. How long he'd been working for the American government, his double life in England, the lies he told his family for years and now his fears for his wife and child, thanks to Brian Althorp.

"I've suspected as much for quite some time," he said quietly when Logan finished.

"I should have known. You seem so calm, considering how my confession could wreak havoc on everyone's lives."

"I'm proud of you, son. Always was." His gruff voice seemed to catch. "I've wanted to help and am pleased you've decided to ask me at this late date." His dark gold eyes shone with intensity and love.

Together they devised a story for Gillian. Henri would stay at the house as long as necessary. He would not take up residence in his home on Church Street, but remain with Gillian until Logan's safe return. With Webster also in residence, Logan felt the women would be safe.

Convincing her was easier than either of the men thought. Still unnerved by Logan's mistaken attack, she was relieved that Logan thoughtfully invited his grandfather to stay with them while he was in

Washington.

Logan left the following dawn leaving his wife, who drowsily stretched on their huge bed, begging in a sleepy voice to be kissed just once more. Wouldn't he like to hold her just once more? she asked as the sheet slipped over her naked thigh.

He left an hour later, carrying her passionate response to his lovemaking deep within his heart.

In the weeks to come he would remember that special morning with sadness and despair.

Chapter Thirty-eight

Gillian felt lonely. Not that she was alone. Henri, Judith, and Helena certainly kept her busy, but nothing was the same without Logan's presence. She knew she was behaving childishly. Oftentimes, he would leave early in the morning and didn't return until late in the evening when she was abed. But there was a difference, for she always fell asleep in his loving embrace. This time, the large four-poster bed with the gold satin sheets was empty.

Three days after Logan's departure, Gillian finally allowed her mother to persuade her to accept an invitation to Hattie Mathews's home for tea. Certain that only a few ladies would be present— most were still on their plantations—Gillian decided to go. "But only for two hours, Mother. No more than that," she warned.

"I shall be honored, ladies, to come for you at the precise time Gillian requests," Henri offered. Judith was safely nestled in her great-grandfather's arms, seemingly mesmerized by the gold chain watch dangling before her blue-gray eyes.

There were, unfortunately, more ladies in attendance than she thought. Gillian silently cursed herself for forgetting that Hattie's niece was Anabelle Blacton, who was—according to the rumors—more than a little interested in Logan. So, too, was Eve Carlton, who smugly sat on the far end of the room, anxious to corner Gillian with more vicious lies.

Gillian did not possess the haughty confidence of Eve or the shrewdness of Anabelle. She quickly looked down at her pale peach India cotton dress, and wished she wore something less revealing. Her full breasts almost spilled over the top and, if she weren't mistaken, her milk began to drip. Quickly excusing herself, she scurried to a dressing room to repair the damage. Fortunately, there was none. Taking a deep breath, she stared at her worried frown in the mirror. "He is your husband. You love him. He loves you. There is nothing these bitches can say to harm you." She spoke with authority to her image.

Eyeing her mother in earnest conversation across the crowded parlor with another matron, Gillian's blue-green eyes remained fixed ahead. She was unprepared for a dual assault.

"Oh, Gillian, dear. Please join us." Anabelle's voice rang clearly in the room. "I wanted to congratulate you. How is the child? A girl, is it not? And you've almost regained your figure. Logan must be pleased."

Don't babble, she warned herself. Look at those two. They're waiting for a faux pas. Be calm, girl. "We are very happy, thank you. Perhaps some day you will understand." She eyed both women.

"Well, Richard has told me how pretty the baby

385

is. Says she looks a lot like you. Logan wasn't too disappointed it wasn't a boy?"

She missed the first reference to Richard Paxton, but not the next one.

"Richard thinks so highly of you, Gillian." Anabelle's light eyes seemed to glow. "But I'm certain you'll be happy for us now, won't you?"

"Anabelle, Gillian has been secluded in her new home with her baby. She has no idea what has been going on in the world around her. I am certain Logan does not tell her everything." Eve's voice dripped venom.

There she goes, Gillian thought. Logan, wherever you are I will thrash you when you return. How could you have been interested in this viper, she wondered. "My husband and I don't concern ourselves with trivial matters outside our home. Surely you must understand how demanding a husband and child can be." Gillian did not flinch. "Oh, but you don't, dear. I seem to have forgotten. You don't have any children and there is no permanent man in your life at the moment, is there?" She spoke in her most official icy English-accented tone. She was so impressed with herself, wondering where in heavens did she learn to be as bitchy as Eve.

"Oh, come now," Anabelle had the good sense to interfere. "We mustn't air our differences in such a gauche manner."

"Of course not." Gillian was warming to the repartee. "I shall tell my husband you both send your best wishes for our happiness."

"When is he returning?" Anabelle asked.

On impulse, she decided to lie. "Tomorrow. He sent a message. Seems as if my husband does not like to be away from us." She smiled brightly. "You might want to try family life, Eve. It's most rewarding."

"Well, I certainly aim to try it. Richard and I have been so happy together," Anabelle trilled. "I love his uniform. It makes one wonder what's beneath."

"You already know, dear." Eve switched to another victim. "If I know my cousin, you must be spending quite a bit of time alone. I'd watch out for my reputation if I were you."

Gillian laughed aloud. "Your reputation? My my, this has been such an enlightening conversation."

"Don't be so smug *chérie*," Eve took her arm. "He was in my bed long before yours and I know how to keep him satisfied. When the novelty of baby and wife wear off, I will be waiting. As I've said, darling, Logan doesn't tell you in detail about all the evenings he has spent, ah, otherwise engaged. He's not a cad."

Instinctively Gillian pulled back. The woman was lying, she was certain of it. But the triumphant look in Eve's dark eyes made Gillian's stomach flip.

"He comes home to me, Eve. Besides, you must know what they say about reformed rakes. They make the best and most loyal husbands. After all," Gillian archly glared at Eve, "they've sampled everything." She promptly spun on her heel and regally walked away.

387

Somehow she managed to make it through the next two hours. Taking special delight in exchanging baby stories with the other women, Gillian smiled at the glowering Eve Carlton.

Only later, when she was alone in the big four-poster bed, she gave in to her doubts and pounded the feather pillow with both fists. She did not know if the imaginary face she pounded was Eve's or Logan's.

The following morning, she received a short letter from Logan.

"I miss you. I hope you and Judith are doing well under Grandfather's stern supervision. I cannot wait to come home to you.

All my love,
Logan."

The timing could not have been better. Some of the nagging doubts were allayed, but only temporarily, for early in the afternoon, just as Gillian and Helena were returning from a shopping trip, a well-dressed gentleman in dark hat and coat jumped out of his coach to hail the ladies.

"Gillian, my dearest, and Lady Marlowe, how good it is to see you both again."

Brian Althorp rushed forward to take some of the boxes out of the ladies' hands, escorting them up the stairs to the Hammond home as if he were a welcome guest.

In a way, he was, for Gillian and Helena were quite ignorant of the drama unfolding around them. Henri Raveneau knew, which was why he had refused Althorp entry into his grandson's home when Althorp appeared on the doorstep less than two hours ago. He obviously underestimated the man who must have kept his coach out of view around the corner waiting for Gillian's arrival.

Henri was standing at the front-door entrance, his large frame ostensibly barring entry to Althorp.

"Grandfather, come greet an old, dear friend of mine. Brian Althorp." She paused and giggled, suddenly remembering to use his formal title. "I meant Viscount Althorp." She turned laughing eyes up to Brian. "We're not so formal in the States, you see."

He did not miss the reference to "we," although Gillian had no idea how much she had revealed about herself with the endearing word she used for Henri and her last statement. Brian suddenly wondered if the situation could get out of control.

As far as he was concerned, Gillian was only temporarily out of his reach. It was simply a minor problem that he would correct within a few weeks, once that husband of hers was either dead or rotting in an English prison.

That Brian had a plan was without doubt. Long before the long, choppy voyage across the Atlantic, he had formulated and calculated. If everything went according to plan, Brian Althorp's journey would be quite fruitful and rewarding.

The surly old man standing before him like one of the king's guards was nothing more than a nuisance and would prove that as well, when the time was right.

"Brian, I'm so happy to see you," Gillian gushed

enthusiastically. Her bonnet fell somewhere near the marble table as she ushered Brian past Henri and into the morning room. "When did you arrive? How was your journey? Have you any letters from Father? Oh, you must tell me about London and the king and your friend Mr. Canning."

Despite his best efforts not to laugh at the bombardment of questions, Brian found himself smiling at her beautiful, bright face. Lord she was a lovely creature. To think that Hammond had her first, that she had his child, were two more reasons to put the noose around his arrogant neck.

"I'm here on part holiday, part official business," he raised a dark eyebrow in Henri's direction, "but I would never miss a chance to see you. I've missed you, too. You ran out of London so quickly, I was unprepared for the void you left in my life." His dark eyes glowed as they focused on her heaving chest. The fine white linen dress revealed a more shapely woman beneath it.

"I insist you stay for dinner. Don't you agree, Grandfather?" She ran to clutch his arm. "Oh, I am so delighted!"

In her heartfelt joy at seeing an old friend, Gillian overlooked her grandfather's dour look. Helena did not. Something was very wrong with Henri. He was never known to be an ungracious host.

"You look the same, Brian." She glanced over his lean, tall frame and dark brown hair. "Ah ha, I see a bit of gray at the temple." She laughed. "Perhaps you take your job too seriously."

Henri groaned inwardly. Gillian was in for a

shock and so was Logan if this friendly reminiscing were allowed to continue. Damn Logan for leaving him to handle this awful situation. Henri suddenly doubted he could keep Gillian away from someone she so obviously respected. What could he tell her? That this man was her husband's nemesis? That he was out to hang her husband, the father of her child who also happened to be an American agent?

Henri acted on his first and only thought. He clutched his chest and leaned forward. "Oh, no," he groaned. "Another one."

"What?" Gillian's alarm was very real. "Grandfather, what is wrong? Here, you must sit down." She aided him to the sidechair. "Let me get help."

"No, no, I'll be fine. Just let me rest a minute. Oh," he groaned a bit louder, "it must have been the stairs. I've forgotten to pace myself, that's all." Under one furry gray eyebrow, Henri stole a glance at Althorp. Judging from his sneer, the man did not approve of his performance.

"Grandfather, let me help you to your room." She looked stricken with fear as she leaned on her knees before him. "You'll be fine. I'll get Dr. Warren."

"No, no, dear, I don't need a doctor."

"Oh, but you must. I'll go myself."

"No," he grabbed her arm, "I would like you to stay with me." His innocent look struck her maternal chords.

"Of course. Of course. I'll send someone else. Brian," she did not even look at him, "I hope you will excuse us. Perhaps you can call on us tomorrow? I really must tend to Grandfather. It must have been the journey here and all the excitement, you know with Judith and all."

Brian could not understand most of her incoherent rambling. Giving this round to the old man, Brian inclined his head a fraction, enough for Henri to notice.

"I understand. Perhaps it was the excitement of seeing me as well that has upset your grandfather. I will be staying at the Planter's Inn, if you should need me for anything at all, at any time." He looked again at the old man.

Grandfather made an amazing recovery after Brian's departure, and Helena again noticed that something was very wrong.

"All right, Henri. You can fool my daughter with that act, but you cannot fool me. Why were you so hostile to Brian Althorp? He's Gillian's oldest friend. And a friend of the Marlowe family, I might add."

Henri struggled to sit up in bed. He hated all those fluffy pillows nestled behind his back. Logan would hear about this, too.

"I don't understand," he began.

"You certainly do." Helena placed herself before the foot of the bed. "Why don't you like Brian? Is it because he had asked for Gillian's hand?"

That wasn't a bad reason, he decided and nodded vigorously. "I know that he and Logan did not get on well in England. I do not know why he is here except to cause some trouble between Logan and Gillian." That much was true.

"Brian is a serious young man, I'll admit. And he takes his responsibilities to heart. But I cannot believe he would cause Gillian harm or interfere with her marriage."

"Take my word for this, will you, Helena? I would like to keep Althorp away from Gillian until Logan returns home. That's all I ask. A few more days. Will you help me?" His voice held a new tone. If she weren't certain that Henri was a man of confidence and power, she never would have guessed that the man's voice trembled with panic.

"Logan should be home in two days. I suppose that is not asking very much."

"No matter what, keep Judith away from him."

"Judith?" She was surprised. "Whatever do you mean?"

"I cannot imagine this Brian, no matter how fond he is of Gillian, would have the same feelings about Logan's daughter."

Helena's forehead wrinkled. "I don't know. I'll think about this. But, Henri, there are only two days to forestall the inevitable. Brian is a patient man, but he can be a tenacious and relentless fellow, too."

"I guessed that the moment I set my eyes on him."

That night, Henri Raveneau prayed his grandson would come home soon and Brian Althorp be put on the first ship back to England.

Chapter Thirty-nine

Everyone but Brian overlooked Gillian's nightly ritual of walking along the Battery. Logan had taken to accompanying her on the evening stroll. It had become their private moment, when Logan protectively draped his arm around Gillian's shoulders as they talked about the little events that occurred during the day. They made plans, shared dreams, and sometimes they silently strolled along the high sea wall, watching the night stars and the ships bob in the bay.

Gillian continued to walk, for she found some solace by imagining that Logan was still alongside her. Not bothering to tell anyone but her maid that she would be out for a short while, Gillian draped a white wool cloak around her blue dress and headed across the road to the sea wall.

She was almost at the South Battery near White Point Garden when Brian caught up. "Hello there! Gillian, wait for me." He seemed to appear out of nowhere.

"Brian, however did you find me?"

"There aren't too many women I know dressed in white cloaks that contrast quite nicely against the dark sky, whose long red-gold hair streams behind

394

her as she walks briskly along this path. There are many things about you I recall, Gillian, especially your quick gait. Not very ladylike, you know." He smiled warmly.

"Oh, I know, Brian. You've told me often enough. Well, I could use some company tonight. Care to join me?"

Having no intention of doing otherwise, Brian nodded his dark head and took her ungloved hand in his. Her hand was smooth and warm, like the rest of Gillian, he decided.

"Tell me about London."

"Do you miss home?"

"Yes and no. I like Charleston, Brian. In some ways it's a lot like London, the different levels of society, the seasons when people journey to their summer homes, the gay social and cultural life. Unlike London, I find the city to be clean, safe enough for me to venture out alone, and not quite as stuffy as London society."

"I see." He didn't, but did not know what else to say. It surprised him that she was not homesick. "When are you planning to return to London? I think your father is angry enough to come after you."

"I know. In the most recent letter you kindly delivered," she lowered her head and flashed a winsome smile, "Father mentioned he might have to come and get Mother if she stayed through the summer."

"He misses his family."

"Isn't what's-her-name keeping him busy?" Gillian could not recall the name of her father's current mistress.

"You, young lady, are not supposed to know such things." There was a trace of humor in his voice.

"Logan. Oh, forgive me," she caught herself, "you sounded just like him. Anyhow, what I was going to tell you is that I am not as naive as you think."

Here was the opportunity. "Oh really? Tell me, Gillian, what do you know about your husband?"

Brian could not see the sparkle in her eyes as she conjured up the image of her husband. Since he'd been gone, the image was usually the same. They were alone in bed, underneath the cool sheets. She blushed in the darkness. "Oh, I know a great deal. He's not the London dandy, the notorious rake we once knew. He's an intelligent man, Brian. I'm sorry you do not know him. You might have been friends." She paused to lead Brian over some stones in their path. "Logan is witty, he is devoted to his family."

"What about to his country?"

"Whatever does that mean?"

They stopped to allow another couple to pass. Gillian decided to lean against the brick wall, offering her patrician profile to Brian.

"I think your husband is a very complicated man." He heard her delighted laugh, but continued. "What I mean is, well, what do you think he does whenever he travels?"

"Business. The Raveneaus own quite a bit of property, you know. And at least three banks that I know of. One factory in the North and various shipping activities. It keeps Logan busy. Brian?" She faced him. "Why are you so interested in Logan's business acumen?"

"Sweeting," he sighed. "It's not that. I don't believe you know everything about your dear Logan."

"You're just jealous," she accused.

"I admit I am, but I think there is something you must know. Gillian," he took her arm, "we've known each another most of our lives. I love you. I wanted to marry you. I'd still marry you."

She laughed. "That's not possible at the moment, Brian."

"Gillian, please be serious. I don't know how to say this."

A frisson of alarm ran up her spine. "Pardon me?"

Brian wanted to shake her. Never being particularly subtle with her, he chose this moment to reveal all.

"Gillian, you don't really understand what I do for His Majesty's government. I'm not saying you should. I've always been aware of your interest in politics, and have encouraged it. But tell me, what do you think about people who misrepresent themselves to others? Let's say these others are influential in one government and could pass along very pertinent information. Let's also say that this information is vital for the security of a nation."

"Why, that's treason!" she gasped.

"Precisely." He began to smile. "My job is multifaceted. One of my responsibilities is to ferret out these agents, arrest them, and bring them to trial."

"I remember," she whispered in a subdued voice.

"I've been after a particularly difficult chap for quite some time. Oh, he is good. He would stop at nothing. He's injured a number of people along the way. He's ruthless, Gillian. A killer."

Her hands rose to her throat. "No!" She shook her head and repeated the word over again. "That's not possible." She convulsively caught her breath. "I don't believe you." She turned away from Brian. She was going to run home, to the security of her house, to her bed, and wait for Logan.

"He's the best. Has been for a number of years."

"No. Not Logan. You must be mistaken, Brian." Brian knew her well enough to discern the tremor in her voice. "I cannot accept such an accusation simply because you say so. God, he is my husband!"

"People often deceive one another," he smoothly countered. "I thought you would force my hand. And I can prove it to you, if you'll let me explain some things to you now. I can also provide the physical evidence. But not here, not tonight. I will bring it to you tomorrow. You will have plenty of time to study it in the daytime."

Her head was spinning. She felt alternating chills and heat. How could she not trust Logan? On the other hand, Brian had never lied to her. Why would he do so now?

"Let me explain, Gillian." Brian suggested they continue to stroll, but she preferred to remain in place, facing the inky waters of the Ashley and Cooper rivers. His skill at piecing together Logan's other life was impressive, and he carefully, methodically related Logan's travels, which coincided with certain political situations. He described Harold Carter, again pointing out the unusual circumstances under which Logan and he would meet.

Still the nagging doubts persisted in Gillian's mind. Brian sensed it and smiled to himself. He was saving the best for last.

"Do you remember the night you were formally introduced to Logan?"

"Of course. It seems like the other day."

"Do you remember the incident that preceded your introduction?"

"Yes, Brian." She was annoyed. "Why do you keep asking these questions?"

"Be patient," he responded calmly. "Now I know you recall that you found yourself listening to a very dangerous conversation between two agents. One was passing information to another. Correct? Wasn't it possible that one of the voices belonged to none other than Logan? Wasn't it also possible that he chose that night to become better acquainted with you because he wanted to know how much you heard?"

She shook her head in denial, but Brian would not let the matter rest. "Wasn't it odd that he began courting you the very next day? You don't have to answer me now, but just think. Didn't Logan ever ask you questions about that night? About me? About your father's associates?"

"No, no, Brian, I don't want to hear any more." She pressed her hands to her ears. "This is ridiculous. This is all supposition. What difference could it make how Logan and I met?" God, she wanted to believe what she was saying, but the intensity behind the words and the fierce loyalty somehow slackened.

"Just let me say one more thing. Please." Brian saw a lone tear travel down the contours of her cheek. He almost thought of refraining from pushing her too far, but knew he was close to planting the final seed. He chose to continue.

"Gillian, about your betrothal. I was angry and hurt, I admit. I'm still uncertain why you chose not to confide in me. This will sound strange, but in a way Logan tried to come back to you when he planned. You see, he had to make that trip. He told you it was a holiday. It wasn't. I have the evidence to show you tomorrow. Logan was injured. In Venice Logan was stabbed. It wasn't a riding accident as he told you. He did break his arm, though it occurred trying to kill his attackers."

"How could you know all of this?" She tried to catch her uneven breath, the pain in her head almost unbearable.

"It's my job. That's what I do for His Majesty's government. I am protecting my country against conspirators and traitors. As I've said, I have known about Logan Hammond for a long time. I've never had the evidence, but I do now. Logan Hammond is an agent for the Americans. I have sworn affidavits from two of his former associates."

"Logan is half American." She feebly tried to defend him, but Brian had been thorough. There was very little left for Gillian to cling to. She was demoralized and beyond humiliation. She had been used and betrayed. What was left? she asked herself. What could possibly be left? How can you know someone as intimately and passionately as she knew Logan, only to discover it was a mirage?

"Logan is also a titled Englishman. Tell me, Gillian, if war were declared tomorrow, which side would you be on?"

"I love my country. I would never do anything to betray England."

"Obviously Logan Hammond feels differently. Can you forgive him?"

"Brian, enough!" she snapped. "I've heard more than enough to destroy all my dreams for a happy life with the man I love and whom I thought loved me. You're telling me he used me, that he never loved me. It was all part of some elaborate charade? I don't know, Brian. Is that what you wanted to hear from me at last? Is that the reason for methodically laying the evidence at my feet?"

"I said I can prove it to you."

"There is no need, you've been quite thorough." She gave an hysterical laugh. "Goodness, Brian. You must be awfully good at what you do."

He was pleased with himself. In a matter of minutes, he had been able to puncture all her silly dreams about the hero she blindly adored. The rest would be simple.

"You can help me."

"I can what?" She stared incredulously at him.

"You can help me. I want to bring Logan back to London to stand trial. I cannot very well arrest him here in the Colonies. Why, he'd be seen as a national hero. No, I plan to leave for England in a month or so. When I am ready, I hope you will help me."

"I cannot. I don't know. Oh, Brian, please." The tears began in earnest. "Don't ask me anything now. I'm going home."

"Let me walk you." He caught her arm as she started to walk away.

"No," she vigorously pulled away, "you've done enough, thank you. I need to be alone."

"Gillian, I'm doing this for you. I still love you." He spoke clearly and without much emotion.

"You also love your country and your position in the government. Tell me, Brian, which is more important to you? Me or your job?"

"Ask Logan," he answered quietly. The wind carried his voice. "What do you think he'll tell you?"

"The same as you. You're not all that different from each other," she called back. "Good night."

Her legs were heavy, and she had no energy. She could have collapsed on the cold stone path, but would not give Brian the satisfaction. She did not want his sympathy. She wanted solace and time to think back on her life in the last year.

Quietly, she dragged her lethargic body into the house, up the long staircase. The white cloak was abandoned somewhere along the way up the steps. She climbed all the way to the third floor, to Judith's nursery. She needed to feel her daughter's warmth as she softly cried on the downy head. She needed to feel wanted. She needed to know that if everything else in her world continued to unravel at this relentless pace, she would at least have her daughter.

Even if her father was a traitor to his country and to his wife.

Chapter Forty

This was not going to be like the other time when Gillian had felt there was no choice but to flee England. Then she had run away from Logan, her friends, and her life because of her shame and despair. Not this time.

Gillian spent the entire night secluded in her large bedroom, alternately pacing, crying, cursing, and feeling more sorry for herself than she ever had in her life. Just as the night sky began to give way to a pink dawn, she resolved how to handle Logan and his family and how to proceed with her family, particularly Judith.

She was leaving Logan, but she would not run out of the back door in the middle of the night. She had her pride and the knowledge that she was right, that she had no other choice but to leave the man who had used her, then betrayed her. But she wanted him to know why she was leaving. Even if he could not understand or care that their marriage vows had been broken, Gillian felt the only way she could be cleansed of Logan Hammond was to spit in his eye.

From the moment she deliberately took her time descending the wide staircase to the formal dining room where the family waited, Henri knew that there was something different about Gillian. And it did not bode well for his grandson.

Dressed in bright pink, her hair tightly coiled at her nape, he knew she was dressed for battle. He had heard her come in late last night and guessed that Althorp had found a way to see her alone.

"Good morning everyone." She forced a cheerful voice that fooled no one.

"What is wrong, Gillian?" Helena was obviously not deceived, either.

"Wrong?" was the shrill reply. "Nothing is wrong. Everything is going to be fine."

As Gillian reached for the silver tea pot, Helena cast Henri a worried frown.

"Did you go out last evening?"

"I did." She seemed to concentrate on buttering her roll.

"You saw Brian."

"Is that a question, Mother?"

Helena hadn't heard her daughter's defiant tone in many months.

"Whatever he told you, I think you should wait for Logan," Henri advised.

That was when Gillian realized her husband's grandfather knew the truth. "I intend to, Henri," she replied firmly.

She hadn't used his Christian name since their marriage and Henri grasped the meaning of her spoken words and gestures.

"Gillian?" Helena was truly confused. "Whatever is bothering you?"

"Ask Henri. He appears to know quite a bit. Let him try to explain away my husband's activities." She suddenly rose. "I think I hear my daughter's cries. I must go to her now."

Helena put down the silver spoon she had left dangling in midair. "Henri Raveneau, you have a lot of explaining to do. And I suggest you do it quickly before Gillian storms out of this house forever."

As diplomatically as possible, Henri tried to explain his grandson's other life to an Englishwoman, a woman whose husband was a respected member of the peerage, whose life and values were dominated by English society and allegiance to the royal family. He had to explain that his grandson believed in another, completely contradictory cause.

He must have aged another ten years. Judging from Helena's horrified expression, not only had *he* aged but she had acquired a few new wrinkles, too.

"I cannot begin to justify this to you," he concluded. "Logan has always been a passionate man. And, despite what you now think, a loyal friend and citizen. Years ago, he chose to remain with his mother's family. I think Richard Hammond had long suspected Logan's loyalties, and prayed nothing harmful would ever come of it."

"It has. You need only to take one close look at my daughter to know that a great deal of damage has occurred. This is only the beginning. Not only does Gillian possess a formidable temper, she does not forget a wrong done to her." Helena wiped a stray wisp of blond hair off her face. Her hands unconsciously twisted her pearl necklace. "I don't know what to say or think. I fear Gillian will leave no choice for the rest of us."

Logan lithely leapt off his stallion before the animal completely stopped. So eager to see his wife and daughter, he handed the animal to the waiting stableboy, shouting instructions as he bounded up the steps.

Some of Judith's things were strewn along the piazza, a poppet, a wooden cradle that was once his, some soft cloths used to prevent Gillian's clothes from soiling after Judith was fed. These were familiar items and it gave him such pleasure to touch them as he sauntered past. Being away made him feel homesick. He missed the freshly painted yellow house with its white trimming and white piazzas. He missed the familiar voices of Hilda shouting orders about the baby and Henri snorting his disgust for being ordered out of one room because it needed to be cleaned and Webster chiding him for some unforseen transgression. But mostly, he missed Gillian.

His trip had been so successful that he was able to leave two days earlier than planned. Harold had met him along the way, which made it easier to relay the information. He knew the names of the English agents, and almost hit himself for not immediately spotting the Charleston agent. It must be love and preoccupation with the woman one cannot wait to hold, he chided himself. Now he understood why so few of the agents were married — or at least happily married.

"Gillian!" he shouted as he pushed the door open. "Where the devil are you? Where is everyone?" He should have noticed that the house was too quiet, but again overlooked the obvious.

Finally his grandfather hurried out of the library. There was a definite slump to Henri's shoulders.

"What is it? Is something wrong with Gillian or Judith?" His eyes immediately lifted to the staircase above. Just as Logan began to dash, Henri stood before him.

"They are physically fine. In fact Judith is in excellent health. Logan, sit down."

"Oh no, you haven't used that tone with me for years, Grandfather." Logan remained standing, impatiently swiping the dust on his leather riding breeches.

"Althorp is here. He has seen Gillian."

The color drained from his ruddy face. "What happened?"

"I cannot say. I know she spoke with him at length, and I know she hasn't been the same since."

He slapped his forehead. He did not know which emotion was more overpowering, dread, panic, or anger. He should have killed Althorp long ago, but now it was too late. He wondered just how late it was for Gillian and him to clear the air.

Reading his mind, Henri offered, "At least she is still here. She must be waiting to talk to you."

"Oh, I doubt that she wants to talk."

Like a man forced to do the unwanted, Logan agonized over each step that led to his bedroom and his wife. He wanted to see Judith, to at least have the reassurance of his daughter's tiny body cuddled in his arms. But Gillian had to come first. He should have made that decision long before he accepted Harold's last assignment.

Knocking softly on the oak door, he did not wait for her to bid entry. His dirty boots made imprints on the cream-colored carpet, but still he walked to her.

Seated on a small cherrywood sidechair facing the window, she kept her gaze fixed on the activities in the bay.

"I know you saw me enter. I am more certain you heard me call your name. Don't you greet your husband?" His voice was rich with longing.

"Husband? Do I have a husband?" She refused to look at his face. "How do I know this marriage is legal? After all, I wonder if there are any laws prohibiting loyal English citizens from marrying American spies?" It was not cold outside, but there was a definite chill in the room.

"Oh, so that's it. You saw Althorp." With some effort, he managed to keep his voice bland.

"Is that all you can say?" She rounded on him at last.

"Would you like to let me talk about it now?"

"What could you possibly say that would make me change my mind?"

Deliberately, he took two steps towards her. "I love you," he quietly said. "Isn't that all that matters?"

"You don't love me, you never did. You used me," she accused, the anger building. "You sought me out the night of my uncle's ball. You, the most famous rake in London, the man who must have seduced more beautiful women than any other man to date, finds the tall, plain spinster and begins to court her for no apparent reason other than finding her witty and charming?"

Unable to contain the mounting fury, Gillian rose at last to look at him. He was dirty and unkempt. "You look like you've had a hard journey. Tell me, dear, were you really doing business for the family, as I so naively believed? Or were your duties more complicated, perhaps another assignment that could very well kill another Englishman?"

"Whether you choose to believe me or not, I am a patriot. I did what had to be done. I tried to save lives, Gillian. I tried to avoid war between two nations that are bound by blood and culture." His hardened voice did not impress her.

"Tell me, Gillian, did your Brian happen to say anything about the number of men he's mistreated in order to seek his truth? He forced confessions out of people. Some never made it to trial. Do you think that is justice?" He stood before her, one arm snaked out to grasp her wrist, pulling her out of the chair. "What can I say that will make you understand or at least accept that I never meant to hurt you?"

"Nothing," she spat, "for I have no desire to live with a traitor, no matter which side of the Atlantic we are on."

"Do you consider Althorp a traitor?"

"No, why should I?"

"Because he is the one who sent British agents to this country? Did he tell you why?" He saw her confusion and seized the advantage. "No, of course not. Why should he tell you that he had men and women come to America to fire up the passions of the northern and southern states — to encourage the southern states to secede. Do you know what the word 'secede' means? Do you?"

She vainly tried to twist out of his tightened grip on her wrist. "Let me go!"

"Not until you listen to me." This time he took both wrists, forcing her to sit on the bed with him. "Your dear friend Althorp wants to promote a civil war between the American states because his superior, your other friend George Canning, thinks it in the best interest of England to add the southern nation to the British empire."

"Let go of my arm," she warned. She was wearing a sleeveless turquoise dress and his imprint remained on her upper arm.

"You're not listening. But I want to tell you something else. Your precious Brian tried to have me killed. That was why I was late coming back to you. Despite what you think, I had every intention of coming back to make you my wife." His mouth tightened with his own mounting fury and his golden-brown eyes glared with the strong emotion. "Maybe you are not grown up enough, Gillian, to comprehend what men and women do for their country. Maybe you've lived too sheltered and pampered a life to understand that some people, even your Brian, will stop at nothing to achieve their goals."

"Are you finished?" she inquired calmly, taking an unanticipated interest in her long nails. "I have some packing to do."

"I'd like to rattle some sense into you. I'd like to shake you so hard, your elegantly coiffed hair would tumble around your face." He sighed heavily. "But I see there is no use. Where do you think you're running away to this time?"

"Away from you."

"And Judith?"

"She is coming with me, of course."

"Not, of course, Gillian." His wrath began to build. "This is my country, remember? I am the noble one here. I'm the one who has risked his life numerous times for his country. You cannot and will not take my daughter away from me."

"Can you follow us to England?" was her sweet retort. "I am most certain you would receive a different, albeit interesting homecoming. And tell me, Logan Hammond. While you are being so self-righteous about your activities for the Americans, what is your father supposed to think of his son the traitor?"

The words struck. Logan had always feared his father's reaction to such news, had once thought of abandoning his ventures for fear of humiliating his father, stepmother, and sister. But he had learned to cast that emotion aside, hoping that someday he could explain what he had not been able to do thus far.

"I suggest you do not discuss this matter with my father. It is something I am going to see to." There was a silken thread of warning in his speech.

"I hope you can live with yourself, Logan Hammond, for I cannot." Pulling her hands out of his, she stood up, to look down on his saturnine features. He was incredibly handsome, she would give him that much, but he was ruthless, too.

"The choice is yours. Either I leave with Judith," she emphasized the latter, "for Raveneau, or you leave this house. I care not where you go or with whom."

"Gillian, this is the last time I will ask you to forgive me and understand. It is the last time I will tell you that I love you. Once I walk out the door, you will have made your decision. It is, from my point of view, irrevocable."

"So be it."

"I will stop at nothing, however, to see my daughter. She will know who her father is."

"We'll see."

He spun to grab her again. "No debates, no negotiations. She is mine, too. You will not take her away from me. Even if you think you'd be safe in England, I assure you, as God is my witness, I will find a way to take her." His thunderous scowl should have been enough to thwart her clever retort.

"Get out of here, Logan. I cannot abide your presence. I am leaving for Raveneau in the afternoon. I will send you a note when it is permissible to visit with Judith."

Logan Hammond had never felt such intense pain or anger, yet before him stood the woman he loved more than his own life, the woman who now scorned him.

"As you wish, madame." His eyes bespoke fury and resolution. Without a backward glance, Logan Hammond spun on his booted heel and walked out the door, slamming it soundly behind him.

Chapter Forty-one

Nothing would ever be the same. Gillian's anger had taken control of her rational mind. Blinded by the overpowering emotions, she could not listen to anyone who spoke in her husband's defense. As far as she was concerned, he had used and betrayed her. Logan had never wanted to marry her, but wanted her only for what he thought she knew. It was as simple as that.

Thirty minutes after Logan marched out of the house, Gillian was still crying, but she was also packing. They would leave for the plantation in a few days. After that, well, she simply needed time to decide how to proceed.

Never had she felt more deserted by loved ones than she did now. Not even her mother, who certainly should have understood why Gillian could not live with Logan, was on her side. Without success, Helena tried to remind Gillian how deeply her husband loved her and their daughter.

Henri fared worse. Gillian was barely civil to him, since he had known about his grandson's occupation. But Henri Raveneau was more philosophical than Helena and believed that, with some time alone, Gillian would come around. That's what happens to people who are passionate about everything in life, especially love, he had told Helena.

Logan, however, was not philosophical. His anger surpassed the boiling point. Daring to think that she loved him bolstered his confidence, for he had wisely chosen his wife. He had decided to give up his dangerous work, because of Gillian and Judith. Now, if he was lucky, he would see Judith on rare occasions. And if the luck ran out, which was more than likely, Gillian would take their child home to England — where *he* could not set foot.

After storming out of the East Bay Street house, Logan — with the ever-faithful Webster in tow — settled himself in his Aunt Liza's home on Meeting Street. For two days he would not speak to anyone about Gillian, preferring the solace derived from excessive quantities of brandy.

Lord he was miserable and more determined than ever to create a trap for Brian Althorp.

On the fourth day of Logan's departure, Gillian received two letters, one from her husband informing her of his arrival late in the afternoon to spend some time with his daughter, the other from Lily Harris, inviting her for tea. Good, she thought, I will not have to look at his loathsome face. To be certain, she left the house before 3 P.M. deciding to walk the short distance to the Harrises' Tradd Street home.

The house was much smaller than her planter's-style home, but as tastefully decorated. Lily escorted Gillian into the upstairs parlor, insisting that Gillian keep her up to date on everything that was happening in Charleston, since she and Peter had been away for the last three weeks. Gillian could not know that Lily was better informed than she, and even knew about her separation from Logan.

Lily's purpose in inviting Gillian to her house was not to gather information from her friend but to be the friendly shoulder that Gillian so obviously needed.

"You look wretched. Are you going to tell me about it?" Lily noticed the faint purple smudges under Gillian's once vibrant eyes. Even the way she walked with her shoulders slightly slumped bespoke of a woman carrying too many burdens.

"I don't know how to begin. So much about me is a lie, I'm afraid it would take too long to explain." Two tears escaped with many more threatening to spill down her cheeks.

"I want to listen." Lily sat next to Gillian on the green damask settee. Her dark brown hair was swept up on top of her head, giving her a taller appearance. If Gillian had looked hard at her friend, she would have noticed that Lily, too, appeared fatigued and less ebullient than her usual cheerful self.

When Lily took Gillian's hand, her self-composure vanished. Once she started to tell her story, everything seemed to pour out of her—including the tears so carefully held in check.

"So you see, Lily," she concluded much later, "I am not entirely innocent. I came to Charleston under false pretenses. I must have hurt Richard Paxton with my slavish devotion to Logan, and now I discover that the man I thought myself to be passionately in love with is a much greater fraud. I cannot forgive him."

"Why?" Lily knew she would be treading in storm-tossed waters, but felt must do something to patch up the differences between her friends. She asked gently, "Ask yourself this, Gillian: Are you hurt because Logan is working against your country? Or is it more plausible that you are deeply hurt because you feel he used you in London, and once he caught up with you here in Charleston, he did not tell you the truth?"

"I cannot say," she sniffed.

"Gillian, you are being too hard on Logan. I know he

loves you."

There was something in the way Lily spoke, with such authority, that made Gillian really look at her friend.

"What are you hiding from me?" she asked suspiciously.

"In my own way I am a fraud, too." Lily's hand shook as she offered Gillian another glass of lemonade. "In time I would like to tell you all about the real Lily Burke Harris. But not now, not when you sorely need a friend. And I am your friend. I know that you love your husband. What else could possibly matter?"

Gillian audibly groaned. "I don't know if I have the strength to think anymore. This has been too awful. Bless you for listening, Lily. I feel so alone and bereft . . . Do you know what?" she hiccuped. "My mother doesn't even agree with me. She thinks I should talk things over with Logan. Can you imagine that?"

"Give yourself time. Perhaps in a few days, you may see things in a different perspective. But, Gillian," Lily took her hand, "don't do anything rash. Don't take revenge on Logan. You will be eternally sorry."

By the time she returned, Logan was still in the house. She knew from the sounds of Judith's happy gurgle that Logan had either arrived late or was unable to tear himself away from Judith.

Praying she would not see him, she quietly climbed up the servants' stairs to the second-floor piazza and sat in a corner rocking chair.

"Ah, you precious bundle. Your daddy loves you so much. I think about you, Judith, you know that? I even dream about your round bald head and sweet cherubic face."

It sounded as if Logan were dancing down the stairs with Judith, for his voice became clear. "You, my sweet baby, are going to be a heartbreaker," he crooned in his

416

uniquely accented half English, half southern drawl.

Gillian stopped rocking. That was Logan's dilemma, she suddenly realized. He was a half member of each nation. He simply chose to be a full citizen of one, and it wasn't her country.

"Your lips are just as sweet and round as your mama's. Did you know that? Ah, the first time I saw your mother, I noticed those lips." Logan continued his chatter, mixing it with nonsensical baby talk and praise over the baby's beauty and sweet disposition.

"Judith, love of my life. I swear I will always be there when you need me, no matter how great the distance separating us from each other. No matter what your mother thinks about me, know this, my little love. I adore you. I always will. And you were born to loving parents. I wish it could have been different for your mother and me." Either his voice seemed to catch, or he was walking away.

"Your mother will be home soon to take you away." He must have kissed her forehead. "Hey, sweetheart, don't close those beautiful eyes on me yet. There, there, thank you." He crooned some more and must have whirled her down the stairs, for they were gone when she finally dried her tears and walked inside to catch sight of them.

That night Gillian again lost some precious sleep. Words whorled through her feverish brain. Everyone was telling her to think about the love she and Logan shared. They told her that nothing else mattered. She remembered every word he had said to Judith, and it made her cry once again. Gillian had no idea she had so many tears left to shed.

And Brian told her to assist the English who wanted to capture Logan Hammond and ship him back to England.

By early morning, she had made two decisions: to

417

spend time alone at Raveneau Plantation and not to give Brian any cooperation.

Life, as Logan Hammond knew it, was unraveling before his heavy-lidded eyes. He hadn't shaved in three days, he drank more than he had in over three months, and he was totally miserable. How could he, of all people, be suffering from a broken heart? It was not possible, he told himself more than once. Now, clutching Gillian's most recent note in his hand, he acted like a lovesick pup, and it was making him careless.

The sun had barely reached its zenith when Logan bounded out the door of Liza's house. Gillian had sent him a note announcing her imminent departure, and it had not sounded as cold as her previous ones. She merely informed him of her desire to be alone, to "sort things out." She expressed hope that upon her return he could join her for tea and a private chat. Logan decided that was very promising indeed.

Thinking it best to see Harold before he went back to Washington, Logan vaulted onto his stallion and quickly rode over to the Planter's Inn—the very place Brian Althorp was residing.

It was inevitable that they would meet again. Logan almost collided with Brian at the entrance door.

Only Brian, whose senses were more keenly alert, reacted. "What a distinct pleasure to see you again, Mr. Hammond. Notice I said 'Mister,' for I believe that by the time you arrive in England—in chains, of course— you will have been stripped of your land and titles."

"A pity you will not be there to see it happen," Logan's lip curled in distaste.

"Well, I seem to have equally important business abroad, but I promised Gillian not to put you on the same ship as the baby and the two of us when we sail

418

home."

"How good of you, but I must apologize, for I will not be sailing with you."

Brian's cold smile did not reach his eyes. "We shall see."

"She is not yours yet, Althorp, and must I remind you that you are in my country? I think you are bluffing, old chap. But if I must hang for treason, there is no reason why I cannot hang for murder, too." Deliberately, Logan bumped his shoulder into Brian's. "It might be worth it. I would enjoy myself."

Harold witnessed the scene from the second-floor balcony. Logan was risking his life, his carelessness could harm all involved, and Harold made a point of dressing him down. "You, my dear man, will destroy everything if you continue to let your emotions control you. We are nearly finished here, Logan, do not ruin it."

"I'm sorry," he ran his fingers through tousled hair, "I just wish I could have a go at him."

"In time. First we must wait for the President's letter. We must wait for him to tell us how to proceed. It is possible that both President Adams and Mr. Clay may not want us to uncover Althorp and his group yet. So you," he jabbed a stubby finger into Logan's shoulder, "will have to refrain from murdering him."

"I am sorely tempted."

"I know, and I promise that you will prevail. But don't be a hothead about such matters. You should have learned that by now."

"I've forgotten quite a bit lately." He stared morosely at his coffee cup.

"She will come around. She loves you."

"It may not be enough." Logan tried to lighten the mood. "Since when does my superior ask me about my personal life?"

"Since your resignation. I hope I can be of some service."

"Not unless I can kidnap my wife and child and bring them to a deserted island and keep Gillian's mouth shut until she forgives me."

"Listen, lad, I know you are preoccupied, but I must ask one more favor of you."

Logan should have known it was coming. But again he blamed his weakness on Gillian. "Now what?" he groaned.

"St. Cecelia's ball. It's tonight. They will be there."

"Both of them?"

"Althorp is a very cocky fellow. Tonight, Logan, you will expose Brian Althorp and his longtime lover and agent, Anabelle Blacton."

"I wish Gillian could see it."

"Who knows? When last I heard, you grandfather and aunt would not take no for an answer. Your wife may be in attendance this evening."

Like a foolish schoolboy, Logan felt a rush of anticipation. Just to see her would satisfy him. And if she smiled at him, or if she would even nod a civil hello, he would be in heaven.

Tonight she would learn about loyalty.

Logan had no idea that his loyalty and love would be put to the limit.

Chapter Forty-two

The St. Cecelia Society was ostensibly an organization founded for the preservation and love of music. It was also one of the most respectable, socially conscious groups in all of South Carolina. A number of social conditions had to be met for admission. Not every upper-class gentleman was admitted to this illustrious group, however, it was often used as an excuse for sponsoring some of the fanciest society balls in Charleston.

Tonight was one of those nights when people came from their secluded plantations simply to be seen.

Logan had no choice but to attend. Gillian, however, had a number of perfectly acceptable excuses for not going, yet a peculiar, probably perverse whim, changed her mind. After all, if she were ever to be seen in society again, she had to make a start somewhere. Now was as good a time as any. With her mother and Brian Althorp as escorts, she might force herself to have a pleasant evening.

Finding a suitable evening dress suddenly became one of the more difficult decisions of her life. Throwing caution to the winds, she selected a less modest creation — one that Logan had insisted she have made. The champagne-colored watered silk was daring in its simplicity. There were no frills or lace around the bodice or neckline, and no jewels adorning the hem. Since the dress was sleeveless, there was nothing to decorate her arms but a long pair of matching silk gloves. The material clung and blended so perfectly with her skin that she almost appeared to be wearing nothing at all.

It was indecent, she decided, but the hour was late and there was no time to select another dress. Her titian-colored hair was piled high atop her head in intricate curls held in place by diamond-and-gold hairpins. Either the matrons accepted her or they did not. Besides, if she understood the membership requirements of this elite club, divorced persons were definitely not permitted entry at any time. She would be in that category shortly, she grimly realized.

Gillian could not find her topaz-and-pearl choker and matching earrings which had been among Logan's earlier presents. They reminded her of happier, albeit stupidly innocent times, but these jewels matched her gown and hair and she wanted to wear them.

"Damn, where have I put them?" It was strange that her jewel box would not contain them, and stranger that she could not remember when she last saw them.

"He must have taken them back," she rashly decided. Since it was convenient to blame Logan for so many transgressions, she found the courage to march into his half-emptied dressing room and search his drawers for her jewels.

Hidden beneath a neatly stacked and starched pile of silk cravats was the beginninga of a long letter to Logan's father. Curiosity prevailed. Grabbing the letter, she sat in the nearest chair, which happened to be the one Logan used when dressing, and perused the contents. It was dated two weeks past, before his trip to Washington, and was unfinished, leaving off in the middle of page five.

She wasn't going to read it, she decided, and for five

long minutes, she stared at the neat handwriting, her heart hammering with indecision. Except for the occasional carriage that rolled down Bay Street, no other sound reached her ears.

Then she saw her name, on the first, third, and fourth pages, and gave in.

It was a letter begging his father to understand, and to someday forgive his son for causing shame to the Hammond name.

"How can I possibly explain to you the great burden I have borne these last five years? I have hidden a great deal from you. You may, in fact, believe that I have betrayed you, but I swear on Mother's grave that that is not so. What I have done was for my country — for America. I believe in freedom, Father, I believe that the citizens of the United States have a right to decide how to live, without interference from another, albeit more powerful nation like England . . ."

It went on to explain how passionately he had come to believe in the preservation of America's freedom.

"I had to choose between family and country. I chose my mother's country, my country, and I pray to God that you will not be shamed by my actions. . . ."

"I love you, Father. I adore Luisa and Charlotte and hope they will be spared pain. Above all, I ask your help."

Gillian's ears were burning, her eyes watering, and still she could not, would not put the letter down. It was Logan Hammond baring his soul. She had no right to peer inside, yet she did so without further thought.

"I ask you to accept Gillian and my daughter Judith. She knew nothing of my actions, and as I write this letter, I shudder to think how I will ever explain these things to her. But I must, for I know that others, less loving, less compassionate than I will try to undermine our love.

"I love her with all my heart and I have chosen to do what I swore I never would. I am no longer working inside the American government. I have decided to quit this life I have loved because I love my wife and daughter more. I cannot jeopardize their future, yet I fear I may cause irreparable damage to my marriage when the truth is revealed.

"Gillian is a fiercely loyal citizen to the Crown. She may reject me and return home. I may be stripped of my lands and title, I will probably be branded a traitor. But she deserves my holdings — everything. If there is anything you can do to assist her in obtaining what is rightfully and legally hers, I hope you will do so."

She couldn't believe it! He knew that something like this would happen? The bastard not only possessed a conscience but a heart? How could a cold and cruel a man write these words to his father, begging for forgiveness.

"One day, Father, I hope you will find some place in your heart for your son. I would give everything to have spared you this impending tragedy. But alas, I have no control. I only pray that there will come a time when you can once again recall some fond thoughts of me. I hope you will tell your granddaughter that her father wanted her by his side. Tell her, if you can, about Logan the boy. Perhaps it will hurt less not to talk about Logan the man you think of as a traitor.

"I hope I will see you again. Just to shake your hand, share a laugh . . ."

It ended there.

Heedless of her carefully applied powders and elegant hairstyle, Gillian dropped her head into her arms and wept bitter tears for a love she helped to destroy. Wracking, heaving sobs tore through her thin body, but they were not cathartic. She felt even worse, for her mind was in turmoil.

Perhaps he did love her. Perhaps she hadn't given him a chance to prove his love and explain himself. Her emotions were too raw, and she was too mired in self-pity and anger to have allowed Logan back into her heart.

"Gillian ?" A soft knock on the door interrupted her anguish. "Are you there, dear? Brian has been waiting for us. Are you feeling well?" Helena's worried voice made her respond.

"No, no," she tried to blow her nose quietly. "I'll be ready in a few more minutes."

She would go to this damn ball because maybe there was a remote chance that Logan would be there, too. This time Gillian was not taking any chances. She was confused and hurt, but she wanted to give him the opportunity to talk to her once more, even if it became the last time they spoke civilly to each other. And he had told her he would not come back unless she made the next move.

Quickly she grabbed pen and paper, asking him to meet her first thing in the morning, then returned to her chamber to repair herself. She gasped in disbelief as she reached for her silver hairbrush and saw the "missing" jewels resting beneath it. How stupid of me, she thought, attaching the necklace and earrings hurriedly. Has that man so affected me that I cannot see what is in front of my eyes? Annoyed and perplexed she scurried down the stairs and handed the sealed letter to one of the slaves, insisting it be delivered to Liza Fenwick's home this evening.

Brian Althorp's mouth dropped open at the sight of the lovely woman approaching him. From the way she moved, Gillian appeared heedless of her beauty and dress.

"My goodness, Gillian," he breathed, "you are a vision."

"Oh, thank you, Brian." She mechanically smiled. "Let's go." She absently handed him her lace wrap. "We're late enough as it is. It is awfully warm out tonight," she commented after realizing her behavior must appear odd. "It's so unusual not to feel any breeze off the harbor, but all day there was nothing."

Henri Raveneau was out for the evening. Disdaining these fancy shindigs, as he put it, he chose to meet two of his old cronies for a long night of card-playing at a private club on King Street.

Like every other place in the heart of Charleston, it took less than ten minutes to ride to the Charleston Society Hall on Meeting Street. The elegant coaches, carriages, and curricles were almost three-deep. But when at last their turn came, Gillian and Helena allowed Brian to assist them.

They were indeed late. The long room was filled with ladies and gentlemen strolling around the perimeters of the dance floor to chat, gossip, or sip their wines. Above, were three massive crystal chandeliers that twinkled from the dozen or so candles surrounding them. Along the sides of the white room more sconces and mirrors were placed to make the room appear large and bright. The highly polished wooden floors reflected the glowing candlelight. The folding doors to a smaller room beyond the hall were thrown open, enlarging the entire area. The small, semi-circular musician's gallery was at the far end of the hall. If one were not in a festive mood before entering the room, one could not help but be caught up in the splendor and gaiety once within the four walls.

Gillian's mood lightened marginally and she hurriedly looked around the crowded room, in dreaded anticipation of spotting Logan. What would she do if she saw him? What were those ladies gossiping about behind their fans? Did they know? What would she do if he didn't arrive?

Her nerves were frazzled, her mind unable to function clearly. She wasn't even aware that she had consumed two glasses of champagne within the first five minutes of her arrival.

"Gillian, are you feeling well?" her mother inquired yet again.

"I'm not certain," she nervously giggled. "I think I might have made a mistake," her eyes vigilantly scanned the room.

"It's not too late." She smiled encouragingly. "I've been told that he will be here tonight, if that will make you relax."

"Why didn't you tell me?"

"I did not think you wanted to know."

"You're right," Gillian decided, unable to keep her eyes focused on anything.

Unfortunately, Gillian did notice two others. Eve and Anabelle. And Captain Richard Paxton, who was standing at Anabelle's side. The women seemed to be the new set of Siamese twins and they descended upon her and Brian with the quickness of a hawk having sighted its prey. Mercifully, Richard remained behind.

"Why, hello, dears," Eve cooed. "How nice to see you again. Where is your darling husband? Don't tell me he's had enough so soon?"

"He'll be here shortly," Gillian briskly replied, unaware of Brian's sharp look.

"Do introduce us to your friend." Eve had no intention of leaving.

Gillian politely made the introductions. In her state of confusion, she missed two things: Brian held Anabelle's hand a trifle too long and Anabelle's green eyes never left his face.

"My, my, it looks like love at first sight. Whatever will Richard think?" Eve missed nothing.

"Oh, Eve, do be serious. I do enjoy meeting a fellow countryman. Your American accents are strange to my ear." She smiled sweetly.

"Lovely dress, Gillian." Eve's eyes scrutinized Gillian's silk dress. "I assume your husband had nothing to do with the selection."

"On the contrary," interrupted a deep, familiar voice, "I insisted she have it made. It suits her perfectly." Logan's gaze was riveted on Gillian's bodice. "I knew it," he whispered more to himself than to the others.

"Logan," Gillian took her first real breath of the evening, "what a surprise!"

"I know you did not expect me to arrive this soon, but I discovered that I could accomplish most of my business this evening."

The musicians stopped playing, and for a moment everything and everyone in the room seemed frozen. Gillian began to fret, for among her many problems, she did not like the way Brian glowered at Logan, who seemed oblivious to the drama unfolding around him.

"Hammond, I believe we have much to discuss."

"I think not. I would prefer to ask my wife to dance

with me. Perhaps another time?" He looked down at Brian as if he were nothing more than a nuisance.

Leave it to Logan, Gillian thought, to look so damn handsome that his presence seemed to fill her senses. For Gillian, there was suddenly no one else in the room but this tall god dressed all in black, except for the white lawn shirt underneath. As the candlelight twinkled above their heads, Gillian's attention briefly focused on his diamond stickpin. The initial "S" jolted her. It was so familiar to her, yet she could not place where or when she had seen this piece of jewelry before.

His tawny hair looked a bit long, almost touching his neck, and her hands wanted to smooth the locks. If she stood very close to him, the combined scent of tobacco and alcohol assailed her nostrils. To her, these were all part of his magnetic allure.

"Dance with me." It was half command, half request. "I'd like to hold you in my arms."

Her knees trembled and without so much as a backward glance to the others, she allowed her husband to lead her away.

"I've come for you, Gillian. Don't say no. I will not ask again."

Chapter Forty-three

"Why are you being so obedient?" he inquired as he continued to navigate their twirls around the crowded dance floor.

"That, Logan, is a very poor choice of words." She looked to her side, mindful of their direction.

"I apologize, madame. I seem to be doing so much of that with you that is has become second nature to me."

"Oh, and does that mean you apologize simply because I want to hear it? Or do you ever admit you can indeed be at fault." Instead of looking at him, she nodded to a couple alongside them. "Smile, your friends are watching us."

"I don't have any friends," he paused to reconsider, "except for you. Well, I *thought* you were my friend."

Damn him for catching her off guard. He actually sounded vulnerable. But where was that hardened man who so effortlessly became a notorious American agent?

"Who are you?" she spoke aloud.

As if he could sort and read the confused thoughts in her mind, he answered, "Your husband, the father of our sweet little girl, and an American." His arm tightened around her waist. "Any other questions?" He had the nerve to smile as if he hadn't a care in the world.

"In that order?"

"Yes, Gillian." His smile vanished. "Are there any other tests? Shall I walk on nails, or through fire? Shall I lay down my life for you?" He spun her dizzily around a corner of the room. "I will. If that's what you want, so help me God, I will."

His words frightened her. "I . . . I don't know what to say."

"Say nothing now. Just let me hold you while we dance. Let's forget everything for just a few more minutes. Let's pretend that I spotted you from across a crowded room, a naked vision in pearls and topaz, whose bright hair and smile beckoned me like a beacon of light out on a dark, storm-tossed sea."

Oh, that voice. It did not matter that he was one of the most experienced men on both continents who could easily seduce a woman with a dark, sultry glance and husky words. He was looking down into her face and he was smiling and she wanted him in her life.

They remained locked in each other's arms for the next three dances: a lively Strauss waltz that left them laughing and breathless, a quadrille, in which Logan refused to give Gillian's hand to another, and a slow, enchanting waltz that made her feel as if the musicians played for her alone.

When she felt the floor beneath her feet rumble, she dismissed the feeling as one more sensation Logan could conjure from her wobbly limbs.

But when the chandelier above shook, she glanced at Logan's worried frown. "What is it?" She stopped. "What's going on?"

"I cannot be certain. It may be nothing."

They felt the ground move again. "That is not nothing, Logan." She would not let go of his hand.

He had no intention of letting her slip out of his sight. Many others had begun to realize that something unusual was happening. He knew what it was. He had experienced an earthquake in the Spanish Americas two years ago.

"Gillian," he took her by the elbow, "listen to me. Under no circumstances do you leave my side. Do you understand?"

"But, Mother?" her voice rose in panic.

"We will find her together."

But that was not possible, for someone shouted, "Earthquake! Everyone get out of here!" and two things happened at once. People stampeded out of the room, screaming wildly with fear, while the chandelier in the middle of the room rocked to and fro before crashing to the floor.

People ran into Logan and Gillian. They were instantly separated, and as she screamed his name above the din, she thought she heard him call out but lost sight of his tall head.

"Oh, God," she said in a surprisingly calm voice, "I'm going to die. Alone."

She felt herself propelled backward by the surging, panicky crowd. Everywhere there were screams, then she heard a loud explosion, and she could have sworn that the building was shaking. The other two chandeliers crashed to the floor. She saw a satin-clad leg minus a fancy dance shoe and what must have been a man's arm. The bile rose in her throat, but this was not the time to get sick or lie down and cry as some others were doing. She had to get out of here. She had to find Logan, her mother, and get Judith.

"Oh, God, Judith, please let her be all right. Take me, but not her. Not Logan. Please," she said aloud, looking above her. She could see the stars. The roof was caving in around her.

She was drawn to the back of the hall, past the doors, but there were no doors. Gillian was about to grab a white column when it swayed before her horrified eyes and folded like a great wave. More voices screamed. Others were trapped beneath rubble.

"Logan! Logan!" she screamed, desperate to evoke his image.

Just when she thought she would be crushed by the screeching mob, someone lurched forward, grabbing her arm, shielding her from the disaster.

His face was covered with white plaster, dust, and paint, but he never looked more wonderful. "I despaired of ever finding you." Logan roughly pulled her into his arms in a hurried embrace. "Let's go. Judith . . ."

"Mother?"

"When last I left her she was outside the building with Paxton leading her away."

Once outside, Gillian and Logan turned for one moment, only to see the building collapse. It was not the only one. Church bells clanged incessantly, horses ran wildly through the streets, fires sprang out of nowhere.

"This must be hell," Logan murmured.

"Don't leave me."

"I won't. I swear, but you better run faster. Because I'd hate to waste my strength carrying you."

How he could manage to say something amusing was beyond her ken. But it elicited a slightly hysterical laugh before she started to sob. "My baby. I want her."

"I know, sweetheart. We'll find her."

As they ran down Meeting Street, they felt as they were running into another inferno. They lost their footing in the street as the ground around them tremored.

"Hold on. Do you hear me?" he shouted. He tore at his cravat and quickly tied it around their joined wrists, then pulled her along.

"Logan! Logan, no matter what happens I want you to know I love you, I always will," she screamed into the smoke-filled air. "I love you."

"I know. I love you, too. Keep running."

The carnage around them did not improve as they neared East Bay Street. One corner house seemed to sway in the windless sky before the piazza side separated and crumbled. The once-still night air was filled with cries and shrieks and the rumbling, crashing sounds of falling buildings.

The Hammonds kept running. When they approached their home, Gillian cried, "Oh, my God! Thank you, God!"

It was still standing, but Logan could not tell her that all would be fine simply because the house still stood. There were more earth tremors to come.

"Stay outside. I'm going in to get her." His hands nimbly untied the knotted material at their wrists.

"Not on your life. I'm not going anywhere without you."

"You'll be safer. Oh, hell . . . come along."

They ran inside, calling Hilda's name. From out of the darkness, Henri popped out behind the stairwell. "We're here!"

It was a beautiful sight. Judith, nestled in blankets, blissfully slept in her great-grandfather's arms. The other servants and slaves appeared one by one.

Gillian grabbed her daughter, sobbing into her little chest.

When she looked up, she saw the tears running down Logan's cheeks. "Let me, please." He took the bundle into his hands, lifted her up to the sky. "Thank you," he quietly said.

"Everyone is safe. The house is sturdy. I don't know what else we can expect. We're as safe here as anywhere else," Henri declared. "Just stay on this floor."

"I'm going back." Logan gently handed his daughter to Gillian. "Take good care of her."

"You're not leaving!"

"I must. I'll be fine. I swear it." He kissed her grimy nose, then bounded out of the house before she could continue to protest.

"He'll be killed."

"I think not, dear. He has everything to lose." Henri smiled through his watery eyes.

"What were you doing at home?"

"I had enough of losing for one night. I decided to come home, change my clothes, and find you two at that silly ball. I thought I could help."

"Oh, Grandfather," she cried. "I'm so frightened."

"I think the worst of this thing has hit. We won't know the full extent of the damage until morning, if then."

The earthquake had struck Charleston at 11 P.M. on a sultry Thursday night of April 22. So much damage, so many lives forfeited, dreams destroyed, fortunes lost.

For the rest of her life, Gillian would always remember how blessed she and her family had been. She had witnessed the horror, would never forget the screams of the maimed and dying. Nor could she ever forget her panic upon being stranded and the overwhelming joy upon seeing her beloved husband — his tall frame above the crowd, his authoritative voice rising above the din, calling for her, rescuing her from being crushed to death by a frenzied mob.

This night when God had forsaken so many, Gillian had come to realize that her one everlasting love was Logan. What he had done before was irrelevant. She would remain by his side, determined to spend the rest of her life proving to him how much she loved and needed him — above all else, above everyone else.

Somehow she made it through the rest of the night. Helena, extremely disheveled and shaken, was brought home by Richard Paxton, who grinned in relief upon seeing Gillian and her family.

"You'll never know how much I am indebted to you," Gillian tearfully said to the man, "for so many reasons, not only for tonight." Her throat was sore, but she rasped the words that needed to be said. "Perhaps if there never had been a Logan Hammond, we would have found each other. But I know you will find your kindred soul." She kissed his ruddy cheek. "I will always be your devoted friend."

"I know." He mopped his brow with a dirty handkerchief. "As I am yours. And I've already told your scoundrel husband he better take excellent care of you, for I shall make his life miserable if he doesn't."

"I hope you two can be friends again."

"Someday." Richard's army jacket had long ago been thrown aside. Dressed in a tattered dark blue shirt and trousers, he no longer looked like the immaculate soldier, but it was there in his proud stance and his unblinking green eyes. He was a good man.

"I'm going back."

"Not you, too."

"I must. Besides, I am fortunate that my family is safe in their home in the mountains. But many of our friends are not."

"Richard," she called to him, "whoever needs help, bring them here. We have room."

"And plenty of bandages," Helena added.

Gillian had no intention of going to sleep without Logan. First she stood on the piazza, then paced the area, then finally went into the street to see if he was coming.

Quite a number of people continued scurrying about the streets. Wagons creaked along. Some with families, hauling their belongings to new locations. There were carts for the injured and dead. There were those hundreds of volunteers, like Logan and Richard, who cleared rocks, wooden beams and, furniture with their bare hands. There were children huddled in groups, waiting the fate of their parents. There were slaves praying. Some fell in the middle of the street, lifted their heads to the heavens, and prayed for it to be over.

It became obvious that Logan was not coming home — not for a long time. As long as the baby was safe with the family, Henri and Gillian decided to bring the bandages, food, water, and clean clothes to Logan and the others.

Walking up Tradd Street, they saw the remains of two houses. Fortunately, the Harrises' home was not among them.

Looking to the east, Gillian saw the dark night turn pale. How could some things remain constant, she wondered, when a world is falling apart?

When she saw a shirtless Logan, his muscles straining under the weight of lifting a chunk of marble, her step quickened and she ran forward to hold the man who would always have her constant love.

Chapter Forty-four

"You shouldn't have come. It's not a pretty sight." Although annoyed that Gillian had disobeyed his order, Logan kissed the top of her head.

"We wanted to do something, too." She gestured to the rest of the family.

Logan directed them towards a harried-looking Dr. Clayton Warren. "He's swamped. There aren't enough physicians to go around." Glancing at her serviceable dark pink cotton dress, he said. "That dress will get mighty dirty this morning. Looks like I'm obligated to replace the ruined gowns." At least there was something to make him smile.

Willing to do anything as long as she could keep Logan within her sight, Gillian listened to Clayton's instructions. Some of the injured suffered from superficial wounds and were off to one side of a once-lovely manicured lawn. There were others, too, those who lay writhing in pain, begging for assistance. Gillian's stomach roiled when she saw the faces of the dead and two other men whose limbs seemed beyond saving.

She immediately recognized one of the seriously wounded patients, and the sobbing, nearly hysterical woman draped over his body.

"My God, Brian!" She ran to him.

His face contorted with pain, his breathing so labored that it echoed through the air, Brian did not look as if he would live. Anabelle Blacton would not let anyone near him. "No! Don't touch him. What do you know?" she shrieked at Clayton when he tried to examine Brian.

"I don't know who you are and I don't care. This man needs my assistance now, and unless you are his wife, I suggest you step aside." Clayton had no time for debates.

"We're going to married as soon as we return to London. It's all been arranged." Anabelle's dark hair looked matted with grime and blood, her light eyes vacant with fear. What remained of her elegant dress had been covered by some kind soul, who must have thrown his jacket over her shoulders.

At first, Gillian dismissed her hysterical words. But Anabelle persisted in declaring her love, forcing Gillian's attention to what should have been obvious before.

"Anabelle, Brian needs help. Step aside." She tried to nudge Anabelle's hand that kept a viselike grip on Brian's waist.

"No, I said no!"

"He'll die if the doctor doesn't see him."

"He'll die anyhow. Oh, I just know it. I knew we shouldn't have come to this godforsaken country. I told him so. I told him to let me stay in London with him. We could have finished our work there."

The words were semi-coherent. Gillian understood enough. Brian and Anabelle. Longtime lovers? Somehow involved in the same wretched business as Logan?

"Come with me." Gillian grabbed Anabelle's arm. "Brian will be safe with Dr. Warren. I promise. Brian is my friend."

"He loved you," she spat, her hair falling around her

face. "What did you do? You fell for that monster! That liar. That . . ."

"Enough!" Gillian shouted. "Brian was and always will be a good friend. Nothing more. You love him."

"I've loved him forever, but it was always your name that was between us. I never wanted to come here. I wanted you to stay with Logan. At least you were both out of England. I told Brian that. What difference could it make to expose Logan Hammond when he was living in this place?"

Someone handed Gillian a drink, which she held for Anabelle. Her voice droned on, getting higher with agitation and hysteria. The woman was going to lose her mind if Brian did not live.

"No. Brian wanted it all. He wanted Logan stripped of everything. He wanted to shame Logan in front of the king, in front of you."

"Please, Anabelle, you must control yourself." Gillian's words made no impression. "Brian will be fine."

"Why did he keep wanting you? Why?" She paused to collect her distracted thoughts, "I would do anything for him. I've done more than you!" she accused.

"You have. And Brian must know it. He loves you."

Mercifully the laudanum-laced drink began to take effect. "I must sit." Anabelle almost collapsed. Henri, who was standing nearby assisting another, had heard enough. Taking her by the arm, he coaxed her into a waiting coach, directing the volunteer driver to Hattie Mathew's home.

"She was the one Logan had been looking for. She's of no use to anyone today." Henri spoke more to himself than Gillian.

"What was Logan going to do?"

"Bargain with the British. Embarrass Canning into recalling all English operatives in America."

"Oh, Lord. It's worse than I thought. Brian, Logan,

women . . . How many people are involved in this thing?" She threw her hands in the air.

"More than I care to know about. Now there will be one fewer representative. Logan is taking a long sabbatical."

"I know. He's doing it for me." She turned her shiny eyes up at the dear man.

"Good," he grunted. "As long as you know."

"This will take a long time to sort out."

"As long as you do it together."

Gillian could have said much more, but Clayton called her over to Brian.

"He'll live. Some broken ribs, a head injury, too, but I've seen much worse tonight. We've got to move him. St. Michael's Church has set up a ward for the injured." Clayton cast a sidelong glance at Gillian. "Know him well?"

"An old friend, so I thought."

"He's mentioned your name and that woman's."

Eventually she would sort and make sense of this mess. But none of it mattered now, for off to her left, the most beautiful sight in the world filled her vision.

Her husband.

Hours later, when the hot Carolina sun beat down upon their uncovered heads, when it became obvious that many of the volunteers could no longer stand on their feet, Logan came for her. Sitting on the ground, her legs curled beneath her now-bare feet, Gillian was sharing a canteen full of cold water with Lily Harris.

"Lord, I'm sore all over. But glad to be feeling it," Lily chortled.

"I'm going to sleep for a whole week."

"Not alone, I hope." Despite her fatigue and numb limbs, his deep voice made her skin tingle.

"Oh, never alone." She displayed her most brilliant smile.

"Let's go home, wife." He offered one arm to pull her up. "I see your man scanning the area for you," Logan offered to Lily, and she was gone in a few seconds.

"They are such nice people," she inanely commented when there was clearly so much more to discuss.

"Another time I'll tell you all about your friends."

"Oh no," she groaned in mock despair. "If this has anything else to do with your spying, I don't want to hear about it." But she was smiling up into his laughing golden gaze.

"Whoever said anything about spying? Such a tawdry word." He affectionately squeezed her shoulders. "I want a long, hot bath. I want a hearty meal, and I want our daughter propped up against my bare knees."

"Precisely. As I recall, that marble tub has room for another." Her arms locked around his bare torso.

Much later, after they hugged and fed Judith, frolicked in the tub, ate a large lunch, retired to their room, and fell onto the bed together, they slept. But not before Logan took Gillian in his arms, kissed her face, and lifted her chin up to his adoring face. His hair was still damp from their long bath, and his face freshly shaven.

"I want us to start anew. You can think what you want about me, but know this. I shall always love you."

Her gaze remained fixed on his handsome face. "I know. I hope you can forgive me for ever doubting you. I don't care anymore about who you were — although I understand you enjoyed a unique reputation for being one of the best agents." She impishly grinned and touched the tiny cleft in his chin. "I should have believed in you and I didn't. I think I understand your motives now. I suppose I could do the same," she saw his hand rise, "but never would," Gillian immediately corrected herself.

Her soft hand located and tenderly touched the two old knife wounds on his matted chest. "Brian was responsible for those."

"He was."

"I listened to the wrong people."

"I know."

"I'll never do that again." She lowered her lips to kiss the scarred skin.

"I know. I won't let you," he groaned into her hair.

"Logan? I've been thinking of nothing else these last few days except kissing your lips."

"Happy to oblige, madame." He none too gently took her shoulders and lowered her onto the bed. Raised above her ebullient face, his eyes darkened and his mouth parted to reclaim what never should have been lost.

Later they would talk about everything else . . .

Much later she told him about coming across the letter to his father. He couldn't possibly be angry, not with Gillian prominently positioned above him.

"I hope we can visit them someday. With your permission, I would like to write to your family."

Touched by her sensitive gesture, Logan wrapped his arms around her smooth shoulders, pulling her down to kiss her swollen lips and simply hug her.

There would be time for further explanations and arguments, and always time to make up.

Epilogue

September 1827

Politically it had not been a good season in international relations between the fledgling nation and her former mother country.

Secretary of State Henry Clay had kept his meeting with Foreign Secretary Canning. And according to plan, Clay handed the politician a complete list of the names of the individuals who were plotting against the young nation. Brian Althorp's name was on the list. So was Anabelle Blacton's.

Canning's surprise was worth all the effort. Elections were to be held shortly, and the foreign secretary could not afford any scandals. Although Canning did not agree to a new West Indian treaty with Clay, he did not rule out future negotiations. However, he did agree to drop all charges against all Americans who were involved in a similar effort and the one Englishman.

Lord Logan Hammond was never officially charged with treason nor were his lands and title stripped. His father, the Earl of Stanton, never received a letter, for Logan had wisely decided to wait before sending a courier with such important news. Lady Helena Marlowe, who was reluctantly sailing home after the hurricane season, was going to deliver all messages personally.

The Hammonds were blissfully settled in their East Bay Street house. Sitting on the joggling board with Judith between them, Gillian and Logan laughed at their daughter's futile attempts to grab Logan's diamond stickpin.

"I should hate that pin, but I don't. I suppose if I had never walked out into that balmy London night — out of sheer boredom, mind you — I wouldn't be bouncing on this contraption with you."

Logan turned his laughing eyes away from Judith to admire her mother. "Best thing that ever happened. I gather you have not experienced too much boredom since that night."

"And you?"

"Not with you and this sprite." He kissed Judith's fuzzy head. "I'm waiting for the riot of raspberry-gold curls. Gracious, I hope something happens. People will think she's a boy."

Gillian lifted one thin curl. "I'll put a bow in this tomorrow."

Judith squealed at her father's face. Logan responded by making another silly face and hugging the child to his chest. "Babies are wonderful."

"I'm glad you said that." She mischievously smiled, angling her bottom along the board to get closer to her husband.

"I'd like a dozen children," he chuckled at her gasp, "but I'd settle for three or four. We've certainly been, ah," his eyes scanned the cloudless blue sky for the words, "active in the baby-making area. And this time, I intend to see that flat tummy grow, inch by expanding inch."

"As long as you stay in our bed."

"I never thought of leaving." His warm smile stirred her senses anew.

"I think it's time for Judith's nap." Her bright eyes

focused meaningfully on his trousers. Lifting his daughter in one arm and placing the other around his wife's still-slim waist, they laughingly walked inside the house.

Earthquakes test the earth's fragile core. The heaving and volcanic revolutions offer proof of nature's fickleness. But like all revolutions, this one came full circle. Turbulence gave way to equilibrium. Nature rested from her ordeal.

Gillian and Logan suffered from love's unpredictable convulsion. Searching for tranquility, they had traveled a road of unpredictability, yet the mutual attraction and their shared destiny could not be denied. It was merely a question of time before serenity could be secured.

The clouds passed the windswept bay. A cascade of light left the water below shimmering. Renewal was in the air. All was not quite right with nature as the devastation of the past suggested. But there was hope, hope for a new day, hope that Gillian and Logan shared.

A bird landed on a precariously bent limb, chirping furiously, giving rise to the belief that life could not be easily extinguished. This palpable sign of life presaged a new day.